GEMSTONE WARS

A FANTASY-WESTERN ADVENTURE

THE HIDDEN KINGDOM

CHRIS JONES

FOR MY PARENTS,
KEN AND KAREN

Table of Contents

The Hidden Kingdom of Tavter

A new light emerged across the horizon's rim, painting the overhead skyline aquamarine with a thin palette of fuchsia caressing the land. The auburn-colored desert below awakened to a splendid display of colors reflecting on the rugged shapes of the sandstone formations, broken mesas, and high buttes that stood alone in the vastness. The angry winds swept in from the west, bringing a rising, scorching heat.

Two adventurers, Suzu and Hogart, streaked across the desert. They had been riding all night for hours, but it felt like an eternity. Their throats were parched, and their eyes stung from dust. They ventured into the desolate lands of sienna sand and ochre rocks on a self-imposed quest that they didn't even know the meaning of—all they knew was that an important task had to be completed before the dawn of the new day.

They raced against the sunlight as if it were their enemy. They knew that if they failed, they would never get another chance. There were other fortune seekers that had figured out what they were up to and were looking for them. If they succeeded now, they would witness something miraculous and give themselves fortune and glory beyond their wildest dreams. With positive prospects in mind, they did not speak or look back at one another; they only urged their horses forward, faster and faster.

Suzu, a young and petite woman from the far lands of the east, surveyed the land with a serious expression. Her fair light-olive complexion and bright lips were vulnerable to the rising, scorching sun, but she did not seem to mind. Her face was flawless and striking, with piercing brown eyes. She wore a long-sleeved tan tunic with a V-neck. A mocha leather quiver bag on her back and a bronze satchel bouncing off her hip were draped together over her shoulder and across the chest. Black pants, with a wide black belt draped with pouches for tools and items, were tucked into her black boots. She gripped the reins of her horse firmly, ready for any challenge that may lay ahead.

Hogart was not far behind, a man who looked like he had seen a decade more of life than his counterpart. His towering, imposing, hefty frame stood out in any crowd. But his relaxed posture and casual, wavy, long charcoal hair that reached his shoulders betrayed his gentle nature. His face was pale, round, and lightly scruffy. His chestnut eyes showed serious intent but also signs of worry. His long beige coat hung loosely over his untucked maroon button-down shirt. Baggy black pants were tucked into his black boots, which filled the entire stirrup. A dark brown satchel, just like Suzu's, draped across the chest but was mostly hidden by the length of the coat.

Finally, appearing on the horizon before them, a solitary monument stood on an oversize, square, taupe stone base—an eroding and chipped statue of a muscular male warrior carved from dark grey stone. A veil of dust covered the form that had weathered many storms and seasons. The figure wore a mohawk-adorned helmet, hiding his face from view. He was clad nearly entirely in armor, ready for battle. In his right hand he raised a circular shield, prepared to block any assault, and in his left, a long spear, poised to attack. The spear was broken at the tip, its blade lost. He eternally gazed at the open sky, day or night, as if challenging the gods. Lars Sill, a member of the legendary Company of Heroes, stood at the edge of a cliff. He seemingly served as a silent sentinel guarding a desolate valley below.

The monument was the only witness to the unlikeliest, most mismatched pairing that had approached in years. The statue's long shadow loomed over Suzu and Hogart as they halted their horses at its base. The animals whinnied and stamped their hooves in approval, glad to have a break from the long journey. The two riders surveyed the empty desert valley stretching for miles before them, then looked up at the diminishing peach colors about to be lit sky blue by the coming sunrise.

"This is it. This is where we cash in," Suzu said.

"Let us hurry! The rising sun is almost on us. The Red Rose Death Gang is only one hour behind at best! If they catch us, we're dead!" Hogart said. The rotund man jumped off his horse with surprising agility. He was either overly eager, in a feverish state of nerves, or both as he hurriedly tried to scurry up the statue's leg. He didn't get very far, though, as his girth prevented him from getting a good hold on the dust-covered stone. He slid down the calf of the leg to the sandaled foot.

"Clumsy oaf," Suzu said. She chuckled lightly, trying not to insult her friend. "I'll make it up in time."

Suzu reached down to the horse's saddle and grabbed her faithful weapon of choice: a short repeating crossbow. The young woman then went into one of her pouches on her black belt, pulling out a piece of silver metal that extended outward into a hook. She quickly fastened it onto the tip of an arrow shaft, tied a rope to the end of the arrow, and placed the arrow in the vertical box magazine on top of the crossbow. With one shot, the grappling hook flew up and wrapped around the outstretched, muscular left arm holding the spear. The lean, petite woman attached the small crossbow to her belt and quickly climbed the rope from the saddle seat.

Successfully reaching the broad shoulder, Suzu carefully lay down on her stomach. She slowly crawled along the stone statue's arm towards the clenched hand holding the long spear shaft. Once within reach, she took out a clear, crystal-bladed spearhead from within her leather satchel. Her fingers carefully placed the spearhead on the missing tip.

The two adventurers held their breath as they gazed earnestly at the tranquil valley below them. The crystal spearhead shimmered in the morning light, emitting vibrant rainbow colors—crimson, tangerine, jade, cobalt, violet, and mustard—that sprang and streamed forth, cascading in oceanic sparkling waves over the barren rust landscape.

The dormant sands in the valley began to shift and stir by its touch, rising and swirling into the air as if guided by an invisible sculpting hand. A colossal wall of pastel dust and tan stone emerged from the ground, obscuring their view of the valley. Behind the curtain of twirling sand, they could see the faint black outlines of buildings and monuments taking shape, as if an entire city were being reconstructed from scratch. The artifact's twirling and sparkling rainbow lights orchestrated the miraculous transformation, restoring a civilization lost for nearly a century.

"The hidden Kingdom of Tavter!" Suzu shouted.

In the quiet valley, magnificent domes, spheres, and towers appeared where nothing had been before. The cessation of the rainbow's vibrant hues marked the end of the reconstruction. The blade lay dormant, its purpose fulfilled. The sands danced their last in the fading rainbow light, their movement a silent symphony to the forces that had stirred them. As they settled, the valley seemed to exhale, its duty done.

Suzu quickly descended the rope and settled on her horse's saddle as easily and quickly as she'd left it. "Hogart, my friend, the gamble you took in Kenjam for that highly questionable artifact actually paid off."

"I told you it would, Suzu."

"I'm happy you recognized it had potential."

"I wasn't too sure about it, but I had a good feeling. That fisherman obviously didn't know what he caught in his net when he placed his bet. But that member of the Red Rose Death Gang at the gambling table suspected its potential too."

"We don't have much time. News of Tavter being resurrected will reach all the civilized lands by the end of the day," Suzu said. "Let us find our riches and be gone before anyone notices us."

"Fortune and glory await us!" Hogart said. He laughed at the prospects.

"Fortune and glory," Suzu repeated. A wide smile spread across her lips, and she happily joined her friend in the celebratory laughter.

In minutes, Suzu and Hogart found a suitable slope descending towards the awaiting city. As they approached the edge of the lost realm, they felt an odd mix of astonishing awe and possible dread. Tavter, a once noble beacon of peace corrupted by the Demon-God King during the Dragon Wars, loomed before them—an old, sprawling city of impressive domes, tall towers, and elegant buildings that once shone with vigorous life.

As they approached the fringe, the only sound heard was the clatter of their horses' hooves on the sand-swept stone streets, breaking the eerie silence. Up close, the city looked like a ghost town, with evident signs of disorder, decay, and the ravages of warlike destruction everywhere. Scattered merchant carts lay abandoned, rubble lay piled up in mounds, and sand covered everything in sight. Suzu and Hogart had hoped to find a hidden treasure but only saw a sad reminder of a lost civilization.

"Rather desolate place," Hogart said.

They rode their steeds through the desolate city in a careful trot, guiding their mounts around huge boulders, broken wood beams, and multiple debris piles. A loud creaking sound came from nearby; the middle section of a three-story tan structure buckled, crumbled, and collapsed into a small river below. The distant sounds of creaking stone and snapping wood could now be faintly heard, followed by loud thuds and the sight of billowing plumes of tawny smoke. Since Tavter had been relocated to a new geographical site by magic, it seemed like the city's landscape was now coming alive, and some buildings were adjusting to their new surroundings.

"We leave our mark no matter where we go," Suzu said, shrugging at the sight of another partial collapse of a building dropping into the small river.

They reached a vast plaza, where a cracked ivory water fountain stood dry and dusty. Beyond the fountain, they saw a dignified sage temple carved from a single massive stone. It looked like a beacon of hope amidst rot. But as they approached, they noticed four grim stone-grey gargoyles perched on the roof, seemingly staring down at them with cold, unflinching eyes.

"This is the building we're looking for," Hogart said confidently.

"Are you sure?" Suzu said.

"I have traveled far and wide in my time, young lady. I know an entrance to the treasure vault when I see it."

In disbelief, Suzu rolled her eyes, swung her leg over her horse, and jumped to the ground. She took her repeater crossbow and attached it to her belt, then walked towards the entrance—a large oval arch carved with intricate patterns and symbols. Suzu was about to enter the structure but recoiled as a small pebble hit her head. She looked up and gasped. A few small stones and a light stream of sand fell in front of the entrance, the cracking and splintering rock heard above. The four gargoyle stone statues that adorned the top of the arch were transforming. The grey stone turned into a sickly dark olive skin, eyes burned like rubies, and their monstrous features became more vividly twisted and grotesque. Suzu grabbed her crossbow and shouted to her companion. "Hogart! The gargoyles are awakening!"

"There's still remnants of magic here?" Hogart said, alarmed. "The Sorceress Laurisia was a force for good. Her spells must have been tainted somehow."

The two intruders were terrified: four living gargoyles screeched and hissed at them from the edge of the building's rooftop. The beasts dug their flaxen razor-sharp claws into the ledge, sending a small shower of rubble down to the courtyard. They spread their obsidian wings outward, flapped, and took flight. The winged creatures took turns swooping and swirling over the heads of the frozen-in-place pair, trying to intimidate their prey.

One of the gargoyles shrieked and finally broke away from the collective swirl, shooting straight at the smallest of the two victims. Suzu fired a single arrow from her crossbow that pierced the gargoyle's chest, sending it crashing to the ground. She searched the sky for the next threat, but before she could react, another gargoyle swooped in from behind, grabbed her with its yellow talons, and lifted her off the ground.

Instinctively, Hogart reached down to a sizeable stone that fit in his hand and hurled it with great speed at the creature's head. The solid jade object hit the gargoyle, magically shattering it to lifeless pieces. Suzu dropped downward a short distance in the air, twisting her body in acrobatics, and safely landed on top of the building ledge like a graceful dove.

Sensing that the bigger of the two intruders was now the more significant threat, a third olive-skinned gargoyle lunged at Hogart. They grappled, each trying to overpower the other. Hogart managed to avoid the beast's sharp fangs but could feel its claws scratching at his chest. He pushed back with all his might, hoping to break free.

Perched on the ledge above the courtyard, Suzu watched helplessly from above as her friend fought for his life. But then she heard a chilling, loud screech and the swooshing of mighty wings behind her, just in time to turn to see another gargoyle flying in her direction. It opened its toothy mouth wide, claws outstretched, ready to tear her apart.

Suzu reacted quickly and dodged the snapping bite, but the gargoyle's body slammed into her petite form and knocked her off the ledge. She screamed as she fell, clutching the gargoyle's neck as it fell with her. She twisted midair and landed on the creature, cushioning her fall.

Hogart heard Suzu's scream and looked up. He saw her falling with the gargoyle and feared the worst. A fit of rage overcame him at the sight of his friend in deadly trouble, and he threw his ghastly opponent against the stone wall with a loud crack. The gargoyle shattered into pieces, seemingly by magic, leaving only beige dust behind. Hogart ran to Suzu's side, hoping she was still alive. "Suzu! Are you alright?"

Suzu slowly rose from the rubble beneath her with a soft chuckle. "The only thing broken is the gargoyle."

"Let's get our gold and leave this cursed place quickly."

Suzu returned to her horse to grab a coil of rope, draping it across her shoulder and torso. Hogart waited for her and the pair walked towards the entrance. The silver iron gate opened easily, perhaps too welcoming, with a gentle push.

Overeagerness taking over, Suzu dashed ahead of Hogart and stepped into the first room—a magnificent turquoise foyer only illuminated by the rising canary sunlight at the entrance. The room had a high stone ceiling with auburn wooden chandeliers holding flickering white candles. On both foyer walls hung faded, tapered, and torn tapestries depicting scenes of glory and conquest, surrounded by dusty, dingy, and corroded grey iron statues. The only way forward was a gloomy stone archway opposite the gate they came from. Two lit black metal torches marked the entrance to the next room, beckoning them to venture deeper into the darkness.

"Don't touch anything," Hogart instructed, taking a torch. The large man took the lead, stepping forward for a few paces into the dimly lit, eerie corridor. "Step where I step."

"Hogart, stop!" Suzu said curtly.

He obeyed without hesitation, freezing in his tracks. He wanted to question the order, but felt something slithering over his broad back and sliding under his long, wavy coal hair before he could utter a word. A soft hiss tickled his ear, making him shiver in a cold sweat. He dared not breathe or twitch a muscle, fearing the worst. Suzu carefully and gently removed the long, slender cerise snake from him.

"Is it poisonous?" he asked.

"No." She placed the snake down on the ground. "But some of them might be."

Hogart cast his bright torch towards the vast arched hallway and sucked in his breath. He only saw a scene straight out of his worst nightmares. The ochre ground of the long corridor constantly shifted and moved around in the dank darkness. Multiple shadows writhed and twisted around the floor and along the walls. The slight illumination spread across the corridor floor. It revealed a gathering of hundreds upon hundreds of various snakes, vipers, and serpents blocking their path.

"You go first?" Hogart said.

Suzu grimaced. "No. Together."

The duo had no choice but to enter the twisting and hissing snake-filled corridor, holding their torches high and hoping to scare them off. But the snakes were not easily intimidated. Some retreated into the cracks and holes of the walls and floor. Others stayed and coiled, ready to strike. The duo had to move forward back-to-back and in a slow circular motion. They swung their torches at any snake that came too close but knew they could not fight them all. They had to reach the end of the corridor, where they hoped to find a way out. They continued to move in a slow spiral, inching forward and turning around, facing the danger from all sides. It felt like an endless ordeal, but they did not give up.

Hogart and Suzu breathed a sigh of relief as they stepped out of the first chamber. They hoped the next one would be easier, but they were unprepared for what they saw. The second chamber was an elongated, wide hall with no decorations or features and devoid of columns, statues, or even tapestries. There was a strange color on the floor—silvery, almost like ash, that nearly matched the color of the stone walls.

"There's nothing to fear here," Suzu said. "Step where I step."

Her foot plunged into thin air as the floor dissolved into a foggy illusion. She gasped loudly as she started falling into a bottomless inky abyss hidden under the deceptive surface. But before she could scream, a firm hand gripped her tunic and yanked her back to safety.

Hogart pointed at the floor, a vast spider web spanning the entire chamber. The web was so delicate and pale that it looked like solid ground from a distance. But up close, it was a deadly trap for unwary travelers.

A circular opening glowed at the chamber's far end with a soft celadon light. Long, slender brown vines hung from the opening, creating a thick curtain.

"How were we supposed to get across?" Hogart said.

"I have an idea," Suzu answered.

She took her trusty crossbow and the coil of rope that she remembered to bring with her. Like with the statue, she shot an arrow with the rope attached across the pit to the opposite wall. Hogart, picking up on the idea, helped her secure the rope to a giant boulder on their side. He tested the rope's strength and gave her a thumbs-up.

"I'll go over first." Suzu grabbed the rope and started to cross over the small, dark chasm. Hand over hand on the rope, she made it across to the other side without any trouble.

Hogart peered down at the murky abyss, the cool draft giving him shivers, and sighed profoundly. At first hesitant due to the apparent danger, he had an intense love for gold and jewels that propelled him reluctantly on. He followed Suzu's lead, moving along on the rope slowly and carefully, hand over hand. He was halfway across when the tip of the boulder the rope was tied to, strained by the heavier weight, unexpectedly broke off. Hogart swung forward, screaming at the sudden drop, and collided with the rocky wall of the chasm. Instantly, his black-booted feet scrambled on unstable, loose rocks and slippery gravel to climb upwards.

"Hogart! Are you alright?" Suzu grabbed the rope and tried to pull her friend up to safety.

"For the moment," Hogart said, panting heavily. "I have to climb up."

Another chill gripped the body as he heard a strange scratching noise from below. He lowered his gaze and gasped in horror. A monstrous black spider, as giant as a horse, was climbing up from the darkened depths of the void. Its four tiny eyes glowed bright crimson with malice, its great fangs oozing teal venom, and its long, hairy legs scurrying rapidly. From another shifting shadow, Hogart felt a splash of liquid on his feet and looked down again. A second gigantic black spider creeped steadily upwards alongside its mate.

"Spiders! Two large spiders!" Hogart screamed. He tried to find a solid foothold on the jagged wall. He kicked with all his might to get a good climbing grip, accidentally dislodging a sizeable rock that dropped onto the head of one of the spiders, sending the fearsome creature plummeting into the darkness below.

Hissing its fury, the second black spider spit a strand of milky webbing, latching onto Hogart's thick leg. It tried to tug and pull its easy meal downward to its waiting, hungry jaws. The strands of webbing gripped Hogart like a coil of a serpent. As the spider continued to yank its prey down, Hogart's tight grip on the rope began slipping.

"Hang on, Hogart!" Suzu yelled. She pulled at the rope when she heard a sudden sharp crack behind her. Suzu turned to see that their misfortune had increased. A stone slab began to slowly slide down at the promising entranceway.

To make matters worse, the arrow stuck in the stone wall began to bend, buckle, and slip out under the pressure of the extra weight and the frantic tugging. Loosening out of its socket, the arrow caused Hogart to slide down the rocky surface for a few inches. The arrow moved again by the increasing strain. Hogart almost lost his sweat-soaked grip entirely and plummeted to his death.

"Hurry up, please!" Suzu held the rope firm and eyed the stone slab gradually dropping behind her with genuine concern. It was halfway closed.

Realizing that it was a matter of seconds before the embedded arrow would loosen from the rock wall, with a desperate effort, Hogart reached out and grabbed a thick leafy vine. As he clenched his mighty fist around the vine, the arrow popped free. The loose rope slid along the ground and over the cliff's edge. The dislodged arrow hit the monstrous spider in the head, making it lose its grip and tumble into the chasm.

With both spiders dead, Hogart hastily climbed the thick sturdy vine. When he reached the top, Suzu's helping hand greeted him. They ran towards the entranceway, the stone slab nearly at the bottom. Both partners slid under the closing door, barely making it through to the next chamber before it shut with a loud thud.

"That was too close," Hogart said. He picked himself up.

"Agreed. But I think we found it!" Suzu replied.

The duo hastily pushed aside the leaves and vines to further expose the open rounded entrance, almost acting like giggling children eager to find their holiday gifts. But as they parted the thick curtains of foliage, they felt disappointed. The chamber was dimly lit by a few fiery chartreuse torches, revealing only mundane objects. There were a few pieces of colorful, exquisite artwork, vases of the finest craftsmanship, silver and bronze plates and cups, elegant oversize tapestries, and furniture crafted from skilled artisans—but not the splendor of jewels, emeralds, or gold. Nothing sparkled or shone in the dank gloom. Nothing looked valuable or rare. They had risked their lives for this? A collection of dusty relics and trinkets? What was supposedly a glorious chamber filled with disgusting wealth beyond anyone's imagination was a profoundly upsetting letdown.

"Disappointed!" Suzu said. She kicked a silver cup away in annoyance.

"This can't be the treasure room," Hogart said. "There's nothing of great value here at all." The burly man rummaged through the unworthy finds like a dog sniffing out a bone.

Fed up with the vault's lack of true treasure, Suzu scrutinized the room for anything worth taking. Her sharp eyes landed on a shiny silver sword with a golden hilt embedded in a maroon wooden chest. "Maybe this will be useful someday," she mumbled, reaching for the blade.

"Wait! Don't!" Hogart yelled, springing forward to stop her.

But it was too late. Suzu's fingers wrapped around the sword's hilt. In an instant, at the slightest touch, the sword surprisingly plunged deeper into the wooden chest. The sandy floor cracked open under their feet, and the bumbling duo both tumbled helplessly into a dark pit.

The pair dropped a short distance into the blackness and landed on a smooth, curved aquamarine surface. Immediately, they tumbled forward and slipped uncontrollably down a polished, steep, slick natural rockslide. After a few nasty sudden twists and turns, they came on an opening at the end of the circular tunnel and were hurled harshly to rough grey cobbled stone.

Groaning softly as they stood up, they found themselves in a clammy, benighted chamber at the beginning of a mazelike catacomb. Even with the help of lit torches nearby, it was too dim and murky to see ten feet ahead of them. The stale air was dank and musky. There was the screeching sound of dozens of rats and the sight of an army of tiny sable spiders crawling around the floor and walls. Amongst those living creatures were the scattered taupe skeletal remains of the dead.

"This is all your fault," Hogart said. "I told you not to touch anything."

"Where are we?" Suzu said.

"Lost. We can't go back up that way."

The partners in plunder had no other option but to venture deeper into the catacombs. They grabbed some of the torches mounted on the walls and walked warily forward. The tunnel ahead seemed like an underground cemetery consisting of a subterranean gallery with recesses and niches for tombs. The underground corridor, winding and bending, was adorned with countless bones and skulls along the edges.

The two friends pressed themselves flat against opposite sides of the arched stone corridor as they proceeded, careful not to step on the many rats scurrying around the floor and into the small pools of water between them. They shuffled through the confusing, twisting, and turning labyrinth, unaware of the possible danger that may lurk ahead in the dark. Rounding another pitch-black corner, they heard indistinct squelching followed by a low, soft rumbling sound behind them.

"Please tell me that's your stomach," Suzu said.

"No, it's not."

The low rumbling sound came again, followed by a threatening hiss. They froze in terror, realizing they were not alone in this dreary place. Something followed them, something large and hungry. They glanced at each other, their eyes wide with trepidation. They slowly turned their heads together to see a shocking sight that paralyzed them where they stood.

From behind a broken partial wall stepped a large, scaly teal bowed leg with sharp, rending dark grey talons on its enormous brown foot. This was followed by a slender forked cherry tongue that slithered out of the rounded snout of a long flat head like an agitated snake. The robust and agile neck and scaly, sturdy green-blue limbs shifted forth in a slow side-to-side movement, seemingly searching the air for distinct smells or the slightest of sounds, as a substantial, muscular, spiked mahogany tail swung around menacingly. What appeared to be a thirty-foot-long monster, some strange midsize emerald dragon, had been awakened. The terrifying creature spied the duo with a slitted yellow eye, growled louder with intense hunger, and advanced towards its long-overdue meal.

"Dragon!" Hogart cried.

Their survival senses quickly returned along with the movement of hurried feet. Hogart and Suzu, the fear of death gripping their hearts, ran away through the murky, twisting, and turning tunnels, stumbling and bumping into each other and sometimes colliding with the grey stone walls of the dark passages. The dragon roared and snorted, following as quickly as its massive body would let it squeeze within the restricting walls, its hunger driving it to chase the fleeing prey. The large, curved, serrated teeth snapped continuously behind the scurrying meals, inching closer, encouraging and urging them to pick up their pace or suffer a gruesome fate.

"Faster!"

The beast's frustration was noticeable as it let out a loud, annoyed wail that reverberated throughout the tunnels. It drew a deep breath within its mighty breast, preparing to unleash its fire on the fleeing duo. Hogart and Suzu sprinted ahead of the monster as fast as they could, hoping to find a way out before they were roasted alive. A hellish roar erupted from the beast's jaws, hurling a wall of scarlet fire along the sides of the tunnel towards the running pair.

Suzu and Hogart saw a soft glimmer of amber light ahead, indicating a more extensive space beyond the tunnel. Luckily, just as the red-hot flames were about to lick the napes of their necks, they reached the opening. Tossing themselves to the sides of the tunnel entrance to avoid getting burned alive, they evaded the flames that followed them and spewed into the vast room. The heat singed their hair and clothes, but they were safe for the moment.

Helping each other scramble to their feet, Suzu and Hogart dashed across the immense beige hall. Their eyes darted around for a way out, but they found none. They were trapped like rats in a giant cage, with an oversize hungry cat on the loose.

"Over there!" Hogart spotted a narrow shadowy gap behind a thick round maroon column with a high pile of debris and rubble stacked next to it. It almost looked like a small cave built into the wall. An excellent place to be temporarily unseen, and it would provide a little time and space between them and the stalking beast.

Suzu and Hogart sprinted across the chamber and squeezed into the hiding spot, hoping to escape the predator's sight. They gasped for air and tried to keep their hearts from pounding, but they knew they couldn't stay there long. They had to find another way out, or they would be doomed.

"We brought back to life a lot more than just a city," Suzu said.

"It's a dragon, I tell you!" Hogart growled. "I hate dragons!"

"I don't think it's a genuine dragon. They're scarce."

"If it has fire spewing through its jaws, Suzu, then it's a dragon!"

The smaller-than-average dragon broke free of the constraining walls and steadily emerged from the tight, suffocating passage, gliding like a slithering serpent into the grand hall. The forked cardinal tongue flicked and licked the air in a fresh hunt for its quarry. The scaly teal body shook with delighted relief from leaving the constricting passage. Then it crept slowly deeper into the hall, its huge head always searching left to right, the enormous, barbed orange-brown tail carelessly thrown around in an effort to flush out the concealed duo. Another brief blast of flame burst from its maw and across the room, setting the lobby partially ablaze.

"We can't stay here forever," Suzu whispered.

The dragon's spiked tail smashed into the maroon pillar with a thunderous crash, unleashing a deadly avalanche of rubble and stones on the cowering pair. They barely escaped being crushed to death, darting out of the hiding spot and sprinting away from the enraged monster. The dragon let out a deafening roar, its slitted eyes gleaming with bloodlust as it chased after its helpless prey, which was out in the open and on the run once more.

Hogart and Suzu ran throughout the lobby, hoping to find a way out or secure another safe hiding spot. Their hearts were pounding hard again, and their breaths were ragged. Panic started to overcome them in their aimless mad dash. Then, Suzu spotted an oval wooden door that might lead to some form of exit. "Over here!"

The pair sprinted towards the wooden door and tried to open it, but it was heavy and seemed fused to the stone wall. The partners in adventure pushed and shoved together against the door but found that it was hardly budging and very difficult to open. They pushed harder, using all their strength, but it barely moved a few inches. They felt a surge of panic as they heard the dragon roar behind them, getting closer and closer.

"Hurry!" Suzu shouted. "It's coming for us!"

"It's stuck!" Hogart said, grunting.

The dragon trudged towards them, moving in for the easy kill, ravenous for their warm blood. Hogart used all his might with a last-effort shove, opening the burdensome wooden door, and the duo flopped in a collective heap onto the hard ground inside the next chamber.

They rose from the ground and slammed themselves against the thick oval door, hoping to seal it shut before the dragon could get them. But the door was obstinate and slow, and the dragon was nimble and furious. It thrust its slimy green-blue snout through the opening, roaring and snapping at its promised tasty meal.

Hogart and Suzu clung to the door, trying to push it closed, but the dragon was stronger. They could feel its blistering breath on their faces and see its jagged teeth inches away from them. However, the dragon's immense body was too large to get through the smaller entrance.

The dragon's rounded snout slammed into the doorframe with a deafening crash a second time, sending splinters of wood, shards of stone, and dust flying in the air. The door cracked and buckled under the relentless assault of the monstrous creature, which roared with rage and frustration. Thrusting and thrashing against the weakening door, the dragon used its razor-sharp teeth to snap inches away from the terrified duo cowering behind the door. But despite its best savage efforts, the oversize brute was still too big to fit through the narrow gap.

Now the oval door was partially broken from its hinges, and the stones were loosened around the frame. The two friends continued to desperately push back together on the door and close it on the dragon's snout. The dragon's slender tongue, long and forked, darted out from its mouth, whipping around and probing the edges of the weakening doorframe, looking for a soft spot to exploit and get at the elusive pair. It spewed out small jets of ginger fire into the room, setting ablaze anything that caught its flame.

The dragon's relentless assault on the door sent Suzu's lithe form tumbling across the room. Highly annoyed by the dragon's unwavering persistence, Suzu looked wildly around her immediate surroundings for anything to help her fend off the beast. Her brown eyes landed on a bow and arrow on a nearby ivory-colored marble table. She snatched them and ran to a corner, where a torch burned brightly. She quickly wrapped a piece of cloth around the arrowhead and set it on fire, developing a flaming projectile.

"Whatever you're doing, make it quick!" Hogart yelled.

Taking careful aim, Suzu drew back her bow with a steady hand and released the fiery arrow into the beast's gaping, toothy maw. The dragon recoiled in sudden pain, stung by the arrow and singed by the flames. It stomped off and retreated into the dark shadows, letting out a pitiful wail of agony.

But the danger was not over yet. Suzu and Hogart found themselves surrounded by growing patches of ruby flames of fire with no apparent way out. The clumps of fire slowly spread, the heat rising and soon becoming unbearable, and the whisps of sooty smoke started to fill their lungs. They had to act fast, or they'd be roasted alive.

"Put the fires out!" Suzu yelled. "Grab that . . ." She paused, stunned at the sight just inches before her boots.

The treasure room was a feast for the eyes, a spectacle of glittering and gleaming objects that dazzled and overwhelmed the senses. Suzu and Hogart had never imagined such a sight in their wildest dreams. They stared in awe and wonder at the mountains of gold coins and bars, the sparkling jewels of every color and shape, the rubies that glowed like wildfire, the sapphires that shone like the stars in the sky, the emeralds that radiated like the deepest forest, the precious metals that reflected the light, the tapestries that depicted scenes of history and legend, the art pieces that showed the skill and creativity of various cultures, the paintings that captured the beauty and mystery of nature, the artifacts that revealed the secrets and mysteries of ancient civilizations, and the various multiple weapons that ranged from simple swords and daggers to exotic devices.

They had finally reached their destination: the treasure room of Tavter, a practical storage facility for accumulated and hoarded treasures from various lands and diverse regions. More than enough wealth was in this vault to satisfy anyone in any land. They felt a rush of exhilaration and curiosity as they looked around the room, eager to explore and claim their portion of the wealth.

Hogart grabbed a heavy tapestry hanging over the wall and tore it off with a loud rip. He wrapped it around his arms and ran towards the blazing inferno threatening to consume the room. He tried to beat down and smother the flames with the heavy fabric, but there were too many clusters, and they were growing too fierce. He could feel the heat scorching his skin and lungs. "Hurry! Take all that you can!" he said.

Suzu let out a delighted squeal, ignoring the fiery danger as she began to rummage and plunder the priceless hoard gleefully, stuffing her sturdy umber cloth bags with as much treasure as she could carry. But then an unusual sight amongst the luminous treasure trove and shifting, fiery amber shadows attracted her keen eyes. She peered closer through the drifting streams of ecru smoke and saw a strange sight unlike anything she had ever seen.

"What's that?" she whispered, curious and intrigued.

At the farthest end of the vault, a glorious, glittering golden throne was seemingly embedded within the tan stone wall, placed on a small beige pedestal that resembled an extension of the stone wall as if carved from the same rock. The golden throne was adorned with intricate patterns and sparkling, colorful jewels, reflecting the faint light that entered the vault. On the royal throne slumped the skeleton of a man who was once the king of this realm, his rusty crown still sitting on his skull and his torn, tattered jade regal robes with porcelain-colored trim lining still covering his withered bones. His empty eye sockets seemed to gaze at everything that happened in the vault as if he were still alive and very curious about his visitors.

Deeply entranced by the strange, eerie vision and undeterred by the looming danger, Suzu felt a strange pull towards the gilded seat. She ignored the crackling, flickering cherry flames, the long whips of curling and swirling flint smoke, and the increasing heat of tangerine embers surrounding her. She tuned out the shuddering cries of the beast raving nearby. With each careful step forward, Suzu studied every aspect of the sitting figure resting peacefully in silence and, oddly, seeming to almost be waiting for her with anticipation. She examined the ashen skeletal remains, which were still erect, upright, and imposing, in defiance of the passing of time, sensing that this man had endured much sorrow and strife in his life and beyond.

Suzu noticed a faint jade glimmer softly emitting from the ancient king's rawboned, clutched right hand resting on the arm of the throne. She reached out and gently pried the emerald gemstone from his skinny, sticklike fingers, feeling a tingle of power and wonder as she brought it into her possession. Once the Land Elemental Gemstone was removed, the king's right hand collapsed in welcome relief, and the skull drooped downward in apparent weariness as if the ages-long commitment, responsibility, and perhaps punishment had just now been fulfilled. He had been seemingly waiting for decades for this moment to arrive, to pass on this terrible burden. The troubled, haunted soul could finally seek release and rest in peace for eternity.

Suzu gazed at the green gem sparkling like a tiny star in the palm of her hand. She felt a surge of pride and joy with her newfound, hard-earned reward, knowing that this particular gem was the most valuable prize in the vault, and decided to keep it. But where could she hide it?

She remembered a secret puzzle-box necklace, a round silver ornament with tiny sapphire stones on the top and bottom and tiny ruby stones on the left and right sides, that hung around her neck. A secret compartment within could only be opened by a unique sequence. She pressed the blue stones on the top and bottom, then the red stones on the right and left, and heard a soft click. She carefully placed the gem safely inside the pendant, closing it with another click, and smiled at the soft weight of her treasure on her chest, hidden from the world.

"How were we supposed to carry our treasure out safely? If we try to run, the sacks will weigh us down," Hogart shouted.

Hearing her friend's choking, hoarse voice brought Suzu out of her tranquil trance and back to harsh reality. "We don't even know where there's a way out yet. If there is one."

"We have to get rid of that nasty beast first," he said. "This will help us." He proudly lifted a sizeable battle axe from the chamber's plentiful assortment of varied weapons.

"No, wait. I don't want to kill it," Suzu said sternly.

"You don't?"

"No. I have a plan."

Outside the treasure vault, the monstrous guardian of all the invaluable riches within roamed around in pain and fury. The dragon snorted and scraped its long round snout against the stone walls, trying unsuccessfully to get rid of the piercing flame arrow still lodged within its jaws. The narrow nostrils flared in anger until they filled up with a particular scent—something familiar and enticing. The unique stench of his elusive prey was nearby. The dragon turned its agile neck slightly to spy the larger meal of the two standing out in the open and waving his arms around like a fool to gain attention. The dragon's slitted eyes narrowed. It licked its lips with its forked tongue and prepared to pounce on the tasty snack.

"Oh, just how is Suzu able to talk me into these things?" Hogart bemoaned. "Suzu! You better be ready!"

No answer from his faithful counterpart was heard. Instead, the dragon's full-throated, deep, angry cry echoed through the lobby, shivering down Hogart's spine, prompting him to cry out and scamper off swiftly. Hogart sprinted ahead of the pursuing dragon as fast as his thick tired legs would let him. He zigzagged and dashed across the lobby floor, dodging and running between columns, furniture, and statues that hindered his path.

Not one evasive move slowed down or deterred the dragon. The beast smashed through a table, then tossed another table with its claws and teeth, creating a trail of rubble behind it. Determined to catch its prey, it lunged at Hogart at every opportunity.

Hogart felt the dragon's hot breath on his neck and screamed in terror. He tried to outrun the dragon, but he knew it was hopeless. The dragon was faster, stronger, and hungrier than him. It would be just a matter of moments before Hogart was snatched up within the monster's jaws.

"Now!" Hogart cried, rounding a corner of the lobby and purposefully running between two specific round pillars.

Safely hidden behind one of the wide columns, Suzu stood ready, clutching a long sword with a razor-sharp edge. She waited for the right moment, then slashed at the cords holding a massive banner hanging over the lobby. The large streamer came tumbling down, landing on the dragon's long flat head and instantly covering its sight.

The vision was obscured; the dragon roared and thrashed its robust neck, violently trying to shake off the heavy fabric. However, it only succeeded in tightening it around its head with every jerking, shaking movement. Blinded, the dragon roared in fury, lashed out, and smashed into the crumbling architecture. Its sturdy, powerful limbs and spiky tail demolished the old pillars and columns, weakening the stability of the lobby. The floor began to shake, and the walls cracked with a low rumble, escalating into a deafening roar. Huge chunks of stone broke off from the sides of the chamber and high ceiling, free-falling and raining down on the enraged beast.

"Fool!" Hogart yelled. "This is your grand plan?"

"Grab the gold!" Suzu shouted.

The pair reunited at their few bags of collected loot, gathering them up in their arms in haste.

"Let's go!" Suzu said.

"Go where?!"

The grand chamber collapsed, and they had nowhere to run for their lives. Huge boulders, heavy stones, and streams of loose dirt continued to fall from the ceiling and crumble inward from the surrounding beige walls like quicksand. Thick greyish dust from the fallen debris and black smoke from multiple red-hot fires rose, limiting any clear view and causing the friends to choke. Large sections of wide maroon columns and pillars splintered off and crashed dangerously to the ground nearby, almost crushing the fleeing twosome to death. They dodged and veered through the turmoil, hoping to find a way out before it was too late.

The tremendous, bulky weight and the beast's savagery cracked and broke down long-standing barriers. The oversized brute, blinded by the banner wrapped around its head, lost its balance, stumbled, reeled, and toppled over into a partition wall that had stood for decades, shattering it like brittle glass. Lashing out furiously to help it regain footing, its long tail whipped around and smashed into another wall section. Streams of canary sunlight shone through the gap, revealing a possible escape route. But to reach it, the two friends would have to get past the mighty thrashing dragon that blocked the way.

Forced to flee the increasingly unstable, crumbling structure, Hogart and Suzu braved their fate and darted as fast as they could across the grand lobby together towards the promising golden glow. As they sprinted forward, both watched the lumbering, unpredictable movements of the behemoth between them and blessed freedom. Sticking together every step of the way, Hogart and Suzu moved carefully through the shifting obstacle course. Avoiding the long, spiked tail swinging around everywhere in the air and being stomped to death by any one of the erratic, shifting, razor-taloned feet, the duo scrambled to get past the blinded and unaware beast with all the riches they could carry in their arms. They ran through the only exit in the chamber, accidentally provided by its lethal guardian.

Invasion of Mills Point

Staggering out from a crack within a wall and onto the abandoned, sandy streets, Suzu let out a piercing whistle that echoed through the restored, empty, old city. Within seconds of the command, the galloping, loyal horses neighed and dutifully came running through the thick veil of syrupy dust. Suzu and Hogart wasted no time loading their bags of precious loot onto the horses' backs, then mounted them and spurred them into a fast gallop. They intertwisted through the streets, as if being chased once more by an unseen force, escaping with their prize.

Without a backwards glance or a single word exchanged, Suzu and Hogart fled from the realm of Tavter, their horses racing at full tilt. The city's towering spires receded from view as they surged eastward, putting as much distance as possible between them and the resurrected city. Only when the highest peaks of the spires vanished from sight did they ease their pace to a leisurely trot, exhaling a collective sigh of relief, their bodies finally relaxing.

"Easy, girl," Hogart said softly to his horse, patting the head gently. "Shouldn't we retrieve the spearhead from the statue of Lars? Will Tavter disappear again?"

"No," Suzu said, calling out over her shoulder. "Tavter is no longer lost. Since it has been moved from its original native lands by magic, there will be disputes over rightful ownership. We should keep riding away and never return."

"Agreed. We have enough gold to last us for quite some time. Let the Red Rose Death Gang fight that dragon for the rest of it."

"What are we going to do about this unique gem that I found in the treasure room?" Suzu said. She rubbed the jewelry box on the silver chain, hiding the gem.

"Not sure yet," Hogart answered.

"I think we should keep it hidden at all times. It's the best out of all our newfound treasures. I'm sure it's worth quite a lot."

"Quite a lot of trouble, you mean."

"We could take the gem to the Kayawa Kingdom. Present it at the capital city of Valsco. It will prove that we were the ones who found Tavter," Suzu suggested.

"They will reward us handsomely with more gold for resurrecting the hidden kingdom. Disputes be damned!" Hogart said excitedly. "The poems and songs that will be written of us!"

"Mills Point is a week's ride to the east," Suzu continued in an even tone. "We can buy passage on a skyship to Kayawa. In the meantime, we should avoid the main roads and interaction with anyone."

Hogart laughed. "Fortune and glory!"

"Fortune and glory." Suzu smiled knowingly at her robust, overjoyed friend, joining in on the laughter. Ever since they'd met years ago, Hogart had had an uncanny natural ability to bring her willingly along in foolish pursuits of glorious riches and fabled tales.

For the next couple of days, the mismatched twosome traveled east to the river town of Mills Point. They traversed the dry, bleak sienna desert valley and entered a land of gently rolling, grassy viridescent hills. A soothing, peaceful relief came to both their hearts as they breathed in the crisp, sweet fragrance and saw vibrant, vividly colored flowers—lilacs, lavenders, and sunflowers--surrounding and adorning thin, leafy mint-green trees. They heard the cheerful songs and chirping of radiant, bright birds darting and flitting about amongst the brown tree branches and the gentle trickle of winding, sparkling azure streams that stretched across the land.

The journey was full of unique encounters with the wild creatures of the land. They marveled at seeing a group of stegosauruses munching on the verdant grassy hills, their spiked tails casually swaying in the warm breeze. They softly progressed through and admired the majestic bison herd that roamed the wide valley, their thick chestnut fur shining in the sun. They held their breath as they witnessed a fierce battle between two huge black bears and a single grey triceratops near a stream. The bears used aggressive teamwork to bring down the horned dinosaur, taking many swipes with their sharp claws against the lone animal. The thick-skinned, very strong, and equally resilient triceratops successfully fended off the furry twin attackers with its powerful, long ivory horns of solid bone, and the observing humans silently cheered for its triumph. Satisfied with the victorious result of the beastly challenge, Suzu and Hogart decided to give a wide berth and ride around the contestants to avoid any unnecessary confrontation.

As they rode along the pleasant path, Suzu had to endure listening to Hogart's endless, various stories of adventure in finding hidden treasure and lost gold, encountering wild creatures like the giant sea serpents and a deadly *Tyrannosaurus rex*, visiting magnificent foreign lands and glorious exotic cities, and his deep loathing of dragons. There were so many tales to be told and a story for every occasion, whether sitting by a campfire's soft, glowing amber light or walking under the blue sky; the days and traveled distance seemed to slip past easily. Suzu enjoyed some of his stories; a few were too farfetched and unbelievable; and others were highly questionable.

It was nearly a week into the trek. The melodious chirping and tweets of various brightly feathered little birds, shrouded in leafy evergreen, plum, and peach tree branches, seem to call forth the approaching morning sun and the waking eyes of the slumbering pair below them. Early lemon and pearly rays of the sun peeked through the drifting white fluffy-cotton clouds, and a warm, balmy wind crawled across the land. Still half-asleep and dreaming, Suzu and Hogart leisurely rose from their blankets and broke down their basic, crude camp. As the sun ascended before them, Hogart started to prattle on about any subject matter, half-coherent and half-not, before they'd even mounted their steeds and rode on to the east.

Suzu barely uttered a word for the first hour. She was too tired from only a few hours of sleep and sore from sleeping on the uncomfortable, rough ground. The dazzling, sparkling golden rays of the sunrise that pierced her brown eyes had a hypnotizing effect and made her feel sleepy again. Her thoughts drifted, and Suzu imagined herself in the wonderful, fantastic stories that her friend had shared with her the previous night while Hogart's continuous funny remarks and jokes in the present flew over her head. That was until, in the far, faint distance, Suzu heard the faint, melodic, soothing sounds of flutes, the thumping and tapping of drums, and a collected chorus of voices in harmony and merriment. It was like nature had developed a small band and was playing beautiful music to fit her mind's vague, tranquil thoughts. "Do you hear that, Hogart?"

The strange musical melody drew them to the top of a grassy lime-green hill, where they beheld a remarkable sight. A dusty road stretched below them, and a colossal brachiosaurus was coming towards them. It looked like a giraffe, but much bigger, with a long neck that reached the sky and a head that seemed too small for its grey-skinned body. Its hind legs were shorter than its front legs, giving it a slanted posture. It bellowed softly and moved with a gentle sway amongst the tops of the trees as if it was enjoying the trip or at least the beat of the music.

A lone rider, a Dino Driver, sat in a tawny leather seat at the base of the dinosaur's neck, holding the reins attached to a hickory noseband and bit around its small head. He looked like he was part of guiding the brachiosaurus but also trusted it to know the way. Positioned and strapped on the back of the brachiosaurus, almost like it was a horse's saddle, was a three-row, flat, open carriage. It rested on a saffron blanket, protecting the dinosaur from rubbing friction as it walked, strapped down by a massive-girthed band and back straps over the garment. Filling these seats were members of a jazz band, about ten musicians playing horns, flutes, guitars, and drums.

Behind it, the brachiosaurus was harnessed by silver tug chains to pull two forty-foot-long, box-shaped wooden stagecoach carriages. Each carriage, also attached to each other by silver tug chains, rolled along on four massive, thick grey iron wheels. At the front of the wagon was the driver's box, consisting of the driver and an additional man meant to make sure the carriage being tugged along was proceeding without pause, keeping an armed lookout for raiders and handling the front brake to keep the wagon at a halt when necessary. Each boxcar wagon was painted burgundy with goldenrod trimmings. They had a single square wooden door, outlined in goldenrod trim, for entering and exiting on each side. Oiled magenta curtains draped the windows, usually covered to keep the rain and dust out. The curtains were rolled up so the crammed-in passengers could see the beautiful passing scenery. Some of them wanted a better view of the landscape and climbed up to the roofs of the carriages, which were made of old wooden planks that creaked and swayed with every step. The roofs were also loaded with various items the passengers had brought, such as boxes, chests, jugs, pieces of luggage, and other personal items. They were all tied down to the railings that ran along the sides of the carriages, which were also made of cedar wood and silver metal bars, preventing them from falling off.

As the first transport made its way through the stretch of long seafoam grass and tall trees, another brachiosaurus followed closely behind, also carrying two carriages of the same type bursting full of passengers. They waved and shouted at each other, played music, sang, and clapped along, sharing their excitement and wonder about the peaceful expedition.

The two towering, grey-skinned brachiosauruses bellowed softly and lumbered along the dusty road, their massive, long necks swaying with each step. The Dino Drivers on their backs continued to urge them on with loud cries of command and an occasional flick of a ten-foot-long whip whistling in the air, guiding both the dinosaurs and the heavy carriages they towed behind them in a northern direction.

"They look like good people," Hogart said.

"At least they're in tune," Suzu said. "We should go say hello."

"What happened to staying off the roads and not interacting with our fellow man?"

"We have to rejoin society sometime. Besides, there might be reports about Tavter by now. It would be good to know what exactly the people are saying."

Suzu and Hogart rode their steeds down the slope of the hill, moving into an easygoing, friendly trot alongside the last carriage of the slow-moving procession.

"Good morning!" Suzu called out.

The festive group inside the last wagon greeted the petite, black-haired horse rider with friendly waves and salutations.

"Mind if we join you for a little while?" Suzu continued, bringing her horse to a slow walk. "My good friend here talks so much his tongue can get a sunburn on a rainy day. I need a new conversation on this beautiful morning to keep me awake."

The merry group of passengers laughed loudly at the spirited jest. They even tooted their horns and banged lightly on the drums in approval.

Hogart smirked at the playful insult, slowing his horse to a walk behind Suzu. "Where were you coming from?" he asked the wagon full of passengers.

"Hennsonn," one voice answered.

"Talinia," another yelled.

"Far from home. What happened?" Hogart asked.

"The Zamana Empire," a third person yelled in disgust, "has been slowly advancing westward from its lands in the far east. They have nearly taken the Poma Kingdom and started its new campaign of terror by invading the lands of Itonia."

"What of their defenses? What of the king?" Suzu asked.

"The Zamana Empire advanced quickly over the northern Vergery Mountain Range, and the Itonians stationed at the border were taken by surprise by the unprovoked attack."

"The Itonians have fortified their positions. Now, it's a stalemate. King Jelia still sits on the throne, but who knows for how long?"

"We heard hundreds of soldiers perished. The captain of the Itonian guard is dead."

"The princess was coming home from a diplomatic trip abroad, but her party went missing. More than likely dead as well."

"We were now refugees traveling to Rizi Springs in Orado."

Hogart rode up next to Suzu's side and spoke in a low tone. "Nothing about Tavter."

"The Zamana Empire. For weeks, they have been broadening their borders westward," Suzu said softly, almost whispering to herself. "Now they have reached the Vergery Mountains and are continuing westward."

"We should get to Kayawa as fast as we can."

"We'll reach Mills Port by midday. Let's ride along and blend in for a few miles in case anyone is looking for just the two of us. Then we'll politely say goodbye and ride off on our own."

Suzu and Hogart peacefully rode along within the crowded safety of the musical caravan. Having kept to themselves for days, keeping a low profile and avoiding trouble, the pair enjoyed the temporary company of other fellow travelers on the open road. Hogart had a new audience that would listen to a story or two, entertaining the crowd with fun fables of heroism and danger. Suzu was delighted to join the band in a song as they played in payment for the tall tales. They made friends and shared laughs, but they knew they couldn't stay for long. After a few fleeting miles of the dusty, uneven road passed, the oddly mismatched duo gave their best wishes to the cheerful passengers for a safe journey, split off on their own once more, and began to ride a different path to the east.

A few hours later, Suzu and Hogart arrived at the edge of Mills Point. Many other travelers depicted it as a bustling port on the edge of the plain. It rested at the meeting of the Reno and Savena River valleys, as the two main watercourses flowed many miles down directly to the sea. Mills Point was a city with tall towers that pierced the highest clouds, diverse buildings of various sizes that housed all kinds of people and businesses, and bridges and walkways leading to more great piazzas. The city port didn't have a central dock for water ships, relying on individual hangars and strips for landing and departure.

Skyships such as schooners, barges, dirigibles, carracks, and galleons, both great and small, personal and commercial, grand and dingy, could freely depart and land out of different sections of the town. They mainly used the riverfront and the mooring towers dotted across the city as their bases of operation. A maximum of six defensive watchtowers remained scattered amongst the buildings, mixed with the mooring towers, guarding the town from hostile threats.

Hogart and Suzu rode their steeds through the bustling, crowded streets of Mills Point at a careful, measured, leisurely pace, taking in the sights and sounds of the city. The active, vibrant atmosphere starkly contrasted with the vacant, lifeless Kingdom of Tavter. The main road cut through the city's heart, where pedestrians of various races walked along the wide, stone-paved street. Following the grid pattern, many other streets and alleys sprang from this central road.

Everywhere they looked, they saw clusters of tiny, cheerful, colorful birds flitting happily amongst the elegant buildings, which glowed with warm hues of copper and apricot in the radiant canary sun. The refined terracotta-roofed buildings were adorned with oval entrances and chalky balconies, giving them a graceful and stylish look. The arcaded streets were paved with wide tan cobblestones and lined with lush, leafy evergreen trees, bushy fuchsia flowering shrubs, and rows of colorful plants. Brightly colored tents and awnings, mixed with descriptive banners and market store signs, were proudly placed in front of the building structures, announcing the myriad goods and exemplary services of the various merchants and artisans. Even the air was fresh and clean, unlike the stale and dusty air of Tavter.

The community itself was vibrant and animated. Mills Point was home to thousands of diverse inhabitants, where different backgrounds and origins peacefully coexisted and interacted. The city consisted of various races, nationalities, cultures, and languages, evident by the distinct, inaudible chattering of numerous foreign dialects mixed with what was known as "the common tongue." The clothes people wore reflected their cultures and identities, creating a colorful and eclectic scene. Mills Port was a place where anyone could find a home, a community, and a voice.

They shared the road with the city populace and an abundant mixture of animal traffic. Single riders on horseback effortlessly weaved through the fluid, erratic traffic every day. Wooden carts and beautifully decorated carriages of different shapes and sizes, drawn by teams of horses that ranged from two to six, carried distant travelers and local pedestrians. Others carried goods for the market, such as wooden barrels, crates, jugs, vases, or stone art pieces. The most impressive sight was the giant dinosaurs that also calmly lumbered along the roads, hauling massive industrial wagons and personal, private carriages behind them. These majestic creatures, such as brachiosauruses or apatosauruses, may have been slow but they could carry dozens of people at a time and hundreds of pounds of cargo. Some smaller dinosaurs, like the docile triceratops or stegosaurus, were also used for transportation, labor, or as personal mounts by more adventurous souls. Some other animals, whether horses or dinosaurs, rested and fed out of a trough or patiently waited while hitched to a post at the side of the road. The streets were a varying symphony of movement that continued traveling the gridlike roads all day and night.

Suzu led the pair through the lively streets, where they witnessed some curious scenes of daily life. A triceratops with a pale jade hide, saddled with large wicker baskets full of fruits on its broad back, was being stubbornly dragged along the street by its weary, exhausted owner holding the reins. Up ahead at an intersection, another woman rode on the saddled neck of a chartreuse-skinned stegosaurus hauling a cart full of crates, chests, and jugs, arguing nastily with a driver of a six-horse passenger carriage. They caught snippets of the conversation as they leisurely passed by and learned that the stegosaurus in front of them had accidentally blocked the carriage and spooked the horses with a casual swipe of its tail. A burly, bearded blacksmith busily tended to the horseshoes of a horse near a large pen that held two towering white-and-mint-skinned brachiosauruses. In front of the famous Homebound Hotel, a staple of Mills Point, an idle mauve-skinned apatosaurus with a long neck had been outfitted with a yellow double-decker carriage that carried passengers on both sides. The driver, perched on a chocolate-brown leather saddle at the base of the neck, shouted rude instructions at the people climbing a wooden ladder to get into the overcrowded, cramped passenger carriage. A dark grey brachiosaurus, pulling a wagon full of carved stones for construction, slowly sauntered around a street corner, making everyone stop briefly and wait for him to pass.

The sweet smell of the town's famed rich cuisine struck Hogart's nostrils, and his hungry, pained stomach growled loudly enough to be heard. "I didn't realize how hungry I was until now," he said, breathing in the delightful aroma, trying to hold it in for as long as possible.

"I smell it, too," Suzu said. Her stomach was now growling just as loudly. "I believe a market area is around the next corner."

The crowded, traffic-filled street spilled into an even more densely populated market square, a living kaleidoscope of colors, sounds, and smells, where a diverse crowd of people and creatures converged and interacted. Scattered throughout the area were the kind of pleasant, welcoming sights that should be found in a community. In this dynamic and jubilant place, everyone could find something to enchant their senses and savor the music, the food, and the camaraderie.

In the middle of the square, a splendid three-tiered oval ivory fountain gushed streams of water in elegant curves. Around the fountain, a harmonious mix of transport modes cohabited. Single-rider horses, various docile dinosaurs put to work hauling cargo or used for recreation, horse-drawn passenger carriages, and sturdy work carts revolved in a counterclockwise circular motion.

The pedestrian portion of the square, surrounding the traffic circle, was a four-section stage for entertainment and culture. Playful children and their dogs scampered in festive mischief, giggling and woofing. Multiple singers and bands played various forms of upbeat music, sometimes interfering or drowning each other out even if they were distanced far enough apart. Street performers entertained gathered crowds with whimsical magic tricks and acrobatic feats. Artists involved in paintings, sculptures, and crafts lined up in rows, showcasing their skills and creativity.

Also along the periphery of the square, multiple vendors tended carts, stalls, and tables displaying a cornucopia of goods like fresh fruit and vegetables, baked loaves of bread, cheese, meats, silky fabrics, sparkling necklaces, vases, carpets, and various tempting sweet treats. More colorful tents, awnings, and specifically designed market signs attracted attention to stores featuring the finest clothing, the most beautiful florists, light meal eateries, full-service restaurants, and the most appreciated taverns.

"A drink at The Tipsy Ferret?" Hogart said happily.

"I'd rather keep an eye on our horses and the sacks they're carrying," Suzu warned.

The twosome guided their steeds to a less populated and quieter area of the bustling square, dismounted, and hitched their horses at a post next to a wooden trough full of refreshing, cool water. Nearby, a merchant vendor sold bread, smoked meats, cheeses, and much-needed water. Buying a combined assortment, Hogart made two generous sandwiches to keep hunger away from both of their bellies for the rest of the long day. The water drenched any thirst caught in their dry, sore throats. After their meal, the next stop was a vending cart full of fresh fruit to buy apples and carrots for their hungry horses.

"There's a mooring tower on the city's north end," Hogart said, closely inspecting the fruit. "There's usually one skyship that travels to Kayawa every day. Even though we don't need the money, we should sell the horses to a stable I saw coming into town and . . ."

Suddenly, a single low horn bellowed from one of the defense towers, sounding like a tepid siren. The entire populace froze, and a quick, sudden hush came over them. More distant horns from watchtowers around the town joined in, raising the alarming sound so high and piercing that no ear in the piazza could ignore the dire warning. The sound of noisy bells ringing added to the cacophony, confirming the town was in imminent danger.

"That can't be good," Hogart said.

"Let's get to that mooring tower," Suzu answered.

As if the alarm were the start of an unwanted race, Hogart and Suzu ran at full speed towards their hitched horses. Trying their best to create a path through the crowds of wildly bolting civilians, both partners got bumped by elbows and pushed around by shoves. A small wave of people accidentally knocked into Suzu, making her trip over her feet and fall harshly onto the hard ground. As always, faithful Hogart protected her from further harm, shielding her from the crushing stampede, and picked her back up on her feet before she was severely injured. They were a loyal team, always looking out for each other.

The piercing sound of the alarm shrieked through the air, startling the horses that were hitched to the post. They tossed their heads restlessly and whinnied nervously, sensing danger. The two riders rushed to their mounts, softly stroking their manes and gently whispering calming, soothing words. They freed them from the wooden post and swung onto their backs. Suzu quickly nudged her horse forward, leading the way, while Hogart followed closely behind. They galloped away from the scene, hoping to escape the brewing trouble.

As they raced towards the north mooring tower, Suzu and Hogart had little choice but to cut across the crowded plaza and face perilous challenges. The terrified locals scattered in every direction in a fluster, creating a tumultuous scene of collisions and commotion before their horses. A hapless vendor and his produce pile tumbled onto the tan cobblestone road, blocking their path and forming a tricky, slippery barrier in front of them. Suzu and Hogart urged their mounts to leap over the obstacle, barely clearing it in time. They continued their frantic dash, swerving and bypassing objects through the unpredictable hazards that sprang up from every direction.

Zooming around the colossal three-tiered fountain in the center of the square, the duo faced a barrage of challenges that pushed their skills and teamwork to the limit. They split apart for a short distance, allowing an olive-skinned brachiosaurus pulling a long alabaster carriage full of screaming pedestrians to pass harmlessly between them. Quickly regrouping, the pair suddenly found they must crisscross and interweave, collectively and individually, between several other individual horse riders buzzing around aimlessly, both horse and dinosaur-drawn wagons running straight at them from the opposite direction, frenzied citizens darting across their steeds' path, and more merchant debris carelessly being thrown about the square. At the square's fringe, a rickety chestnut merchant wagon full of lumber and pulled by a team of six horses snapped its hitch and toppled in front of them. The long pieces of wood spilled off the wagon, splintered, and scattered on the road, creating a labyrinth of logs. Suzu and Hogart had to maneuver carefully but quickly around the rolling, shifting pieces.

Reaching the north end of the market square and entering a wide street, Suzu and Hogart commanded their horses to pick up their pace. The increase in speed made the ride even more challenging. The frightened civilians ran around and along the street, darting in and out in front of them. A hazel apatosaurus and a green-spotted triceratops, both hitched at posts, began to stir around due to the high-pitched screams and sudden movements of the people around them. A driverless grey parasaurolophus, a docile peach triceratops, and an indigo stegosaurus recklessly and aimlessly roamed the wide street. They were joined by more horse riders and horse-pulled wagons that sped along in a panic going up and down the avenue. Merchant carts, baskets, vases, and other merchandise that were once neatly arranged on the sidewalks were now scattered on the street.

As they turned the corner at full speed, Hogart and Suzu encountered a huge driverless apatosaurus with a milky underbelly rampaging on the street. It seemed to be deliberately targeting smaller creatures, such as single horse riders and pedestrians, purposely pushing into and sometimes hurling them around the confines of the street with its massive body. One of its victims was a magenta-skinned, blue-horned parasaurolophus and its saddled rider, who were both thrown to the ground right in front of the approaching duo. Determined and unhindered, Suzu didn't hesitate and confidently steered her horse past the tangled mess. As Hogart passed, the apatosaurus's wild, swinging tail unfurled and brushed lightly against his speeding horse. Still, the mare recovered nicely from the glancing blow and ran on unharmed.

Suzu and Hogart dashed through the narrow market alleys, avoiding the crowds and carts that impeded their way, and rounded another street corner. They had to reach the north mooring tower before the skyship departed. It was their only chance to escape the city and its unknown dangers. The tan stone tower loomed over the red-tiled rooftops, a grand pillar reaching the snowy clouds.

The umber wooden Nao-styled skyship that awaited them, still tethered to the outstretched observation platform by thick ropes, was a marvel of craftsmanship, engineering, and magic. It gently floated above the ground, buoyed by the radiant glow of magitite, a rare mineral. The magitite was stored in a large coral balloon that crowned the ship, resembling a giant blimp in the sky. The vessel was made of sturdy wood, carved and painted to look like a nautical ship, complete with three masts. Like sailing ships, some skyships had sails atop their deck to catch more wind for higher speeds. But unlike a standard ocean-faring ship, all skyships had long, curved sails that could extend from the sides of the hull, catching the air and giving the vessel extra lift and maneuverability.

"One last skyship!"

But as they approached the single mooring tower, the hot-air-balloon craft detached from the extended platform and drifted away. The single rear wooden-bladed propeller rotated, most likely by pedal power from a couple of crew members, in a clockwise motion and picked up speed. The sapphire propulsion sails from both sides of the hull extended fully outward when they cleared the platform, catching the slight wind to propel the ship forward.

"No! Wait for us!" Hogart cried out.

"They can't hear you, fool!" Suzu said.

They halted their horses and gazed helplessly at the scene in a broad pearl-colored piazza. The mooring tower loomed in the middle, and a large crowd who had hoped to board the skyship was left behind at the base. They watched in despair as the vessel faded into the distance, taking their chance of escape with it. Peaceful people, panicked and angry, stirred uneasily about their unknown fate. Rabid consternation spread amongst the masses like a contagion.

"Now what?" Hogart asked.

"The river port!" Suzu yelled. "Come on!"

They zigzagged across the plaza, shunning the clusters of crowds, Suzu in front with her usual confident stride. She felt she knew the way to the river port, where they could find a sailboat to escape the city. They had to hurry. They were not safe yet, but they were close. They had made it this far with their treasure from Tavter; they could make it a little farther.

The horses galloped down another nameless cobbled street, eluding the multiple blazing fires and sooty smoke erupting from the front of the building and spreading onto the street. Suzu and Hogart could barely see where they were going as the air was filled with hot flint ash and floating, scorched debris. They had to diverge numerous times to avoid the numerous obstacles appearing out of nowhere, like a few stray civilians or dinosaurs great and small suddenly emerging from the swirling, oily smoke, staggering or running aimlessly in the horses' path.

Along the way, Suzu and Hogart encountered more obstacles, such as a bewildered claret parasaurolophus with a wounded rider slumped on its back. They had to steer around it, hoping the massive animal wouldn't charge at them. They saw other horse riders hurtling in and out of the smoke, some friendly and shouting words of warning as they passed, some hostile and cursing that they almost collided. A wagon train of four carriages pulled by terrified horses came straight at them through the inky smoke. They had to squeeze through the narrow gap between the rushing wagons, hoping the carriages wouldn't tip over on them as they frantically passed by. They witnessed an amaranthine-skinned, blue-spotted brachiosaurus, blinded by the fire and smoke, smashing into a statue of a bird that toppled over, crumbling to pieces. They were forced to ride under the falling stones and rubble, praying they wouldn't be crushed. Sadly, they passed by a grey-striped light-tangerine stegosaurus lying dead in the street, riddled with arrows sticking out of its scaly hide. They both had to look away, feeling a pang of pity and a swell of anger for the innocent animal.

They raced into a surprisingly nearly empty, hidden corner of the city, a nonmarket section of town where a wooden bridge was under construction. They started to cross over the approach slab, but the wood of the dilapidated, rickety overpass creaked, groaned, and cracked at the very first step. Significant bits of splintered timber broke off, and entire girders collapsed into the small river below, making loud splashes that sprayed upwards with each downed wooden board.

"It's collapsing! Hurry across!"

The duo was halfway across without a problem when an agitated brachiosaurus stumbled and collided with the bridge support beams behind them. The entire under-construction wooden bridge tilted and shook violently. One section of the wooden decking suddenly dipped down, sinking towards the river below.

"Mercy!" Hogart cried.

The frail structure began breaking apart; another section of the decking dipped down even more underneath them. The bridge's entire length buckled and sank under the horses' hooves, forcing them to instinctively sprint forward faster to the end of the decking and safely jump forward in a tremendous leap off the collapsing bridge just as it gave way and disintegrated into the river.

Leaving the remnants of the broken bridge in their wake and shooting into a tight, narrow street, Suzu and Hogart's celebratory chuckling was cut short when they came face-to-face with a new danger. A massive black-and-white-spotted apatosaurus, yoked to a metal industrial cart that had flipped over, was stampeding down the road towards them. The cart dragged behind the beast, spraying small waves of sand into the air, threatening to crush anything in its path and acting as a secondary weapon.

The two friends had to act fast. First, they avoided the apatosaurus by steering their horses underneath the snow-colored belly and between the towering dinosaur's moving legs, dodging its long, swinging tail. Then they saw the cart coming, a metal monster ready to devour them.

Suzu and Hogart urged their horses to leap onto a chestnut wooden porch along the street's side. The cart slammed into its wooden pillars holding up a balcony, sending splinters flying everywhere. The overhang caved in behind them, barely missing their heads as they rode along the porch. They breathed a sigh of relief as the horses leapt from the porch and rode out of the short, slender street and into another open city road.

"I think we're past the worst of it," Suzu said, almost laughing at their good fortune. But as soon as those words were spoken, an unforeseen arrow struck the breast of Suzu's horse, instantly causing the mare to fall to the street in a dusty heap.

"Suzu!" Hogart shouted. He immediately stopped his horse and dismounted, taking his sacks of gold off the saddle. He rushed to his friend's aid, setting the loot bags down. "Are you alright?"

"I'm alright. But my leg is trapped underneath my horse."

Hogart gritted his teeth, rubbed his hands together, and placed his arms underneath the carcass that pinned Suzu to the ground. He strained to lift the massive weight, hoping to free his friend from the trap. But the animal was too heavy for him alone, and he felt his muscles giving up. He surveyed the area for anything that could help him: a branch, a rock, a rope. He spotted a bronze metal rod sticking out of a pile of rubble nearby. He could use it to pry the animal off Suzu or at least create some space for her to squirm out. He let go of the carcass and ran towards the rod, praying it wasn't too late.

The duo were on the outer fringe of a bustling, pedestrian-filled plaza. None of the citizens surrounding them seemed interested, sympathetic, or concerned with their perilous situation; their attention was drawn elsewhere in the area.

A few singular screams were heard, followed by a loud wave of murmurs that overcame the crowd. A few individuals started skittering around, pushing into other startled, motionless fellow citizens or toppling over unattended vendor carts and stalls. Soon, the hysteria heightened and spread to the rest of the masses. At one end of the market square, an appearance horrified the crowd and caused them to flee.

A fearsome sight greeted the terrified eyes of the spectators as they beheld a triceratops, reaching thirty feet in length, standing motionless on the far end of the plaza. The skin of its body was a striking orange-tinged color, with a champagne underside contrasting its dark legs and tail. Its enormous head was the most impressive feature, sporting a broad and bony tangerine crest that extended from its forehead to its neck and three sharp, pointed ivory horns that jutted out from its face. The white horn on its snout was above its nostrils, and two equally sharp four-foot-long yellowish horns were above the eyes. As if forged from iron, a silver metallic luster covered the rest of the beast's body, forming an additional protective armor that enhanced its already intimidating appearance.

A commander of the Zamana Empire, Tomap Sruz, was already making a name for himself and becoming a legend. Saddled on top of this beast, Tomap was a midsize, imposing, and striking man with pale white skin and short jet hair that contrasted with his fiery emerald eyes. His upper body was draped entirely in light scarlet, and his lower in pitch-black armor, creating a striking impression of blood and shadow. He appeared youthful but with a hint of being aged by battle, leaving his age uncertain. His muscular build conveyed power and self-control. Handsome and intense, he made unflinching eye contact with a smolder inside that would boil and get angry at the snap of the fingers. Considered a very ambitious and determined individual throughout the Zamana Empire, he never backed down from a challenge or an enemy. With his clenched fist gripped tight around a long silver sword that gleamed in the golden sun, it was evident why this man inspired fear and demanded respect from his foes and allies alike.

With a fierce battle cry and a crazed look in his dark green eyes, Tomap commanded the armored triceratops to charge purposely into the helpless, screaming, frightened crowd. The horn on the snout tore into flesh and bone. A wave of mangled, bloodied bodies flew aimlessly and carelessly high into the air. The immense armored creature easily toppled over carts and wagons. Horses, scared by the presence of the sharp horns, tossed their riders cruelly to the hard street.

To make matters worse, the scene behind Tomap was a blossoming nightmare for the huddled, distraught masses. The three branches of the Zamana army marched behind the commander, each showing affiliation with a uniform of a different color.

The most feared of them were the top tier: the Allosaurus Riders, comprised of elite men and women warriors who had captured and trained the savage beasts for war. They wore crimson armor: light shoulder armor, arm armor, gauntlets, breastplate armor, and thigh armor that left their limbs free for movement. Over the thin armor, they wore ruby robes with hoods and a cowl around their mouths that masked their faces so only the eyes were seen. Black leather boots filled the stirrups hanging from the saddles of the dangerous animals. Each rider carried a round, spotted silver shield and a sword held in a sheath, ready to strike at any enemy.

Two monstrous allosaurus dinosaurs, clad in black armor and carrying armed riders on their saddles, loomed over the crowd. These beasts were naturally dark grey and measured thirty feet in height and length. They walked in the courtyard on their powerful hind legs while their small front limbs had hungry, sharp, sturdy claws. Both allosauruses' heads swung like axes at their prey just as much as their long and muscular tails.

Following the Allosaurus Riders, fifty cavalry trotted on horseback. These horse riders were the Lancers, the elite spear wielders of the

Zamana Empire. Their uniforms matched the rest of the army, except for the dark grey that signified their military rank. They held round silver shields in one hand and long spears in the other, ready to pierce through any enemy that stood in their way.

The Zamana Troopers, at least three hundred strong men and women, were the most dreadful sight, marching in perfect formation behind the Lancers, the elite of the elite, chosen for their deadly skill and unwavering loyalty. They wore gleaming, thin white armor reflecting the sun, and wielded long, sharp silver swords that could easily cut through most enemies with one stroke. They were the pride and glory of the Zamana Empire, and they knew it.

Each Allosaurus Rider screamed an unclear command to their reined beast. Instinctively, the allosauruses sprang forth on bipedal legs and tore into the unarmed crowd with knifelike teeth. The firm, sharp black claws grabbed the torsos of people, bringing them to their waiting jaws to munch on. The active predators preyed on and attacked anything that moved before them.

Hogart's horse, agitated by the noise and danger, let out a loud neigh and bolted away from the scene. "Come back here!" Hogart yelled.

A fearsome allosaurus, with a Dino Rider saddled on its back, emerged from the scattering crowd with a shrill, high-pitched roar. The Allosaurus Rider spotted the two stranded friends amidst the crowd, one person struggling to lift the horse's carcass off the other. He pulled his reins to direct his beast towards them. The allosaurus snarled and closed in on the pair, ready to strike for an easy kill.

"Hogart! Watch out!" Suzu screamed.

The Zamana Empire Allosaurus Rider was about to shout the command to strike when a sudden burst of vermilion fire hit the side armor of his dinosaur, stunning the beast and forcing him to stagger back. The Dino Rider saw a barrage of flaming arrows raining down from the sky. The dinosaur roared in pain and agitation as most arrows bounced off the black armor, but some pierced its grey scales and set its flesh on fire. The Dino Rider tried to calm his mount, but it was too late.

A small group of Mills Point soldiers had arrived on the plaza, riding four giant silver-armored rhinos that were ten feet high and long. The four battle-ready rhinos charged at the single allosaurus, using their massive ashen bodies and sharp ivory horns to ram and gore the enemy. The Dino Rider was thrown off his saddle and trampled under the rhinos' hooves. The riderless allosaurus tried to fight back but was outnumbered and outmatched, snapping its jaws at any of the four smaller creatures that dared to get nearby.

The four thick-skinned rhinos were huge but also fast, covering a lot of ground in a short time. The distinctive horns on their noses were used as weapons, prodding and stabbing at the underbelly of the dinosaur when an opportunity presented itself. Extremely loyal to the Mills Point soldiers, who had trained and protected them from poachers, the rhinos and their riders worked together as a team, coordinating their movements and attacks. They quickly circled and overpowered the single allosaurus, saving their fellow townspeople from certain harm or death.

The plaza was a scene of havoc and resistance as the town defenders finally arrived and held their ground against the invaders. Either a rhino rider or a foot soldier, the Mills Point soldiers were dressed in caramel and aqua armor, pewter metal helmets, and black boots. Every man and woman appeared equipped with a weapon, whether a shield, sword, bow, arrow, or crossbow. The Mills Point soldiers formed a blockade, swords on the street, and archers positioned on the rooftops at one square section. More flaming arrows from the small assemblage of town peacekeepers soared through the area, striking their targeted marks precisely.

"Come on, you overgrown lummox! Lift!" Suzu screamed.

With a loud grunt, Hogart lifted the mare's hide again, trying to dislodge Suzu from the lifeless heap. He heard her gasp softly as she finally freed her leg from the weight. They snatched their sacks of stolen goods, aware that the Zamana Troopers were closing in on them.

On the edge of a war-torn plaza, Suzu and Hogart dashed away with desperate urgency, their feet barely touching the cobblestones. The air was brimming with the tawny dust and din of battle, a cacophony of clashing steel and war cries that echoed off the sandstone facades surrounding them. They darted like shadows down a street, slipping through the calamity, their minds singularly focused on the immediate mission of escaping.

"Suzu, stop!" Hogart hollered. "You're spilling!"

Suzu halted and let out a loud scoff of annoyance. One of the two cloth loot sacks that she was carrying was torn. "This is the worst time!"

Hogart and Suzu quickly tried fixing the hole by tying the ends off but couldn't do it due to the hefty size. They tried to ignore the trail of glittering coins and gems they were leaving behind, hoping no one would notice. But their luck ran out when a small group of greedy people spotted their treasure bags, ignored the bestial dangers and the enemy troops, and circled the duo to attack them. Multiple hands sprang out, grabbing and ripping at Suzu's valued sack, making it burst open and spill its contents. Gold coins, jewels, and rubies were all over the street.

"Gold! Treasure!" voices in the crowd cried.

"Get off me!" Suzu shouted. Both she and Hogart fought back, but their defenses were limited since they gripped their treasure tightly. They were quickly outnumbered and overwhelmed by the crowd.

No one saw the allosaurus approaching them down the street, drawn by the people's loud noise and wild commotion. The enormous armored dinosaur only saw an easy feeding frenzy assembled in one area. It lunged at the distracted crowd, snapping its sharp jaws around several people and tossing them aside. The masses screamed and ran for their lives as the dinosaur chomped down on the pedestrians, leaving Suzu and Hogart alone with the remaining three sacks of treasure. With the momentary break from being grabbed and pummeled, Suzu and Hogart took the opportunity to escape the greedy mob, the hungry dinosaur, and the fierce battle.

The bumbling duo, arms laden with loot bags, sprinted through the tumultuous streets on foot. They were an unlikely pair, one tall and girthy, the other short and lean, but together, Hogart and Suzu moved with an unexpected grace amidst the confusion. The street was bursting with obsidian smoke and the sharp tang of cherry embers while the sounds of the city in distress filled their ears. They ducked under a falling, black-charred wooden beam and the remnants of a once sturdy turquoise awning, and sidestepped a blazing, rolling cart. They carefully cut through the shifting, panicked crowds, people who were too caught up in their survival. A woman clutching her child close, a man shouting for his lost dog, and a group of youths who looked like they might be considering a venture into opportunism—the streets were a tapestry of desperation and disarray.

Suddenly, a loud rumble made Suzu and Hogart stop and look up. A wall of a three-story building had collapsed before them, the fallen stones blocking their way. They quickly turned around and ran in the opposite direction. As they did, they immediately saw a tilting defense tower engulfed in cerulean fire and thick grey smoke. The structure weakened and finally toppled over, sending a shower of stone shards flying in their direction. They were forced to change direction repeatedly to escape harm.

They scurried aimlessly around the corner of an intersection and found a street filled with ashen smoke like a cloud, but it seemed empty of people. They were stunned by the image that emerged through the clotted smoke. The brachiosaurus was a massive beast, towering over the city's trees and buildings, bellowing in agony. It had escaped from the command of its Dino Rider and was now lumbering through the streets with a mauve pedestrian carriage full of travelers still hitched to it. In its state of agitation, the dinosaur unknowingly crushed anything and everything under its feet.

A terrible roar was heard. A Zamana Empire Allosaurus Rider, saddled on top of a smaller but faster predator, also emerged from the whisps of smoke to chase after the runaway herbivore. He wielded a long spear tipped with a sharp metal blade. He brought his mount alongside and aimed for the brachiosaurus's neck, hoping to pierce its vital artery and bring the beast down quickly. During the pursuit and conflict, the Dino Rider urged his allosaurus to leap over the obstacles in the path, dodging the carts and debris.

The pedestrians, families, and individual foreign travelers within the wagon screamed. The Allosaurus Dino Rider had no time to swerve or halt its attacks. The allosaurus crashed its head into the wagon, sending it flying off the hitch and into a stone wall. The brachiosaurus bellowed in terror and continued to stumble down the street to escape its attacker. The wooden door to the toppled carriage popped open, and people started to climb out, helping one another to safety.

The Allosaurus Rider looked up and saw that the brachiosaurus had stopped running and decided to confront its attacker. It swung its long tail, hitting his allosaurus on the side. The impact sent the allosaurus and rider tumbling to the ground, rolling over several times. The Allosaurus Rider lost his grip on his spear, losing it, and his helmet flew off his head. Lying on the sandy ground under his mount, the rider felt blood dripping from his nose and mouth. He tried to get up, but his allosaurus was too injured to move. It groaned in agony, its ribs broken and its skin torn. The mighty brachiosaurus loomed over them, ready to finish them off with a stomp. The Allosaurus Rider closed his eyes and waited for the end.

Hogart and Suzu barely had time to react to the bestial fight as a wall of flame erupted in front of them from one of the damaged buildings, sending white sparks and ashes into the air. They felt surrounded. The town was a blazing inferno, the heat intense, with multiple fires consuming the wooden buildings and creating thick midnight smoke that choked their lungs.

The two friends, relentless in their desire to escape, rushed down another nameless, smoky street and found themselves trapped amongst the remaining horse riders and wagons speeding dangerously around them. The remnants of a once orderly procession now careened in a desperate bid for safety, the air dense with the dust and distress they kicked up in their wake. Sensing the urgency and terror, the horses responded in kind; their instincts overrode training as they reared and lashed out, their riders struggling to maintain control. They sidestepped a particularly frantic amber stallion, its eyes wild with fear, and narrowly avoided the crash of a flipped wagon.

Suzu and Hogart turned to find themselves in a heart-stopping encounter with a stegosaurus that had been set ablaze. The beast charged at them through the streets. Its scales, once a part of its grandeur, now served as kindling for the flames that engulfed it. The heat radiated off its body in waves, the fire crackling with a ferocity that mirrored the creature's horror and anguish. It headed straight towards Suzu.

Hogart, with reflexes honed by countless close calls in this unpredictable world, reacted with lightning speed. His soft, firm grip on Suzu was both a lifeline and a silent vow that he wouldn't let harm come to her. As the stegosaurus barreled past, its spiked tail a fiery whip that slashed through the air, Hogart pulled Suzu away to safety.

As the stegosaurus disappeared into the distance, its cries echoing in the smoky haze, Suzu and Hogart stumbled into a narrow alley between tall residential buildings. Wanting to leave the upheaval in the street, they sped through the labyrinth of alleys. Hogart, with eyes wide as saucers, kept close behind Suzu. Up ahead, the alley opened to reveal ivory steps, a glimmer of hope amidst the despair.

Hogart and Suzu exited the alley and reached the steps of a broad, grandiose white staircase. As they stood on the staircase, panting heavily and bewildered, they felt the weight of uncertainty bearing down on them. With its twisting steps, the staircase seemed to ascend and descend into the unknown. The distant screams continued to meld with the beastly bellows, creating a surreal symphony that added to the confusion.

"Which way? Hogart said, still breathing hard.

"Follow me," Suzu said. In an instant, she bounded up the staircase.

As the lost, mismatched misfits ascended only a few steps with their loot bags cradled in their arms, they met two Zamana soldiers on the stairs who had just turned the corner of another side alley. On seeing the two civilians with their cloth sacks of loot, the invading pair of military men draw their swords in unison, spinning and twirling them in a stylish, lethal manner with flair and skill. Finished with the excellent swordsmanship display, they aimed the sharp tips of their blades at the two hapless "thieving" peasants who had unexpectedly crossed their path on the stone-white stairs.

Silently, without a second thought, Suzu smiled and tossed her single bag of treasure over her shoulder to Hogart, who bobbled the bag with his large hands, already full of two sacks, but managed to catch it. In an instant, Suzu's sword left its sheath, finding its first target, who slumped to the ground. The other soldier jumped back in surprise, fending off a series of strikes that became increasingly hard to block until the sword was struck away from the hand that wielded it. The unarmed Zamana soldier turned, yelped, and ran up the stairs, fearing for his life. Suzu brandished her sword in the air, screamed in a horrific, bloodcurdling style, and chased the frightened soldier up the stairs.

Hogart watched his friend sprint a short distance up the staircase, suddenly stop, turn, and sprint back downward. "Run!" she screamed.

Almost like a huge tidal wave engulfing a tiny sailing ship before it, a sudden rush of screaming Zamana Empire troops, horses, and spears swept down the wide staircase. Hogart instinctively spun around and ran down the stairs, hoping to find a way inside the buildings along the staircase and out of the wave's path.

Suzu quickly joined Hogart at his side, matching his pace. Then they heard another chorus of screaming and roaring from the town's defenders, who rushed up the stairs to meet the foreign Zamana invaders.

Caught between the two warring armies, Hogart and Suzu pressed themselves against the side wall as the swords and spears clashed. Blood splattered, and screams echoed around the pair. Unnoticed, they slid along the edge, avoiding conflict with any of the soldiers, who tore into each other, and clumsily found a massive wooden door. Hogart pushed against it, opening it just enough to let them escape the conflict unseen.

Leaving the sounds of battle on the staircase behind, they ran through another tight, slender alley to the top of a U-shaped sandstone staircase devoid of people or soldiers. They looked around, wondering where they were and how they got there. Thankfully, the stairs led down towards the river port.

Suzu led the way. "I lost one sack of our loot."

"It's alright," Hogart said. "As long as you're unharmed."

"I can't believe our rotten luck right now. Who was that guy on the triceratops?"

"Don't know. But the Zamana Empire has advanced farther to the west than we anticipated."

"We're almost to the pier. Keep moving."

Scampering down the U-shaped staircase, Suzu and Hogart, panting heavily, felt a surge of relief when they smelled the salty breeze of the river. There was also the welcomed sight of two long hot-air balloons floating above them, the last skyships in the city. Each Nao-crafted vessel was approximately seventy-five feet long, but they had different balloon designs. One had a cylindrical maroon hot-air balloon with a simple black rudder sail to steer it. The other balloon was just as long but with a pitch-black top and a pure white bottom. A narrow gold trim separated the two contrasting colors. It had white propulsion sails on the bow and stern of the skyship, with a narrow strip of a rudder sail on top of the stern, making it look like a large killer whale. The cawing of seagulls overwhelmed the ears, and the sight of a few of them circling the waiting crafts renewed their hope and rejuvenated their spirits as they reached the riverbank.

The long, narrow wooden pier, extending from the shore to the river water and between the two docked passenger skyships, was a scene of utter unruliness and perturbation. Crowds of people desperately tried to get on board the skyships, waiting to take them away from the city under attack. The skyships were tied to wooden poles that stuck out of the pier, and they swayed gently in the wind as if they were eager to break free and fly away from the destruction unfolding around them.

The pier was crowded with people stuck close together, unable to move much at all. They were pushing and shoving to get to the single ramps that led to the deck of each skyship. The ramp was a wooden plank attached to the pier by ropes, tilted upwards to allow people to climb up to the deck. It was jammed with frantic and terrified people who did not care about being polite or orderly, only about saving their own lives.

Plumes of pitch-black smoke rose over the tops of the red-tiled roofs, followed closely by the glowing amber and burgundy embers of flame consuming entire buildings. It created a somber and ominous atmosphere for the once peaceful town of Mills Point. Buildings collapsed and burned, sending mustard sparks and flaming black debris flying. Distant screams echoed in the streets as people were injured or killed by the Zamana soldiers or by the surrounding, inescapable fire. It was a nightmare that had come true, and the only hope for survival was to flee on the last two skyships.

Each person on the pier held firmly onto some form of baggage or personal belonging, hoping to get on board. With their sacks of loot held tightly in their arms, Suzu and Hogart surprisingly looked no different from anyone else in the crowd carrying their possessions. But unlike the others, their bags were filled with stolen treasures, not sentimental items. With his wide girth as an advantage, Hogart gently pushed and squeezed through the blockade of assembled people. Suzu followed closely behind her friend, holding tightly on to the back of Hogart's long brown jacket, not separating one inch as he delicately cleared a path for them. Luckily, they finally made it on board the main deck of one of the air vessels, the skyship with the maroon balloon named the *Intrepid*.

"I think we're safe now," Hogart said.

"If only we would lift off into the air, we'd be safer."

As the crowd of passengers surged aboard the ship, Suzu and Hogart felt a sudden push towards the aft observation deck's starboard side to make room for more people trying to board the vessel. They stumbled into a pair of wooden barrels lying idle on the deck. The barrels rolled and rattled, spilling some contents on the floor. Suzu and Hogart looked at each other in dismay, wondering what they had just disturbed, and then got a bright idea that lifted their spirits.

"We can safely stash our loot in these barrels," Hogart said. "Hurry! Before anyone sees us."

The pair hid their sacks of loot in a couple of the empty wooden barrels.

"We'll have to stay nearby at all times and guard our hidden treasures from the crowd," Suzu said.

"Mark them. So we know which barrels are ours and don't lose them," Hogart said.

Suzu removed her knife from her belt and swiftly slashed her silver blade across the deep-brown wooden casks that held their hard-earned gold coins, marking them with a bold *X* to help them later identify their stash. She then grabbed a thick rope hanging from a sturdy beam near the front corner of the rear lookout platform and quickly tied the marked barrels to the wooden beam along the front right side of the aft observation deck. Hogart stood before her, providing a shield with his long brown coat, blocking any curious glances or casual prying eyes from the rest of the pedestrians and crew. He gave her a wink and a smile as if to say they were almost home free.

As the *Intrepid* filled to capacity, it loosened and lifted its ropes from the wooden platform. The craft, able to traverse both air and water, began to float gently away from the dock and along the river's tranquil surface. Some people who missed their chance to board the vessel were still frantic about catching it. They leapt from the edge of the ramp to the receding ship, clinging to the ropes that hung over the hull and plunging into the water when their strength gave out.

A few outcries could be heard on the main deck, fingers pointed to the river. Two man-of-war vessels were arriving, blocking the waterway entrance towards the open ocean. The flags of the Zamana Empire sailing warships waved menacingly, showing the emblem of a golden dragon spewing scarlet fire. The man-of-war vessels were powerful, made of sturdy wood and measuring two hundred feet long. Propelled primarily by black canvas sails, the man-of-war had three masts, each with three to four sails. They could sail at a speed of eight or nine knots, faster than most ships, and were coming in fast.

In response to the sight of the two approaching Zamana Empire sailing warships, the fleeing civilian skyship slowly rose from the river water. The *Intrepid* buckled and shook briefly, the wood creaking and moaning from its hefty load. The collected civilian crowd gasped in unison, clinging to the railing and each other, trying to steady their balance on the shifting deck. The rear propeller splashed water behind them as it spun, pushing the craft forward even when it emerged from the water. Pale white propulsion sails extended outward and rotated into position to give the aircraft an extra push into the sky and hope to reach the safety of the clouds before it was too late.

The *Intrepid* was in a tight spot, sandwiched between two enemy ships closing in rapidly. The distance between them decreased by the moment. The captain had no choice but to gamble on a daring maneuver. He ordered the crew to tilt the skyship's white sails vertically, hoping to catch a gust of wind that would lift them higher and faster.

The *Intrepid* surged forward, steadily rising and turning towards the looming Zamana warships. The passengers on the deck held their breath as they approached the mighty warship masts, praying they would clear them. The *Intrepid* soared over the sailing ships, narrowly avoiding a collision, and flew harmlessly over the top of the masts.

The river below sparkled in the honey sunlight, reflecting the navy-blue sky and snow-white clouds. The skyship cut through the air with elegance, a sleek and sturdy vessel that could navigate the winds. The massive propeller at the ship's rear spun steadily, energized by pedal power, pushing it forward with increasing speed. The black rudder sail pivoted to the right, while the left propulsion sail adjusted its angle upwards slightly, altering the ship's direction from over the river to above the land.

From the deck of the skyship, the citizens peered over the wooden railings and watched the pandemonium unfold as the *Intrepid* sailed over the streets and buildings of Mills Point. Their fellow townspeople left behind ran around the streets aimlessly with nowhere to go from the horror. Dinosaurs lay slain on the streets, spears and arrows sticking out of their scaly hides. Streams of umber smoke and patches of scarlet fire scattered across the city like low clouds. They had never seen such a spectacle before and felt dismay and sorrow for their community.

The pedestrians on deck pointed into the distance, murmured indistinctly, then shouting out in unison. The fleeing passengers caught sight of a terrifying silhouette in the azure sky. It was none other than the *Iron Talon*, the most dreaded military skyship of the Zamana Empire. The colossal galleon vessel had a sturdy three-hundred-foot-long mahogany-colored wooden hull. Its single gigantic cylindrical white hot-air balloon was encased in a light silver armor framework. The skyship boasted three masts with four billowing black propulsion sails. Two additional black propulsion sails extended at the fore and aft for extra thrust. The Zamana emblem, a twisting golden dragon spewing scarlet fire, was displayed on the smaller black sails. The *Iron Talon* was notorious for its relentless raids and merciless attacks on anyone who dared to defy the Zamana Empire.

Already an intimidating vision in the sky, the *Iron Talon* led a pair of smaller troop deployment transports floating with purpose behind it. The troop transport shared the same design as the flagship, with two masts on each ship, one at the stern and one at the bow, supporting a single armored hot-air balloon filled with scorching air. The balloons were covered with light grey metal plates protecting them from enemy fire. Four black sails of different sizes, two at the back and two at the front, provided thrust and speed. Troop transports were armed with harpoons and basilisks, ready to engage in aerial combat or board enemy ships.

Keldace Vildan, Mistress of the Dark Arts and the revered leader of the Zamana Empire, occupied the most prominent position on the bow of the *Iron Talon* as if daring anyone to challenge her authority. She surveyed the vast expanse of the sky with a piercing gaze, looking for signs of trouble or opportunity. Her attire was simple but striking: an obsidian hood and robe that enveloped her lithe body and an iron-grey mask that obscured her entire face, except for two narrow slits that revealed her icy aqua-colored eyes. She carried a long sword in a mocha sheath, partially hidden by the cloak. She did not need any weapons to command respect; her presence was enough to instill fear and awe in those who encountered her.

Vildan extended both arms outward and started to wave them purposefully, as if creating or molding some sculpture, painting, or invisible forces around her, uttering arcane words from unseen lips. She was the influencer of the wind and bent it to her will with her dark magic. The air responded as if it was a living entity, swirls and twists forming patterns and shapes that only she could see. She was in harmony with the element, which obeyed her every command.

The *Iron Talon* unleashed a dozen mooring lines that slithered towards the civilian aircraft like hungry serpents on the wind. The thick ropes latched onto the unsuspecting *Intrepid* and became secure. The passengers screamed in shock as they realized the enemy was capturing them.

But the mysterious, black-robed figure was not satisfied with just one prize. Not only was the *Intrepid* captured, but she quickly magically fastened the mooring lines to another civilian skyship that escaped the sailing warships and flew nearby. The skyship also docked at the port, the *Orca*, was unwillingly dragged along with the *Intrepid*. The Zamana Empire had seized two skyships full of Mills Point townspeople in one fell swoop.

The giant galleon skyship of the Zamana Empire, the *Iron Talon*, loomed over the two smaller civilian skyships like a predator over its prey. The passengers and crew of the fleeing Nao skyships had no choice but to surrender, as they were outnumbered and outgunned by the Zamana forces.

THE SILVER MOON SHARKS

Ever since he was a young boy, Hogart had been fascinated by and appreciated the names of sailing ships and skyships. He had a collection of books, maps, and posters that featured them, and he dreamed of one day boarding one of them. Since his first voyage, Hogart had been to many lands and cities, interacted with many cultures and people, and had many adventures. But he never expected that one day, his dream would come true in such a terrible way.

He and Suzu were idly standing on the upper deck amongst the unlucky assorted passengers of the *Intrepid*. They were dragged along by the *Iron Talon*, which dwarfed their hot-air-balloon craft. Hogart looked at the other Nao skyship that smoothly sailed across from them and shared their fate, the *Orca*. It was an apt and fitting name for a vessel that looked like a whale in the air, but also a cruel irony for a prey that a predator caught. Hogart wondered what would happen to them when they reached the Zamana territory. He hoped they would find a way to escape or at least survive.

Suzu and Hogart had no choice but to stay close by their precious cargo, two chestnut wooden barrels full of glittering loot secured to the front right side of the aft observation deck, in fear of someone discovering it. They leaned on the flying vessel's thick wooden taffrail, gazing at the peach sky slowly fading into a soft lavender.

"I have no idea how we're going to get out of this one," Hogart bemoaned.

"Cheer up," Suzu said, half happily. "At least our barrels are marked, hidden, and safe for now. As long as we stay by them, we're alright."

"And that special gem you have on you?"

Suzu touched the necklace underneath her long-sleeved tunic. "No one knows about it but us. Let's not speak about it in front of mixed company."

Hogart turned from the banister and glanced at the faces of the "mixed company" clumped and huddled together on the upper deck. He saw fright, confusion, and dismay in their eyes. They were not warriors, thieves, rogues, or even adventurers. They were ordinary, innocent people, some with children in their arms, some with spouses by their side, and some alone. All brave. He noticed the details amongst them that increased the despair: the lone old woman with a cherry shawl wrapped around her shoulders, shivering from the cool breeze and clutching a single wooden box; the young couple holding hands and whispering prayers; the boy with a mustard straw hat and a slingshot, looking at the fuchsia horizon with curiosity and utterly unaware of what was transpiring; the short ebony man with a scarred face and a limp, carrying the ravages of war already; the olive-skinned, midnight-haired girl with a periwinkle flower in her hair and a smile on her lips, singing a soft melody in an attempt to calm the crowd. They were all different but shared a common bond: they were prisoners of the Zamana Empire.

Feeling sadness, Hogart turned back and returned to the wooden railing along Suzu's side and gazed at the early night sky. He saw a few white stars twinkling like diamonds amongst the fading ocherous clouds, which looked like soft pillows of fire. But his eyes were drawn to the distinct, flickering, ruddy lights that drifted closer towards their skyship. He wondered what they were and hoped they were friendly, but he feared they were not. "It seems another ship has been captured and is joining our unhappy convoy."

"I don't think so," Suzu said. "That's a Zamana shuttle transport."

From the upper deck of the *Intrepid*, Suzu and Hogart watched as four brightly lit lanterns faintly outlined a very small, slender skiff skyship approaching. It almost looked like a sleek, graceful, oversize blackbird looking to find its nest in the early twilight. The dark brown wooden hull was about twenty-five feet long and narrow. The dark blue rudder sail almost acted like a feathered tail, moving side to side, changing the direction of the craft as it closed in. The cerulean propulsion sails, acting like wings catching the soft drifting wind, were extended entirely outright. Against the apricot glow of the four lanterns, the silhouette of a single pilot could be seen steering at the back of the skyship, and there were two more crew members at the sides of the deck handling the propulsion sails. Another lone figure, the features too vague and obscure to make out in the creeping darkness, stood motionless on the extended, sloped front deck.

As the Zamana transport shuttle approached the *Iron Talon* from astern, a sail-like airbrake lifted upwards, slowing the craft to a gentle glide. The pilot adjusted the rudder slightly, and the propulsion sails moved up or down for last-second adjustments to align alongside the galleon. Nearing the hull of the *Iron Talon*, the propulsion sails finally folded inwards so they avoided damage and did not break. Mooring lines were passed between the crew members of the two skycraft as the skiff docked itself next to the *Iron Talon*. The mooring lines were secured, and a wooden gangplank with rope rails was extended from the small skyship to the main deck of the *Iron Talon*, creating a bridge between them.

The same individual leading the attack on Mills Point, Tomap Sruz, confidently crossed the sturdy wooden beam. He was very young, but not a boy. His white skin and short jet hair contrasted sharply with his crimson armor. He stepped onto the upper main deck of the *Iron Talon*, finding that the loyal troops on board were already in military formation and feeling their eyes on him. He marched between the rows of assembled soldiers towards the entrance of the captain's quarters and stopped outside the cabin's wooden door, drawing a silent, heavy breath. A carefully measured eye and an equally stern look were cast on all assembled men and women watching him. Forced to swallow his pride in front of his subordinates, Tomap performed the humiliating act he hated to do the most for any being in this life, but knew he had no choice. A gesture of submission he would never make for anyone else in this world. He lowered himself down to one knee and bowed his head.

As if acknowledging the humbling act, the door of the captain's quarters slowly creaked open. From the shadowy depths of the cabin, the Mistress of Darkness Keldace Vildan, emerged. Her stature was imposing, her attire regal. Her tall figure was draped in an obsidian-hooded cloak with a scarlet lining that billowed behind her like a banner of blood. The cloak was a fitting mantle for an empress, and the dark grey armor that clad her shoulders only added to her aura of authority. A black belt with a ruby clasp circled her waist, a subtle yet potent symbol of her power. Only her icy artic eyes were visible, piercing the night with their malice.

The most notable feature was the mask. There was the basic version of the mask she wore most often, the one she wore tonight, made of thin silvery metal. It had a sinister and imposing design, with a hoodlike shape that obscured her facial features. The mask was expressionless, giving Vildan an aura of unyielding determination, and featured narrow eye slits, allowing her to see while maintaining an air of mystery. It served as a shield, concealing her emotions and the scars that marred her teal skin. Each mask she magically conjured was different, reflecting her mood or the occasion to conjure the dark arts of magic.

"Empress, an update on Mills Port." Tomap Sruz stood. "We have won the city but have not advanced farther into the territory. I want to start a campaign to take over the area immediately by . . ."

"No." The raspy voice emitting from behind the mask was grave and ghastly. The argent iron accessory magically transformed into stark ivory. Under the left eye slit, a streak of crimson representing blood rolled down the cheek and stopped at a dagger's point. Under the right eye slit, a streak of aquamarine representing a watery tear stopped at an equal distance on the cheek and ended with the same pointed tip.

"M-my empress?" Tomap staggered. "With a thousand men and women at my command . . ."

"There has been a recent change in plans," Vildan said. "There are reports that the lost Kingdom of Tavter has now been found."

"T-Tavter?" Tomap said. His usually stern voice was in disbelief. He felt an urgency to seize the opportunity. "All the more reason to advance into those lands now that we have Mills Port."

"The reports also state that thieves have already plundered valued treasure from the king's vault," Vildan said, "more specifically, the Land Elemental Gem."

Tomap's handsome face tightened, and his stance became firmer. "Then let me conquer those lands in your name and find the people who took the gem."

The empress shook her head. "The Zamana Empire has taken Fenbrig and Witwardia in the last week. Since we must control those newly acquired lands, we do not have the resources and soldiers at the moment."

"A thousand of my best men and women!" Tomap growled. "I promise you, in my command, I will—"

"Silence!" The gruff voice grew darker and impatient.

An evil moment of deep dread swept across every man and woman assembled on the upper deck.

Vildan stepped closer to the commander. "Most civilian prisoners from both captured skyships will be transferred to the *Iron Talon*. Place them in the hold. They will be transported to Black Rock, where they will serve as slave labor to finish the construction of new skyships. The completion of these aircraft is critical and will strengthen the Zamana Empire's rule of the skies."

"The majority? What of the others?" Tomap asked.

"There's not enough room in the hold for all. Some will have to remain behind on civilian skyships until they reach Black Rock. At that point, those chosen will go on to the Kiptoon Mines."

Tomap flinched. He believed he would also stay at "the Mines" and command boring administrative tasks beneath him. "My position? Is it my understanding that I am also meant to go to the Kiptoon Mines?"

"No." The voice behind the mask resumed its even tone. "You have served me well lately, young Tomap. As a reward for the victory over Mills Port, I appoint you command of the *Iron Talon*. Once you successfully bring all the prisoners back to Black Rock, and I do mean every single one of them, you will take command of one of the newly constructed skyships. The *Blade Guard*."

A cruel smile came across Tomap's face in his happiness that his recent military accomplishments were finally being rewarded. "It will be done, my empress. You have my word."

"We shall see. In the meantime, I'm needed elsewhere. I will meet you at Black Rock in three days," Vildan said, pointing a single steady finger at the underling. "Do not disappoint me."

She departed from the *Iron Talon* and walked across the gangplank connecting the two ships, and onto the small transport shuttle Tomap had just arrived in. The skiff detached from the larger skyship, drifted off in the open air far enough to extend its dark blue propulsion sails, and flew into the deepening mauve night sky.

Shortly, after the ships spent nearly half a day being left alone to be towed along helplessly, members of the Zamana Empire began boarding both civilian ships. The propulsion sails on both craft were ordered to be pulled inward and locked tight. The rudder sails stayed motionless. Heavy mooring ropes with metal grapnels were tossed over from the *Iron Talon* and forcibly attached to the smaller skyships. The Zamana Empire Troopers pulled on the mooring lines, dragging the *Intrepid* and the *Orca* closer to the *Iron Talon*, showing no mercy as it reeled in its prey.

The *Iron Talon* loomed over the *Orca*, the first of the two passenger skyships to be boarded. The two skyships were joined by a wide wooden gangplank, similar to the one the shuttle used, that served as a bridge of doom for the captive civilians. The Zamana Empire Troopers acted like ruthless wolves, driving the helpless sheep across the plank with their weapons and shouts. They ignored the cries and pleas of the terrified people, who were forced into the *Iron Talon*'s dark and cramped cargo hold.

Once the transfer of most civilians from the *Orca* was completed, the airborne captives watched in horror as the same gangplank was next extended to the *Intrepid*. The nefarious Tomap came on board and went through the crowd with another military officer, a tall, physically imposing ebony woman who appeared to be his trusted first officer. They glanced over the gathered crowd of prisoners with cold, calculating eyes as if they weren't even people. Tomap pointed towards specific crowd members and quietly talked to his second-in-command, First Officer Mosley, selecting who would go to the *Iron Talon* and who remained behind on board the *Intrepid*. Whispered words and phrases—Black Rock, Kiptoon Mines, war skyships, and slavery—spread quickly amongst the huddled crowd.

"Why are they splitting us up?" Hogart said.

"They're selecting people to go to a place called Black Rock," Suzu said, overhearing the crowd's murmurs.

"Black Rock?!"

"To work on skyships for the Empire. Those who remain on board go to the Kiptoon Mines to dig for magitite."

Tomap stopped before the mismatched, bumbling duo and looked them over. "These two will stay behind. The big guy is good for lift-and-carry jobs. The little one can get into small, difficult places."

Suzu moved slightly forward, obviously wanting to strike the insulting person no matter who it may be. Hogart quickly held her back by placing his large, comforting hand on her slender shoulder before it was noticed.

"I don't know which place is worse. Black Rock or the Kiptoon Mines. Both are horrifying places," Suzu said softly.

"Luckily, we are still near our gold!" Hogart whispered.

Exhausted from the day's events, the uncanny pair of friends fell asleep a few hours later on the journey across the sky. Their backs rested on their scratch-marked barrels with gold and jewels safely hidden inside. Hogart's girth and long brown coat hid most of the unknown loot. Suzu rested, using his bloated stomach as a soft pillow, her lean body stretched out and hiding the rest of the barrels.

Throughout the hours of the night, the weather turned for the worse during their sleep. Flint storm clouds had gathered and deepened. The breezy winds had picked up tremendously and faintly howled like a wounded beast, sweeping across the soft, pale moonlit sky. A stray strike of marigold lightning flashed, piercing the darkness and illuminating the surrounding storm clouds for brief seconds, closely followed by a distant, gentle roll of thunder.

Another sudden jolt and shudder of the Nao skyship by a nearby lightning strike, followed by a louder rumble of rolling thunder, stirred Suzu awake from her deepest dreams. Her tired eyes slowly opened and blinked, and she noticed the unlucky change in the weather and dark graphite clouds looming over them. She looked around and saw the other passengers huddled under blankets or coats, trying to stay warm and dry. The Zamana Troopers were nowhere to be seen, probably busy trying to steer the ship away from the storm or seeking shelter. She wondered how long they had been flying and how far they must go. Single raindrops began to pelt the wooden deck, followed quickly by light, misty rain, dampening her clothes and sending a cold chill through her body. She cursed their rotten luck. Their gross misfortune seemed to continue and worsen all the time.

Gazing sleepily out into the hefty bank of swiftly moving storm clouds, Suzu soon appreciated the enchanting dance of whisps and swirls the ever-changing, whipping air movement allowed. The wind howled and whipped the clouds into different shapes, creating a dynamic and captivating spectacle. Suzu felt a strange attraction to the clouds, as if they were inviting her to join them in their dance. She leaned closer, trying to make out the images that the clouds formed. She saw animals, faces, buildings, and landscapes that changed and morphed with every gust of wind. Her mind was soothed, and her tense muscles relaxed. Mesmerized by nature's will, she welcomed slumber once more. But as her lazy lids finally almost shut and let the clouds lull her back to sleep, Suzu's keen eyes spied something extremely odd moving in and out amongst the shifting grey storm clouds that made her softly gasp. A flash of silver with a viridescent tint caught her eye, moving swiftly amongst the clouds. It looked like a fin, similar to a shark's, but much larger and smoother. It darted in and out of the clouds as if playing hide-and-seek with them. The faint triangular outline seemed acutely aware, like an animal, and ran alongside the *Iron Talon* and the helplessly towed *Intrepid*.

Suzu couldn't believe what she was seeing. Was it a creature? Magic? A hallucination?

She sat up and rubbed her eyes with her tiny fists. The only answer was a quick series of white light flashes spreading across the cloudy sky, followed quickly by low rumbles of thunder. She gazed more intently for evidence of the odd triangle shape drifting within the cloudbanks. Waiting patiently for another flash of lighting to use as a guide, she spied the outlines of a sizeable turquoise-hued triangle effortlessly breaking through the parting storm clouds for the briefest moment. It almost appeared as if it were a sizeable physical creature silently hunting the captive *Intrepid*, getting eerily closer to its oblivious target and ready to swallow it whole.

"Hogart," Suzu whispered. She dug her elbow into his belly to rouse him. "Wake up. I think we're in trouble."

The burly man snorted and mumbled something incoherent about the Thieves Guild, the Cursed Mask of Arda, and the beautiful Horsewomen of Gon.

"Hogart, my friend," Suzu hissed. She dug her elbow harder and deeper into his belly numerous times to wake him. "There's a creature out there in the storm!"

Jostled awake, Hogart sat up and looked into the smoky clouds. He did not see anything at all through his weary eyes that gave a hint of a giant creature. "The excitement of the day has gotten to you. Go back to sleep."

"It looked like a dorsal fin of a shark."

"A shark??!! Ha!" Hogart said, laughing out loud. "The thinner air is playing tricks with your mind." Satisfied with his answer, he rested his back against the marked barrels. A wide smile spread across his lips as pleasant dreams came over him once more about how to spend his newfound gold. But then, a terrible, dreadful thought darted to the forefront of his mind, springing his eyes wide open in alarm. "The Silver Moon Sharks!"

The Silver Moon Sharks were notorious for being one of the worst groups of sky pirates to prowl and plunder the open skies. Their specially modified skyship was named *The Lunar Nymph*. They had one main craft, as long as a three-hundred-foot sailing galleon, with a single massive hot-air balloon resembling a great white shark. A light-blue armor was draped over the balloon for protection. Inflated pectoral fins extended outward from the main body of the balloon, with razor tips on the end that could cut through other skyships' sails and balloons. The tail caudal fin acted as a massive rudder, steering the craft with precision and speed. The main nest was built around the top dorsal fin for a couple of crew members. The elongated, razor-sharp spear at the end of the nose could pierce any obstacle or enemy craft. The skyship's wooden body, painted in sapphire and grey, was crafted almost like a smaller shark swimming underneath a similar hot-air balloon. A balloon-slicing blade stretched along the underbelly of the sleek hull, ready to tear down a foe from the skies. Dark blue propulsion sails, with blades lined at the end, acted like pectoral fins from the hull, and it featured two main masts on the upper deck, aft and fore, each bearing the insignia of a shark. Two smaller lifeboats attached to the sides, one port and one starboard, hung there for emergencies and escape from enemies. *The Lunar Nymph* was an infamous vessel of war and pirating that struck terror into the hearts of anyone who saw the deadly predator in the sky.

Before a single voice or horn could raise any alarm, this colossal skyship silently breached the stormy cloud bank as if it were bursting through a tidal wave of ocean water to reach its unsuspecting prey. As another flaxen flash of lightning, longer than the last, spread across the skies, Hogart and Suzu could now plainly see the details of the sky pirate vessel. The sudden frightening sight of the dreaded *Lunar Nymph*, crossing directly in front of the helplessly towed *Intrepid*'s bow, caused Suzu and Hogart to freeze in place amidst the cold light rain. They felt no cold, only dread. They had no chance to escape or fight back.

The Lunar Nymph brazenly attacked the unsuspecting *Iron Talon*, ramming directly into the starboard midsection of the equally sized galleon skyship. The figurehead of the sky pirate vessel, a wide opening equipped with protruding sharp knives that acted like the mighty jaws of a dangerous shark, literally bit and cut through the wood and metal of the burdened *Iron Talon*. Coupled with the twisting and turning storm winds, the determined invader started ripping and tearing into the wooden hull like a terrifying, savage beast. *The Lunar Nymph* was not here to negotiate but to plunder its prey.

Pirates manning *The Lunar Nymph*'s ballistae at the upper deck's aft and fore unleashed a barrage of harpoons with grappling hooks. The iron spears sank deep into the wooden upper decks of the *Iron Talon*, piercing through the wood and catching a firm hold even against the waning storm.

The stern of *The Lunar Nymph* was caught in a fierce blast of wind, which hurled it towards the *Intrepid* like a battering ram. Tightly tethered to the upper decks of the *Iron Talon*, the stern of the pirate skyship swung back and forth in the gusty winds, gaining momentum with each swing until it slammed into the *Intrepid*'s prow with a deafening impact. Wood shattered, metal twisted, and people shrieked as the two ships collided, sending splinters and sparks flying.

Like being struck by a massive wave of water, all the *Intrepid* passengers were helplessly thrown around the shifting, slippery upper decks like ragdolls. Hogart and Suzu were amongst them, clinging onto each other as they were tossed across the rain-soaked wooden deck. They smacked into the port wooden taffrail, which stopped them from going over the side. They were left gasping for air and holding on to the railing for dear life. A couple of other passengers next to them were not as fortunate, unable to stop themselves and practically flying over the top of the wooden guardrail; their terrified screams and cries were heard until they faded and disappeared entirely into the howling, swirling, misty storm clouds.

Hogart and Suzu tried to gather themselves, gravely clinging onto the port taffrail with all their strength. "We're swinging towards the *Iron Talon*! Hold on!" Hogart shouted.

The *Intrepid* was now set in motion from the decisive blow, swinging recklessly towards the left. The front end of the *Intrepid* slammed harshly and violently against the aft end of the *Iron Talon*. Once more, every soul on board was flung mercilessly across the upper decks like puppets cut from their strings, and a few unlucky souls were tossed into the unforgiving, raging sky.

As the two massive skyships fiercely collided, so did the smaller ships. The *Orca* could not escape the assault as the *Intrepid* rammed into it with full force. The mooring lines were slack enough to allow the *Intrepid*'s stern to swing around and hit the *Orca*'s side. The third collision was less brutal and violent than the previous ones, but the *Intrepid*'s hull was already cracked and buckled from the impact.

The howling winds continued to gust, swirl, and twist around all the skyships, which acted like leaves caught in the wind. The *Intrepid* drifted back to the right and was caught helplessly between the behemoth war-mongering *Iron Talon* and *Lunar Nymph*, bouncing back and forth against the two massive hulls like a small child's toy. The *Intrepid* was forced to endure and suffer unwanted punishment. Wooden pieces of the hull, sails, and small sections of the passenger skyship were starting to break apart and plunge into the merciless storm.

Despite the storm's turmoil, the Silver Moon Sharks were relentless in their pursuit of the *Iron Talon*. They hurled more grappling irons over the wooden banisters and onto the upper decks, hoping to catch and drag the fleeing vessel closer. Once they had a firm grip, the sky pirates pulled the *Iron Talon* closer and latched onto it. The Silver Moon Sharks were ready to unleash their infamous boarding strategy, which involved swarming the upper decks with an aerial assault.

The Zamana Empire Troopers, scrambling on the rain-soaked upper deck of the *Iron Talon*, were under siege from either flame arrows, spears, or javelins. From the fore and aft castles of *The Lunar Nymph*, unseen expert archers took aim from the high vantage points, raining death on the soldiers and quickly diminishing their ranks. The sky was filled with volleys of scarlet flame arrows arching from *The Lunar Nymph*'s upper deck, streaking through the open air with a serpentlike hiss towards the targeted *Iron Talon* and at the two helpless passenger skyships caught in the crossfire, striking them all with deadly accuracy.

Suzu found little adequate cover as she dodged from the barrage of flying flame arrows. She saw an arrow strike a Zamana Empire Trooper through the neck in front of her, making the man fall face-first to the wooden deck, gagging, dark red blood spilling from his throat. She heard a bloodcurdling scream as another arrow hit a nearby civilian passenger in the shoulder, sending him spinning overboard into the foggy abyss. She turned around and gasped as a spear barely missed her loyal companion, Hogart, in the head, firmly embedding itself in the wooden wall of the aft observation deck behind him.

The Lunar Nymph loosened its vicious hold on the hull of the *Iron Talon*, spitting shards of wood out of its serrated silver steel jaws like dripping blood and leaving a gaping wound wide enough for a few soldiers to fall out to the open air. *The Lunar Nymph* straightened out, running alongside its intended target, and raised itself slightly above the upper decks of the *Iron Talon* like it was riding the crest of an ocean wave.

Along the bulwarks of *The Lunar Nymph*'s upper deck, men and women sky pirates brandished swords, spears, and spotted shields in their hands, chanting and hollering at the top of their lungs to show they were more than ready to take the *Iron Talon* by brutal force. They roared and cheered as the small miscellaneous army of Silver Moon Sharks dropped down on the upper decks of the *Iron Talon* like graceful predators, eager to plunder and kill any person in sight. At the same time, a heavy wooden plank with a piercing metal spike dropped deep into the *Iron Talon*'s upper deck, providing a gangway for more hostile boarders that swarmed over like a horde of hungry locusts.

The capture of the imperial flag skyship of the Zamana Empire was the ultimate goal, but the greedy Silver Moon Sharks were not content with only that. They also set their sights on the innocent civilian skyship *Intrepid*, which was trapped in the deadly crossfire of their relentless assault. *Intrepid* suffered the same boarding techniques. The Silver Moon Sharks hurled another heavy wooden gangway on its rickety, splintered upper deck and surged over it with their sharp weapons and savage war cries. The loyal Zamana Empire soldiers, the cunning sky pirates, and the frightened civilians took to arms and clashed in a bloody melee on the slippery, tilted deck.

Suzu and Hogart, unable to find a safe hiding place, knew they were in big trouble. The deck crawled with soldiers and pirates swishing their swords, screaming, and dying. Innocent civilians cried in terror and scattered to find a place to hide from the carnage. They looked at each other with trepidation, having no choice but to defend themselves any way they could if they wanted to survive. Suzu and Hogart stood together, ready to face any attackers, knowing they had to rely only on themselves.

With a swift motion, Hogart seized a sky pirate by the collar and flung him over the side railing in one movement, snatching the silver battle axe that fell from his grasp in surprised fright. He marched boldly towards three more Silver Moon Sharks, who looked at the single sturdy man with question and hesitation. They knew they were no match for his strength and skill with such a formidable weapon. Impatient for any of the three to make a move, Hogart grew tired of their cowardice and decided to end the fight quickly. He swung his axe at a nearby rope, releasing a massive unfurled mast that swept wildly across the deck, knocking all three pirates off their feet in one hit and sending them screaming into the storm.

Suzu was unarmed and defenseless, looking for any weapon to defend herself with, when a sky pirate charged at her with a long sword in hand. Suzu barely avoided the deadly strike passing over her head by rolling forward and noticed a sword sliding towards her on the wet deck. She had one chance to grab it, or she would be doomed. She got up to her feet, kicked the blade up with her foot, and caught it in midair, grabbing the hilt of the sword. She turned around and faced her attacker, twirling the sword with finesse.

The two women exchanged furious blows, their swords clanging and sparking alabaster on the dark rainy night. Suzu used her martial arts skills to deliver a powerful kick to the sky pirate's chest, but the ship suddenly jerked and tilted as she did. The sky pirate gasped loudly as she lost her footing and fell over the wooden banister, her scream echoing as she disappeared into the sooty rain clouds below.

The two partners in pillaging bumped into each other and found themselves fighting back to back. "We're surrounded!" Suzu yelled.

In what would seem like a natural act of defiance, one last canary lightning strike reached out from the pastel heavens of the dissipating storm. The jagged, streaking electrical bolt darted from the clouds and hit the *Iron Talon*'s bow, causing an instant fiery cherry explosion that engulfed and heavily damaged the entire fore of the upper deck. The colossal Zamana Empire skyship buckled and swerved from the direct hit, placing both feuding skyships in a tangled disarray. The light rain was not enough to quench a sizeable blazing tangerine fire that erupted and rapidly spread across the bow's upper deck.

All the people on board the *Intrepid*, sky pirates, soldiers, and civilians, were barbarously tossed around the deck like ragdolls from the enormous lightning blast, giving Suzu and Hogart a brief respite from being surrounded by the blades of their enemies. But the entire situation was going from bad to worse; in addition to the heavy damage already placed on the *Intrepid*, the grappling hooks latched on started to tear and rip apart the civilian airship. With each drastic push and shove of the ever-changing, whistling wind, the sharp mooring hooks would also tear farther and deeper for a short distance into the hull of the *Iron Talon*, ripping through chunks of metal and wood, and then halt. With every heavy gale burst, this vicious cycle would repeat, causing more disruption and disorder with the hand-to-hand combat and sword fighting on the decks. The sudden shifts, bucks, and jerking movements of the *Intrepid* trying to break loose like a wild animal caught in a trap caused added mayhem and confusion to all on board fighting for their lives. To survive, they had to sever the rest of the mooring lines and the grappling hooks that bound them together or face certain doom.

"Hogart!" Suzu shouted. "Cut the mooring lines, or they'll shred the ship apart!"

With a nod and a heavy grunt, Hogart brought his axe down on the coarse rope, hacking away at the sturdy strands holding the skyship. He felt the tension in his arms as he swung repeatedly, slicing through the fibers with each blow. He knew he had to hurry before the guards noticed their improvised escape plan.

Tomap felt his blood boil as he savagely fought amidst a sea of swarming sky pirates. He saw the burly brute on board the *Intrepid* wildly trying to cut the mooring lines that held them together. He knew he had to stop him, or Keldace Vildan would not be pleased he lost a ship to sky pirates. His loyal crew would be doomed.

Angered and screaming at the top of his lungs, the young militant cut and carved, hewing and hacking his way through the seemingly endless waves of Silver Moon Sharks, the pirate scum that had dared to ambush them. He didn't care about their bloodcurdling screams or their scarlet blood spilled on his blade; he only cared about reaching Hogart in time to stop him. He swung his sword at anyone in his path with skill and fury, parrying, thrusting, dodging, and lunging until he was close enough to lock eyes with Hogart, who grinned wickedly and raised his silver axe.

"Do it!" Suzu yelled. She provided fighting cover, expertly dispatching a sky pirate and a soldier with her sword as Hogart cut through the final mooring line.

The *Intrepid* continued to shudder, groan, and wail like a great captured animal, determined more than ever to pull away from its snare. The sharp metal hooks tore through splintered, cracked wood like an undeniable, hot knife. Taut mooring lines started to snap, unravel, and give way. The tiny *Intrepid* finally broke away from the ongoing, anarchic fight with a sickening, loud snap, dragging a motley crew of Zamana Empire Troopers, Silver Moon Sharks, and innocent bystanders unwillingly for a wild ride.

The last remnants of the rainstorm disappeared in the distance, leaving behind a clear, starry, pale sky. But the few white stars were not the only lights in the night. The bright, burning golden flames and plumes of ivory smoke erupting from both combative skyships could be seen against the last gilded flashes of the diminishing rainstorm. The lumbering Zamana Empire skyship and the attacking Silver Moon Sharks, locked into an unflinching hostile battle with one another, continued with their warlike fight in the air. Behind them, the *Orca* was caught in the crossfire. It hung from its mooring lines, unable to escape or fight back, twisting and turning in the wind like a wounded whale. The battle appeared fierce, and neither side showed any sign of backing down.

In the dawn skies above the *Intrepid*, *The Lunar Nymph* looked like a monstrous great white shark trying to tear and pull the rival skyship down under the pearly clouds like it was dragging the craft underwater. Large splinters of wood plunged into the mist from *The Lunar Nymph*'s bow, and the aft swung wildly like an energized tail hungry for more destruction.

The beaten and battered *Intrepid* drifted aimlessly, swung, and spiraled away in the dying storm. The heavily damaged civilian skyship was now entirely out of control, flying solo, untethered to its captor. Like some wounded beast annoyed with its escaping prey, the gathered winds howled and gusted one last time to swat the small vessel across the early, glowing light.

Ironically, as if guided by fate, the wandering and unruly *Intrepid* veered straight for a series of vast ashen peaks and snowcapped pinnacles that ran like a resplendent backbone down the rugged countryside. Everyone on board seemed oblivious to the impending danger of possibly colliding into one of the looming mountains, as they were too busy fighting for survival on the wayward vessel's slippery deck.

Swords continued to clash, and bare fists flew on the *Intrepid*'s upper deck. Every individual was fighting for their very life. Suddenly, the skyship's bottom hull scraped and ground against a rugged, rocky peak, sending a violent jolt through the whole structure. It hurled everyone off their feet and cruelly tossed all passengers across the rain-drenched deck. The impact was brutal, and no one was spared from the upheaval.

"Our situation has not improved," Suzu moaned.

The *Intrepid*'s pilotless voyage continued as the port hull struck and bounced off another mountainside, sending shock waves throughout the vessel. The sound of splintering wood and metal split the ear as the impact tore apart the ship's port side. All combatants were savagely thrown around the upper deck. Most were thrown harshly onto the wooden planks or into each other. Some held on to something solid to stabilize themselves, but a few unfortunate souls were flung over the guardrails to their inevitable demise.

Suzu gripped her sword firmly as she saw a Zamana soldier approaching her and a stunned Hogart, his eyes filled with malice. Suzu was determined to protect her friend, even if it meant risking her own life. She sprang to her feet and lunged at the soldier, clashing her blade with his. The sound of metal on metal echoed in the air as sparks flew from their swords. Suzu was faster and more agile than the soldier, dodging his swings and countering with her own. She saw an opening and kicked him hard in the stomach, making him gasp for breath. He stumbled backwards, losing his grip on his sword. He reached the wooden railing and fell over it, but not before he grabbed Suzu's beige tunic with his hand in a last-ditch attempt to save his own life. He pulled her, hoping to take her down as well. Suzu felt a jolt of alarm as she realized what was happening. She was falling over the ship's starboard side into the unknown below.

"Suzu!" Hogart cried out, rushing over to peer over the bar.

He found the dainty young woman in a distressed and fevered state as the wind whipped through her long black hair and the rope burned her hands. Suzu was hanging from the bottom of the *Intrepid* like a pendulum, swinging back and forth over the jagged, ghostly peaks of the ivory-covered mountains. She could see the cracks and crevices in the rocks, the white snow and cyan ice that covered them, and the dark shadows that lurked below. But the damaged *Intrepid* sailed on aimlessly, oblivious to her plight, heading deeper into the mountain range. "Hogart, you dolt! Pull me up!"

The sharp rocky spires rose menacingly and loomed closer, stretching outward like cruel talons eager to snatch their powerless, flying victim from the sky and tear her apart. At the brisk speed they were flying, colliding with the immovable rocks would mean certain death. Hogart heaved and hauled madly on the rope, hand over hand with all his might, each pull bringing Suzu a healthy distance upwards. At the same time, Suzu cooly and peacefully ascended the rope, hoping to escape nature's waiting, deadly clutches. Between the two working together, their contrasting efforts paid off as Suzu passed over the piercing, jagged tips of the rocks by a hair's breadth.

Hogart, unaware of Suzu's fate, continued to heave on the rope, ignoring the fighting disarray, screaming shouts, and every immediate danger around him. He felt his heart pounding, hoping to see Suzu alive again. Finally, after what seemed like an agonizing eternity, he saw her slender fingers grab a firm hold of the starboard wooden rail and pull herself up to the upper deck.

"I thought I lost you," Hogart said. He stood panting, wiping the sweat from his dark brown brow.

"Are you kidding?" Suzu said. "You still owe me money."

The moment's victory was fleeting as the damaged *Intrepid* whipped up speed and rapidly descended through the treacherous peaks of the mountain range, heading straight for the broad side of a mammoth snow-fringed cliff.

"The propulsion sail! We must change course, or we'll crash into the mountainside!" Hogart rushed over the upper deck to the port swing-arm sail. He mustered up what was left of his strength, gripped the long handle, and pulled backwards, praying to change their course and avoid a direct hit against the mountainside. He dug his feet into the floorboards and grunted loudly, straining and exerting every muscle as he pulled.

"It's damaged," Suzu yelled. Noticing that her friend's best efforts were barely enough to change the dangerous direction away from the looming mountain, she jumped to Hogart's side and grabbed the long wooden sail handle. She knew they had only seconds to avoid a fatal crash and pulled with all her might alongside her big friend, hoping to tilt the damaged sail enough to change their course. Working together, they directed the port-side propulsion sail, damaged or not, to tilt gradually. With each tiny and forceful budge, the ship's nose was directed slightly away from the craggy wall.

Hogart and Suzu may have avoided a direct collision. Still, they could not adjust the projected course as the *Intrepid*'s fore port side struck along the snow-covered rock face. The propulsion side sail snapped off from the violent impact, throwing the two friends brutally backwards across the upper deck and slamming them into the pile of barrels and crates secured to the aft observation deck. The entire port side of the wooden hull scraped and ground against the unforgiving mountainside a lengthy distance, causing a cascade of rocks and waves of heavy snow to fall around the deck and almost bury them.

The *Intrepid* spun out of control between the mountain walls, trailing cardinal flames, inky smoke, and debris as it plummeted from the sky. It finally crashed, the bowsprit of the skyship digging sharply into the frozen landscape with a loud boom, shattering the snow, ice, and rock around it. The people on board, a ragtag mix of Zamana Empire soldiers, civilians, and Silver Moon Sharks, were hurled forward by the collision's impact, grabbing onto anything they could on the upper deck of the doomed, wrecked vessel to stop their momentum from forcing them overboard.

The *Intrepid* slid forward in the icy, chalky snow for a short distance, tilted backwards to a nearly vertical position, and then skidded down the steep snow-fringed slope, bouncing and twisting as it collided with a collection of large pallid rocks and tall evergreen trees. With each slide and collision, some of the passengers lost their grip and were thrown over the side, screaming as they plunged into the gaping chasm hundreds of feet below, where a swift river roared and awaited them. The terrifying ride ended abruptly when the *Intrepid* rammed into two giant boulders on the cliff's brink and settled precariously alongside the sloped escarpment.

The doomed vessel was a wooden coffin ready to be placed into its grave, barely holding together as it teetered along the unstable mountainside, swaying dangerously back and forth amongst the shifting cliff rocks. One of the giant boulders shifted and started to crumble under the weight of the massive hull. The wind howled and tore at its wood-and-metal skin, ripping off chunks that flew like deadly shrapnel, making lethal, drifting projectiles for those still on board to avoid. The crew was a flock of terrified birds, flapping and flailing in vain, clinging to whatever they could and praying that the ship would not tip over the abyss. The swaying stopped with the starboard side of the *Intrepid* tilted alarmingly over the chasm.

Hogart's blood ran as cold as the whipping wind as he heard a horrific sound of wood snapping and metal shrieking. He looked up and saw the colossal pole that supported the ship's sails shattering in two. The wind was relentless, the damage deep, and the mast was succumbing to its fury. The mast plunged towards the deck, smashing everything in its way. "Suzu! Look out!"

Suzu saw the central mast snap and hurtle towards her, threatening to flatten her. She had only seconds to react. She held on to a thin rope and dashed across the slippery deck, scrambling sideways along the deck, dodging the debris. She spotted another rope that dangled from the sails, reached for it, and clung to it with all her strength. She swung herself out of harm's way just as the falling mast crashed down where she had been a moment ago. The mast smashed into the side of the tilted aircraft, making a deafening noise and sending shards and splinters of wood soaring everywhere.

Suzu gasped as she hung from the rope, feeling relief to be alive. She glanced around and witnessed the carnage of the mast collision. Several pirates and soldiers had been flung overboard by the impact, plummeting to the depths of the gorge. She turned her head to see a sky pirate holding on to the shattered wooden railing when the weakened banister inexplicably snapped off and also sent the pirate free-falling into the void.

Multiple massive wooden crates and barrels began to shake loose from their bindings, sliding and tumbling into two Zamana Empire soldiers, who screamed horrifically as they were swept helplessly away from the *Intrepid*'s rain-soaked, slanted, slippery deck. The shattered wooden planks near the ship's tilted edge simply broke away under booted feet, sending three more victims tumbling into the air and screaming to their inevitable deaths.

"Will this never end?" Hogart moaned.

"We need to get our gold and get off this ship!" Suzu shouted.

The *Intrepid's* bow sank forward, the hull shifting to the left in a rolling motion. It settled momentarily, leveling the upper deck enough for Hogart, Suzu, and everyone else to walk on it. Completely ignoring the immediate imperilment and instability of the skyship, the hand-to-hand fighting between all conflicting parties ensued on the destroyed upper deck. Since both Zamana soldiers and Silver Moon Sharks sky pirates were occupied with each other in a deadly fight or precariously hanging on to something solid to save themselves from falling to their deaths, Hogart and Suzu slipped through the entropy unnoticed and unscathed to get to their precious barrels filled with treasure.

"Still here!" Hogart said. Both gave heavy sighs of relief to find them still safely tied to the aft observation deck.

The owners hastily unfastened the *X*-marked barrels. But as soon as the last knot was undone, the *Intrepid* underwent an unforeseen shift. The wooden barrels broke free from their bindings, slipped out of their fingers' grasp, and rolled carelessly around the ever-changing, churning upper deck.

The *Intrepid* was now a massive death trap, a twisted ruin of wood and metal, with the terrified survivors on board clinging to the broken remains. The heavy weight of the fallen mast and the shattered planks of wood acted like an anchor, gradually pulling the wreck inexorably back to the right towards the mountain's edge.

The ill-fated skyship steadily slid closer to the edge in short violent spurts, twisting and turning with every shift of the ground. With the rocks loose and unstable, constantly and sporadically shifting underneath the hull, the vessel teetered uncontrollably back and forth whenever it moved. With every shift, parts of the vessel splintered, snapped, and broke off entirely due to the strain. It was also taking the fortunate remaining survivors still trapped on board unwillingly to certain death.

As the *Intrepid* slid towards the cliff, the bumbling twosome tried to save their rolling *X*-marked barrels from going over the side. One of the barrels escaped Suzu's grasp and rolled away. She instinctively chased after it when there was a sudden upwards shift on the deck, causing the barrel to roll backwards towards her and threatening to squish her. Suzu jumped out of the way, cursed, and resumed her pursuit. Hogart chased after the second marked barrel that was freely rolling and zigzagging around the upper deck. He lunged forward to grab the barrel and almost wrapped his arms around it, but an abrupt, unexpected tilt caused the barrel to move in another direction at the last moment. Hogart fell face-first and ate the floorboard, his arms wrapping around empty air. Undeterred by running around the constantly tilting upper deck, Suzu and Hogart collided with each other as they chased their separate barrels.

"Got yours?" Suzu said.

"Not yet." Hogart's eyes brightened with delight as he spotted a barrel with a familiar symbol scratched on it. He lunged towards it, but before he could grab it, his foot was snagged by a rope net tangled with other barrels. The surprise netting coiled around his foot like a waiting snake. It pulled Hogart down to the deck with its hefty weight, making him fall flat on his face, stunning him, and then dragging him across the deck. Hogart looked up and noticed he was helplessly sliding towards the broken-off wooden rail and the gaping hole in the ship's hull that yawned ahead. He panicked and wildly tried to kick free from the net, but it was wrapped too tight. He dug his nails into the wood and clawed the flooring with his stout fingers, desperate to stop, but it was too slippery. He felt himself sliding closer and closer to the edge, where the distant river awaited him with hungry waves. "Suzu! Help!"

Suzu saw her friend in mortal peril, caught in a snare that dragged him closer to his doom by the moment. She instinctively abandoned her pursuit of the prized barrel, evaded the endless fighting between soldiers and sky pirates on the deck, and leapt over shifting obstacles to nimbly forward roll over to Hogarth's side. Springing up in one movement, with a swift and precise strike, Suzu severed the entangled line of rope that ensnared him with her razor-sharp blade, saving him from the deadly trap.

"The barrel . . ." Hogart said, breathing heavily.

"True friendship means more than gold, my friend," Suzu said. She smiled at him and extended her hand.

Hogart laughed heartily in unspoken agreement as Suzu helped him get untangled from the rest of the netting, slicing away at the confining ropes with her sword. He barely had time to stand up before the ground beneath them shifted and trembled, the loose rocks underneath the hull finally giving away. The crashed skyship lurched downward towards the cliff's edge. This was it, they realized—the *Intrepid* was going over the edge, and it wasn't stopping this time. It picked up rapid speed as it slipped along the loose stone, shale, and gravel.

"We have to jump!" Hogart cried.

As the *Intrepid* tilted to the right and started to topple over the edge of the precipice, Suzu and Hogart knew they had only one chance to survive. They ran towards the opposite side, hoping to find a spot to jump off. They saw an opening in the broken railing in front of them, and without hesitation, they leapt from the upper deck of the *Intrepid* into the open air, feeling the wind rush past their faces. At the exact moment of their collective leap of faith, the *Intrepid* finished its undeterred slide and toppled over the cliff.

Suzu and Hogart landed on the hard ground, rolling and tumbling until they stopped. They were alive and started to laugh until the dreadful thought seeped into their minds about what they had just lost. "Our fortune and glory!" both friends cried in unison.

The scene unfolded before their eyes like a bad dream in slow motion. The skyship they had boarded with their ill-gotten gains from the heist of Tavter's treasure vault was now falling hundreds of feet. They saw the chestnut barrels containing their gold, diamonds, emeralds, and jewels plummeting with the debris destined to crash into the rushing river far below. All their daring plans, cunning schemes, and risky, lucky gambles had come to nothing. They had lost everything. The stolen loot from Tavter's treasure vault was now lost, just like the city once was.

A high-pitched, shrill scream pierced the vacuum of silence, interrupting the temporary moment of sorrow and woe to reveal more immediate trouble. Suzu and Hogart turned from the sudden drop and gaping chasm where the *Intrepid* had fallen, only to witness a surviving, small group of Zamana Empire Troopers, Silver Moon Sharks, and civilians still exchanging blows with swords and fists on a broad, flat outcrop on the mountainside.

The scene was anarchic and violent, as the last of the innocent civilians from Mills Point shouted and fell to the ground, pierced by blades. The remaining fighters scoured the area for any sign of movement, eager to kill or be killed. Unnoticed for the moment, the two friends stood silently at the cliff's edge, cowering in dread, hoping to escape the madness. They were unarmed, outnumbered, and helpless, and they knew it. But their luck ran out when, seemingly needing to fight anyone in sight, one of the crazed, bloodthirsty sky pirates, a hulking, pale, brutish, auburn-bearded man with a long sword, spotted them and grinned wickedly. He turned his attention towards the cornered duo and approached them menacingly, savoring their combined terror, as they slowly backed away until their heels reached the very edge of the cliff.

The Stranger

The russet-bearded sky pirate approached them with a wicked grin and derisive laughter. He raised his long silver sword to strike. But before he swung his blade, his eyes widened, and he screamed in horror. A tiny lavender dragon swooped in above his cornered victims' heads and breathed a stream of highly intense vermilion fire straight at the single sky pirate. Caught aflame, the large man howled in agony and ran amok in a fiery hysteria. Quickly forgetting his surroundings, the flame-engulfed sky pirate stumbled and fell over the side of the cliff to his doom while the duo watched in surprised awe and awkward relief.

"Dragon!" Hogart screamed. "That's a dragon!"

"Yes," Suzu said. Her voice was calm. "A dragonet."

It looked like a miniature dragon but was much more than that. With two tiny leathery wings on its back that enabled him to fly around, the dragonet was about the size of an average house cat, covered entirely in scaly light-purple-hued skin that shimmered in the golden morning sunlight. He had a small triangular head about half a foot long, with two small curved horns protruding from the back of it, and piercing canary eyes with black pupils. He appeared to be able to smell everything, including the wretched stench from the humans, with his elongated oval nostrils. A small forked claret tongue slid between razor-sharp teeth, protruding outward from his upper and lower jaws. A quadrupedal animal, his forelegs resembled and functioned as arms with five fingers, each ending with sharp claws. The dragon also appeared to be able to stand on his much longer hind legs, which had three clawed toes each that could scratch and tear. His lavender tail was long and flexible, ending with a spadelike tip he could use as a spear.

The petite dragon inhaled, filling his lungs with air, and then breathed another intense scarlet stream of fire from his jaws. The blazing inferno swept over and scorched the dry, rocky soil with a wall of flame that deterred the enemy soldiers and pirates from approaching the last civilians. They recoiled in horror and retreated from the cornered pair, who finally gained some ground to move.

"Come on! That dragon has given us a chance!" Hogart said, immediately picking up a discarded sword amongst the cluttered debris of the skyship wreck. Hogart clashed his sword with the first soldier foolish enough to stand in his way, punching him in the stomach and slamming him headfirst into a wooden crate.

Suzu pounced forward, grabbing a sword from its sheath on the ground. She swung it at the first person to approach, proudly dispatching one enemy with one stroke. She looked around, expecting more enemies to come. She didn't have to wait long. Three more soldiers emerged from the smoking, burning debris, running towards her with their blades raised. They looked bloodthirsty and determined to end her life, but Suzu was not afraid. She tightened her grip on her sword, ready to face them. But fate had other plans.

A loud rumble echoed through the air, followed by a long sable shadow that covered the ground. Suzu saw a massive ochre boulder rolling down from the rugged crag above. It was heading straight for the three soldiers, who had no time to react. The boulder smashed into them, flattening them like pancakes. Suzu watched in disbelief as the ashen dust and albino flakes of snow settled, revealing the carnage. A mysterious miracle had just saved her.

Suzu looked up and caught a distorted glimpse of a single towering figure on the escarpment above her. The image looked like a woman, but her proportions were distorted and unnatural. Before she could react, the shimmering figure vanished in the bright, blinding flaxen sunlight like an illusion. Suzu blinked and rubbed her eyes, wondering if she had imagined the whole thing.

Hogart approached her. "Suzu! Are you alright?"

"Yes. I just thought . . ." She glanced up at the long rock shelf above her again.

"Thought what?"

"I thought I saw a woman after the boulder dropped, but she's not there anymore."

"The thinner air must have done a number on you. You're hallucinating."

Suzu spun around instantly and angrily pointed her narrow finger at the larger man's chest. "Was I hallucinating when I said a shark was—"

Two arrows whistled sharply past their heads, snapping Suzu and Hogart back to the harsh reality of the fight they were currently in. Hogart instinctively grabbed a small throwing knife from his belt, turned to throw it in the direction the arrow came from, and skimmed the horizon for the target. He saw a Zamana Empire Trooper thirty yards away, hastily fixing another arrow on his bowstring. Hogart took measured aim, ready to hurl the knife at the enemy, but something strange happened. The Zamana soldier's head suddenly jerked back violently as if struck by an invisible hammer, and he simply collapsed on the ground like a limp ragdoll.

"Did you see that?" Hogart said.

"See what?"

"That soldier just dropped to the ground. I didn't throw my knife yet."

A few Zamana Troopers hollered and screamed, waving their weapons at the small, violet-scaled dragon circling just above their heads. As they distracted the creature, three Silver Moon Sharks gathered a fishing net from the wreckage. The three sky pirates waited for the right moment, then hurled the thick net over the dragon's leathery wings, bringing the tiny beast crashing down to the harsh, rocky, snow-flecked ground.

A terrible, fierce roar was heard throughout the entire gorge, as if a furious lioness had been secretly watching from the dark shadows and was now angered by the armed men endangering one of her kin. The Zamana Troopers and Silver Moon Sharks collectively stopped their conflict at once, freezing in worriment. They held their breath as they searched the drab rocky walls and snow mounds but saw no trace of the unseen, fearsome creature.

A lone, beautiful young woman suddenly materialized amongst them from nowhere, practically out of thin air, as if by magic. She was a towering, lean figure, standing nearly six feet tall, with long, wild, curly raven hair and smooth light-golden-brown skin. A deep-plum cloak concealed her travel attire: a maroon shirt, ashen pants, and a pair of belts—one bronze with pouches, the other burgundy, supporting a sword sheath. Silver gauntlets gleamed on her forearms. She furrowed her dark eyebrows, fixed her intense gaze on the men with piercing brown eyes, and stood ready to unleash her wrath.

In a sudden burst of speed, the stranger moved forward with deadly intention and purpose, ripping a long silver sword out of her sheath. She single-handedly engaged the three stunned sky pirates gloating over their netted prize. Her movements were that of a trained professional swordswoman—clean, swift, graceful, and accurate. She showed no mercy or hesitation. She was amply skilled, undoubtedly able to handle her own. Three quick well-placed strokes of the sword caused the three Silver Moon Sharks to slump to the ground dead within seconds.

In response to the outcry, the little lavender dragon did not hesitate to free himself from the net that trapped him. With a swift flick of his long tail, he unleashed a jet of ocherous fire that melted the thick ropes in seconds, then soared into the air and landed gracefully on the woman's shoulder. She lovingly smiled and stroked his head, whispering something in his ear. The dragon nodded and looked around with deadly purpose, ready to defend her.

The last two Silver Moon Sharks and the last two Zamana Troopers, who had been fighting each other moments ago, now turned their attention to the solitary woman and the dragonet. They sensed an opportunity to capture a rare prize or perhaps perceived the new duo as a threat to their safety. The four of them silently formed a loose, temporary, sinister alliance, forgetting their previous quarrels, and advanced towards the armed woman with their blades drawn. They did not know who she was or why she was there. All they knew was they wanted her and what she had.

"We want the little dragon," one pirate hissed. "Extremely rare."

"And valuable," a scraggly soldier added.

"A woman that beautiful, boys," a second pirate said, chuckling derisively, "they'll both get a great price."

"You cannot have the dragon, nor me." The swordswoman growled, steadily pointing her sword tip at them all.

"You can't take us all on."

Suzu and Hogart looked at each other, shrugged their shoulders, and sighed softly. They knew they were no longer the primary target, not much of a valued prize, nor the most significant threat to the newly formed, dastardly group. They rushed over and quickly joined forces with the stranger, standing on both sides of her, creating a united front of three. "You can't have us either!" they cried out together.

The young woman and her faithful dragon both turned their heads in unison to look at the other uncanny pair in disbelief.

"Take them down, boys!" one of the pirates yelled. At the command, the two Zamana soldiers and two Silver Moon Sharks rushed in together in one movement, screaming at the top of their lungs with brazenly raised swords.

Suzu found herself in the crosshairs of the two sky pirates sprinting towards her with their swords flashing. She ducked and evaded the first pirate's strike, which whistled past her ear and grazed her long black hair. She retaliated with a powerful punch to his tender belly, making him stumble backwards, wheezing and groaning. She then shoved him with all her might into his companion, who toppled over and impaled himself on an upright, jagged sword dropped by a slain soldier.

Enraged by his role in his mate's demise, the final Silver Moon Shark launched a furious assault on Suzu. The clash of steel rang out throughout the mountain range as they exchanged blows, each looking for an opening. Suzu danced around his strikes, using her agility and skill to avoid his brute force. She saw a chance and lunged forward, driving her blade into his chest.

She quickly inspected the scene, looking for the mysterious woman who had come to their aid. Suzu spotted her on the rocky outcrop, surrounded by the wreckage of tossed crates, white sails, and barrels. She expected to see her wielding her sword with as much skill as before, but instead, she saw the stranger's weapon being ripped away from her hands by a hulking ebony soldier. The woman was defenseless, her back pressed against a stack of crates.

The soldier raised his sword high, ready to swing downward. But the grape-hooded stranger was not giving up. She lifted her arms and crossed them in front of her, revealing her gauntlets. She used them to deflect the soldier's sword, creating a loud clang. She then swung her fist and smashed it into his face, breaking his nose and making him stagger away. He groaned in pain and lunged at her again in anger, hoping to catch her off guard.

But Suzu was watching. She had already nocked an arrow and aimed it at his neck. She released it with a smooth motion and watched as it flew through the air and pierced his throat. He gasped and choked, clutching at his wound, then fell to the ground, joining his dead comrades. The mystery woman bent down and picked up her sword, wiping the blood from her face. She looked up at Suzu and gave her a grateful nod, a smile on her lips.

Both women heard heavy grunting that made them spin around. Hogart fought his own battle, locked in a fierce struggle with the last of the enemy soldiers, right at the brink of the precipice. Hogart, grappling and entangled with his opponent, lost his footing and went over the cliff side. At the last moment, as they fell, a large burly hand lashed out and clutched a rope that hung from the ship's broken mast. The rope quickly uncoiled and slid down with them over the side until it snagged on a large wooden plank from the shipwreck, holding firm and stopping their descent. The soldier fell, losing his grip, screaming all the way to the river below.

"Hogart!" Suzu raced to the cliff's edge, where Hogart hung by a thread. She grabbed the rope with both hands, feeling it burn her skin. She looked up and saw the stranger instantly beside her, clutching the rope with a grim expression. The two women pulled with all their might, straining to lift Hogart from the natural abyss. But the hefty Hogart was like a dead weight. The rope didn't budge due to the heavy anchor. Suzu felt a cold sweat on her forehead, fearing she would lose her friend. "Climb up!"

"I can't!" Hogart screamed. The girthy man was scared stiff of falling to his death, his shaky voice echoing within the gorge.

"Mozo," the stranger said to the dragonet. "Fly down and give the big guy a little inspiration."

Mozo flapped his lavender leathery wings and drifted downward towards a highly alarmed Hogart.

"No! No dragons! Shoo! Go away!"

With one hand clutching the rope, Hogart swung his other hand at the pesky dragon just beyond his reach. Mozo, seemingly irritated and annoyed by the futile attempt to swat him down from the sky, flew under Hogart and gave him a fiery snort from his nostrils, barely singeing his oversize tush.

"Yow!" Hogart cried from the slight burn, quickly scrambling up the rope and climbing over the cliff's edge.

"Hogart!" Suzu said, alarmed. She rushed over to help him to his feet, checking to see if he was severely burned. "Are you alright?"

"I'm fine."

"You always say that."

Mozo soared into the air with a flutter of his wings and circled the rocky grey ledge. He felt joy and freedom as he flew, enjoying the warming breeze and the morning sunlight. He glanced down and saw his human companion smiling at him, her eyes sparkling with amusement. He swooped down and landed gently on her shoulder, nuzzling her cheek with his snout. She giggled and stroked his head, whispering something in his ear that only he could hear. They shared a moment of laughter and happiness as if they had a secret bond that no one else could understand.

"Not very funny, lady," Suzu growled. The petite woman turned and squared off against the slightly taller woman a few years older than her. "My friend doesn't care much for dragons."

"My apologies. We needed a laugh," the stranger said, continuing to chuckle. "My friend and I have been through quite a lot together in the last few days."

Suzu's face tightened, her posture more rigid and her voice far sterner. "As have we."

The stranger stopped her laughter, recognizing that the younger woman was swiftly getting annoyed. "Then perhaps we can help each other out," she said. Her voice was calm and even, trying to ease the escalating, tempestuous situation.

"Perhaps," Suzu said. She stood steadfast, not backing down.

Hogart placed his soothing hand on Suzu's shoulder. "Ladies, we should gather anything we need from the wreckage to survive and leave the area immediately. I'm sure both of you will agree that the Silver Moon Sharks or the Zamana Empire will be looking for the *Intrepid*. And they'll be looking for it soon."

The stranger kept her voice level and tranquil. "I agree."

Suzu turned to Hogart, keeping her voice low, almost a whisper. "Hogart, what were you thinking?"

"She did save our skins, Suzu. I believe she can be trusted, even with that little beast resting on her shoulder. And we do need to leave this area immediately before someone comes searching for us."

"We can go our own way," Suzu said, her voice encouraging.

"We'll have a better chance of survival if we stick together," the stranger said aloud, as if she was overhearing every word.

Suzu snapped her head around and shot a dirty look of annoyance at the source of the comment. But then she softened when she saw her partner in plunder walking over and standing at the cliff's rim, gazing down at the river below with a sad, remorseful, solemn expression on his scruffy, round face. "Our treasure. Everything we worked so hard for is gone," Hogart said aloud weakly and gave the heaviest sigh.

Suzu walked over to stand by his side, placed her arms around her friend as much as she could in a bear hug, and then slyly motioned to her tan tunic with a broad, knowing grin. At first, Hogart's long sad expression changed to one of befuddled confusion. But then he remembered that Suzu still had the unusual emerald gem hidden inside her jewelry box. A knowing grin appeared to match his partner in pillage. "Fortune and glory!" they said together as if they were sharing their own private joke.

Hogart turned to address the stranger in a renewed, joyful spirit. "We travel together until we reach a town. Then we go our separate ways. I go with my friend. You go with yours." He motioned to the dragonet, almost to shoo him away again.

The swordswoman smiled. "Very well."

"Let's see if we can find anything useful out of this mess," Suzu said.

All four members of the new group wasted no time expeditiously searching through the debris strewn about the rugged stone escarpment. Thankfully, they were lucky to salvage some necessary items from the wreckage. Suzu reclaimed a small serviceable Zamana repeater crossbow, a forest-green quiver for small arrows, and a light, sturdy silver sword. Hogart only chose a sizeable, sharp silver axe and a few small throwing knives, preferring simple and effective tools. After obtaining armaments, they gathered some fruit and canteens of water from the broken-up wooden crates and barrels spilled onto the area.

The two uncanny pairs departed immediately and traveled together cross-country as a foursome through the Vergery Mountain Range, a region of snowcapped peaks, verdant valleys, and soft blue lakes. They were not friends or enemies but allies of convenience.

The mysterious woman and her dragon took the lead. The two pairings were close enough to one another but kept their respective distances. Throughout much of the day, they maintained a distance of about forty yards apart and only gave an occasional casual glance back to see if they were too far ahead.

As a group, they moved swiftly along the winding mountain path. Mozo flew ahead low to the ground, scouting for every turn in the course and spotting any possible trouble from man or beast. He returned, landing dutifully on the woman's shoulder and nuzzling his snout in her ear. Such an act did not faze the woman; she whispered soft words back to him as if the two were communicating with one another in a secret language.

"Interesting," Suzu said, keeping a keen, watchful eye on the interaction.

"What's that?"

"Those two seem to understand one another."

Hogart studied their interaction. He was panting slightly and wiping the sweat away from his bushy brown brow. "That shouldn't be surprising," he said.

"Do you think we can trust them?"

"I don't see a reason why not."

"The nameless wild woman of the mountains and her odd dragonet?" Suzu said.

The party froze as the stranger signaled them to stop when she held up a tightly clenched fist, crouched down low, and hid behind the tall, bright fern-green grass. She pointed to a clearing up ahead, about a hundred yards away, where a gruesome scene unfolded. A pack of five velociraptors were feasting on the remains of an ivory-tusked grey elephant carcass for their late-morning breakfast. The sound of their crunching bones and snarling growls resonated. The party watched in disgust and fascination, hoping the predators wouldn't notice them.

"That's handy. The dragon can tip her off when other dangerous predators are nearby," Hogart said softly.

"Regardless," Suzu said. "Once we get to a town, we'll say our goodbyes."

The foursome moved silently away from the danger.

The journey seemed endless as they trudged through the mountain landscape for hours. The sun was relentless, beating down on their weary heads, getting higher in the sky. They had not seen any sign of life for miles until they spotted a glimmer of navy blue in the distance. It was a stream, a small but precious water source, flowing down a channel. They quickened their pace, imagining how refreshing it would be to dip their feet in the cool stream, splash some water on their faces, and quench their thirst. They reached the stream bank and felt a surge of relief and joy.

"Let's stop here for a moment. We can get fresh water," the stranger said, "and rest." Her bronze skin had lost some color, and she looked pale with beads of sweat above her black brow. She silently clutched her right hip and winced as if in a little bit of pain.

"And get dinner," Hogart added.

Hogart and Suzu had a peculiar way of fishing. It would start with Hogart taking off his long beige coat and boots. He would wade into a calm pool, spot a school of small fish, and then slam his fists or feet into the surface, creating a shock wave that stunned the fish. Then, he would quickly grab as many as possible and toss them onto the shore to Suzu. They called this technique "smash and grab." It was loud, messy, and wasteful, but they enjoyed it. However, their efforts had yet to bear any proverbial fruit.

The stranger observed this humorous spectacle from a distance, sitting on a sizeable cream-colored rock overlooking the flowing stream. Mozo was also huddled on the rock nearby, lazily enjoying the rest and the late-morning sun.

"Don't think about it," Suzu said. "Just reach out into the water."

Hogart softly waded across the gently flowing stream. He stopped momentarily and shot his burly hands in the water but missed his elusive underwater target. "They're quick."

"No, you're too slow and cumbersome," Suzu said. She took out her crossbow. "I can shoot one from here."

"No, no, no," Hogart said. He chuckled to himself. "I'm graceful and smooth, like a delicate wind or a ripple on the water. I'll catch one." He plunged his arms into the water, hoping to finally catch a nearby fish. But he miscalculated his momentum and toppled over, losing his balance. He landed with a loud splash, startling the fish and himself.

"Hogart!" Suzu cried out. She was relieved when her friend resurfaced, shaking his long, curly charcoal hair away from his face and spitting out a stream of water. Then she heard the stranger laugh softly to herself, trying very hard not to be too obvious. Even the cat-size dragon had a toothy smirk on his face. At first, Suzu was annoyed at the mockery but found that she couldn't help but join in on the laughter. "Let me help you," she said.

She removed her boots and stepped into the pool to help her friend catch fish. First, she took a big narrow stick from the ground and handed it to Hogart. "When you see a fish, try to hit it with a stick. Or at least stun the water so I can grab it."

Hogart nodded and waited for the perfect opportunity. He grunted softly as he hit the water hard with the stick, creating a big enough watery splash that it erupted upwards from the stream and hit Suzu in the face. Drenched by the unintentional splash, Suzu looked at her friend in annoyance and spit the stream water out of her mouth.

They could faintly overhear the stranger and Mozo sharing another round of hearty chuckles. Suzu and Hogart pretended to be oblivious to being the subject of their amusement and continued to focus on their fishing. They got several plump trout out of the stream and onto the shoreline through their usual teamwork.

—— ◆ ——

In the late afternoon, a long cylindrical hot-air balloon, pitch-black on top and pure white on the bottom, drifted slowly through the snowcapped peaks of the Vergery Mountain Range. The skyship had alabaster propulsion sails on the front and tail ends, with a narrow strip of a rudder sail on top of the tail, making it look like a giant killer whale searching for its early dinner.

The *Orca* had painstakingly followed the collision markings and the broken pieces of the *Intrepid* throughout the range, hoping to find some of the escaped enslaved people amongst the wreckage or camping nearby.

Tomap stood at the bow of the *Orca*. His eyes searched every ashen mountain ridge, white snowy peak, lining of evergreen trees, collection of rocks, and oily crevices. He was furious that the Silver Moon Sharks, the lowest kind of scum, had managed to hijack his captured skyship and crash it into the Vergery Mountains. He had worked hard to rise in the ranks of the Zamana Empire, and he would not let a crew of lousy, lowlife sky pirates ruin his chances of a grand promotion.

First Officer Mosley approached the ill-tempered commander with caution. She was loyal to him, but he could sense her hesitation. "Sir, we have followed the debris trail deep into the Vergery Range. If the storm didn't destroy the *Intrepid* and all on board, then these mountains certainly shredded the craft apart. We should return to the *Iron Talon* and complete our journey to Black Rock."

"I cannot arrive at Black Rock and report to Empress Vildan without the *Intrepid*. She was expecting two civilian skyships, not one. It's my duty, my mission, to find out what happened to the craft and find any survivors."

An incoherent shout was heard, one of excited discovery. Tomap and First Officer Mosley walked to the port-side rail, where a soldier pointed to a craggy pewter outcrop just below a pearly snow fringe. Numerous crates, barrels, and a portion of a mast with the sail still attached were scattered around the area in twisted, distorted clumps.

"Get the ship close to that flat bench. Ready the horses," Tomap said.

"Sir," First Officer Mosley said. She nodded dutifully and left to fulfill the order.

The *Orca* gracefully glided between the rocky walls and settled over the flat, long protrusion with the skyship debris. A portion of the wooden hull dropped down, creating a sturdy ramp, and landed solidly on the mountain shelf with a loud thud. Tomap casually rode out of the *Orca* atop his chestnut horse, followed by four mounted Zamana Empire Lancers. First Officer Mosley brought up the rear of the search party, riding an albino horse.

The *Intrepid* crash site was a gruesome sight, but incomplete. The wooden deck portions of the *Intrepid* were splintered apart, small remnants of the hull twisted and charred black. Slain bodies of Zamana Empire Troopers, Silver Moon Sharks, and civilians were scattered everywhere, some half-frozen, some still lightly smoking from fire.

Except for his Troopers, Tomap felt no pity for them. They were enemies, and they deserved to die. He dismounted his horse and walked around the crash site, looking for any signs of life. He hoped to find at least one person alive so he could interrogate them.

"Sir, the *Intrepid* appears to have crashed on this overhang and then fallen to the bottom of the gorge," First Officer Mosley said. She looked at the dead bodies of her fellow Troopers and the dreadful sky pirates scattered amongst the debris. "There are no survivors. They killed one another."

"Look closer," Tomap said sharply. "The debris here has been picked through for supplies."

First Officer Mosley, usually stoic and considered amongst most to be equally as intense as Tomap, bristled at the sharpness of her commander's words and stammered, "C-could be bandits. S-scavengers."

"Sir!" a Zamana Lancer called out. He motioned his superior officers over to the area where he was standing. "We found foot tracks leading away from the crash site. There's also this." The soldier pointed to the ground, which showed an outlined stretch of scorch marks from intense fire.

"What do you make of it?" First Officer Mosley said.

Tomap knelt and placed his black-gloved hand on the ground. "Not sure."

"There are no reports of a dragon residing in these mountains."

"No, there's not."

"What are your orders, sir?"

"Take the *Orca* and search the rest of the area for possible survivors," Tomap said. He stood up and walked to his waiting horse. "Meet us at Clitton in two days. I'm going to follow these tracks. See where they lead and to whom. "

"Yes, sir. "

The legend-in-the-making commander of the Zamana Empire galloped through the trees and rocks of the mountain pass with four Zamana Empire Lancers following close behind him. Following the faint tracks of a small group that had escaped and fled from the wreck, Tomap was determined to get all the fugitives back. Every single one of them. He could not face Keldace Vildan without them.

———❖———

The group of three humans and one small dragonet continued on the carved-out dirt pass through the Vergery Mountain Range. But after several hours of walking alongside a small gorge, they realized something was wrong. The beaten path had vanished, leaving them in a maze of graphite rocks and leafy, chromatic trees. They looked around, trying to find any signs of where to go, but they saw nothing. The path seemed to have disappeared, or they had lost their way.

"Where's the path?" Suzu said.

"It's been wiped away by a storm," Hogart said, "or maybe a landslide."

"What do we do? We can't go back."

"I think I see a path developing below us," the stranger said. She was peering over the small ledge to the shelf under them. "We have to find a way down."

Left with no choice but to descend to another area, the trio looked around for a safe way to the next ledge below them. As they approached the edge, they noticed a large chalky barked tree, with long rust-colored limbs full of sea-green leaves, that must have been uprooted recently and was teetering near the brink.

"I have an idea," Hogart said. He shrugged off his long sandy coat and draped it over a nearby stump. He eyed the massive tree that leaned precariously on a rocky ledge like a challenge or adversary. With a heavy grunt, he pushed against it with all his might, sending it top-first sliding down the slope. The tree tip crashed into the ground like a spear, forming a makeshift natural ladder of tree limbs to the next section of the trail.

"Nicely done, Hogart," the stranger said.

The trio carefully descended the jagged slope, climbing down on a few boulders, with Mozo always flitting nearby. They reached the first massive arm of the tree stretching out like a welcoming embrace. Grabbing the tree's limbs with both hands, they gradually and safely lowered themselves. The group followed a natural route to the next level of the mountain ledges.

As they reached the end of the descent, Suzu noticed a trail of scarlet blood on the leaves behind them. She turned to the stranger, who was clutching her right side and panting heavily. The unnamed woman clumsily dropped from the last tree limb to the ground below, staggered a few feet, and fell to the hard ground. She groaned softly and held her right side tenderly.

"Are you alright?" Hogart asked. His face was full of alarm. Being a person of good character, he dropped from the tree limb and helped her up. The injured woman grunted aloud at the slightest touch. Not wanting to anger the dragonet that watched intently nearby and reared his small triangular head with a nasty look at the outcry, Hogart cautiously backed away.

"We're obviously not going to hurt you," Suzu said. She dropped from the last tree limb and stood next to Hogart.

"I know," the stranger said. She turned to the dragon. "Mozo, it's alright. They will not harm us." The dragon seemed to understand, nodding oddly in agreement and backing off.

Suzu knelt on one knee and pulled the stranger's dark maroon shirt up near the right hip. She saw the black-bluish marks and cherry blood splotches of an untreated injury. "There's a nasty scrape. The color of your shirt hid your injury."

The stranger straightened up. "It's from my previous encounter before I met you."

Suzu scoffed lightly. "Previous encounter. It doesn't matter. You should have said something before." Her voice was raised and noticeably angry.

Hogart politely stepped in between the two opposing women, noticing that relations were getting tense and hostile just when they were doing so well. "We shouldn't travel farther until your wound is addressed. We can use the tree as protection against the night winds and anyone searching for us. We'll make camp here for the night."

Suzu mumbled something incoherent, obviously belligerent, but not much else was said. Without one word of debate, Hogart helped the injured, nameless woman settle underneath the leafy protection of the downed tree. There wasn't any fear that the mighty tree would dislodge and fall farther. It seemed stuck in its upside-down position. Its limbs creaked slightly and swayed happily in the warm breeze.

Suzu set out to gather certain herbs in the immediate area to distract herself with a task. Despite her burning desire to purposely hurt the stranger, she hoped there were enough ingredients around to develop some remedy to soothe the nasty scrape. In the meantime, Hogart gathered some thin branches, dry leaves, and a few large rocks to build a campfire.

The butterscotch sun rested for the day, and the chill of the late-evening wind settled over the small gorge within the Vergery Mountains. Beneath a star-flecked, heavenly sky, the half-moon rose high, casting a soft frost glow over the openness of the gorge. Despite their misfortunes, they all felt a sense of peace and wonder with their crude campsite, as if they were finally safe for the moment and the only ones left in the world of Arthea.

Suzu sat alone with a tiny bowl taken from the skyship wreckage in her hands. She mixed some herbs she'd found earlier with water from a canteen to create a soothing healing cream for the stranger's injury. As Suzu churned the herbs as if twisting a knife, she kept half an eye on what she was doing and the other half watching the stranger resting peacefully against a large moss-covered log.

Hogart was determined to make a campfire, even if he had to do it the old-fashioned way. He had gathered some dry twigs and leaves and piled them within a small rock circle. He then took two rocks and started to rub them together, hoping to create a spark. He rubbed and rubbed, but nothing happened. He tried harder, faster, louder, but still nothing. He looked at the rocks in frustration.

Maybe they were the wrong kind? He switched them with two other stones and repeated the process. This time, he saw a tiny spark fly out of the rocks and land on the ground. Excited, he continued to strike the stones with more force. More sparks flew, but none of them reached the pile of twigs. He leaned closer to the pile and tried to aim the sparks at it, but he only succeeded in burning his fingers. He yelped and dropped the rocks, shaking his hand in pain and glaring at the pile of twigs, which remained cold and unlit. He felt like giving up, but decided to try it again. Picking up the rocks once more, he smashed them together with all his strength. A big spark flew out of the rocks and landed on the pile of twigs. Hogart held his breath and watched as the spark slowly faded away. Nothing happened. The pile of twigs did not catch fire. He sighed and threw the rocks away in defeat.

Mozo calmly walked up on his hind legs and showed off his fire-breathing skills by igniting the crude fire pit with a short blast of flame through his nostrils. Seemingly mocking the human with a toothy smile, he flew over to the silent stranger and snuggled in her lap like a house cat.

Hogart let out a soft chuckle. "Mozo is a unique name for a dragon. Where did you find your little pet?"

Mozo sat up, looking pensive and slightly annoyed by grating his teeth. It was evident that he understood human language, specifically the "common tongue." The problem for Hogart was if the dragon took offense to the words "little" or "pet."

The stranger, noticing the agitation, stroked Mozo's head gently. "Mozo is not my pet. He's a friend. He chooses to stay with me of his own free will."

"He's rather loyal," Suzu said.

"Yes, very. We've been together ever since I was little," the woman said.

Mozo lifted from the woman's lap and spread his tiny leathery wings. He flitted upwards to the fallen tree that provided the group natural shelter, settled on a thick leafy branch, and seemed content to watch over them all from there.

Suzu sat beside the mysterious woman and gently lifted her dark maroon shirt just enough to see the mulberry scrape above her right hip. She gingerly dabbed the herbal ointment she had created on the stranger's wound, trying not to cause more pain. The stranger groaned and clenched her teeth but did not resist. Suzu felt sorry for her and her pain, but she was also curious about her identity. The woman cried out and winced a second time. Mozo stirred within the shifting leaves above them. Suzu and Hogart exchange a terrified glance and froze in place.

"You have nothing to fear from him," the woman said.

Suzu and Hogart sighed softly in relief. After applying the cream and a clean lilac cloth to cover the wound, Suzu sat beside Hogart near the campfire. The eight fish caught earlier in the day were now taken out of the tawny burlap bag and set to roast on a spit over a lively crackling pit. Within minutes, the fish dinner smelled delicious, and their stomachs growled with hunger.

Suzu cleared her throat and spoke directly. "It's occurred to us that we've been traveling all day, friend, and we don't even know your name."

The stranger looked at her sternly and studiedly, as if she was not used to being talked to in such a tone. "Mia."

"That's a nasty scrape, Mia," Hogart said. His voice was one of honest concern, trying to counter the tension between the two women.

Mia remained silent and rummaged through a burlap sack she had salvaged from the skyship crash, looking for something edible. She found two bruised but still fresh apples. She took one out and bit into it, savoring the sweet-and-sour taste. She threw the other apple to the branches where Mozo was hungrily waiting. The creature caught it with his teeth and devoured it in seconds, making happy noises. A polite, knowing smirk came across Mia's lips.

Unintimidated by the display, Suzu smiled, continuing her direct tone of voice and stoic demeanor. "It will start to heal soon. Good as new in a few days."

Mia suspected that the two unlikely friends had done this sort of curious banter routine many times before, playing off each other to get answers from a person. Suzu and Hogart had an uncanny knack for interrogating people with, in their mind's eye at least, witty and clever exchanges. They would take turns asking questions, sometimes teasing, sometimes pressuring, sometimes flattering the person they were questioning. They knew how to read each other's cues and play along with their roles, which they had practiced and perfected over time. Mia thought momentarily about this and then responded carefully. "Thank you."

"How did you get it?" Hogart asked. "It wasn't at the *Intrepid* crash site."

"You said you have been alone for a few days in these mountains?" Suzu added quickly.

Mia made another hard study of the pair, seemingly asking herself if they were to be trusted with the truth or not—or, at least, part of it. "I was sent on a task to seek aid from a friend against the Zamana Empire. My party was attacked on the way. Mozo and I alone managed to escape."

"The rest of your party?" Suzu said.

"Not sure. Dead or captured." The soft coral glow of the campfire seemed to etch and highlight the look of remorse and sorrow on her beautiful golden face.

"Sorry." Suzu recoiled momentarily from her direct tone and questioning, showing respect.

"As Mozo and I broke down our camp this morning, we saw your skyship fall from the sky," Mia said. "I felt compelled to help any survivors when I saw it was a civilian skyship."

"Well, we're happy you came to help us," Hogart said. He hummed softly to himself and stirred the blazing merlot embers of the campfire with his long stick, raising the blush flames higher to cook the sweet-smelling, sizzling fish faster.

Mia couldn't help but stare at the odd couple. They were the unlikeliest pairing and had nothing in common. A tall, stocky, scruffy white man in his early thirties who had traveled the world and nearly seen it all. A slim, elegant, olive-skinned young woman from the far eastern lands in her late teens who was beginning to explore life and its possibilities. They came from different backgrounds, cultures, and generations, yet they shared a bond of friendship stronger than any difference. "What were the two of you doing on a civilian skyship full of Silver Moon Sharks and Zamana Empire Troopers?"

Hogart stopped humming and poking the fish with his stick, looking nervously over to his counterpart for any answer. Suzu was surprised by the sudden turn in questioning and started looking uncomfortable herself. "Um . . . huh?"

"Are you wanted by the authorities?"

Hogart scoffed. "Wanted?"

Suzu shook her head and chuckled lightly. "No. No, not us."

"Who would want us?" Hogart said sheepishly and then shrugged his shoulders. "Look at us."

Mia glanced up at the dragonet perched on the branch above her. She dug into her burlap sack and threw another apple in the air. The dragon caught it with his mouth in one snap and swallowed it whole. Mia nibbled on her apple and gave her new traveling companions a friendly, polite smile.

Suzu's black eyebrows furrowed in a frown at the suggested threat but felt conversation and diplomacy would be best. Unamused by the change in the conversation, her tone of voice returned to even and direct. "The city of Mills Port was attacked by a Zamana commander named Tomap Sruz. We tried to flee the city on that passenger skyship, the *Intrepid*. Then it was captured."

"There was a witch who used magic to take hold of the skyships," Hogart said. "Don't know her name. She was dressed in a hooded black cloak and wore some form of an iron mask. Creepy lookin' lady if you ask me."

"Keldace Vildan," Mia said softly, almost to herself. The slight smile on her lips was wiped clean, and deep dread was fixed on her face.

"Who?"

"Keldace Vildan. The empress of the Zamana Empire. Mistress of the Dark Arts."

"What do you know of her?" Suzu said.

Mia shrugged. "Not much is known about her. That's the problem. Some say she's a lost warrior; some others say a vagabond. Most say a merciless demon sent from the darkest pits of the Netherworld. No one even knew of her existence until about three years ago. Stories of a black-robed sorceress, covered in armor from head to toe, that came down from the Northern Mountains with just a few loyal followers. Within days, Keldace Vildan overthrew the monarchy of Ture, claiming to be absolute ruler by right."

"Why didn't anyone stop her?" Hogart said.

"Most people are content with their personal affairs, their lakes and lands, and not overly concerned with what happens to another land thousands of miles away. Besides, Vildan seemed only intent on overseeing the reconstruction of her realm at the time. A campaign of law and order to an uncivilized land. Only in recent months has the Zamana Empire begun to branch out and aggressively take new territory."

"There was another passenger skyship called the *Orca*, along with ours, being taken to Black Rock," Suzu continued. "It was filled with innocent people from Mills Point."

Hogart sighed softly. "The people from Mills Point will be used as slave labor to construct new Zamana Empire sailing ships and skyships. Men. Women. Even a few kids were on board."

"On the way to Black Rock, in the middle of a thunderstorm, the Silver Moon Sharks attacked the convoy," Suzu said. "Our skyship broke away from the battle. That's when you saw us crashing."

"Black Rock?" Mia fell silent, shuddering at the name of the terrible place, and mused silently to herself. She appeared deeply troubled by this dreadful news and the people's plight. She didn't say a word as she was handed two cooked fish for dinner. Mia blindly tossed one more fish upwards to the trees for Mozo, who quickly caught and slurped the fish down his gullet in hungry delight. She returned to her plate and slowly ate her dinner while deep in thought.

A couple of hours later, Suzu and Hogart sat wearily at the campfire. They rubbed their full bellies, rested their backs against a hollow log they'd dragged close to the pit, and relaxed their guard for a few minutes. Both casually looked around the rugged outcrop to spot any sign of their traveling companions amongst the large rocks, softly swaying, leafy trees, and long, shifting sable shadows in the pale moonlight.

"Do you see her?" Hogart said.

"No," Suzu answered softly.

"I think she's gone off with her dragon for the moment." Hogart looked around, scratched his scalp under his hair, and saw nothing in the darkness.

Suzu smirked. "They haven't left us. I can feel it."

"Quickly! I have a plan!" he said excitedly.

"You, of all people," Suzu said in disbelief and then laughed, "a simple-minded oaf, have a plan?"

"Yes!" Hogart beamed with pride. "And it's a good one this time."

"This time? Show me."

Hogart grabbed a long, narrow wooden stick from the nearby bushes and dug into the dirt. Using the stick like a writing instrument, he created three connecting square areas; one box was more significant and next to the other two that seem stacked on top of one another. "The squares are lands: Dexarocco, Kayawa, and Zamana-controlled territory. We are here in Dexarocco." He dug a deep hole in the first smaller square to represent their position. "To the south, Kayawa. This is our ultimate destination." He created a large *X* on the second smaller square below the first.

"I understand," Suzu said. "Go on."

Hogart then made a wavy pattern between the squares representing Dexarocco and Kayawa. "The wavy lines represent the Zamana Empire Lancers that now heavily guard the Kayawa-Dexarocco border." Hogart tapped the wavy lines between the two neighboring squares.

"I'm with you so far."

He created another pattern, short straight lines running along the long border between Dexarocco, Kayawa, and the Zamana-occupied lands. He pointed the tip of the stick to the deep hole that represented their current position on the map and began to drag it across the dirt to the unmarked third square. "There's no way anyone would want to cross into Zamana territory willingly, so there will not be so many troops guarding the border. It should be open. So, we will purposely cross the border and enter Zamana territory from our position here."

Suzu inhaled sharply, ready to debate the crazy idea.

"We stay close to the Vergery Mountain Range, practically hugging it, heading south," Hogart continued, dragging the stick in a southern direction to show precisely what he meant. He then stopped the stick and crossed it back to the right, indicating a new direction away from the Zamana lands. "The Zamana-Kayawa border must be easier to cross than the Kayawa-Dexarocco border. We will safely cross from Zamana territory into Kayawa territory at a less guarded point along that border. We will then continue our journey safely and reach our destination, the capital city of Valsco." Hogart smiled broadly as he lightly pointed towards the giant *X* on the makeshift map.

"Hmpf. *X* never ever marks the spot, my friend," Suzu mumbled.

Not far away, a woman burst into near-derisive laughter. An unstable human outline shimmered and emerged from just beyond the dancing marigold campfire light and the evening's shifting inky shadows, like a ghost made of pale moonlight. Mia laughed delightedly and clapped her hands approvingly at the scheming pair, apparently secretly listening to the entire conversation.

"Ingenious," Mia said. Mozo came swooping out of the darkness, landed on her shoulder, and nuzzled into her hair. Mia said something incoherent to her small companion, and he instantly flew up to a tree branch like before. "But I will add to your plan. We will all travel to the Zamana Empire lands together. We will rescue the enslaved civilians from Black Rock, dismantle or steal the new Zamana Empire sailing ships and skyships, and then safely pass into the Kayawa territory through the mountain range to complete the journey."

At first, Hogart and Suzu couldn't believe what they had just witnessed. Their eyes met in a silent exchange of shock and awe. They were frozen in place for a long moment, unsure how to process the absurd scene. Then they heard the new version of their plan from someone who wasn't even involved. A faint chuckle escaped Suzu's lips, followed by a snort from Hogart. Soon, they were laughing lightly, finding humor in the ridiculous situation.

"We do not want to be viewed as rude or ungrateful, but you and the dragon are nowhere in these plans," Hogart said, pointing the stick at the lines in the dirt.

"We do not want to be viewed as cowards or unsympathetic to the people of Mills Point, but we're not going to Black Rock either," Suzu added.

"We barely escaped with our lives with the one encounter."

"Not doing that again."

Against the backdrop of crackling amber flames from the blazing campfire and the soft white light from the moon above, a distinct, twisted look of anger and disgust came over Mia's face. She reached into her belt as if to draw her sword but threw something else. She flung her hand forward, and two golden shards gleamed and sparkled against the evening moonlight. The shards of gold landed with a clink at the feet of the adventurous, bumbling duo. "I'm hiring the two of you fools."

Suzu looked down and picked up the golden shards. She turned to Hogart and whispered, "We're with her one day, and she knows our weakness."

"Those are just shards. Once we reach the capital city of Valsco in the Kayawa Kingdom, you'll have a promised payment of five gold bars," Mia announced.

Hogart moaned as if he had just been given a stomachache. "Five gold bars?"

Mia nodded. "Each."

Suzu looked directly at Mia. "Each?"

Mia nodded again in the same manner.

Hogart groaned again, shaking his head. "Suzu, please don't . . ."

Suzu pointed her index finger at Mia. "One moment."

"C'mon, Suzu!"

"You come on! Get up, dolt!" Suzu said. "We need to discuss this in private."

The pair pick themselves up, leaving the warmth of the flames and the company of their new companions behind, and ventured into the shadows of the night. They needed to discuss their plans privately, away from prying ears and curious eyes. They found a secluded spot amongst the swaying trees where they could speak freely and honestly. They had a lot to say and a lot to decide.

"Think about it, Hogart! We can regain our small fortune that has been lost with five gold bars each," Suzu said softly. She looked over her shoulder to make sure she was not heard. "Once we are at Valsco, we can still try to sell that hidden gem we have on us and increase our fortune."

"I don't know, Suzu."

"We've been in situations like this before, big guy. Come on!"

"There is the glory of rescuing the innocent people of Mills Point," Hogart said, pointing out the positive of the situation. "We're doing a good thing."

"Yeah, sure. There's that too. Think of the songs that will be sung of our adventures," Suzu said excitedly.

"We can still have our fortune and the glory!" Hogart said. "Let's do it!"

In the final agreement between them, Suzu turned from Hogart and walked directly up to Mia. "Alright, you got yourself new partners. Five gold bars. Each. And if you don't pay up"—Suzu glanced over to Hogart, who was out of earshot—"the big guy said he's gonna wring your scrawny little neck. And not even your little pet dragon will be able to help you. Understood?"

Able to understand the common tongue, the insult, and the threat, Mozo lowered his head and growled softly. Mia rubbed his head in comfort, soothing the tiny beast from responding. "Very well," she said politely. "We leave first light tomorrow morning for Clitton."

Elephant Chase

The copper sun rose over the puffy cream clouds and snow-peaked mountains. Suzu and Hogart took the lead for a change in their journey across the mountainous expanse. They walked along a twisty, narrow trail through the sage rocky terrain, followed by their two new companions. Soon, the mountain pass elevated to a stroll along the parakeet grass-lined base of a mountain ridge. The spontaneous burst of wind brought a settled coolness, making the trek pleasant.

Suzu gazed at the cobalt sky, where an unusual caravel hot-air balloon floated amongst the puffy milky-white clouds. The bowsprit was painted bright canary, and the bow of the skyship was pitch-black as night. The hot-air balloon was completely bright cherry. The propulsion and rudder sails were the same color but with black streaks, almost representing feathers. The underbelly of the hull was stark white. It had the markings of a civilian skyship, a vessel used by either traders or travelers, shaped like a cardinal bird, with its wings spread out as if ready to soar. "That's a good sign. We're heading in the right direction."

"Do either of you even know how to pilot a skyship?" Mia asked.

"I do," Hogart called back. "Suzu doesn't."

"Not yet, anyway. I was hoping you could teach me, especially after our encounter with the Silver Moon Sharks."

"I will be happy to teach you," Hogart said merrily, ready to take on the challenge. "You might need the skill one day to get us out of trouble."

"I'm afraid I do not have enough gold to buy a skyship," Mia said, proving still that she had excellent hearing.

Hogart scoffed. "Never mind buying a skyship. It might be difficult just to pay a decent fare to get to Black Rock, no matter how much gold you may have on you. Not many want to go to such a dreadful place willingly."

"We can stow away," Suzu suggested.

"No. Too long a journey," Hogart grumbled. "I don't want to be cramped hiding away for a long time."

Suzu looked over her shoulder to a visibly concerned Mia and smiled. "We'll think of something. We always do."

The foursome continued along the beaten mountain path to the promised port. Using the slow-moving skyship above as their unaware guide to follow, the group was forced to move along at a steady pace to keep it in sight. Following the flight path of the caravel skyship for the entire afternoon, they finally found themselves on the outskirts of Clitton.

Perched atop and along the slopes of a towering headland, the port of Clitton was a unique mixture of aviation and commerce. The hardworking trade town was a vital link between the Vergery Mountains' rich mines and the lowlands' bustling markets, mainly relying on skyships to transport goods and passengers across the treacherous terrain. The port was divided into several natural tiers with distinct character and function. They were all connected by a few narrow, twisting and turning, man-made dirt roads that snaked around the contours, occasionally disappearing into tunnels carved into the ecru rock.

The first tier was the square, where the merchants and traders conducted business and negotiated. The square was a spacious stretch of square three-story buildings that occupied most of the headland's summit, surrounded by a couple of watchtowers that offered a panoramic view of the port's activities and the looming valley landscape. The square was filled with stalls and booths where merchants displayed their wares and haggled with buyers. The square was also where the port's authorities and officials had offices and chambers, overseeing its operations and regulations.

The second tier was the town, where most residents lived and worked. Nestled amongst the verdure of trees and shrubs, the section was a collection of residential buildings and houses clinging to the sides of the headland and the slopes, defying gravity and the elements, connected by mocha wooden bridges and grey stone stairs. The town had its shops, taverns, inns, stables, workshops, and other facilities catering to the needs and preferences of its inhabitants. The quaint structures evoked a sense of charm and wonder. They were not mere buildings but crafted works of art that blended seamlessly with the natural foliage surroundings. Each had its unique design, color, and features, reflecting the personality and culture of the mountainous people.

The third tier was the dock, where the larger merchant galleon and schooner skyships docked at the natural rock ledges that jutted out from the mountainside, forming a network of ports and platforms. Others were smaller, more personal, or passenger carracks, prams, and cog vessels that could only land at the wooden ports built as extensions of the mountain slopes. The skyships were secured to the docks by ropes and hooks to be repaired or serviced by cranes and lifts, and to load and unload their cargo. These ports were connected by wooden bridges that spanned the gaps between the rocks, creating a web of pathways and stairs. Far below them, the river roared and splashed, cascading down in several aquamarine waterfalls that sparkled in the medallion sunlight. The only way to reach the river was by a long stone stair carved out of the mountain, leading to a pier where some people fished or traded with the river folk. The dock was always busy, with skyships arriving and departing at all hours.

The lowest tier featured the city's gate, where the few roads and paths that connected the port to the rest of the world converged. The gate included a fortified celadon gatehouse that guarded the entrance to the port, controlling the traffic of people and vehicles that passed through. It was also where the port's defenses were located, including ballistae and watchtowers, and was manned round the clock by soldiers and guards, who protected the port from any threats or attacks.

Below the gate, built on the side of the precipice, a cluster of dwellings defied gravity and logic. They were not mere huts but elaborate structures of varying shapes, colors, and sizes, each with personality and charm. Some were long and slender, others were short and squat, but all were supported by sturdy wooden beams that dug into the rock. The residents had also built cozy wooden pavilions and gazebos where they could relax and enjoy the open fresh air and scenery. To reach them, one had to climb a series of ladders, staircases along the rock face, and rope bridges that crisscrossed the chasm.

Some adventurous and artistic souls, and many considered to simply be skyship enthusiasts, had even built their dwellings on two nearby mammoth buttes that rose from the valley floor, like giant fingers pointing to the sky. They used wooden ladders, staircases, and bridges to access the houses and shops carved in the rock face. The walls and roofs were painted with bright patterns and symbols, creating a cozy and colorful community. The townspeople flew in their personal skyships, which were personally decorated with colorful flags and streamers, and docked their craft along the cliff sides or on the rooftops of the buildings. A gondola system connected the main town with the two isolated pinnacles, offering a scenic ride and a thrilling view. The passengers could see the valley below them, dotted with farms, forests, and rivers.

Mia reached into her satchel and took out small binoculars. She looked at the town through the device for a minute and sighed heavily. "We have a problem. There are Zamana Empire Troopers at every gate."

Hogart took the binoculars passed over to him, peered through the lenses, and surveyed the town below. He saw several groups of Zamana soldiers roaming the streets, some stationed at each of the three gated entrances. Two gates were located at the top level for the only two roads into the town. One entrance at the bottom level, a part of the sage stone gatehouse, led out to a very narrow road along the mountain slope. Hogart noticed, to his amazement, that the soldiers seemed relaxed and bored, not paying much attention to their surroundings. "Once we get past one of the gates, we should be alright."

"We need to get closer to see what we can do," Suzu said.

The foursome carefully descended the naturally carved-out rocky path, keeping a low profile and moving fast. They knew they had to reach the mountain road before anyone spotted them, and they knew the trail was dangerous, where one slip would cost them dearly. The road was used by the miners and traders, who transported their precious cargo with the help of massive mottled elephants. The beasts had huge slightly curled ivory tusks that could pierce through anything, and they were fiercely loyal to their drivers standing in large open carriages on their backs. The group hoped to avoid any confrontation with them, but as they neared the road, they saw three elephants coming their way. Two were dragging heavy wagons loaded with magitite, while the third carried golden hay for the horses and elephants in town.

"There's our way in," Suzu said, pointing at the last wagon. "Let's go."

The three elephants bellowed softly as they made their way to the gated entranceway, walking slowly and sullenly in a single file. Above them, on a rocky outcrop, the three travelers waited for the right moment to pounce as they passed underneath. They spotted the last wagon full of hay passing them on the road below, the driver seemingly oblivious to his surroundings. They seized their chance and leapt from the ledge, landing softly on the hay.

"Come on!" Mia called out softly. Mozo flew into the safe confines of the haystack, flying in low from behind the cart.

Quickly burrowing into the pile, they avoided detection hitching a free ride to the town.

The brief journey was rough and noisy, with every bump in the path and turn of the wheel making the wagon creak and groan. After a few minutes, the lumbering animal convoy came to a soft halt. The voices of the driver and the soldiers were muffled and unclear, but they were exchanging some friendly words. The wagon then rolled forward and resumed its course, shaking and rattling into Clitton. They had easily and quickly passed a checkpoint at the gate, unnoticed by the guards.

The three giant elephants continued their single-file, slow walk into the top tier of the village, loudly trumpeting their arrival. As soon as they reached the streets, the hidden stowaways spilled out of the back of the wagon. Still unnoticed, they quickly scampered off to the side of the street and into an alley. They immediately dusted hay from their clothes and hair, erasing any evidence of how they got in, hoping no one had seen them. Mia held Mozo close to her chest, hiding the dragon within her cloak, where he curled up in her arms like a cat as the trio prepared to integrate themselves with the townspeople.

They slipped into a passing crowd of workers and followed the winding road that snaked along the peak, leading them to the upper part of the village. There, they saw the white-armored Zamana Empire Troopers patrolling the town's perimeter, but they didn't seem to bother the villagers much, who were busy haggling and carrying on with their daily lives. The road had a few single-rider horses, two-horse personal carriages, and long passenger wagons, but they were not very large or luxurious. The wagons were small and primarily used for work, such as carrying food, wood, or tools. They didn't see any dinosaurs here, like they had in Mills Point. Instead, there were more tusked ashen elephants, giant and hairy creatures that suited the mountainous climate and terrain. They could be trained to walk in a line along the narrow streets, safely carrying loads of goods or carriages of passengers. The village was full of specialized merchants, blacksmiths, general stores selling necessary goods, and craft workshops, from which came the sounds of hammers and saws. There were also multiple tiny houses and mills made of stone and wood, with red chimneys that smoked black. A huge rogue water wheel spun by the narrow blue river that ran through the village and provided power and water. The river then cascaded down the buff cliff side, creating a spectacular waterfall that sparkled rainbow colors in the sun.

"Ah, civilization," Suzu said.

"We should arrange our fare immediately," Mia said softly.

"Why the hurry?" Suzu asked. "There's nothing to worry about."

Mia looked around her surroundings with high reserve. "I don't want to risk being spotted, that's all."

"Spotted?" Hogart said. He snorted and laughed. "No one is looking for us."

The bumbling duo chuckled and carried on flippantly, acting as if they were visitors passing through and did not have a care in the world. The authorities didn't want them. No one knew about them or their latest exploits. They could be as carefree as they liked to be. However, Mia appeared worried, restless, and fidgety for an unknown reason. She was constantly looking over her shoulder as if she would be pointed out amongst the crowd.

"You need something to eat," Hogart said.

"And drink," Suzu added. "I'm thirsty."

Suzu, Hogart, and Mia descended the rough-hewn stone stairs that led to the bustling marketplace. The markets were spread out in different sections on the uppermost level of the city. They could smell the enticing aromas of freshly baked bread, roasted nuts, and spiced meat as they crossed the rickety wooden bridge over the narrow chasm to the designated food market area. After their long journey, they were hungry and eager to sample the local delicacies. They stopped at a stall that sold skewers of grilled chicken and vegetables dripping with a tangy sauce. Suzu paid the vendor with a handful of coins and handed each of her companions a skewer. They bit into the juicy meat and savored the explosion of flavors in their mouths. For a few minutes, all was good with the world, and they were at peace.

Out of nowhere, a shout was heard directed at them. "You! Halt!" Two white-armored Zamana Empire Troopers were across the food market area, pointing directly at the trio.

Suzu and Hogart froze in their tracks, taken aback and unsure what to do. They looked around but couldn't see anyone else that the Troopers might be pointing to. Confused, they pointed at one another. "Us?"

The two soldiers rushed towards them, drawing their swords. Two more soldiers quickly joined them, making a war party of four. "We said stop!"

"Why are they coming at us?" Suzu said, alarmed. "We didn't do anything."

Hogart turned around to see Mia and her dragonet were gone. "Where did she go?"

Suzu looked at the spot where their new friend had been standing and then glanced around the immediate market area. "She disappeared on us."

"She was standing right there," Hogart said, scratching his scalp.

"Well, she's gone now! And, more importantly at a time like this, so's the dragon!"

Hogart's shoulders slumped, and he exhaled softly. "Oh, that is so not fair."

Hogart and Suzu, known for getting into dangerous situations in a quick minute wherever they might go, worked as a team as usual to fend off the four assailants. Hogart spotted a sizeable ceramic basket of food nearby and hurled it with all his strength at one of them, sending the soldier tumbling to the ground. Suzu seized the opportunity to disarm another soldier, grabbing his arm as he was about to slash her with his sword and flipping him over her shoulder. Hogart dodged a blow from a third soldier and landed a solid punch in his gut. He then slammed the head of the soldier against the wooden stand of a merchant. Suzu parried a sword thrust from the last attacker, delivering a swift jab to his nose. She then stomped on his foot and kicked him aside. Having quickly dispatched the four foes, they took flight and sprinted through the village.

"Run!"

Suzu and Hogart dashed through the crowded marketplace, blending in and bypassing the colorful stalls and the noisy, distracted shoppers. They could hear the shouts of the Zamana soldiers behind them, getting closer and closer. They had to reach the wooden rope bridge that spanned the deep ravine and cross it before the Zamana soldiers caught up with them.

Hogart crossed the bridge first, waited for Suzu, and grabbed his axe from the strap across the back. He raised it high and brought it down hard on the thick ropes that anchored the bridge to the cliff. He repeated the motion, hacking away at the ropes until they snapped. The rope bridge swung wildly and fell apart, sending planks and ropes crashing into the ravine. Suzu and Hogart watched as the Zamana soldiers on the bridge screamed and flailed their arms as they plunged into the abyss.

Barely escaping the soldiers chasing them across the wooden bridge, Suzu and Hogart ran through the busy streets of the designated merchant district, hoping to find a safe place to hide. They dodged a couple of horse riders and a small two-horse-drawn carriage in the street, scrambling to find any hiding spot amongst the surrounding buildings.

Their luck ran out when they saw a small group of horsemen entering the gated town from the opposite direction. It was Tomap Sruz, the ruthless commander of the *Iron Talon*, and his four loyal Lancers. Somehow, amongst a sea of faces, Tomap spotted Hogart, and an instant flash of bitter recognition came over him. "You two! Halt!"

The young warrior singled out the escaped prisoners amongst the rabble and commanded the Lancers to charge at them with their horses. Hogart and Suzu had no time to react. They faced the deadly assault head-on, but it was over quickly. A giant spotted elephant crossed before the charge, giving the fugitive pair time to blend in with the confused, screaming crowd.

More Zamana Troopers appeared on the street and were closing in on them. Suzu and Hogart had nowhere to run, soon surrounded by the enemy's blades and arrows. But then a sudden burst of sanguine fire erupted between them and the Troopers, creating a natural barrier. The flames were so intense that everyone could feel the heat on their faces. Suzu looked around and saw Mia and Mozo, their allies, standing discreetly in a short nearby alley. They had created the ten-foot firewall, but before Suzu could call out to them, they vanished in thin air as if they had never been there.

The flames of the fire spread uncontrollably and reached the nearby stable, where a herd of four elephants was resting in an enclosure. Startled by the threat of the fire, the four elephants thrashed against the wooden beams of their pen and broke free. They ran amok into the merchant area, knocking over carts and stalls and further blocking off Tomap and his four horsemen from pursuit.

One of the escaped, startled elephants bellowed and charged directly at a cornered Hogart and Suzu. Alarmed, they barely had time to react as the massive beast bore down on them, its white tusks gleaming in the firelight.

"There's nowhere to go!" Suzu shouted.

"Over the garden wall!" Hogart said. He helped his pint-sized friend reach the lip of the garnet stone wall and pushed her upwards. He quickly climbed up and stood at the top by her side. "Jump!"

They leapt from the garden wall, leaving behind the charging, angry elephant. They hoped to escape harm by landing on a lower plum roof, but they miscalculated the tiles' angle and wetness. They slid down the roof like toboggans, unable to brake or steer, towards the next street level. Screaming, they flew off the roof's edge and crashed into an open carriage basket strapped to an elephant.

The elephant was startled by the sudden impact and let out a roar, shaking its trunk in protest. It charged into the busy town street, sending unsuspecting people and idle carts zooming everywhere. As the elephant charged through the crowded plaza, the two hapless adventurers clung to the open carriage basket strapped to its back. They had hoped for an easy escape, but instead, they found themselves in a turbulent scene of destruction. The elephant smashed into stalls, carts, and barrels, sending fruits, vegetables, and pottery flying aimlessly. The terrified townsfolk scattered and screamed, trying to avoid the rampaging beast and its unwelcome passengers.

Hogart grabbed the reins into his hands. "This can't get any worse."

Suzu and Hogart soon realized that their troubles were not over. They felt a sudden rush of wind as two arrows whizzed past their heads, barely missing them. They looked back and saw four Zamana horsemen galloping towards them, their bows drawn and ready to fire again. They shouted and aimed their arrows, trying to catch up with the runaway elephant.

"It just got worse. You drive the beast. I'll take care of the horsemen." Suzu's crossbow could fire multiple arrows in rapid succession and reload faster than any of her foes. She aimed carefully at the incoming projectiles and pulled the trigger. With a satisfying thwack, she knocked down each arrow fired at them. She then sent an arrow flying back at the pursuing horse riders, hitting one of the soldiers in the hip. He slumped on his horse, clutching his wound.

With a thunderous roar, the stampeding elephant smashed into a wooden cart. The wagon spun wildly around on its wheels like a top, sending splinters and planks of wood soaring haphazardly. One of the wooden beams struck the already injured Zamana Lancer riding by on his horse, hitting him with such force that he flew clear off his saddle and landed on the street with a loud crash. Unfazed by what happened, the horse didn't miss a stride and galloped to safety.

Undaunted by the fate of the first rider, a second Zamana horseman spurred his horse to match the elephant's speed, galloping alongside the beast. He reached out and grabbed the girth band, the strap that secured the basket to the animal's back. Getting a firm hold of the thick strap, the horseman leapt from the saddle of his horse and swung himself onto the side of the running elephant. Hanging on to the girth band for balance and support, the Lancer struggled to climb upwards towards the basket. But when he reached the top, Suzu punched the soldier in the face, and he fell back down to the passing street, nearly getting trampled.

Suzu's brown eyes darted from side to side as she heard two more arrows fly by, barely missing her. She quickly reloaded her crossbow and aimed at the wooden crates and barrels that lined the street. Firing at them in hopes of creating obstacles for the two horse riders still chasing her, she smiled as she saw one of the barrels explode, sending a shower of nails, metal rods, and wood splinters skyward. The horse rider behind it screamed as the debris hit him and fell off his unscathed mount. The last rider tried to dodge the falling objects, but Suzu had another arrow ready. She shot it at a rope that held a large advertisement sign above a shop. The arrow cut through the rope, and the sign swung down and smashed into the horseman's head, knocking him clean off his horse as well. Suzu breathed a sigh of relief and chuckled as she saw the last two pursuers lying on the ground, motionless.

"Suzu! Duck!" Hogart called out.

Suzu turned around in time to see them about to go under a low stone archway. She quickly ducked down with Hogart, crouching in the carriage, as they barely cleared the archway passing overhead. She turned her head to look behind them and saw that they had shaken off their pursuers. Letting out a triumphant laugh, she hugged Hogart. "That has to be the end of it!"

Suddenly, a lone elephant emerged from a side street with a threatening blare of its trunk to signal its arrival and malice. It rammed into the side of Suzu and Hogart's elephant, jolting them violently in their open carriage. The enemy elephant was not alone. It had a driver who steered it closer to their target, and three more Zamana Troopers stirred within the basket, ready to strike. One thin albino-armored soldier drew an arrow and aimed at Hogart with his bow. Suzu saw the danger to her friend and proved to be a faster shot, unleashing two arrows from her crossbow into the soldier.

At the same time, the second Zamana Empire Trooper bravely jumped from the back of his running elephant and landed in the opposing carriage. The soldier fought with Suzu within the confines of the flat platform in a fierce struggle, each trading punches with the other, while Hogart tried to keep control of the reins. The pair of elephants dashed through a neighborhood of residential houses, one behind the other, barely avoiding colliding with the walls.

"Suzu, watch out!" Hogart cried.

As the Trooper wrapped his hands around her throat, lifted her upwards, and started to choke her, Suzu looked ahead and saw the clothesline stretched across the residential road. She reacted quickly, landing a knee under the Trooper's chin, making him lose his grip and drop her. This gave her time to duck low in the open carriage. Hogart followed her lead, lowering his head as well. The Zamana Empire Trooper was less lucky. The clothesline hit him hard across the throat and sent him flying off the platform to the street below. The discarded, stunned soldier barely got up before being crushed by the feet of the Zamana elephant chasing them.

"Here they come again!" Suzu shouted.

The Zamana elephant trumpeted its trunk and surged forward with a burst of speed, narrowing the distance with the leader. The two elephants were evenly matched now, slamming and smashing into each other with their massive bodies as they raced along the twisting residential village road. The sound of their thundering feet and clashing tusks was ear-splitting, and the people watching from the streets and their windows were terrified.

The third and last Zamana Empire Trooper tried to leap from his elephant's back to the one carrying the two fugitives. But the two beasts were constantly colliding and jostling with each other, making the jump difficult. The soldier misjudged his leap, failed to land in the carriage, and instead grabbed the harness straps that held the elephant's headgear. He was now dangling from the front of the charging elephant, trying to climb up as it sprinted forward.

With his life on the line, the Trooper scrambled up the elephant's rotund neck, digging his feet against the rough skin and clutching the leather harness for balance. He reached the front of the carriage and drew a knife, stabbing away at Hogart. The blade went wild and missed its mark. The soldier tried to slash the burly man multiple times, lunging and swinging out with the knife in one hand when he was not holding on to keep himself from falling with the other. He lost his grip and let go of the harness after one final strike, sliding down underneath the moving beast, crushed by its stomping feet.

A battle cry came from a passing rooftop above as a Zamana Empire Trooper jumped into the carriage from up high, his face twisted in rage and his sword drawn. He immediately lunged at Suzu, but she dodged his blade and punched him in the jaw, sending the sword spiraling away to the street. They exchanged fists and blows, each trying to gain the upper hand. The soldier grabbed her by the hair and pulled her head back, then wrapped his arm around her throat and squeezed. Suzu gasped for air, feeling her vision blur. She clawed at his arm, but he held on tight. She was losing consciousness.

Suzu's elbow smashed into the stomach of the soldier, who gasped in pain. She swiftly performed an over-the-shoulder toss, flipping and hurling him out of the carriage like a sack of potatoes. He flew and landed on the cobblestone street in front of the colossal elephant carrying the Zamana driver. The beast had no time to stop, and its massive foot came down on the soldier, squashing him like a bug. The impact made the Zamana elephant lose balance and swerve off the road. It stumbled to the side of the street, bellowing, and slammed into a stone building. It collapsed helplessly on impact, blocking the curvy street with its enormous body.

◆

At the sky docks, on the lowest level of the village, life went on as usual for some of the townsfolk who were oblivious to the calamity unfolding elsewhere. Amongst them was a solitary merchant shipman, a sun-drenched man with a bushy, peppered beard. He was slightly tipsy from his drink, getting his cog skyship, the *Minnow*, ready for departure the next day. His elongated, specially designed vessel, about eighty feet long, was weathered, aged, and battered, with a single flint balloon that kept it afloat. The ruddy propulsion sails were folded inward. The cabin towards the aft served as a living quarters and it had a very inviting, comfortable bed that was waiting for him when he was done.

The shipman took a sip of his bottle and sang a hearty song. As he approached the gangplank, a peculiar sight occurred in front of his eyes. It was as if a ghost were playing a comical magic trick just for him. A short, thick piece of wood lifted on its own from the lumber stack on the pier in front of him, magically and comically spinning around in midair. He rubbed his eyes in disbelief, wondering if he'd had too much ale or if the bright sun was playing tricks on him. But no, there it was again. Two more planks of wood flew up from the pile, and they all danced around in the air, forming a strange and whimsical juggling orchestra. The shipman laughed and clapped his hands, enjoying the show. However, the merchant's merriment was over when two pieces of wood dropped to the pier like stones. The third piece of wood twirled and came crashing down on his head, knocking him out.

"Sorry about that, my friend," Mia said, removing her purple hood to make herself visible. "I need your skyship."

Mia clutched Mozo close to her chest as she crossed the wooden gangplank and stepped onto the *Minnow*. She found a cozy spot for Mozo on a wooden box, placing him on top of the crate, then hurried to untie the mooring lines that kept the dingy boat anchored to the dock. She dashed to the back of the ship, climbed the ladder on the side of the cabin to reach the helm, and grabbed the pilot controls.

Free from its moorings, the *Minnow* slowly drifted away from the pier. When far enough away from the decking, the red propulsion sails extended outward to catch the slightest wind gusts. The cog skyship drifted lazily forward through the port.

"I'm a little rusty at this, Mozo."

The *Minnow* carefully navigated through the busy port's multiple bustling air vessels and stationary piers, looking for a safe flight path.

Mia gasped when she immediately spotted a frigate that resembled a screaming great eagle approaching a dock on her starboard side. She pushed the rudder sail to the right and adjusted the propulsion sails, changing her flight path and tilting the skyship just enough to let the more significant aircraft pass by alongside her unhindered. Quickly adjusting the sails, she set the skyship on a straight course. Another merchant skyship, a dirigible that looked like a turtle, seemed to come out of nowhere on the port bow and cruised directly in front of the *Minnow*. Mia adjusted the propulsion sails to capture a sudden gust of wind and force the skyship to climb upwards, nearly scraping the top of the hot-air balloon of the unsuspecting skyship. Mia was past that obstacle when a long wooden bridge suddenly appeared in the way. With one more adjustment with the propulsion sails, she guided the skyship to dip down sharply and fly underneath the bridge.

Relieved and grateful to have passed a few aerial dangers, Mia heard a far-off creature bellow. She looked down and saw a spiraling column of midnight smoke rising over the rooftops, followed by panicked voices and shouts. What was happening down there? She skimmed the streets for any sign of her new friends, hoping they were safe. Then she spotted them, riding on the back of a rampaging elephant smashing everything in its path. She had to find a way to help them before it was too late.

"Think we should bail them out, Mozo?"

Mozo nodded in approval.

———— ·‹‹ ———— ‹‹◆››· ———— ››· ————

A lone elephant with a tan open carriage strapped to its back barreled through a narrow side street, sending people and carts flying. Its trunk blasted a loud warning, telling everyone to get out of its way or face its wrath. Atop the platform, a man with a fierce expression gripped the reins tightly—Commander Tomap Sruz. He guided the elephant around a corner and moved in behind the two fugitives.

"This guy is just annoyingly persistent," Suzu said.

"Hold on to something!" Hogart yelled.

"What?" Suzu asked.

Before an answer came, the charging elephant rushed through some hastily erected, feeble, makeshift barricade constructed by the village pedestrians in a vain attempt to stop them. Baskets, wooden stands, and barrels that stood flimsily up in a thick, seemingly forbidding pile were broken apart into splinters within seconds. The carriage shook violently at the sudden jolt, causing Suzu to lose her balance and tumble over the railing of the basket, barely grasping the leather girth strap that secured it to the elephant's back. She hung on with all her strength, feeling the wind whip through her hair and the ground rush by below her feet.

Helplessly swinging and bouncing around while holding onto the girth strap, Suzu felt like a helpless ragdoll as the unaware and uncaring elephant surged forward. She saw the terrified people who had tried to block the beast's path with the barricade scattered like ants whose anthill had just been kicked. They then seemed to cast themselves aside to the edges of the street as if they did not have a choice. They had to avoid something else coming up on the road, something else that was approaching fast.

Suzu realized with horror that they were heading towards a thin stone bridge that spanned a deep chasm. She could not climb back up as the elephant innocently shook and swung her around wildly.

Crossing the slender bridge, she clenched her teeth and gripped the girth strap tighter as her feet dangled over the natural abyss.

Tomap urged his elephant to chase the fleeing elephant in front of them across the stone bridge. Once across, he caught up with the lead animal on the left side, matched speeds, and rammed his beast into his opponent. The two colossal, tusked creatures roared in vexation, smashing and bumping into each other.

Suzu's heart was pounding like a drum in her chest as she clung to the side of the speeding elephant, still trying to hoist herself into the carriage. She felt the elephants jostle each other with their massive bodies colliding, making her grip loosen and slide down a little on the girth strap. She peered ahead and flattened her body against the beast's hide, barely eluding a short stone wall, coming inches from being dragged along the stone structure.

She gasped loudly as the elephants collided violently again. She lost her grip and slid farther down the leather strap, feeling the rough road scrape the heels of her black-booted feet like sandpaper. She slowly climbed back up the girth strap, lifting upwards at moments and avoiding the obstacles that whizzed by underneath her feet in the street—carts full of material goods, barrels spilling water, and tables laden with food. She wondered how long she could hold on before she fell off and got trampled to death by the stomping hooves.

With thunderous bellows, the two elephants charged at each other again, their massive bodies colliding in a continuous fierce battle. They snorted and trumpeted, their ears flapping and their tails swinging, exchanging powerful blows with their sharp ivory tusks. Neither was willing to back down or admit defeat, determined to prove their dominance and strength. The clash climaxed when the two combatants locked their entangled weapons, unable to break free or push the other away.

Realizing that the elephants were locked together by their tusks, Tomap swung his sword at the large man in the carriage next to him. Hogart ducked his head and picked up his axe from the floor. As the beast carnage surged on, an equal amount of the sword swinging against the mighty axe played out between the drivers.

The narrow road that cut through the village became a deadly bottleneck, forcing the adversaries to be closer and collide more in their relentless fight. Metal shards scattered as razor-sharp blades clashed with deafening noise, each strike met with an equally skillful parry.

"Hogart! Stop fooling around and help me!" Suzu shouted.

Hogart felt anger and frustration as he saw his petite friend trapped in peril. He swung his axe with all his might, lashing out with a desperate strike, hoping to disarm Tomap. His gamble paid off as he struck Tomap's sword solidly, sending the blade flying into the passing street. The elephants, ironically sensing an opportunity, broke free from their tangled tusks and separated at the same time.

Hogart reached down from the carriage and grabbed Suzu by the tunic. "Need a hand?"

"Hurry, Hogart!" she shouted. "There's a tunnel coming!"

Hogart searched the street ahead. He spotted a looming, gloomy tunnel cut through the hillside that was approaching swiftly. Suzu still hung precariously from the elephant's side. She wouldn't make it past the narrow opening without being smashed against the rocks. He summoned all his strength and yanked her up, barely getting her into the flat platform as they plunged into the gloomy, eerie obsidian shadows.

The tunnel trembled with the elephants' pounding feet, and their trumpeting bounced off the walls like sonic booms. They charged ahead with unstoppable force in the darkness, smashing anything in their way. The jade stone gatehouse loomed ahead at the end of the tunnel, armed with four Zamana Troopers.

"Close the gate!" Tomap shouted.

The Zamana Troopers hustled and struggled to execute the command in time. But the first elephant to burst out of the obscure tunnel, carrying two unknown individuals on its back, easily smashed through the fortified entrance. The gate's iron bars dropped right behind the first elephant passing underneath it. The second elephant stopped short at the closed gate, enraging Tomap.

"Ha! We finally got rid of him," Hogart said happily. He watched as the commander screamed at his troops to open the iron gate, allowing him to continue the pursuit. "We're safe now."

"No, we're not! We're coming to the end of the road!" Suzu shouted, pointing ahead.

Hogart's eyes broadened. The road they were on curved sharply around the mountain, shrinking to a thin trail with a sheer drop ahead. The massive elephant was still charging towards it, oblivious to the looming danger and showing no signs of stopping.

"Hey! You two bumbling fools!" a woman's voice cried out from nowhere.

Hogart and Suzu, already frightened and unsettled enough by their out-of-control predicament, were equally startled to see an aged cog skyship with ruddy propulsion sails emerge from behind a rocky outcrop. It rose upwards and flew parallel to the road. Mia was seen at the helm.

"We have to jump!" Hogart shouted, climbing up onto the carriage's wooden rail. Shaking back and forth on the sturdy banister, he reached down to help Suzu join him.

Both partners balanced themselves on the railing of the basket, holding on to each other on the back of the speeding elephant. Neither seemed ready to leap over open air into the stolen skyship. If they missed, they would fall to their deaths.

"The road is running out!" Mia shouted. She turned the rudder slightly to fly the skyship closer alongside the elephant, decreasing the gap between them.

"You first!" Hogart shouted.

"No, you first this time!" Suzu yelled.

"The both of you! Now!" Mia cried.

As they shouted in unison with genuine terror, Hogart and Suzu mustered the strength to hurl themselves out of the open carriage and into the navy-blue sky. Clinging to each other and shrieking in their daring leap of faith, they landed clumsily and awkwardly on the skyship's upper wooden deck. Stark horror turned to relief as the two friends realized they made it safely, laughing merrily and embracing one another in triumph.

Mia smirked. "I like you two. I think I'll keep you around."

The wild, rampaging elephant abruptly halted at the end of the carved-out mountain road. It lifted its elongated, wrinkled grey trunk high and noisily blared a heartfelt "goodbye." Or maybe a more appropriate, very fond "good riddance." Either way, none of the passengers on board the *Minnow* could tell for sure as they sailed onward to the east in the coming clouded lavender-maroon evening.

BLACK ROCK

Mia, her lean, nearly six-foot frame aching from the trials of the past few days, had barely slept. When she'd finally succumbed to exhaustion the previous night, she'd been reluctant to wake. She found herself on a cot in the captain's quarters of the *Minnow*. Pushing her long, curly black hair away from her light-golden-brown face, she slowly opened her eyes to see buttery light streaming through the wood planks, casting a warm glow on the quarters. Judging by the angle of the sunlight, she estimated it was around noon.

Mia was abruptly awakened by the loud creaks and groans of the ship's wood as if the ship was struggling with some turbulence. The slight tilting and shifting of the cabin underneath her confirmed her suspicion. Maybe they had encountered a storm, or perhaps the ship was old and rickety. Either way, the *Minnow* was not precisely flying steady.

She gradually became aware of the stench of the untidy quarters, the cawing of birds, and the amusing sounds of constant friendly bickering nearby, which was also a factor in waking her out of slumber. At first, Mia thought the subject matter might be about her, the little dragon, and what to do about them. But the chattering was too indistinct and fast with the back-and-forth, playful exchanges.

Mia leisurely rubbed her weary eyes and got out of the lumpy cot. She flinched momentarily, the right side above her hip still sore and tender but better from Suzu's ointment. She slipped on her black boots and draped the purplish cloak over her shoulders, then made her way up a couple of steps to the upper deck, emerging from the captain's quarters. The honey sun blinded her for a second, making her squint. She saw a vast expanse of pale sky dotted with fluffy pearly clouds. A gentle, cool breeze wafted over her face, and she pulled the cloak closer to her body to resist a chill.

On the main deck of the *Minnow*, Hogart was busy teaching Suzu how to fly. There was quite a bit of bickering between the two, mainly regarding pilot controls and paying attention to the weather at all times. Mozo was on the bow of the deck, curled up in a cerise blanket on top of a chestnut wooden crate like a house cat, half sleepily watching everything that transpired.

Noticing that Mia had joined them and could now hear every word they were saying, Hogart stopped in midsentence, tugged the ruffles out of his long beige coat, and straightened his posture. "Good morning, Mia."

"Good morning, Hogart. What's going on?" she asked.

"Taking the opportunity to teach Suzu how to pilot a skyship. She wants to learn."

"Always good to learn new things."

"It also provided a distraction."

Mia looked surprised. "A distraction from what?'

"Killing you in your sleep."

Mia looked over at Suzu, whose face looked calm and serene at the helm, almost like she was actually enjoying herself. A joyful smile spread across her bright lips as the wind flowed through her lengthy black hair. "Why would Suzu want to do that?"

Hogart's brown eyes narrowed at Mia directly, disapprovingly. "The disappearing act that you pulled on us back in Clitton. She's still a little sore about that."

"Oh, that," Mia said. Her light-brown cheeks blushed rosy, and she almost laughed out loud in front of the man twice her size but held her composure. "I can understand."

"I told her it wasn't possible, but Suzu swears that she has seen you disappear into thin air," he said. "Like magic. Twice."

Mia's cheeks blushed a little brighter. "She's not far from the truth." She walked a few steps towards the ship's bow and turned to face her two new companions. She wrapped the cloak around her frame, flipped on the hood, and passed her hand over the brooch. Within an instant, Mia completely disappeared. After a few seconds, she reappeared in the same spot.

Hogart gave a heavy scoff. "An invisibility cloak."

"Hogart!"

He closed his eyes, placing the palm of his large hand on his scruffy white face. "Here it comes," he says.

"I told you!" Suzu shouted. "Don't you dare ignore me, Hogart! I told you!"

Hogart shook his head in dismay. "I'm never going to be able to live this one down."

"Thin air, huh? Just my imagination, huh?" Suzu continued. "I ought to . . ." She stepped away from the helm. The skyship teetered and tilted.

"Get back to the pilot's position!" Hogart growled.

Annoyed, Suzu blew a raspberry at her partner and returned to the pilot controls. The *Minnow* straightened back out and resumed its wobbly cruise.

"I have my reasons for keeping this secret to myself," Mia said softly to Hogart. "I'm sure you understand."

"I do understand," Hogart said. He then looked over his shoulder at Suzu, giving a knowing, soft smile. "We understand."

"Don't you ever doubt me again, you overgrown buffoon!" Suzu yelled.

Hogart gave a deep, heavy sigh and smiled halfheartedly at Mia. "Excuse me for a few minutes. I have to smooth things over with my good friend."

"Of course." Mia turned away from the pair and walked to the front of the skyship. She felt a light thud on her shoulder as the house-cat-size dragon woke up from his snug bed of blankets and joined her. They both stared at the magnificent sight of the noon sky, one in which the glowing marigold sun and the faint outline of the quarter silver moon shared the same admiral sky with puffy cream clouds.

Hogart walked over to Suzu at the helm. "Yes?"

"Hogart!" Suzu hissed. She grabbed him by the maroon button-down shirt and pulled him close so only he could hear. "We cannot trust her!"

"I disagree, Suzu. She let us in on her little secret. She didn't have to do so."

"An invisibility cloak?" Suzu said, her tone unusually raised and full of dire warning. "She'll disappear on us again at the first sign of trouble!"

Hogart softly sighed. He seriously pondered the idea that their new companion might put them in a tight spot. "I don't think so."

"You trust too much," Suzu scolded.

"I remember a long time ago being in a bad situation myself when I trusted you on blind faith."

"That's different." She let go of the shirt and pointed to herself. "I'm trustworthy."

"So I found out. Nearly the hard way."

They both silently observed Mia, with Mozo on her shoulder, who was busy looking into the noon sky.

"I do not know what it is yet," Hogart said. "But I sense that young Mia here feels some weighty responsibility and is in way over her head."

Suzu snorted and shook her head. "Fine. We stay true to our side of the bargain and help her. Just make sure we get paid."

As the radiant sun cast its lemony beams over the land, the dark outlines of Black Rock came into view. It used to be a peaceful port of travel for people all over the world. Nearly a year prior, the Zamana Empire had seized it and converted the city to something more sinister.

The coastal section of Black Rock resembled a small industrial city that was sprawled along the coastline, nestled behind dangerous foothills and a towering one-hundred-foot snow-white seawall. The coastal land seemed to be divided into zones: the hull zone, where the wooden frames of the ships were built; the mast zone, where the tall poles that supported the sails were made; the lumberyard, where the wood was stored and cut; the sailing zone, where the fabric was dyed and sewn; the paint zone, where the ships were painted with colors and the dragon insignia of the Empire; the tool zone, where the hammers, nails, ropes, and other equipment were forged and repaired; the assembly zone, where the ships were put together and tested; the barracks zone, where the soldiers who guarded and operated the ships lived and trained; the kitchen zone, where the food was cooked and served; the stable zone, where the animals that helped with transportation and labor were kept and cared for; and the dry dock zone, where the ships were launched and docked.

The seawall stood like a colossal barrier, not only protecting the buildings of the city from the sea elements and invasion but also serving as an entrance to the section known as The Piers. A massive spear-tipped iron-bar gate, a hundred and twenty-five feet high, was embedded in the seawall. It was the only way in and out from the coast to the many platforms of The Piers. The gate's iron bars were adorned with intricate carvings of sea creatures and mythical beasts.

A long, broad, sturdy jetty paved with smooth stones acted as a natural dock extended from the iron gate into the bay, like an arm reaching out for the colossal fortress that ruled the dark water. The central jetty ended at an intimidating barbican with heavy iron gates in front of the foreboding fortress, ready to repel any invaders. The obsidian fortress loomed over the bay, a gloomy and menacing presence that inspired nightmarish awe. A solitary sable lighthouse stood to its south, shining a weak and pale light over the restless salt-crested sapphire waves.

The Piers were like small individual cities on the water, carved from stone and wood. Branching off the central jetty were six double-decked wooden piers built on natural stone formations, three on each side of the main wharf. Schooners, galleons, cogs, and various other skyships at The Piers came and went at all hours of the day. Some were for trade, carrying goods and passengers from faraway lands. Some were for war, armed with soldiers ready to fight. And some were still being built, with scaffolds and ropes around them.

The people who worked and lived here were diverse. Some were free, earning their wages and living in modest residential quarters. Some were enslaved, forced to labor under harsh conditions, and chained in pens at night. Some were soldiers, wearing the uniforms of the Zamana Troopers and Lancers, patrolling and guarding The Piers. And some were trolls, huge and hairy creatures that helped the Zamana Empire with the heavy lifting and keeping the subjugated workers in line with whips. They all had their roles and tasks in this bustling place. The Piers had everything they needed. Workshops where skilled artisans made and repaired ships; storage areas where piles of lumber, metal, and tools were kept; supplies of food and water for distribution; and even a simple outhouse to relieve themselves.

The water was dotted with a healthy mixture of various frigates, barges, and man-of-war sailing ships. They came and went from different ports, depending on their size and purpose. Some ports were made of stone and could accommodate large vessels, while others were wooden extensions that hosted smaller ships. A floating workshop was also visible, where repairs and maintenance were done. The workshop was busy, with workers climbing up and down the ropes and ladders, carrying tools and parts. The ships had different flags and insignia, indicating their origin and affiliation, but all were allies of the Zamana Empire. They carried cargo and passengers, or sometimes patrolled the nearby waters for pirates or smugglers.

At the mouth of the bay, where the sea met the land, two watchtowers stood guard over the horizon. The salt of the ocean and the wind weathered their stone walls, but they still retained their majesty. From their vantage point, they could see everything that happened on the water: the air and water ships that came and went, the storms that raged and calmed, the sea creatures that lurked and leapt.

Hogart approached the helm of the *Minnow*. "Let me pilot to the docking area, Suzu."

Suzu nodded in silent agreement, stepping away from the pilot controls and towards the wooden railing. She trembled at the view of the massive foreboding harbor named Black Rock but calmed her nerves when she saw a series of unfortunate events as they flew towards the docks. She saw a man carelessly slip and fall off the pier into the water below. He splashed around and cursed at his rotten luck as he tried to swim back to the shore. On one of the upper piers, she saw a brachiosaurus crash into a pile of crates, sending them flying in all directions. Some of them hit the workers, who screamed and ran for cover. Some of them hit the Troopers, who chased after the brachiosaurus, trying to keep the beast from escaping the area. Finally, she saw a scaffolding collapse under the weight of a giant wooden beam falling from a crane. The beam smashed into a nearby skyship, causing a loud bang and a thin, spiraling cloud of black smoke.

"Mia, I suggest you and Mozo disappear," Hogart said. "Follow Suzu and I."

"I hate to ask," Mia said. "Do you have a plan?"

"Not yet. Suzu and I make it up as we go along."

The *Minnow*, designated by its flags as a harmless merchant skyship, soared confidently through the air. Approaching the upper southwest pier, the skyship seemed to naturally mix with the other craft in the area. It flew past a fellow merchant cog skyship, over the masts of a sailing warship, and between the upper piers until it gracefully landed at the upper southwest pier platform. A small group of three Zamana Empire Troopers seemingly awaited them. Amongst them was a single grey-skinned, rotund, brutish troll, standing about ten feet tall, towering over the soldiers. Trolls were known to be ugly, slow-witted, and might behave exactly like the worst human beings at times. This one was no different, its thick arms and legs draped in silver armor, holding an iron-spiked club.

There was only a crew of two on board the *Minnow* when it docked.

"Hello," Suzu said.

"Hello yourself, little one," one of the Troopers said gruffly.

Suzu cringed, wanting to strike out at the guard for the insult, but held her resolve steady.

"Cargo?" another Trooper said, just as roughly.

"Medical supplies," Suzu answered in a forced, even, and friendly tone.

"Good," the first guard said. "We need it. But with all our construction accidents lately, we'll probably burn through it by the end of the week. Load up on this wagon. Deliver the supplies to the storage facility near the medical area at the lower southeast pier."

"Yes, sir." Suzu bowed to the officer. She motioned for Hogart at the helm to come forward.

The Troopers carefully watched the amusing mismatched pair loaded the wagon. The big man hoisted the heavy cargo with ease and gently placed it in the wagon, while the small woman shifted and arranged the items neatly to fit more. They had a unique rhythm and an unspoken rapport that made their work efficient and amusing. The Troopers couldn't help but admire their teamwork and wonder what could have brought them together. Impressively, they both worked in synchronicity to get the job done effectively.

Bringing an amusing, hearty laugh to the Troopers and even a loud snort from the troll, Hogart awkwardly lost his footing during the loading process and clumsily stumbled forward for no reason. It was like a gust of the ocean wind caught the burly merchantman off guard and almost blew him over. He looked around bewildered and appeared slightly annoyed. Noticing the Troopers were watching him, Hogart laughed halfheartedly at his innocent folly and returned to loading the wagon.

"Watch who you're pushing into," Hogart growled low.

"Sorry. Mozo wanted to burn the troll's face off. I had to hold him back," a soft female voice said, the speaker unseen.

Suzu and Hogart glanced at each other, exchanging a silent look of disbelief, and shook their heads. Between them, filling the wagon up to capacity with crates, barrels, and sacks took nearly a half hour. Satisfied with the load, the two climbed into the driver's seat. With a polite wave to the Troopers and the grunting, ugly troll, they departed on the two-horse wagon and traveled along the upper southwest pier.

Suzu exhaled slowly. "The first part is done."

"Take a look at the central north pier. It looks like the *Iron Talon* survived their encounter with the Silver Moon Sharks. It's under repairs," Hogart said.

As Suzu and Hogart rode amidst the bustling shipyard, their eyes locked onto the once stately *Iron Talon*. Its hull, shredded from grappling hooks ripping through the wood, blackened and twisted from the flames that had consumed it, lay moored to the dock like a wounded beast. Around it, a swarm of workers moved with a sense of urgency, their hands and tools a blur as they cut away damaged sections and welded new wooden planks onto the skeleton. The air had the scent of molten metal and the echoes of hammers against steel and wood.

The wagon traveled down a flat ramp to the central jetty. They turned away from the tall speared-tipped gates and towards the dark fortress. The initial journey along the broad dock area, almost like moving along a city street, was a grim sight of the realities of war and slavery. From the heaps of wounded bodies, only faint moans could be heard. They were barely clinging to life, their blood staining the stone and wood with dark crimson patches. Above them, birds of prey cawed and circled, waiting for their chance to feast. Suzu and Hogart skimmed over the gaunt, tormented faces, wondering what horrors they had endured, knowing they could never understand their pain nor ease it.

"I hate to say it, my friend," Suzu said. "We must succeed in helping these good people at all costs."

Hogart only grunted softly in acknowledgment.

The wooden wagon, pulled by two sturdy horses, continued along the central jetty. Suzu and Hogart were forced to remain silent at the sights along the way. A brachiosaurus pulled carved stones on a flat cart, guided by a troll. A squad of armed soldiers marched past them in formation, ready to board a galleon skyship for the next conquest. The captive workers moved like a hive of bees, constructing the next weapons of destruction. When they got a short break, they sat huddled and tired from the long hours with nothing to eat.

Finally, the wagon reached its destination: the medical storage facility. The facility was a moderate-size building at the base of the lower southeast pier, almost like a warehouse, where ships docked and unloaded their goods.

Hogart jumped off the wagon's driver's box and knocked on the facility's large wooden barn door. A single guard answered by sliding the door ajar, acknowledged Hogart, and checked his papers. The guard grunted, nodded, and let the expected wagon in by fully sliding open the door. Hogart led the two horses and the wagon into a spacious warehouse, where rows of shelves were partially filled with boxes and crates. He parked the wagon near an unloading area, where they encountered a second guard and two workers. The warehouse's barn door closed behind the wagon, providing privacy from the outside world.

Without a word, Hogart delivered a swift punch to the jaw of one guard, sending him flying to the ground. Suzu sprayed a cloud of lilac mist from her hand, making the two innocent clerks nearby fall harmlessly asleep on the floor. Mia, invisible to the naked eye, grabbed a wrench from a table and hit the last guard on the back of his head, knocking him out cold.

Mia took the hood off her head, becoming visible. "Quick! Bar the door!"

Suzu placed a wooden beam across the door. "Do a quick survey of the area, Hogart."

Hogart looked through a crack in the wall. Through the wooden slat, he could see soldiers and workers passing by without notice of them. The horse carriages and brachiosauruses pulling carts and passengers continued along the central jetty, seagulls cried and twirled above in the sky, and wooden cranes lifted lumber up and moved around a galleon skyship being built.

"What do you see?" Suzu asked.

Hogart whistled low. "What a beauty. I see the new aerial flagship being constructed on the northeast pier directly before us. The markings name her the *Blade Guard*."

"Anything else?"

"A lot of familiar unhappy faces. I recognize quite a few from the *Intrepid*."

"We need to split up," Mia said.

Suzu looked alarmed and glared at Hogart briefly before focusing on Mia. "Split up?"

"Yes," Mia said. "I will use my invisibility cloak to get Mozo and myself inside the fortress. We'll find the jail cells within Black Rock, get to the prisoners, and release them."

"What are we supposed to do?" Hogart said. "Just sit here and wait for you?"

"No. The two of you need to create a distraction involving the Main Gate on the coast so that more Zamana Lancers and Troopers do not enter the dockyard."

"How were we supposed to do that?" Suzu said.

"I don't know. The two of you will think of something, I'm sure. You always do," Mia said with a smile.

"Nice." Hogart grimaced.

"I'll meet you back at the *Minnow*. Good luck." Mia held Mozo in her arms like a house cat. Her hand passed over the brooch, and she flipped the purple hood on her head. In an instant, whether the pair wanted to stop Mia or not, she disappeared.

Suzu waited until even the spiritual presence of Mia was long gone before she spoke. She turned to her faithful companion with a disapproving look. "She's going to get us killed."

Hogart was busy looking through the thin crack again. "We must move along the pier discreetly and get closer to the Main Gate somehow."

"And deliver"—Suzu threw her hands up and shrugged—"what?"

"Something different from medical supplies if we're to get anywhere."

Suzu's voice was barely audible as she muttered something under her breath. She searched the facility's shelves, looking for anything that might be of use. There were rows and rows of bottles, jars, and vials, each containing some mysterious substance. Some were labeled with names like "Acidic Solution," "Explosive Compound," or "Neural Enhancer." Others had no labels at all, only symbols or codes. Suzu wondered what would happen if she mixed them. She could create a powerful weapon or a distraction with some chemicals. She reached for a random bottle and examined it.

Hearing the clattering and tinkering behind him, Hogart turned away from the wall. "What are you doing?"

"Looking for anything in this warehouse that might help us later." Suzu placed a few small glass vials in her pouches on her black belt.

Hogart returned to the thin crack within the wooden wall, trying to solve the mobility problem. After a half minute, he saw a possible solution: an unattended two-horse wagon twenty yards away. "There it is. Follow me."

The duo slid open the warehouse door enough to slip out, step onto the pier, and close it behind them. They had just raided the medical depot, but no one could tell from their calm demeanor. Suzu and Hogart acted as if they were meant to be there as they strolled towards the two-horse carriage, blending in with the crowd of workers, merchants, and soldiers. They climbed aboard the unattended wagon, settled in the seats, and nodded reassuringly to each other. With a flick of the wrist, Hogart urged the horses to move, passing by the oblivious sentries without a hitch.

Hogart waited until they were away a short distance, heading away from the fortress and towards the Main Gate, before he spoke. "What's in the back?"

Suzu peeled back the olive flap covering the cargo. "Magitite."

"Perfect," Hogart said with partial relief. "We can act like we need to deliver it to a skyship. Get as close as we can to the Main Gate."

<hr>

A brooding shadow loomed over the sprawling coastal city of Black Rock as one of the Zamana Empire's most feared vessels descended from within the depths of one of the graphite clouds. The *Invader*, a colossal three-hundred-foot galleon skyship held afloat by twin oval magenta hot-air balloons, four massive masts with white sails, and four white propulsion sails, sailed over the rooftops like a silent predator. An ally, it peacefully docked at the fortress's east platform. Mooring lines were thrown over to attach the warcraft to the exclusive elongated fortress platform. A wooden ramp fell with a thunderous clang.

Keldace Vildan was a fearsome sight to behold, a woman of veiled mystery and unholy power. She may have reverted back to the primary form of the iron mask that hid her face, but it didn't hide her undeniable authority. Her obsidian hood and cloak were trimmed with regal red, a sign of her imperial status. Her shoulders, arms, and legs were covered with achromatic armor, ready for armed conflict. Her keen mind held the knowledge of dark magic that was taught to her by her master. She was the empress and the ruler of the Zamana Empire. No one dared to question or challenge her. She only inspired the deepest dread and the greatest reverence.

Vildan departed the *Invader*, crossed the platform unescorted, and descended the spiral grey stone staircase to the fortress grounds. She headed without pause for the Southeast Tower, a grim and imposing structure that loomed over the bay. The tower was made of smoky stone, covered in slick lime-green moss. It had no windows, only narrow slits that let in a faint light. The Southeast Tower was the prison where the enslaved were kept until work the next day. It was also where the Zamana Empire's worst enemies were locked away and tortured.

The empress had no pity for them nor mercy. She walked past the guards, who saluted her with respect, and past the working prisoners, who trembled in fright. She confidently entered the Southeast Tower and ascended the spiral stone staircase until she reached a heavy iron door. Behind it was her most prized captive, the one she had been chasing for the last couple of days. The one she needed the most to achieve her goals since the discovery of Tavter.

Vildan entered the unique cell and stood at an outer ledge of the shaft. A man was held in a round iron cage above a watery pit. A relatively handsome white man in his midthirties, he had a strong jawline, a prominent nose, and piercing brown eyes. His hair was dark and wavy, often casually falling over his forehead, and a light scruffiness garnished his face. He had a lean and muscular physique, honed by years of living a nomadic lifestyle, and was dressed in a button-down blue shirt, dark brown pants, and black boots.

She studied the man for a moment before she spoke. "Garrison Ogan, the Relic Hunter. Or is it, Relic Raider? Matters not. You are needed in a great pursuit. Join me"

Garrison looked through the bars and down the shaft at the watery ditch below him. He was trapped in the cage, which hung suspended from a single heavy metal chain over a pool of hungry reptiles. He could see the scaly bodies and the snapping jaws of the alligators and crocodiles twisting around in the lapis water, waiting for him to fall into their domain. "Join you?" Garrison said. "I'm not a soldier or a carpenter. I'm an archeologist. The skyships you are building here are for conquest. I don't see how I can be of use to you. Other than to be food for your pets below."

"My attention is focused on more than just the construction of skyships. They are a means to an end."

"What end would that be?" Garrison said.

"The Kingdom of Tavter is no longer hidden."

Garrison straightened up in the confined space, his rugged face displaying interest and concern. "Tavter?"

"Yes. The alleged final resting place of the Land Elemental Gemstone."

Mia held Mozo close to her heart, ensuring he was covered entirely by the invisibility cloak even when he fidgeted in her arms. She crossed the length of the pier and easily sneaked past the guard at the barbican gate, who was busy chatting with another soldier. She made her way through the upper bailey, where she saw the miserable faces of the construction workers who were forced to build the tyrant's fortress. She also noticed the two huge brachiosauruses that hauled stones in carts and the wooden scaffolding that supported the unfinished walls. She reached the Southeast Tower, which she'd overheard held the prison, without being detected and slipped inside the dark cells where the civilian prisoners were held captive.

Still holding a shrouded Mozo, Mia softly crept along the pewter corridors, avoiding the security patrols. They reached the heavy wooden door leading to the prison pens, hoping to find a way to release the people. But two armed guards were blocking their way. They were sitting at a small round table and playing a game of cubes for money. The game involved rolling six-sided yellow dice and trying to match the symbols on them. It was a popular pastime amongst the bored and the reckless.

The guards rolled the cubed dice, grumbling loudly or howling delightedly at the outcome. Mia, who was invisible, watched them intently from around a corner. She saw an opportunity to create confusion and distract them from their duty.

She crept next to the table without being seen or heard. The guards continued their game and rolled the cubes that settled on the table. "Ha! I win again!" one of the guards said.

Mia, while invisible, lightly rolled one of the dice over with her finger to a new result.

"Hey, did you see that?" the second, losing guard said.

"What?"

"I won! Baw-haw!"

"You're cheating! You switched the dice when I wasn't looking!" The first guard looked at his opponent with suspicion and irritation.

"What did you say?"

"Don't lie to me, you dirty cheater!" the first guard shouted. He lunged at the other guard, grabbing him by the back of the head, slamming him headfirst into the table, and knocking him out. The lone guard laughed derisively at the alleged "cheater," oblivious that an invisible Mia was nearby. She grabbed ahold of a wooden club lying near the table and swung it at the back of the guard's head, knocking him out cold in mid-laughter. He also fell face-first unconscious to the table.

Mia pulled back her hood, revealing herself to the dim cream light of the dank, dim chamber. She spotted the jail keys on the table, glinting like a promise. Releasing the feisty Mozo, who was thankful to stretch his wings finally, she grabbed the keys and headed to the massive wooden door that separated her from the prisoners. She inserted the key and turned it, hearing a loud click. Pushing the door open, she stepped into the next room, followed quickly by faithful Mozo floating above her head. Rows of cages lined the stone walls, each one holding clusters of people in a miserable state. She felt pity and rage as she walked along the corridor, looking at the innocent faces of men, women, and children.

There was finally a glimpse of hope as Mia spotted a familiar face. "Pedro!"

A short, pale-skinned man with brunet hair pressed through a few people and clutched the iron bars of his cell, instantly recognizing the young bronze-skinned woman before him. "Your Hig . . ."

"Sshhhh!" Mia said. "Now is not the time."

Mia's heart was pounding as she reached the jail cell, where Pedro and a couple of others in her traveling party were locked up. She knew they had to hurry before more guards arrived, but she couldn't help feeling a jolt of joy at seeing her friend again. She hugged him through the bars and then fumbled with the keys, dropping them twice. The seconds seemed like minutes ticking by as she tried to find the right one for the lock. Finally, she heard a click, and the door tumbled open.

"I'm so relieved to see you," Pedro said, hugging Mia as he exited the cell. "I thought you were dead."

"I used the invisibility cloak to disappear. Mozo and I got away."

Pedro chuckled and rubbed Mozo's snout. "Good boy."

"I want you to—"

"I-I must tell you," Pedro stammered. "There's a unique person of great importance to the Zamana Empire recently brought in. Garrison Ogan, a Relic Raider."

"Garrison?" Mia thought to herself for a quick moment. "I've heard of that name. There's been a few stories about him, but he's just an antique collector. Why him?"

Pedro shrugged. "I don't know why he's of interest."

"If the Empire wants him so badly, then I must free him too."

"There's a spiral staircase nearby. I'll go with you."

"No," Mia said. She handed Pedro the keys to the cells. "Free the other prisoners, get to The Piers, and take over as many sailing ships and skyships as possible to escape. Fly west."

Pedro chuckled nervously. "But the Main Gate—the Zamana Lancers and Troopers will be pouring in from the mainland . . ."

"I came with a couple of new friends. They're an unusual pair, but they'll take care of the Main Gate," Mia said. She flipped on her hood and disappeared.

———— ··◄———◄◆►———►·· ————

"It's impossible," Garrison said. He stirred uneasily within the iron bars of his suspended cage. "The Elemental Gemstones were scattered around the world in unknown locations. Lost. You'll never get them all."

"That's why I need you," Keldace Vildan said. She circled the outer rim of the deep round chasm. "I've been told by more than one source that you know more about the Elemental Gemstones than anyone else. It's your life's pursuit."

Garrison flinched as if the empress had inadvertently touched on a sensitive subject. He wanted to shrink away deeper into the shadows of his dangling prison if he could. "You've been misinformed."

"You're lying."

"Nearly a hundred years ago, gathering those four gemstones nearly destroyed Arthea. I will not help you find them."

Vildan scoffed lightly. "I do have the power to give a man or woman anything they could ever want in this life. I can give you your heart's burning desire."

The heart's burning desire. What does drive a person? What do they want more than anything in this life? What makes a person the happiest? Garrison momentarily mulled over the enticing offer, knowing the single answer to all the questions. Misery suddenly appeared on his scruffy, pale face, reflecting that he might take the seductive offer from the wicked witch for a second, even against his better judgment. But then, just as quickly, renege. "No."

"A disappointment," Vildan hissed. "I have no choice but to keep you in that cage until you are adequately motivated to come to your senses. But know this: I know what I want and am not a very patient woman." She raised a black-gloved hand, and crackling emerald energy ignited like a living flame.

A blaring alarm came suddenly throughout the prison walls. The Mistress of the Dark Arts stopped her hand, and the sizzling green light faded away. Without another word, she turned to go, leaving the Relic Hunter behind in his imprisonment.

⸻ ◆ ⸻

Suzu and Hogart continued their journey by wagon along the central jetty with their self-imposed delivery assignment. On the way to the Main Gate in the hopes of finding a way to bar it from opening to the coastline, they skillfully navigated the bustling pier full of soldiers, merchants, workers, trolls, horse-drawn wagons, and a couple of brachiosauruses pulling large carts full of carved stones. With her sharp eyes and quick reflexes, Suzu remained ready for any possible trouble. Hogart's eyes were fixed on their looming approaching destination.

"I just came up with a plan," Suzu said.

"You have a plan? Oh, this has got to be good," Hogart said. "Okay, let's hear it."

"I douse the ore in the cart with this chemical I found in the medical supply room. We get the cart as close as possible to the gate and set it on fire. The explosion will cripple the gate, preventing any more Zamana Lancers and Troopers from entering the pier area."

"Sounds good enough for me," Hogart said. "Except for the 'how do we escape after' part."

"I haven't figured that out yet."

Hogart smirked. "Typical. Let's do it."

Suzu turned in the driver's seat of the moving wagon and took a few of the glass vials she had collected at the warehouse from her pouch. She then wet the ore with the chemicals, splashing the liquid around.

As the wagon approached the Main Gate, four armed soldiers standing alongside a single ten-foot troll directed the duo away from the Main Gate and up the ramp to the upper northwest pier.

"What do I do?" Hogart asked.

"Do as they say for now," Suzu said. "We don't want to raise the alarm just yet."

The wagon's two horses did precisely as they were directed and turned from the central jetty to climb the wide stone ramp to the upper northwest pier. A two-hundred-foot Zamana galleon skyship named the *Reaver* was docked at the top of the ramp. It had finally come home from a glorious victory with livestock and crates of rare material goods. The spoils of war were currently being unloaded onto a large wooden wagon attached to a patiently waiting brachiosaurus. The pair came on another set of four Zamana Troopers and a threatening troll waiting for them near the bow of the *Reaver*. The soldiers stepped in the path and waved the cart down. They insisted that the pair stop their cart full of special magical ore, secretly drenched with flammable chemicals, and get out of the carriage.

"Stay here until we're ready to load your cargo," a Trooper ordered.

Hogart nodded. "Yes, sir."

The mismatched duo stood idly on the pier, silently fearing they would be found out the longer they stood around. They spotted a large square iron-barred cage with three wild allosauruses inside slowly being lowered from the aft of the *Reaver* onto the upper wooden dock by a sizeable crane. The massive feral creatures, growling loudly and snapping within the confines of their cage, exuded an air of deadly menace. Their serrated chartreuse teeth gleamed in the sunlight, and their eyes fixated on the humans walking freely on the stone pier with primal hunger.

Everyone on the pier heard the piercing horn alarm. The sudden blare startled the various members of the crowd, their faces contorting in confusion. Was this just a drill? Had a fire broken out? Was it an invasion? Who would be so bold and arrogant as to attack Black Rock? Zamana Lancers and Troopers shouted commands and scurried around, abandoning their posts and sprinting towards their new battle positions.

Hogart shrugged. "Now what?"

"Slight change in plans," Suzu said. She noticed the Zamana Troopers had left the crane wheel, leaving the cargo of three encaged allosauruses high in the air. "Come on! Help me!"

The odd pairing ran up the length of the pier, past the turquoise brachiosaurus hitched to the post, towards the aft of the *Reaver*. The salty breeze swept around them, their footsteps echoing against the weathered stone as they reached the unmanned wheel crane that stood tall, its slightly rusted metal frame showing months of service. The oversize iron-barred cage dangled precariously from its hook, swaying with the beasts' erratic movements inside and each powerful gust of ocean wind.

Suzu and Hogart grasped the round wooden spokes of the giant wheel. The wheel crane resisted at first, either locked or stubbornly clinging to its position. But with conviction and working together, they began to turn it, muscles straining against the weight. The gears groaned in protest, and the cage slowly descended towards the stone dock below. But then, as the ocean winds gusted, they were unable to control the hefty weight and their grip slipped. Panic surged through them as they lost control of the crane and watched the cage plummet. It crashed onto the solid dock, a resounding thud that echoed across the water. The once sturdy structure splintered on impact, its iron bars bent and twisted.

Suzu and Hogart exchanged a worried glance. The cage was slightly broken apart, but none of the massive creatures within stirred. As they stood there, catching their breath, they realized that perhaps they'd made a mistake. But for now, they stood side by side silently, staring at the wreckage before them—their shared mistake etched into the very fabric of the dock.

"You two! Halt!" Zamana Troopers shouted to the apparent culprits standing at the crane wheel, surrounding them.

The three wild allosauruses within the damaged cage finally stirred around for a moment, growling low after being stunned. They burst out of their imprisonment, the dangerous animals free on the upper pier. One was ash-skinned with black stripes on top and a mustard-spotted underbelly. The second was almond skinned with teal stripes. The third was deep green with black spots. The three predators emerged with primal fury; their powerful hind limbs propelled them swiftly forward. As they stalked the upper northwest pier, they preyed on the few surprised Zamana Troopers and innocent others alike, leaving bedlam and terror in their wake. The salty sea air vibrated with their primal roars as they reclaimed their freedom.

Hogart and Suzu, per usual, yelped in horrific fright and made a run for their lives during the mayhem. No longer concerned about the armed soldiers, the two ran around the area of devastation that they'd helped cause.

The light-green-striped allosaurus chased Hogart across the pier. As Hogart ran, an unaware Zamana Trooper stepped out from behind a collection of wooden crates. Hogart punched the soldier in the face, grabbed ahold of him, and then tossed him into the open mouth of the pursuing allosaurus. The allosaurus momentarily stopped its pursuit, satisfied with the tasty snack.

The black-spotted allosaurus cornered Suzu against the edge of the dock. Suzu frantically dug into one of the pouches on her belt for some of the vials she had collected earlier. The allosaurus roared and stepped menacingly forward directly at her. As the allosaurus was about to munch on Suzu, she tossed two glass vials between them. They broke, and an enormous blast of indigo smoke forced the beast to stagger back.

⎯⎯⎯ ◆ ⎯⎯⎯

Mia and Mozo found themselves deep within the prison's Southeast Tower, where bleak shadows clung to the umber stone walls like forgotten secrets. The air was thick with the scent of damp stone, and the only illumination came from flickering torches. Mia cautiously climbed the spiral stone staircase, still cloaked and armed with the wooden club. Each step forward was progress to reach the mysterious, valued prisoner.

The blaring horn alarm filled the underground corridor like a wailing beast. Mia moved faster, her adrenaline pumping. The high noise level covered her echoing steps, but she was still careful not to be seen.

The guards, burly and unsuspecting, stood watch outside the high-security cell. Their eyes darted between the movement of shadows and the shouts of voices in the distance. They were getting anxious and unsure by the sudden alarm. She had to act fast while they were distracted.

Mia cautiously approached the first guard while draped in the invisibility cloak. His back was turned, and she seized the opportunity. A swift blow to the base of his skull with the wooden club sent him crumpling to the ground, unconscious. The second guard spun around, eyes wide with shock. A small lavender dragon suddenly hovered before him, making him disbelieve his senses. Before he could react, Mia swung the club, connecting with his temple. He collapsed like a marionette with severed strings.

On a teal table were a set of jail keys and Garrison's possessions: a mocha leather satchel, a foot-long hunting knife, and a bullwhip. The guards' keys jingled as Mia, still invisible, unlocked the cell door.

The prisoner inside the cell watched in awe as the door swung open by itself. A cat-size purple-hued dragon flew into the cell area and up to the round, suspended cage with iron bars. The keys to the dangling cell were in one claw, and the bullwhip was in the other. "And who are you, my little friend?"

"His name is Mozo. And my name is," the voice of someone unseen said, "Mia."

Garrison looked like he had seen a ghost when the woman with long, curly jet hair appeared out of thin air. "Do I know you?"

"No, we've never met."

Garrison fit the key into the jail lock and fidgeted it around until he heard a heavy click. He kicked the iron-barred door with his black boot wide open. Taking the bullwhip from Mozo, Garrison unfurled it across the chasm and coiled it around a group of chains holding up the suspended cage. Using the whip like a rope, Garrison easily swung across the deadly chasm and landed safely on the ledge, denying the hungry crocodiles twisting and slithering around the bottom their long-promised meal.

The scruffy middle-aged man looked the woman, who was at least twenty years younger than him, over. "Fascinating. Invisibility cloak. Small, unique dragonet. Were you—?"

"We don't have the time to talk right now," Mia said sharply. "We need to get out of here."

The approach of running feet echoed throughout the spiral staircase, followed by warning shouts. Two Zamana Troopers arrived at the prison with swords in hand.

"Duck!" Garrison shouted.

Mia dropped into a crouch in time as the first guard swung his sword at her head and missed. Garrison punched the guard in the face, grabbed him, and threw him into the prison shaft to a crocodile death below.

Mia got up and turned around to see the second soldier lunge forward at her with his blade, only to disappear before him at the last moment. Unable to stop his rushed momentum, the second soldier also fell downward into the open pit to the waiting, hungry crocodiles. Mia reappeared just feet away from where she was standing previously. "Come with me. There's a skyship on the upper southwest—"

"No."

Mia stood, perplexed. "What? Are you kidding me? Why?"

"I can't leave yet. Not without it."

"Without what?" Mia growled.

"It is of great importance to me personally." Garrison's pale face looked grave and troubled, as if his existence was about to end. "When the Zamana Empire found me, they mistook it for an artifact and brought it to some treasure room. I must get to it."

Mia, still perplexed, said, "What can be so important—?"

"It's everything to me!" Garrison said. He was visibly angry and upset at the same time.

"Fine," Mia said. She did not have the time to pursue the issue further. "Retrieve your item and meet me at the upper southwest pier."

"I will," Garrison said, seeming more at ease. "You have my word."

Mia held Mozo in her arms and covered him with the cloak. She passed her hand across the brooch, placed the hood on her head, and disappeared.

———••◄———••◆►••———►►•———

Amidst the distraction of a wailing horn, the three wild allosauruses roared and continued to rampage on the northwest upper pier. They were now in different sections on the upper stone deck, sharing their equal destruction and attacking any moving object. Their massive forms crashed against wooden cranes, barrels, and crates, splintering them into shards. Zamana Troopers yelled commands; Zamana Lancers came to arms with spears and rushed up the wide stone ramp to contain the gigantic animals. The soldiers scrambled to form a defensive line at the top of the ramp, creating a blockade to the central jetty, their swords and spears at the ready.

The ink-spotted allosaurus lunged angrily at the group of newly arrived soldiers, its jaws snapping shut inches from their faces. The Zamana Lancers dodged and counterattacked, but their weapons barely scratched its thick scaly evergreen hide. The allosaurus tried to circle around the soldiers in hopes of flanking them from behind. Its tail whipped like a battering ram, sending a few soldiers flying into the water and setting part of the upper dock ablaze with fire. Cardinal flames licked at wooden crates and barrels, creating a disorderly obstacle course for the soldiers.

The ash-skinned allosaurus stomped towards the far end of the pier. Its lumbering body took up the width of the dock, cutting off two horses hitched to an empty pedestrian carriage. The dangerous, ravenous beast bellowed a terrible roar at the smaller animals. Frightened by the threatening, enormous creature, the two horses bucked wildly and broke free from the wagon's restraints. They escaped in a frantic run down the length of the pier, past the yellow-striped brachiosaurus hitched to a wagon, their hooves echoing against the stone. The ash-skinned allosaurus watched them go, missing its meaty meal. With a hungry snarl, it bit into the stationary carriage and tossed it away. The unoccupied wagon hurtled towards the opposite end of the pier, sending splinters flying and crashing into the line of soldiers. The grey-skinned allosaurus stood there momentarily, disappointed but still hungry, eyeing the idle oversize brachiosaurus.

But the teal-striped allosaurus stepped out from behind a stack of crates and lunged at the unsuspecting olive brachiosaurus first, jaws snapping shut around its lengthy bronze-striped neck. The two massive bodies collided in combat and survival, shaking the stone pier to its foundations with their fierce fight. The allosaurus and brachiosaurus were locked in a primal struggle for survival and dominance, thrashing around the upper pier. The almond allosaurus's teeth tore into the brachiosaurus's flesh while the herbivore's powerful tail swung like a battering ram in defense.

The swinging tail collided with a nearby crane, weathered by years of salt and wind. The crane swayed dangerously on its wooden supports, its iron hook swinging like a pendulum. The wooden crane couldn't withstand the force of another blow—it splintered and broke off, crashing into the docked skyship, the *Reaver*. The iron hook, now free, swung wildly and found an unexpected target: the deep-purple hot-air balloon tethered nearby.

With a sickening tear, the hook pierced the hot-air balloon's fabric, securing a firm hold. The *Reaver* groaned under the sudden weight of the massive crane as it began to descend. Still entangled in their battle, the monsters stumbled carelessly towards the pier's edge. Their combined mass pulled on the taut mooring lines, thick ropes that had weathered many storms, threatening to tear them loose. The pier violently trembled as if protesting this unnatural alliance.

In a final chaotic twist of fate, the battling allosaurus and brachiosaurus lost their balance. They plummeted into the collection of mooring lines between the *Reaver* and the upper northwest pier.

Their combined clawed hands and feet scrabbled against the stone of the pier and ripped through the heavy mooring lines. The *Reaver* started to follow suit; its bowsprit snapped like a matchstick, secure white sails broke loose and fluttered in surrender, and numerous grappling lines snapped.

Despite the imminent peril posed by the doomed skyship, pandemonium reigned on the upper pier. Hogart and Suzu had no choice but to sprint towards the only exit to safety: the stone ramp leading to the central jetty. To do so, they had to run the length of the pier and an obstacle course fraught with danger. As they ran past it, the grey allosaurus with mustard underbelly and black stripes became a whirlwind of primal fury. Its massive form stumbled and fell to the pier, the unfortunate soldiers beneath crushed by its weight. The next obstacle in their path was the forest-green black-spotted allosaurus. Driven by instinct, it tossed the soldiers aside effortlessly, their armor clinking like tin toys in the predator's jaws. The soldiers collided into a cluster of crates that toppled over, forcing the pair to climb over the splintered wood. Nearby, a solitary troll, towering at ten feet with muscles like coiled steel, stood its ground with a mace. The clash between the troll and the allosaurus was a spectacle of raw power. Each blow from the troll met with a ferocious counter from the dinosaur. A lethal dance of giants shook the pier until the troll was tossed aside.

Done with the soldiers and the troll, the allosaurus renewed its pursuit of the duo. Running past the wagon they'd brought in, Suzu grabbed a lit lantern nearby and tossed it into the cart of chemical-soaked magitite. The lantern and the mix of volatile chemicals instantly combined in a frenzied display of vermilion fire and pewter smoke.

Jaws wide open, the forest green black-spotted allosaurus lunged at her and Hogart. Time seemed to slow down as the cart exploded, engulfing the pursuing dinosaur in a fiery inferno. The ground shook, debris flew, and Suzu shielded her eyes from the blinding light. When the lemony smoke cleared, she opened her eyes and found herself standing amidst the wreckage. The allosaurus lay on the stone pier motionless, its scales charred and smoking. Hogart stumbled to his feet, coughing from the acrid fumes. Suzu wiped the sweat from her brow and grinned. "Guess we won't be anyone's lunch today," she said, brushing soot off her clothes.

Hogart chuckled weakly. "Next time," he said, "let's stick to less explosive solutions."

Suzu nodded. "Agreed," she said. "As long as you don't make bad jokes like that again."

The explosion reverberated throughout the entire northwest pier, both upper and lower docks, further damaging the mooring lines that the initial catastrophe had already weakened. The once sturdy connections snapped free from the upper pier, their frayed ends flailing like desperate tendrils. The *Reaver*, already battered and swaying, tilted its nose steeply downward, breaking away from its moorings with a final defiant lurch. As it plummeted, the equally sized merchant sailing ship named the *Jester's Jolly* docked below suffered its own calamity—the masts, once proud and tall, snapped like the branches of a tree under the weight of the collapsing *Reaver*. The lilac sails fell and covered the crew working on the upper decks. The air bristled with debris and coal plumes of smoke as two vessels—one grand and doomed, the other sturdy but now scarred—met their violent fates.

"Run, Hogart!"

The damaged, untethered *Reaver* surged downward, its wooden hull glancing off the *Jester's Jolly* below. The *Reaver's* descent was uncontrolled, a tumultuous plunge towards the lower pier and the Main Gate. With a resounding crash, its hull struck the stone surface, sending shards of wood and metal soaring. The massive iron gate loomed ahead, its imposing bars standing firm against the inevitable impact. The collision between the *Reaver*, the *Jester's Jolly*, and the enormous gate erupted in furor—a maelstrom of broken debris and wildfire. Flames licked at the *Reaver's* torn canvas while the *Jester's Jolly* groaned under the strain, the wood snapping like matchsticks. The Main Gate, the only entrance to the ships docked at the pier, was highly damaged. There was heavy, twisted silver iron bars weighing hundreds of pounds and a growing fiery blaze blocking the path.

Seeking safety from the massive destruction of the two ships colliding with one another, Hogart and Suzu took cover and crouched behind a large crate on the upper pier. They peeked over the top of the wooden box to observe the mayhem. The sea air smelled of salt and burning wood, and a jumbled symphony of splintering wooden masts mixed with desperate shouts was heard. The once proud vessels now resembled wounded beasts, their hulls ablaze and crackling with fire.

Zamana Troopers rushed up the ramp to contain the fire and the one remaining allosaurus rampaging around the upper deck. But even their combined efforts seemed futile against the further enraged beast. The allosaurus snapped at them like a cornered, hungry wolf, its jaws closing around a screaming soldier who had dared to stand his ground.

"Let's get back to the *Minnow*," Hogart said, watching in horror as the soldier was gobbled up.

The upper bailey was a scene of upheaval and bloodshed as the imprisoned people clashed with the Zamana Troopers who guarded the walls. The people fought with whatever weapons they could find, from swords and axes to rocks and sticks. They had nothing to lose and everything to gain. On the other side, the soldiers fought with alarm and distress, knowing they were outnumbered and outmatched without reinforcements from the mainland. They tried to push the people back to their cells but were met with fierce resistance.

The battle reached a critical point when Zamana Troopers surrounded the confined people on three sides. The only way out was through the gate, which was locked and guarded by more soldiers. The people knew they could not escape, but they refused to surrender. They prepared to make their last stand, hoping to take as many soldiers with them as possible.

The Zamana Troopers closed in, ready to strike the final blow. They raised their swords and spears, aiming for the hearts and throats of the mostly unarmed people. But before they could strike, a sudden blast of heat and amber light stopped them. A wall of scarlet flame erupted at the gate, engulfing the soldiers who stood there. The fire spread quickly like a guided slithering snake, creating a natural barrier between the people and the soldiers. The people stared in shock and disbelief, as they saw their salvation in the form of a creature not seen for a very long time.

The upper bailey was ablaze with the spewing fire of the tiny purple-scaled dragon who darted through the air like a zigzagging arrow. He was no bigger than a cat, but his vermilion flames were fierce and deadly. He scorched the Zamana Troopers, who tried to shoot him down with arrows and spears to no avail. Satisfied, the dragonet finally landed on the shoulder and showed loyalty to only one person: the woman suddenly appearing from thin air. She stood tall and proud atop a pile of rubble amidst the babel, her golden skin glistening with sweat, her long black curls flowing in the sea wind. She wore a billowing deep-purple cloak matching her dragon's hue. She reached a sword hidden under her cloak, which she drew out with a flourish. She raised it high, signaling to her faithful dragon and her new allies that it was time to strike. "Fight for freedom!"

A joyous cry of hope streaked through the people at the sight of the unknown woman who had freed them from slavery. The Barbican Gate could not withstand the force of the desperate and rejuvenated crowd. They smashed it wide open within a minute and rushed inside the lower bailey, hoping to escape the horrors behind them. However, some of the captives did not run away. They stayed to face their oppressors with courage and defiance, even without weapons. They had been prisoners for too long, and they would not give up this one chance at freedom.

———— ⋅◄———⋅◄◆►⋅———►⋅ ————

Tomap Sruz had a clear view of the anarchy in Black Rock as his civilian skyship, the *Orca*, approached the coastal city from the northwest. From a distance, he saw the crowds of rebels and enslaved storming the Barbican Gate, freeing their fellow captives from the tyranny of the Zamana Empire. He also noticed the smoking wreckage of another skyship, the *Reaver*, that had crashed into the Main Gate, blocking any chance of imperial reinforcements.

"Land at the northwest mooring tower. We'll seize the center of the upper pier structure and push the rebels back to their cells," Tomap ordered First Officer Mosley.

"Yes, sir."

The *Orca* confidently soared through the other skyships floating in the sky, over the city rooftops, and descended on the northwest mooring tower, where the fighting was the least intense. On securing the mooring lines, the ship's crew dropped wooden planks onto the pier's top level, allowing the small group of Zamana forces on board to disembark. The first to emerge were six Zamana Lancers, mounted on swift horses and armed with long spears. They charged down the pier at the thin rebel lines on the upper deck, breaking their formation and creating an opening. Behind them came two screaming squads of Zamana Troopers carrying long swords and shields. They followed the Lancers' vicious lead and joined the fight to secure the pier.

❖

Garrison sprinted through the dimly lit grey corridors of the castle, dodging anxious guards and patrols as he made his way to the alleged treasure room. He finally had his trusty bullwhip coiled to the belt on his waist, something he had learned to use for offense and defense at times in his line of business. Taking the whip off his belt, he used it to latch onto a candelabra and swung across the room. He landed on a balcony, where a singular burly, unseen guard was waiting for him with a sword in hand.

Instincts took over. With a swift motion, Garrison disarmed the guard with the whip, the sound of metal echoing off the stone walls. The guard, driven by duty, charged with a ferocity born of desperation, but Garrison was ready. He sidestepped and countered, his fists a blur as they found their mark repeatedly. The final headbutt was a calculated move, a need to end the fight quickly. As the guard slumped to the ground, Garrison stood tall.

The archeologist picked up the bullwhip from the floor, keys from the guard, and continued his run. He hoped to reach the treasure room and his personal keepsake before the alarm that indicated his location was raised. He spotted an iron door with a golden lock and knew he had found his target. He picked the lock open with the keys and entered the room. He gasped at seeing the piles of jewels and gold that filled the chamber.

Garrison rummaged through the priceless items without a care in the world. Ironically, none of the gold coins, sparkling jewels, or rare antiquities were of value to him. Finally, after what seemed like an eternity, he found his objective amongst the artifacts: a simple three-inch-diameter, gold-rimmed disk with a smooth white surface. Once back in his hands, he exhaled sharply and found instant, peaceful relief.

Greatly satisfied with getting back what was rightfully his, Garrison was about to leave the chamber of riches when he heard footsteps behind him. He turned and saw a man in a black cloak holding a sword. The soldier lunged at him, swinging his blade. Garrison dodged the sword and immediately parried, using his whip as a weapon to keep the swordsman back. He managed to wound the soldier's arm with a flick of the whip, but the man was relentless.

He cornered Garrison against a wall, raising his sword for the final strike. Garrison backpedaled until his back hit the wall, caught the sword arm as it was crashing down, and punched the swordsman in the gut. As the soldier doubled over, Garrison lifted his knee into the man's face, knocking him out.

⸺ ·‹⸺‹◆›⸺›· ⸺

The sinful sorceress Keldace Vildan emerged from the sable shadows of the fortress tower, her eyes glowing crimson with arcane power behind the iron mask. She surveyed the battle in the upper bailey, where the enslaved prisoners dared to rise against her soldiers. As magic melded with metal, the iron mask's transformation was a visual enchantment. The faceplate bloomed into a bouquet of burgundy, and its edges reached six inches skyward, igniting into a flaming crescendo of tangerine and fiery cherry. It was not just a change of color but a metamorphosis of purpose, as if the mask were awakening to a higher calling.

On sight and without a word of warning, six rebels fired a series of arrows at Vildan. She made a simple sweeping motion with her hand as if she were swatting away an annoying insect. Like a flock of birds, the arrows unexplainably changed direction in midair and impaled other rebels nearby. Another volley of arrows was fired on the Mistress of the Dark Arts, and again, the direction changed in flight with an unimportant wave of her hand to find different targets.

A small group of four brave citizens, finding strength in numbers, rushed the lone witch. Vildan lifted her hand as if she were raising an invisible object. Dark roots sprang out of the ground and wrapped around the legs and arms of the four rebels, their screams outweighing the sick snapping of wood and bone.

Vildan snarled behind her magical mask and reached into her sword sheath, summoning a sharp silver blade blazing with pure sangria fire that crackled and hissed in the air. She slashed at the nearest rebels, cutting them down with ease. The smell of burning flesh filled the bailey as she carved a path of destruction through the helpless crowd.

Summoning their collective courage, another small group of four rebels rushed towards the wicked sorceress with weapons held high. Vildan created an emerald energy-barrier sphere around her that extended outward like an undeniable wave, knocking the rebels off their feet and away from her.

Nothing able to stand in her way, the empress of the Zamana Empire strode forward to the gate that separated the upper and lower baileys. A group of a dozen slaves was busy holding the gate up to escape, keeping it at shoulder height with their combined effort. Vildan pointed the tip of her flaming sword at them and unleashed a blast of fire, much like Mozo's, that incinerated them on the spot. The gate slammed shut, skeletal remains clinging to the bars, trapping the rest of the remaining rebels inside the lower bailey with Vildan and her troops.

◆

Mia raised her bloodied sword and shouted, "Take over the ships!" Her strong, unwavering voice rallied the people behind her. They had broken free from their chains and seized their captors' weapons.

Most subjugated had escaped the tower and fought through the upper bailey to the lower bailey. They stormed the central jetty, where the enemy sailing ships and skyships that had brought them to this forsaken place were docked.

A catastrophe was unfolding in the industrial imperial city. The galleon skyship under construction, the *Blade Guard*, that was supposed to be the new flagship in a month was engulfed in flames, sending plumes of charcoal smoke into the air. The fire had spread from the bow to the rest of the hull, and there was no hope of saving it. The crew and workers had abandoned the ship, some jumping into the water below, others using parachutes or one-person gliders to escape.

But that was not the only disaster for the Zamana Empire. All across The Piers, other skyships and sailing ships were being hijacked by the massive uprising. Inspired by the sudden breakout of the prison and the confusion of an entire skyship blocking the Main Gate, the rest of the prisoners throughout the area fought to be freed from the chains on the docks and work in factories. Arming themselves with weapons, they stormed the platforms, warehouses, and mooring towers, overpowering the guards and taking control of the vessels. Most flew away, heading for the mountains to the east or the open sea to the west. A few stayed behind, using the ships as weapons to attack the imperial buildings, fortifications, and any incoming Zamana skyship reinforcements.

Mia battled through the crowded central jetty, avoiding swords, fists, and curses, hoping to find a clear path to the upper southwest pier. But as a few bloodied bodies parted or fell to the ground in battle like waves of the ocean, she saw a familiar face blocking her way amongst the masses. Tomap was waiting for her with a wicked grin and a drawn sword.

"Arrogant girl," he said, twirling his blade with practiced finesse. "This is the end for you."

Mia cursed under her breath. She had no time for this. She drew her sword and lunged at him, hoping to catch him off guard by taking the initiative. But Tomap was ready for her. He parried her attack and countered with a swift slash. Mia barely dodged it, feeling the wind of his blade on her cheek.

They exchanged a flurry of blows, each faster and fiercer than the last. Mia tried to find an opening, but Tomap was too skilled and experienced. He matched her every move, forcing her backwards and up the stone ramp to the upper northeast pier.

Despite doing her best, Mia felt a surge of panic. She glanced behind her as she pedaled backwards up the ramp and saw the surrounding mob unintentionally closing in because of the tight constraints of the space. She was trapped between two enemies: Tomap, and the battle around them. She needed help. After a successful thrust forcing Tomap to back off for a needed moment, Mia whistled sharply, summoning her loyal companion.

Mozo flew out of the blue sky and went straight at Mia's adversary. He snarled at Tomap, baring his tiny fangs, stretching out his claws, and spitting sparks of fire.

"Get lost, you little pest," Tomap said, swatting at Mozo with his free hand.

Mozo easily evaded his hand and bit down on his ear, drawing blood. Tomap howled in pain and anger. He slapped Mozo hard, sending him flying across the pier.

Mia gasped as she saw Mozo fall into a collection of crates and barrels. She felt a surge of rage within her breast. She loved Mozo more than anything in the world. He was her best friend in this life since childhood.

She screamed and attacked Tomap with renewed fury. The noise of metal clashing with metal would be deafening but was mixed in with the other cries and clangs of metal surrounding them. Mia and Tomap did not hold out on each other, battling for survival on the upper pier. Mia deflected and struck, but Tomap was a relentless adversary. Impatient for a victory, he hurled a storm of slashes, pushing Mia back to the very edge of the upper northeast pier. He continued to press his advantage, relentless in his attacks until she lost her balance and fell over the upper pier's edge.

As Mia started to fall over the pier, she instinctively reached out and grasped the stone ledge. Barely clinging on with one hand, she hung suspended over the raging bay waters. Mia screamed in agony, reinjuring her wounded hip. The shooting pain was so excruciating that she lost her sword, swung helplessly in the air, and grabbed onto the ledge with both hands.

Tomap cackled evilly and walked over to the pier's edge where she dangled. He raised his black boot slightly and crushed down on her fingers, digging and rubbing in, trying to make her drop to her death. Mia screamed again, in anguish and horror, feeling her grip on the ledge breaking and her hip injury festering.

Mozo heard the familiar cries and launched another assault on Tomap. He circled the man in the air, spitting ruby flames. Tomap raised his shield to block the scorching heat, waiting for the right moment, then threw his shield like a discus at the flying menace.

Mozo was caught off guard and struck by the metal projectile. He tumbled back down to the pier, stunned and wounded.

"No!" Mia screamed. Her fingers were numb and sore from the pressure of Tomap's boot grinding into her. She heard Tomap's cruel laughter as he ground harder, making her lose her grip on one side. She swung wildly over the bay waters from the ledge, trying to find something to hold on to before she fell to her death. She knew he wouldn't stop until she lost her grip and fell into the dark watery abyss below.

"I'll be well rewarded for your death," Tomap said.

"Mia! Drop! We'll catch you!" Suzu shouted.

Mia looked down and saw the grey hot-air balloon of the *Minnow* float around the stone pillar and under the wooden pier underneath her dangling feet.

Tomap raised his black boot, about to stomp on Mia's hand with it. Mia made a split-second decision and purposely released her grip on the pier's edge, free-falling into the open air below. She landed with a thud on the upper deck of the *Minnow*, the junky cog skyship that was proving itself to be their trusty escape from perilous situations.

"Are you alright?" Suzu said.

"Yes. Thank you," Mia said. She got to her feet and grunted loudly, tenderly holding her right hip. "Mozo!"

Mozo snapped out of his daze and dived after her, streaking like a wayward arrow. He landed on her shoulder and nuzzled into her long raven hair.

"Let's get out of here!" Hogart called out from the pilot's position.

"Not yet. Fly close to the fortress," Mia said.

"What? Why?" Hogart asked.

"Just do it!"

Garrison sprinted through the dimly lit corridors of the castle, ducking arrows and spears from the pursuing soldiers. He could hear their shouts and footsteps behind him, getting closer and closer. He had no idea how he had ended up in this hellish castle, surrounded by enemies who wanted him dead.

He reached a dead end with a single large glass window. He turned around, facing a half-dozen angry Zamana Troopers. They wore light, thin white armor and carried swords and shields. He had only one last resort: his faithful bullwhip. He unlatched the weapon from his belt and snapped it at the guards several times, creating a loud sound that echoed through the hall. The soldiers jumped back and hesitated momentarily, not wanting to get cut and startled by the noise.

Garrison then swung the whip around a wooden chair leg and pulled hard, sending the chair flying towards the large window. The glass shattered, and Garrison saw his chance. He ran towards the opening and jumped through the open window. He unfurled the bullwhip to latch onto a wooden beam, part of a scaffolding network, feeling it wrap securely, then swung to a safe landing on the wooden planks.

He paused momentarily to collect himself and catch his breath. He found he was on the second level of a four-level construction scaffolding network, a complex web of wooden planks and metal poles alongside the sable seawall on the upper bailey. The scaffolding, in place for renovations to the fortress, appeared to spread across the entire northwest section of the upper bailey, wrap around a tower, and continue to the lower bailey.

Indistinct shouts were heard. Two Zamana Troopers were climbing up a ragged wooden ladder from the ground to reach their prey on the second level. Garrison ran on the scaffolding to get to the ladder just in time and pushed it forward with all his strength to the open air. Unbalanced, it toppled over. The two soldiers screamed as they lost their hold and fell to the hard ground below.

One level down, on the ground floor, five Zamana Troopers came running up the wooden ramp in pursuit. Garrison scurried across the second level, circumventing arrows fired at him from Troopers on the ground. He spotted a wooden ladder leading to the third level and climbed up quickly. At the top of the ladder, he found a table full of tools and weapons. He grabbed a small axe and threw it at an approaching soldier, hitting him in the chest. Garrison then picked up two knives and flung them at two more soldiers sprinting straight at him, piercing their throats. He saw a mallet leaning against the table and snatched it. He swung it hard at a wooden support beam, making it crack and creak. The ropes holding the beam snapped and broke from the force, releasing it from its place. The scaffolding collapsed, falling on top of two soldiers rushing towards him.

Garrison kept the mallet in hand, ascending another ladder to the fourth and top level. He sprinted ahead until he reached a dead end along a narrow wooden plank. He spun around in time to block the blade of a sword with the mallet. Holding the blade skillfully, the Zamana Trooper pressed his advantage, rattling his sword and making sparks fly against the mallet. The swordsman took a close swing at Garrison's head, causing him to misstep off the plank and free-fall backwards.

Garrison tossed the mallet away and unfurled his bullwhip at a passing support beam in one quick movement, swung towards the second level, and collided with an unsuspecting soldier. The soldier screamed and fell off the scaffolding. Garrison had been on the top level and was now, ironically, back down to the second level where he'd started.

Regaining his footing, Garrison gasped for air, his heart pounding. Numerous shouts and angry voices came from above and below, closing in on him. Garrison quickly realized that he was surrounded in every direction, no matter where he might run.

A single Zamana Trooper got to the fugitive first, roaring like a young lion as he swung his sword wildly at the target's head. Garrison ducked under the attack, but the sword severed a rope that held a heavy basket of square stones to reconstruct the fortress wall. The basket plummeted down, pulling the rope upwards. Garrison seized the opportunity, grabbed the rope, and was carried back up safely to the top level.

Not one to waste his surprising good fortune, Garrison ran towards the watchtower that separated the upper and lower baileys. He climbed a ladder leading to a wooden scaffolding platform that circled the watchtower and kicked the ladder down, hoping to prevent anyone from chasing him. He sprinted along the outskirts of the watchtower, desperate to find any means of escape.

He was halfway around the watchtower when he saw a Zamana Trooper blocking his path. The Trooper held a long sword and a fierce look in his eyes. Garrison acted quickly and used his whip to snatch the sword from the Trooper's grip. The sword flew into the air and landed in the murky water below. The Trooper was not deterred by being disarmed and lunged at Garrison, trying to wrestle him down. Garrison fought back with his fists and landed a blow on the Trooper's face. He grabbed the Trooper by the shirt and flung him over the platform's edge, sending him into the water.

Steering clear of the watchtower guards' arrows, Garrison continued his sprint around the outskirts of the watchtower until he reached another dead end. There was the next network of scaffolding of the lower bailey below him. He spotted a wooden crane hanging over the lower bailey and latched his bullwhip onto it, then swung over the bay waters to a three-tiered construction scaffold along the lower bailey's northwest wall.

Breathing a sigh of relief, he reached the solid wood of the platform, but his respite was short-lived. A door slammed open behind him, and four Zamana soldiers emerged from the watchtower. He ran for his life, dodging and swerving through the maze of wooden planks and metal rods that supported the scaffold.

Garrison heard a loud, bellowing roar and a crashing sound like a tree falling. A colossal brachiosaurus, an innocent victim of the battle, toppled over and smashed into the wooden platform ahead of him, creating a gaping hole in his path. Determined to lose his pursuers, Garrison gathered his courage and jumped over the crumbling section, hoping to land on the other side. He felt a rush of air as he flew over the dinosaur's body crashing underneath him. He landed safely with a thud on the other side, but the same could not be said for his four pursuers. The falling beast crushed them, or they were flung off the scaffold to their doom.

As the battle raged on the lower bailey between soldiers and the rebels, Keldace Vildan witnessed the massive brachiosaurus collapse under a barrage of arrows and spears. Its colossal body crashed into the wooden scaffolding surrounding the northwest walls, bringing down planks and ropes with a loud clamor. Vildan scanned the commotion and spotted her target on the top level of the scaffolding. It was Garrison, the Relic Hunter—the only man who could fulfill her final goal.

Vildan felt a surge of outrage and charged towards him, hoping to capture him. But before she could reach him, an explosion rocked the ground, sending flames and smoke into the air. Another section of the scaffolding gave way, falling on top of the brachiosaurus and creating a thick barrier between her and Garrison. She cursed and looked for a way around, but it was too late. Garrison had escaped her grasp.

Garrison got to his feet on the top level of the scaffolding and climbed up on wooden crates stacked along the sooty seawall. He ran on top of them and jumped a short distance from the scaffolding to the fortress wall, landing on the narrow, flat surface, barely making it. He sprinted ahead, looking for any escape and finding no options. Trapped and desperate, he stood atop the fortress wall. All hope seemed gone until Garrison heard a familiar female voice shouting out to him.

"Garrison! Come on!" Mia yelled.

He searched the aqua horizon and spotted a small merchant skyship, barely eighty feet long, that hugged the fortress wall as it sailed by. Garrison grinned and reached for his trusty bullwhip. He snapped it in the air and caught the hook of a swinging crane that hung over the edge. He jumped off the wall, leaving behind the foreboding fortress. The salty ocean wind whipped his face as he swung over the bay, dangling from the crane. He saw the ashen balloon of the skyship below him, its crimson propulsion sails fluttering in the breeze. He timed his release and dropped onto the wooden deck with a loud thump.

"Southeast, Hogart!" Suzu said.

The *Minnow* flew away from Black Rock, turning slightly in a southeastern direction. Behind them, the construction facility for the Zamana Empire was a devastated mess of wreckage. At the Main Gate, crowds of soldiers gathered at the coastline to try to push into the gate and open it just enough to get to the fighting. But they were blocked by the twisted *Reaver* wreck that settled before the iron bars and a raging inferno that engulfed the area, cutting off any escape and preventing anyone from getting through.

At the fortress, in the middle of the bay, the rebels finally breached the Lower Bailey Gate. The last of the enslaved people were fighting their way out, clashing with the few remaining Zamana Troopers with their bare fists or stolen blades. They had endured too much suffering and oppression and were now seizing their chance to escape.

In between, across the different sections at The Piers, the scene at the docks was one of utter pandemonium. Everywhere you looked, there were people, horses with wagons, Allosaurus Riders, trolls, and brachiosauruses scrambling for safety, some plunging into the cold, dark water below. Clashes of fists and swords continued to erupt between the soldiers and the rebels. Cherry-red flames engulfed parts of the wooden piers, sending inky smoke and bronze sparks into the air.

Many sailing and skyships had been destroyed or hijacked. Whether in the air and water, they freely drifted around and away from the shore. Some of them were in smoky ruins, having been attacked or sabotaged. One empty sailing ship floated away, fully ablaze. Another skyship faltered in flight and crashed into the bay, failing to take off at launch. But most sailing ships and skyships simply drifted in the water or floated in the air at a safe distance, unable to do anything but observe the destruction of Black Rock from afar.

The Skunnimonk Passage

Tomap Sruz, his strong-willed ego more battered and bruised than his physical body from the Battle of Black Rock, stood resolute on the fore observation deck of the *Iron Talon*. His mounting anxiety was concealed. Commanding his battle-damaged skyship, he relentlessly pursued the *Minnow*, the cog skyship that had miraculously managed to elude their clutches. Every evasive move of the old merchant skyship was under his intense scrutiny. A sharp inhale betrayed his growing impatience.

The *Iron Talon*, like a wounded predator, plodded on, refusing to relent in its pursuit of the lone prey. Tomap's capture of the vessel would mean delivering the crew responsible for the Black Rock revolt to Keldace Vildan, a prospect that would undoubtedly please the Mistress of the Dark Arts. Yet the *Iron Talon*'s sluggish pace, akin to an ocean vessel battling against the crashing waves, was a source of hidden irritation for the commander.

The Zamana Troopers, manning a single ballista newly mounted on the bow of the *Iron Talon*, unleashed a volley of flaming arrows at the smaller sky vessel. Their attempts, to their dismay, missed the target by a significant margin. Equally disheartened by the poor results and the prolonged pursuit, First Officer Mosley approached her temperamental commander with caution.

"Report," Tomap said. He did not take his dark brown eyes off the prey.

"We almost have them, sir," the first officer stated.

"Almost?" There was an annoyed growl in the tone.

"Sir," First Officer Mosley said. She kept her tone even but direct. "The *Iron Talon* has taken some significant damage, not only from the attack by the Silver Moon Sharks but also from the slave revolt at Black Rock . . ."

Tomap whirled around, his face turning from pale to bloodred with rage. "I don't want excuses. I want that skyship," he said. His voice was laced with fury.

First Officer Mosley, one of the very few not intimidated by her superior officer, kept her firm composure and even tone of voice. "We're gaining on them, sir."

•‹‹━━‹‹◆››━━››•

Adrenaline surged through Mia as she scanned the cobalt horizon with her binoculars. The meager, dingy *Minnow* was fast but not fast enough to outrun the Zamana Empire's most feared skyship, the *Iron Talon*. She could see the fresh scars and scrapes on its black-charred wooden hull, the result of the Battle of Black Rock and the Silver Moon Shark raid. But it still looked menacing; the image grew within the frame every time she peered through the lenses. "Well, they're gaining on us."

Hogart stood by Mia's side, taking the binoculars in his burly hands to look for himself. "They'll be on us very soon if we don't do something quickly," he complained.

Standing at the helm, Garrison made a sudden, unannounced decision and altered the direction of the *Minnow*. He adjusted the bright red rudder and propulsion sails from the pilot's position, setting the skyship on a new course. Garrison's square-jawed, lightly scruffy face looked focused on flying to a specific destination.

Standing at the bow of the *Minnow* to keep a lookout for anything dangerous ahead in their course, Suzu was the first to notice the change. She felt the skyship shift slightly underneath her feet and the point of the bowsprit move from the previous aerial view. "What are you doing?"

"We have only one chance to escape them," Garrison said. "The Skunnimonk Passage."

"No!" Hogart cried out. "That's too dangerous!"

Mia looked puzzled. "What's the Skunnimonk Passage?"

Hogart's face looked horrified and the blood in his cheeks receded. "A treacherous, ill-advised route. It is an immense cavern that goes through the Vergery Mountains to the Kayawa border."

"I've heard of this passage," Suzu said. "No one has ever successfully gone through the cave tunnel and come out alive."

"I'm telling you," Garrison shouted, "it's our only chance!"

Hogart scoffed. "We'll vote on it. All those opposed to the idea." Suzu and Hogart raised their hands high into the air.

Mia gave a soft sigh. "Those for it." Mia and Garrison raised their hands. "You're outvoted."

"You can't count?" Suzu said. "It's a stalemate at two votes apiece."

"No," Mia said, "The dragon counts as a fifth vote. You're outvoted."

Suzu and Hogart look at the dragon curled up like a house cat on a box crate. Mozo shifted his head, emitted cream smoke from his oval nostrils, and gave a menacing look. The bumbling duo, seeing that they had been outvoted, fell silent.

The *Iron Talon* methodically chased the *Minnow* with dogged persistence, unleashing its aerial arsenal of fiery projectiles. The scorching flaming-red arrows flew through the clear blue sky, creating plumes of midnight smoke that marred the serene landscape. The Zamana Empire narrowed the gap between them and the elusive target. The smaller, nimble craft seemed to anticipate, zigzag, and swerve, attempting to shake off the lethal onslaught. But the *Iron Talon* was relentless and refused to give up.

The *Minnow*, having no choice but to go through with this dangerous route—the only way to escape impending capture, tilted its propulsion sails down and rapidly descended with a burst of speed. Cautiously, but purposely, it approached a long sage valley with a narrow, twisty aqua-blue river leading to the fringe of misty, cloud-covered foothills. Leveling off at a much lower altitude, almost skimming across the placid river, the specially designed cog skyship flew into a trench filled with pure pearly clouds within the mountain range that naturally split the land into two territories.

As the *Minnow* approached the natural gap, a collection of strong, gusty winds grabbed hold of the sails, increasing its speed by sucking the vessel into the broad native breach. Once through the mouth of the trench, the *Minnow* was swallowed by the milky fog, easily losing the pursuing *Iron Talon* within the confines of the heavy, uncanny cloud cover and seemingly entering a new world.

The strong winds ceased, and a light breeze replaced it, gently pushing the skyship forward within the mountain range's taupe walls. Soon, the weather changed, accompanied by increasing patches of bushy fog clouds. A cold, misty rain encircled the *Minnow*.

"I hope you know what you're doing," Mia said.

Steering at the pilot's position, Garrison looked apprehensive about his hasty decision. "Me too."

The *Minnow* flew forward through the deep natural trench, slowly navigating between the cloud-filled, narrow, dark grey rocky mountain walls. The unforgiving fog created a sense of both mystery and peril. There was no sound, not one chirp from a single bird or the distant bellow of a herd of animals. Visibility ahead was less than twenty yards, simultaneously making the dreamlike, creepy atmosphere beautifully eerie and naturally dangerous.

As the *Minnow* gently pushed through the bleached mist, a jagged, distorted, rough form loomed ahead. Garrison grunted loudly to himself, swiftly altering the ship's course and veering away from the hidden danger. He had been caught off guard by the shifting terrain of the mountain trench, where the clouds concealed treacherous twists and turns. The *Minnow* had to cautiously avoid the murky, cloud-hidden rock walls lurking in the fog, or it would mean death for all on board.

"Suzu. Hogart," Garrison said. "Get to the bow of the ship and call off directions. We don't want to crash into a rock face."

Aware of their dangerous situation, the pair followed the instructions and hurried to the vessel's bow. They strained their eyes to see through the abundant fog, hoping to anticipate the next curve.

"Hard to port," Suzu called out.

The *Minnow* glided through the tight space between the towering cliffs, where a few thick leafy viridian trees had toppled over the precipice. The gnarled, long rust branches jutted out over the abyss like crooked fingers, providing a home for some bizarre birds that looked like they belonged in a nightmare. Their realgar beaks were sharp as blades, and their teal feathers were tattered and dull.

The birds resented the intrusion of the *Minnow* trespassing in their territory, and they expressed their displeasure with a deafening cacophony of shrieks and chittering as they soared into the air. The threatening sight and sound of the hideous birds swarming and screeching around the vessel gave the trespassing passengers on board little hope that the mountain forest trench was vacated. The skyship labored forth, unharmed, slowly leaving the angry birds behind.

"Now turn to starboard," Hogart shouted above the terrible cawing nearby.

The air vessel made another turn in direction within the trench and passed through another shroud-filled section. Wrecked remnants of fallen skyships, broken-up burgundy wooden planks, snapped masts, and small, torn flaxen, lime, and cyan sails were littered and scattered along the ledges and outcrops of the surrounding rock face. Some of them were old and rusted; others were fresh and charred. Amongst the skyship debris, two human skeletons dangled from the splintered upper deck of a large frigate, their bones bleached white by the radiant marigold sun and picked clean by the bizarre-looking giant birds. The sight filled the passengers with dread. They averted their eyes and moved silently along the trench, wanting to forget they had seen this ghastly area.

"Straighten out," Suzu said. "I think I hear something."

"It's getting louder," Hogart said.

A low rumbling noise ahead got louder as the craft sailed persistently forward. The *Minnow* glided through the less soupy fog, the sound of roaring water growing louder every second. The drifting, shifting whisps of the ivory clouds surrounding the *Minnow* faded away and changed to a light mist and spray of water droplets. As the ship emerged from the encompassing vapors, a breathtaking sight greeted the crew. Nestled in the lush verdant foothills of the Vergery Mountains, twin, free-falling, resplendent waterfalls cascaded from a stunning two-hundred-and-fifty-foot rust-colored rock face. The waterfalls flanked a narrow gap in the rock, creating a natural watery gateway for the skyship to pass through. Water streamed down both sides of the thin passage, the bottom appearing like some menacing witches' cauldron churning and bubbling white with foam. With clear water streaming down both sides of the narrow passage, the *Minnow* carefully sailed between the glorious waterfalls and avoided the turbulent frost-crested waters at their base.

As the dinky skyship passed the waterfalls, it crept into a natural entrance that marked a forest zone. The roar of the cascades faded away, replaced by the gentle rustle of fern leaves and bone-colored branches. The *Minnow* entered a canopy of lush greenery, where exotic plants and various animals thrived in the moist air. The forest was a wonderland of biodiversity, with colorful flowers, fruits, and fungi dotting the landscape. The rare and remarkable species that inhabited the forest, such as the glowing orchids and the giant butterflies, were evident, along with the singing of colorful birds. The *Minnow* seemed to slow down to admire the beauty and diversity of this natural paradise.

"At last. We can see where we're going," Mia said.

It was pleasant in the woods with a form of music provided by nature. The *Minnow* continued to sail along the mountain trench, able to see clearly ahead but unaware of what awaited them around the next bend.

Suddenly, a single strike of a drum was heard. Seconds passed before another bang echoed through the swaying trees. The single drumbeat became a steady beat and slowly picked up its pace. Soon, as the *Minnow* passed deeper into the forest, other drums joined it, beating rhythmically throughout the shifting trees, almost making a unique dance or a message. A single whistle followed it, then a blaring of horns. It was almost like the trees were extending a call or musical invitation, being sent, heard, and answered throughout the forest. The crew of the *Minnow* looked around nervously, wondering who or what was making the noise and why. They felt an odd dread as if unknowingly drawn into a well-placed trap.

Terrible growls, low roars, and animalistic screeches came from within the shadowy confines of the stocky foliage. The many twisting branches and clusters of leaves of the surrounding trees sprang to life. The branches shook, swayed, and snapped unnaturally, like something was running along the limbs, following or even hunting the tiny skyship as it gradually poked along its unknown path. The ferocious growls gathered more voices and multiplied, becoming more urgent and coordinated, turning to short grunts and huffs as if secret communications were happening around the *Minnow*. The passengers' hearts pounded and their breaths quickened, leaving them wondering if they would ever escape this nightmare as the unforeseen predators grew louder and closed in on their prey.

"Oh no," Garrison said. He looked frightened as if he had made a lethal mistake.

"What is it?" Mia asked.

"Man-apes!"

Six apelike creatures leapt off the branches from the overhanging trees above and attacked the floating vessel—their shaggy forms each at least seven feet tall. Tales told by travelers who survived encounters with man-apes described these mountain dwellers as resembling a cross between a silverback gorilla and a human. They were like apes that walked upright and learned to speak roughly in the common tongue, only to curse and threaten their enemies. The man-apes were dressed in crude garments of fabric cloth draped around the waistline. A form of jewelry adorned their necks like necklaces, consisting of bones and teeth from different creatures in the world. They ranged from dinosaurs to men, signifying fighting conquests. They had various shades of fur, from black, to white, to brown, to grey, but all had the same savage features: ruddy eyes, wide nostrils, and ecru fangs. They attacked with metal weapons, such as spiked clubs and sharp spears, aiming to kill, loot, or capture the airship crew.

"We want your ship," an albino man-ape announced gruffly.

Hogart clenched his fists as he faced one of the snarling man-apes, one with caramel fur and two deep scratches across its chest. Hogart, like everyone else on board, had no choice but to fight for his life and his friends. He sidestepped a swipe of the beast's black razor claws and punched its scruffy, solid jaw. The man-ape staggered back but quickly recovered and lunged at Hogart again. Hogart grabbed its shaggy arms and wrestled with it, trying to push it off the edge of the skyship. The man-ape was strong and fierce, but Hogart had the advantage. He twisted and turned, throwing the savage beast off balance with his weight and momentum. With a final heave, he flung the scarred caramel-colored man-ape over the side of the *Minnow*, watching it fall into the water below. Hogart breathed a sigh of relief but knew he had to keep fighting. There were five more man-apes to deal with.

Suzu sprang into action, twirling and kicking the two man-apes that thought it might be easy to ambush her. She delivered a devastating blow to one of them, sending it airborne over the edge of the *Minnow*. The second man-ape retreated, hissing and snarling, slowly backing away. Suzu drew her small repeater crossbow and faced off with the beast again, glaring at it with fiery eyes, daring it to come closer.

"Kill you, little one." The man-ape growled. It pounced forward until a single perfectly aimed arrow shot from the crossbow had sliced across its upper arm while the man-ape was in midair. The man-ape fell to the upper deck, grabbed its arm, and whimpered. It got up and decided to run away, vanishing back into the thick greenery with a single leap.

Garrison faced the single ferocious albino man-ape that had invaded the pilot's position by himself. He grabbed a sharp sword that rested nearby and lunged at the hairy creature, hoping to pierce its husky white fur. The man-ape roared viciously and swung its massive, strong arms, trying to knock Garrison off-balance.

Man and man-ape struggled at the helm for control of the *Minnow*, which was drifting awkwardly and dangerously towards the rock face. The sword was knocked away from Garrison's hand, clattering to the ground. The albino man-ape saw an opportunity and sprang at its target with black claws stretched outward to kill. Garrison felt a surge of adrenaline at the gruesome, terrifying sight as he reached into his knife sheath and pulled out his weapon in time to stab the beast deep in the chest, making it howl in pain and retreat. Free from the attack, Garrison quickly took over the helm and stabilized the *Minnow*, breathing a sigh of relief as they avoided the rock-face collision.

Mia had the invisibility cloak. She wrapped it around herself and vanished from sight, leaving only a faint shimmer in the air. She crept behind one of the man-apes, who was snarling and throwing rocks at her friends. She stabbed the beast in the upper back with her sword, preventing it from throwing another rock and making it howl in anguish. She slashed another one's leg, making it stumble and fall.

"Where is it?" The last two remaining injured man-apes were confused and terrified, unable to see their aggressive attacker. They backed away together on the deck, hoping to escape the invisible menace.

Mozo saw Mia's shimmer with his acute senses and realized what she was doing. He joined her in the fight, flying over the two man-apes and spitting fire at them. He scorched their brown fur, making them drop their weapons and leap for their lives in the trees.

"Good boy!" Mia smiled and took off her cloak, revealing her face. She hugged Mozo and praised him for his bravery with a language and bond only they could understand. Together, they had driven off the last of the man-apes and protected their friends.

"Is everyone alright? Is anyone hurt?" Garrison asked.

"No, we're fine," Suzu said.

Hogart, wiping the sweat off his face, mumbled something incoherent and turned to the bow of the skyship. He unexpectedly yelled in fright. "Watch out!"

They all gasped and braced themselves for another attack, thinking they had flown into another trap. But as they all turned to the bow, they realized it was just a natural illusion that had scared the big man. There was no cause for alarm.

The *Minnow* had encountered the entrance to the Skunnimonk Passage. Carved into the rock face of the mountain was the gaping opening to the treacherous cavern, a colossal sienna stone gorilla face, with a menacing expression and sharp rocky teeth. The mouth was wide open for about two hundred yards as if ready to swallow the approaching *Minnow* whole. The appearance of the grotesque entrance was a clever disguise to deter all intruders. Still, the *Minnow* purposefully flew towards the dark abyss opening, hoping to find their way through the cavern and a way out.

"I don't know about you, but that certainly looks like we should not go in there!" Suzu said.

Garrison looked to Mia as if waiting for an order but already knew the answer.

"Keep going," she said.

The tiny brave *Minnow* confidently sailed into a vast, gloomy tunnel. The light breeze of damp, cold air immediately seized their bodies, chilling each to the bone. The pitch-black darkness grew around the skyship like a living shadow as sunlight failed to penetrate beyond the twilight zone of the cavern, the region just inside the entrance.

"Tell the dragon to start streaming fire so we can see," Suzu said to Mia.

"It doesn't work like that," Mia said, annoyed. "Even Mozo has his limits. He cannot stream fire forever."

"Light the lanterns. Use some of the oil for torches," Garrison suggested.

Suzu and Hogart worked together to attach the lanterns to the bow and stern of the *Minnow*, ensuring they were secure and stable. Mozo lit them up with a quick puff of his fire breath, creating a bright, warm dandelion light illuminating the dingy skyship. They also gave Mia one of the torches they had made, which she held high as she examined the surroundings. The lanterns and the torch revealed the dangerous rocks that jutted out from the walls and ceiling of the cavern, like knives and spikes, threatening to damage the *Minnow* if they got too close. Suzu and Hogart distributed a couple more lanterns around the skyship, hoping to increase their visibility and safety as they ventured deeper into the mysterious cave.

The *Minnow* glided along the center of the dusky tunnel, aided by the flickering flames of lanterns and torches that cast a warm glow on the jagged rocks. The boat successfully steered clear of sharp edges that could puncture its hull and the uneven floor that could scrape its bottom. Along the way, the *Minnow* thankfully encountered patches of natural illumination, such as beams of buttery sunlight that pierced through cracks in the ceiling, turquoise bulb bushes that respawned randomly throughout the cavern, or clusters of luminescent plants that dotted the walls like pearly sparkles. The sunlight created dazzling reflections on the water droplets along the walls, and the plants emitted a soft lilac radiance that contrasted with the inky darkness.

The *Minnow* entered a significant, unadorned, rocky periwinkle orifice connected to the main entrance corridor. Like light waves lapping the shore, a faint sound came from within the cool air. The eerie sound within the darkness increased, growing louder and becoming more furious as the skyship ventured deeper into the cavern. It was as if the sea was within the cavern walls, roaring in protest at the intrusion.

"What's that up there?" Mia asked, casting her bright torch upwards towards the ceiling.

A high-pitched shrill filled the chilling air. The fury of the lapping waves of the sea crashing on the rocks echoed throughout the tunnel, but the sound came from the flapping of leathery wings. Giant black bats, with bodies as big as dogs and wings as wide as vultures, flew around the chamber and the *Minnow* in a collective swarm. They had sharp claws on their fingers, ready to rip and tear apart flesh, and long hind legs and short forearms, similar to climbing mammals that hang upside down from trees. The bats were more agile in the air than most birds, and they hovered, dived, caromed, coiled, and swayed above the heads of the scared crew. Multiple sets of wings fanned and stirred the stagnant air. A high-pitched, horrific screech combined with terrifying squealing filled their ears.

"Watch yourselves!" Garrison yelled.

The massive flock of furious, grotesque bats besieged the *Minnow*, beating their colossal wings with rage and looming threateningly over the flying craft. The bats maneuvered nimbly and unpredictably in the air, alternating between flapping and gliding, interweaving through the interior and circling the exterior of the skyship. The storm of bats swarmed and swooped, pecking at the crew, creating a noisy thunder of swooping wings.

"Shoo! Go away!" Hogart cried.

Mozo's roar echoed through the cavernous expanse, a primal declaration of protection over Mia and a tactic to scare off the invaders. As the bats descended like shadows, Mozo unleashed a fiery torrent, the scarlet blaze painting the darkness with vibrant streaks. The bats, caught in the inferno, burst into brilliant sparks, scattering like a thousand tiny suns.

With wings like tattered cloaks, the bats swirled in a frenzied dance around Suzu, their eyes glinting like shards of obsidian in the fading light. She stood resolute with crossbow in hand, her silhouette a stark contrast against the luminescent lanterns of the deck. As three audacious creatures dived towards her, she let out a battle cry that mingled with the howling winds and the bats' piercing screeches and let loose three arrows from her crossbow. Two found their mark, while the third missed.

The impact was sudden, a force that threw Suzu off-balance and backwards to the upper deck. She grappled with the creature, defending herself. Her fist met its snout with a satisfying crunch. Her leg arced through the air with a swift motion, delivering a powerful kick. The bat, stunned, retreated into the dark, its squeal fading into the cacophony of its brethren.

Hogart stood, a lone figure against the horde of winged assailants. With reflexes as sharp as a lion's, he turned their momentum against them, his hands a blur as he deftly caught one of the creatures. With a warrior's grace, he wielded the bat like a master swordsman, felling his aerial foes with swift, decisive strikes and knocking them out of the sky. He then tossed his unwilling weapon at a fellow bat, making them both fall from the air. And as quickly as the battle began, it ended, the remaining bats vanished into the shadows.

The swarming aerial assault was brief but terrifying. The enormous, winged creatures seemed to sense some form of danger ahead from the gaping hole leading to another chamber and acted as one flock in a hasty retreat. The battered but unbroken *Minnow* continued its forever forward journey through the orifice and emerged into a chamber with a different atmosphere.

The air was dry and crisp. The chamber they had entered was vast and barren, with sparse vegetation. Before the ship's bow, celadon stalactites, rock-growth formations dangling from the roof downward, and beige stalagmites, growths jutting from the floor upwards, appeared. The *Minnow* was required to carefully navigate and sail around the natural formations placed sporadically within the cavern.

As the adventurers delved deeper into the cavern's heart, the dance of stalactites and stalagmites grew ever more intricate. Shadows played tricks on the eyes. The draft was heavy with the scent of mineral-rich water and the echoes of droplets that had shaped these natural sculptures over millennia. The path wound along a serpentine trail carved by patient and persistent forces. With each passing moment, the cavern revealed new wonders—a hidden pool reflecting the ceiling like a mirror, a narrow crevice leading to unknown depths, and a sudden clearing where the stalactites and stalagmites seemed to meet in a stony embrace.

"The walls are closing in!" Mia shouted.

"No, they're not. The tunnel is just getting narrower," Garrison said calmly.

The crew approached the next section, a cramped passage they could barely fit through. They held their breath and crossed their fingers, hoping to reach the other side unscathed. The *Minnow* narrowly squeaked through the tight passage, and they heard the wooden hull screech against the jagged rocks on the floor. The walls seem to press in on them from all sides like a vise, making them feel trapped and claustrophobic.

The confined passage suddenly sloped down, and Garrison angled the ship to fit the three-hundred-yard-long slope to avoid crashing. They leveled out at the bottom of the slope and flew straight for a few more tense moments, scraping the bottom of the hull again before they emerged into a wider chamber with some welcome relief.

"It's getting a little colder," Hogart said.

Suzu looked ahead in the cavern. "What is that?"

The *Minnow* floated through the tunnel, seemingly drawn in by a dazzling, swirling, bright spectacle of colors. A rainbow of rose, tangerine, canary, violet, emerald, azure, lilac, and ivory swirls pranced to unheard music ahead, inviting the curious travelers to explore its whimsical secrets. As the *Minnow* entered the Rainbow Room, they gasped in awe at the sight of glowing rocks in every hue imaginable. The ceiling was covered with ice crystals that reflected and refracted the rainbow light, creating a kaleidoscopic effect. The walls and floor were beautifully adorned with various colorful stalactites and stalagmites of many shapes and sizes, some forming uncanny natural sculptures that resembled animals or plants. A small aquamarine pool of water sparkled in the center, fed by rainbow droplets from the roof. The water was clear and pure, revealing a blush hue on the bottom. This was a place of wonder and beauty, untouched by human hands, where nature showed its artistic genius.

The travelers marveled at the details of this natural wonderland, noticing how the ice crystals on the ceiling changed color depending on the angle of the light, creating a dynamic and mesmerizing display. They saw how the stalactites and stalagmites had grown over thousands of years, layer by layer, forming intricate patterns and textures. Some rocks had different shades of color, indicating different minerals or elements in their composition. The coolness of the air and the water contrasted with the warmth of their bodies. The gentle sound of dripping water and their breathing created a soothing rhythm. The freshness and cleanliness of this underground oasis was free from any pollution or contamination.

The *Minnow* continued to sail through a tapering aperture, leaving the Rainbow Room behind, and found itself in a hidden paradise: a huge cavern filled with lush greenery, breathtaking cascades, and abundant life. The air was moist and wonderfully fragrant. The surrounding sound of clear streams was soothing and refreshing, emptying into a small reservoir in the center of the cavern. The cave's walls and ceiling were dotted with holes that let in golden beams of sunlight, creating a magical effect. The *Minnow* explored the cistern, marveling at the variety of creatures that inhabited it: frogs the size of house cats that croaked and hopped, their olive skin glistening with dew; elongated snakes that slithered and coiled, their scales shimmering with rainbow colors; lime lizards that scurried along the vegetation and basked on the pearl rocks, their slitted eyes darting with curiosity; small birds that flew and sang happily, their myriad of colorful feathers bright and soft; schools of fish that swam and splashed in the reservoir, their fins sparkling and smooth. It felt like a dream, a secret world untouched by the outside.

However, the crew of the *Minnow* had reached a proverbial dead end. Three tunnels branched off in different directions from the underground reservoir. The crew had yet to learn which tunnel would lead them to their desired destination and which would forever trap them in a maze of peril. They had to make a choice, and fast. The center tunnel looked the broadest and most inviting. But it could also be the most obvious trap. The left tunnel was narrow and crooked, but it could also be a shortcut to the exit. The right tunnel was steep and slippery, but it could offer a rare reward. The crew had to weigh each option's risks and benefits, hoping they picked the right one.

"Which tunnel?" Hogart said.

"I don't know. I wasn't expecting this," Garrison said. He rubbed his narrow chin, thinking to himself.

"Great! You bring us through here and don't know where you're going?" Suzu said.

"We can't go back. You do realize this, right?" Hogart added.

"What do you think, Mia?" Garrison said.

Mia gave a heavy sigh. "Steady as she goes to the center tunnel. Hope for the best."

The lost vessel did not alter course and drifted straight through the dark center passage, following the faint apricot glow of its lanterns. The tan walls were rough and wet, and the aerial boat made sure it was away from the sharp rocks that protruded from them. The tunnel seemed endless, and the breeze was damp and cold. The crew wondered what lay ahead, if anything at all.

The *Minnow* floated deeper into the dingy tunnel, oblivious to the slitted yellow eyes watching it intently once it entered. A long dark shadow slid and slithered around the sharp edges of the beige rocks, along the outcrops of the tunnel walls, near the starboard side of the unsuspecting craft. The unseen creeping menace hissed low, barely audible, as it slithered closer and closer. Not yet ready to pounce on its prey, it silently slipped through a crevice in the rocky wall with lightning speed, disappearing back into the inky shadows.

"What was that?" Suzu asked.

"What?" Mia asked.

"I thought I saw something move along the cavern wall."

Hogart cast the torchlight to the starboard side against the cave wall and saw nothing moving. "There's nothing there. It's just your imagi—" he began to say out loud until Suzu turned to give him a sharp look. "Never mind."

The *Minnow* sailed confidently forward and was greeted by a dazzling sight of various unique rock formations and scattered, glowing flora on mangled vines and dark brown roots throughout a vast, wide chamber. The skyship gracefully cruised around the giant roots and twisting vines that crisscrossed the ceiling and wrapped around a few slender burgundy mesas, some bearing delicate white and blue flowers that cast a celestial light over the scene. Here and there, beams of champagne sunlight pierced through the cracks above, creating natural spotlights for the *Minnow* to navigate by. In some places, clusters of luminous plants lit the walls with creamy light like natural lanterns. Various sections of the stony ground and ceiling were adorned with countless rock-cone formations, some as thin as needles and others as thick as pillars. At the same time, the shadowy gaps between them hinted at possible hidden dangers or a bottomless chasm. The slender mesas spotted around the chamber, between dark, endless pits, were covered with lush vegetation. The atmosphere was filled with a sweet, pleasant fragrance and a gentle breeze that caressed the skyship's hull.

Hogart heard a faint, menacing sound behind him. It sounded like a low growl mixed with a hiss and was getting louder. He knew it was not the wind nor a friendly creature. He quickly turned around and held a torch high in the air, hoping to scare away whatever lurked in the shadows. The hefty man gasped when he pointed the light of the torch at the viny cavern wall. There, amongst the green leaves and the violet flowers, he saw a pair of glowing yellow-slitted eyes staring at him. They belonged to a huge one-hundred-foot snake with forest-green snow-spotted scales that matched the color of the leaves and flowers. The immense, overlong snake had been hiding in plain sight, waiting for the right moment to attack the tiny vessel. It uncoiled its long, sleek, and slender body from the twisted vines and ploddingly slithered towards the *Minnow* with a hungry look.

"It's a giant anaconda snake!" Hogart shouted.

Knowing it had been spotted, the mammoth snake swiftly moved in on the sailing skyship, visibly annoyed at the intrusion within its home. It targeted the most significant meal, Hogart, who was holding a torch in his burly hands to light the way. The snake lunged at him over a wooden railing, but Hogart swung his torch and fended it off. The snake tried again, striking quickly. Hogart lost his balance after another wild swing and fell to the wooden planks, dropping his torch. The snake saw its chance and moved in for the kill. It raised its flat head and opened its wide mouth, its red tongue flickering in hunger, ready to bite Hogart's body. But before it could strike, two arrows flew from Suzu's crossbow, hitting the snake in the body under the head. The snake recoiled in pain and momentarily retreated from the railing of the skyship, leaving Hogart unharmed.

In angry retaliation and with a furious hiss, the giant serpent reappeared and rushed at the *Minnow*, its blunt head striking the starboard side of the wooden hull. The impact sent the skyship veering to the left, barely avoiding a collision with a jagged rock pillar and a gnarled brown root hanging from the cavern roof. The crew held on for dear life as the ship swayed and shuddered, trying to regain its balance.

"Where did it go?" Suzu yelled.

The giant snake appeared again, this time on the port side. The monstrosity coiled its scaly body around a sturdy stalagmite, hissing with a forked cherry tongue flicking at the vessel. This time, the snake's swift head struck the port upper deck with a loud thud. Everyone on board was knocked down to the deck, sprawling, scrambling to get up as the *Minnow* lost control. It was pushed aimlessly around the cavern again, circumventing vines and stalactites in its path.

Mia got up from the deck and steadied herself, hearing the malevolent hissing sound behind her next. She turned around and saw the huge snake coiled around a long stocky tree branch, ready to strike. She froze in alarm, unable to move or scream. Suddenly, a flash of coral flames darted before her. It was Mozo, her loyal dragon companion. He had sensed her being in danger and came immediately to her rescue. Mozo flew in circles around the twisting head of the snake, breathing out a jet of fire that scorched its dark green scales and set a portion of the leaf-filled branch ablaze. The mammoth snake hissed in fury, lashing out at the tiny target, but Mozo was too fast and agile. He kept attacking quickly and sporadically until the snake gave up being pecked at and speedily slithered away into the thick foliage of the vines and sooty roots.

Mia breathed a sigh of relief and ran to hug Mozo, who nuzzled her affectionately. "Thank you." Mozo wagged his long tail happily for the praise of his bravery and licked her face.

"It's not done with us," Garrison warned.

They all felt a surge of dread as they flew deeper into the cavern, knowing Garrison was right. They saw the gigantic beast slither into view and loom in front of their course. Its scales shimmered like metal in the sparse light, reflecting their terrified faces. It had stretched its colossal body across the entire tunnel, leaving no space for them to pass, and coiled itself around two massive rust-colored rock pillars as if guarding a sacred gate. Its yellow eyes glowed with malice, and its mouth opened wide, revealing rows of tiny razor-sharp teeth.

Mozo defiantly soared into the air again, his tiny body full of courage. He knew by animal instinct he had to protect Mia and the others from the monstrous snake that threatened them. The snake roared and spat its forked tongue at Mozo, but he evaded every attack with his swift aerial movements. He darted towards the snake's blunt head, aiming the streams of orange-red fire at its vulnerable eyes, making it scream in agony and put it in a vicious rage. The snake thrashed its tail wildly, unknowingly hitting Mozo with a powerful blow.

"Mozo!" Mia screamed.

A sharp sting shot throughout Mozo's body and he lost control of his wings. He plummeted to the ground, luckily landing on the skyship's deck with a thud. He lay there, barely conscious, as Mia ran to him and picked him up in her hands.

The *Minnow* was in grave danger. The colossal reptile regrouped and coiled around the slender wooden bowsprit that jutted out from the front of the vessel. The crew could only watch helplessly from the deck as the snake tightened its grip on the bowsprit with its muscles, making the wood creak and crack under immense pressure. The snake's flat head, with its fangs bared and its forked tongue flicking, inched closer to the ship's bow, constricting its body and crushing the wood of its bowsprit until it snapped with a sickening crunch.

A thunderous roar rumbled from the concealed depths of the underground tunnel, announcing the arrival of a new monster: a gargantuan ebony silverback gorilla that towered at fifteen feet tall. His body was a mass of rippling muscles, an awesome display of strength and power, covered with sable fur that shone with silver streaks in the faint light. He lifted his massive arms and smashed his huge fists against his mighty, broad chest, creating shock waves that shook the air and the ground. He was a fearsome sight, a primal force of nature that demanded respect and fear.

"We're doomed!" Hogart yelled.

The colossal serpent had the tiny wooden skyship in its deadly embrace, squeezing the proverbial life out of it. But then, the oversized silverback gorilla leapt on the serpent's blunt head, biting and clawing at its eyes. The mammoth serpent let out a deafening roar and released its miniature prey, thrashing wildly to shake off the savage attacker.

The *Minnow* was free from the lethal hold but was swatted away by the two leviathans in their tussle. It spun helplessly around in a circle, having no control over direction, and carelessly drifted towards a massive rock mesa that towered before them. The crew screamed, hoping they would avoid an inevitable collision. They were going to crash and die.

However, at the very last second, Garrison regained control. The *Minnow* veered away, barely scraping against the rocks. The hull of the skyship bounced off the mesa, giving the craft a gentle push back to the center of the wide cavern.

A tense standoff unfolded in the ominous depths of the cavern, now acting like a gladiator arena, where the two colossal beasts eyed each other with primal fury. On one side, the enormous gorilla, its jet fur matted with silver streaks and brown dirt, clutched the rocky ceiling with its powerful hands and feet, swinging from root to vine to stalactite with agile grace. On the other side, the monstrous snake, its forest-green white-spotted scales shimmering with slime, briskly coiled and uncoiled around the jagged pillars and spires of the cave in a constant sliding movement, flicking its forked tongue with sinister malice. The *Minnow* sailed nervously between them, dodging the falling, flying debris and avoiding the stone obstacles threatening to destroy it. The crew knew they were in grave danger, caught in the crossfire of a titanic clash that could erupt at any moment. They needed to escape before the beasts unleashed their full wrath on each other and them.

"Do something!" Mia shouted to Garrison.

To flee being caught between them, the only immediate way to avoid the two monstrosities was to fly the skyship through a stone ring straight ahead. The crimson propulsion sails were adjusted, dipping downward for a steep descent. The *Minnow* responded, diving towards the patchwork ground with a short burst of speed. The wind howled in their ears; the ground and stone ring rushed up to meet them. They could see every crack and crevice in the stone ring as they approached it. At the last moment, Garrison pulled the lever, raising the propulsion sails again. The skyship leveled off, barely skimming the jagged surface of the stone ring as the craft soared through it.

Once clear of the rocky overpass, the giant fifteen-foot silverback suddenly appeared and swung nearby on the port side of the *Minnow*. It grabbed the broken-off end of a stalactite and hurled the pointed rock with all its might at the opposing snake like a deadly spear. The rocky spear came streaking past the bow of the skyship, nearly striking the vessel down from the air. The rock also missed the intended target. The elusive giant anaconda was too quick and agile, slithering along the roots and vines. The rock shattered against the cavern wall.

The snake constantly moved, slithered, and blended into the safe confines of the twisted brown vines, dense green foliage, and mangled chestnut roots. It repeatedly tried to strike at the rapidly prowling, shaggy opponent from a safe distance. The immense gorilla angrily pounced around the chamber, bellowing with rage and flashing its fangs. It pounded its chest like it was tired of playing hide-and-seek and was ready for a straight-on brawl.

The *Minnow* zigzagged forward through the chamber, forced to interweave a course through the shifting battle and the thick and twisted moss-covered roots that hung like vines in their way. First, the vines and roots swayed and snapped as the *Minnow* forcefully brushed past them, scraping and scratching the wooden hull. Likewise, the skyship had to be careful not to crash into the multiple rocks that crumbled from the events of the fight, some as big as boulders falling from the walls and ceiling of the cave. The tumbling rocks echoed loudly as they hit the ground, sending tan dust and debris flying upwards. The dust created a light, unnatural fog covering the chamber full of sharp spikes, some pointing up from the floor and some dangling down from above. The *Minnow* broke through the thin, dusty veil and maneuvered around the spikes, using its propulsion wings and rudder tail to steer and balance the craft.

The skyship flew swiftly through the air, but suddenly, a loud thud shook the craft as the lumbering, mighty gorilla grazed its hull with a massive swinging fist. The *Minnow* forcefully veered off course, smashing into a jagged, elongated root that shattered into splinters, sending debris flying wildly. It managed to break through the entire natural obstacle and regain its balance from the collision on the other side of the barrier, floating away from the immediate danger zone.

An unnatural, chilling, animalistic scream echoed throughout the cavern. The crew of the *Minnow* looked behind them to see the giant serpent wrapped once around the torso of its mighty enemy, sinking its fangs deep into the gorilla's, robust shoulder with unyielding force. In a display of unbridled, raw power, the fifteen-foot silverback gorilla hammered the serpent's flat head with powerful fists. Yet the snake clung on tenaciously.

In a desperate bid for freedom, the gorilla grasped a hefty root with its muscular arm, tearing it from the cavern ceiling. With relentless ferocity, the gorilla attempted to stab and impale the snake multiple times with the sharp root. After three mighty blows, the snake was forced to uncoil itself from the girthy, hairy torso and retreat into hiding within the enshrouding gloom of the thick green underbrush.

Stunned and wounded, the giant gorilla grunted loudly and huffed as he attempted to regroup, channeling his remaining primal strength to navigate the chamber's wild labyrinth. With each powerful swing, he clutched at giant roots, vines, and stalactites, searching for the hidden, giant anaconda. Amidst this swinging, the lethal serpent emerged from its arboreal concealment, striking with the precision of a silent assassin. Its fangs sank deep into the gorilla's left leg, a deadly embrace that sought to claim victory over brawn.

The sinuous specter coiled with deceptive grace around the mighty leg, its green-scaled tail ascending with an ominous intent. But the silverback gorilla, a titan amongst beasts, responded with a howl that echoed through the chamber's depths. He seized the snake by its slender neck with a swift motion born of desperation and fury. The struggle was palpable; the gorilla's grip was an unyielding vise against the serpent's hissing protest.

As the *Minnow* neared the end of the chamber, the entire area succumbed to unbridled havoc. Stalactites snapped from their ancient perches, falling to the ground and grazing the fragile vessel with their jagged edges. Once proud and stoic for decades, stalagmites now swayed dangerously from their foundations or toppled over. They threatened to crush or impale the tiny craft as it methodically swerved and veered around them. Amidst the tumult, a landslide from one side of the cavern was unleashed, creating a wave of boulders that nearly struck the passing vessel down and shrouded the tumultuous scene in a thin veil of pewter dust.

As they left the chamber, the final glimpse of the animalistic destruction by the crew of the *Minnow* was one of primal fury: two behemoths locked in a lethal embrace, their battle undeterred by the secret, hidden world crumbling around them.

The *Minnow*, though bold in its efforts to get through the cavern, was now battered and bore the scars of the colossal clash. Once reaching ambitiously towards the heavens, one mast was now splintered into two. The grey hot-air balloon, the ship's breath and buoyancy, clung to its purpose despite the tear in its fabric. The rudder sail, essential for navigation through the skies, stood wounded yet resolute. Nevertheless, the unique cog skyship embarked towards the next chamber. Hopefully, a haven of safety amidst the perils.

"We're losing altitude," Suzu said in an alarmed tone.

"The magitite burner is damaged!" Garrison shouted.

"Repair it quickly, or we'll crash on those boulders below," Mia said.

A new silent peril unfurled; the brittle vessel faced the insidious threat of a gradual descent. It was as if unseen forces were tugging the skyship downward, each moment bringing it perilously closer to the jagged caress of the numerous rocks that hungered below. The crew, aware of their dire straits, scrambled with genuine urgency. The *Minnow* now teetered on the brink of becoming wreckage.

"Hogart, take the pilot's position. I'll repair the burner," Garrison said. Without a response, he disappeared into the lower decks.

"What's that sound?" Mia asked.

"Sounds like rushing water," Suzu said.

In the cavern's dimly lit expanse, they spotted possible salvation in the form of a vast swift-moving river. Though wounded by its arduous journey and flying perilously low, the *Minnow* limped through the air and slowly descended towards the welcoming embrace of the water. The battered wooden hull barely skirted a treacherous stretch of rocks before it triumphantly cleared the final rocky spires and finally dropped towards the running water. The *Minnow* crashed into the river with a dramatic splash, half by skill, half by sheer fortune.

Berry-blue water furiously crashed over the guardrails, drenching the upper deck in small waves and a wild spray. The relentless, turbulent current seized the *Minnow*, propelling it at an alarming speed through the shadowy tunnel. Moderate waves, adorned with frothy white crests, rose and fell with a rhythmic fury before the broken bowsprit, snapping it free. At the same time, dangerous, jagged rock formations loomed ominously within the rushing water and along the river's edge, ready to shred the ship apart.

Hogart did his best to guide the battered craft, an example of his years of skillful navigation, whether in the water or air. But despite his best efforts, the ship suffered damage. The *Minnow*'s port hull grazed a cluster of jagged stones, rebounding with a resilient shudder that echoed through its fragile frame. As the vessel forged ahead, its bow performed a delicate dance, bobbing rhythmically up and down with the ocean's pulse. Suddenly, the *Minnow*'s port bow collided with the curved arm of a rocky barrier, its wooden skin screeching against the abrasive surface. At the same time, the relentless tide continued to push it mercilessly onward. The bow plunged into the watery depths, scooping up a burst of brine that showered the deck in a salty mist. The crimson port propulsion sail was torn away, lost to the whims of the water, leaving a trail of tattered remnants fluttering in its wake like a trail of blood.

The *Minnow* was deftly swept between two jagged rocks that jutted out like the fangs of some monstrous beast, a quick reminder of the deadly encounter they'd just survived. With a skilled last-second maneuver by Hogart, the ship narrowly avoided the rocks' rugged embrace, escaping the clutches of the twin, craggy jaws.

No sooner did they pass this perilous strait than a colossal rock formation loomed directly ahead, rising ominously from the midst of the turbulent river like a titan from the depths. With another swift and decisive maneuver, Hogart veered towards the solitary sentinel, the vessel's remaining starboard propulsion sail billowing like the wings of an angel. The *Minnow* angled itself towards a slender gap on one side of the monolithic obstacle, its port side grazing the rough surface, kissing the stone with a screech that echoed through the dank air.

Undeterred, the vessel continued its treacherous journey downstream, still flirting with a cluster of tiny stony obstacles scattered wide and far in its path. The broken hull bounced against a cluster of smaller rocks in a futile attempt to avoid further damage or danger. Each contact off a small boulder or stone sent the *Minnow* spiraling, twirling in a ballet of confusion on the wild waters, like a small ball bouncing off pins. After the stretch of small rocks, the skyship was careening sideways down the waterway, lurching violently, churning the waters around it into a frothy maelstrom.

With one jarring impact against the timeworn timber hull, Mia was flung against the ship's guardrail, teetering perilously on the brink over the churning, foamy river below. Suzu's quick reflexes come to her rescue as she snatched Mia from the jaws of the watery void, anchoring her safely back onto the sodden deck. Together, they staggered to hold themselves upright, their feet betraying them on the slippery surface. They desperately clung to ropes and rails, anything that might spare them from being swallowed by the relentless river.

The boat heaved and groaned, its planks drenched as wave after wave crashed overboard, dousing them in the river's icy spray.

Hogart, in a valiant effort, continuously wrestled with the helm, his muscles straining as he attempted to align the bow with the relentless current, and then found that he had to readjust. The *Minnow* shook and trembled as the water below the hull transformed into a wild, swirling pool of frenzied, churning waves that tossed it to and fro.

The waves, infused with the tempest's power, thrust the *Minnow* across the width of the expansive river. Like a behemoth's hand rising from the depths and tossing the vessel away in disgust, a monstrous wave engulfed them, propelling them in a starboard direction towards an uncertain fate. The crew screamed as they glimpsed the foreboding silhouettes of rocks and boulders along the cavern wall. They rapidly approached an unavoidable obstacle course set by nature, helpless to do anything about it.

"Hogart! The rocks!" Suzu yelled.

Despite Hogart's best efforts, the ship's starboard side grazed the length of the rocks with a harrowing scrape, each glancing impact causing its hull to creak and shudder ominously. At the last deflection, the *Minnow* started to pirouette through the rapids, spinning into a dizzying rotation amidst the cold spray and milky foam. Several more times it spun, each turn a dance with disaster in the swift-moving rapids that sought to claim the craft as their own.

The *Minnow* went on, enduring a steep descent, teetering on the brink of capsizing at the nadir. Surprisingly propelled by its inherent buoyancy, it ascended abruptly from the river, only to be thrust forward again in an unrestrained advance. Along its committed trajectory lay several abrupt descents, almost like rolling waves, culminating in a steep plunge that concluded with an immense splash.

Hogart coughed for air. He was soaked to the bone, his long beige coat clinging to him. "Great idea!" he said. "I don't know how much more we can take!"

"We had no other choice!" Suzu yelled.

Mia dashed over to the living quarters and peered downward into the darkness. Water sloshed in the cabin, and the previous owner's personal items drifted around. Garrison was not seen but heard, clanking away with the burner, still trying to repair the balloon. "Garrison, faster on those repairs!" Mia shouted.

Suzu gasped deeply. "Look ahead!"

Every person on deck cast their eyes forward and looked equally terrified at the sight they beheld. The cavern's underground tunnel ended with a three-hundred-yard-wide opening that promised broad golden daylight and navy-blue skies ahead. But a boisterous rumbling was heard—the river swiftly disappearing over the tunnel's edge. A massive waterfall with a four-hundred-foot drop that would undoubtedly destroy the tiny *Minnow* was rapidly approaching.

"Garrison! We're approaching a waterfall!" Mia shouted.

Garrison's hands moved with a feverish urgency on the repairs, the sound of the roaring rapids thundering in his ears. Time was slipping away as the edge of the waterfall drew perilously close. With each passing second, the hope of reigniting the burner dimmed. The ship groaned, its frame sodden and heavy with the relentless grip of the river's embrace. Garrison knew that their chances of reigniting the burner were dwindling rapidly, as scarce as the chances of their survival. Yet he labored on, driven by a will that refused to yield to the looming descent.

Perilously perched at the precipice of the waterfall, the *Minnow* quivered and teetered, a mere breath away from catastrophe. It strained and buckled to resist the raging water current as it was dangerously close to falling over into the stirring, ghostly, foaming waves below. The waterfall's edge acted like a fierce natural boundary between salvation and doom for a brief time, refusing to let the skyship fall but also wanting to tip it over the edge. With each passing moment, the threat intensified; the monstrous roar of the rushing water was a constant reminder of the watery pit that waited below and wanted to swallow the vessel.

"I think I got it!" Garrison shouted. Though not fully mended, the burner miraculously sparked to life, igniting the balloon with a fierce blue-white blaze.

The beleaguered merchant skyship, buffeted by the relentless onslaught of waves against the brittle, beaten hull, was finally thrust from the waterfall's brink. It began a dangerous, tilting descent, dipped sharply downward, and then dived freely towards the churning pit below. Yet, by some stroke of fortune, the patchwork repairs were just enough, in time, and able to hold. With a sudden lurch and a newfound steadiness, the *Minnow* righted itself, narrowly escaping the waterfall's four-hundred-foot drop and the bottom's whirlpool-like, deadly embrace. It flittered through the air, its movements erratic as a bird with a clipped wing, spiraling uncontrollably away from the waterfall's gaping maw and towards the outstretched river's more placid waters just beyond.

The *Minnow* crashed with a loud thud and triumphant splash of water into the middle of the river beyond the waterfall. The skyship, once a simple merchant vessel soaring dutifully through the clouds, now lay crippled and groaning. The remains of the wooden framework were being pushed downstream by the relentless assault from the continuous waves of the waterfall's base. The surrounding forest air was rich with a watery mist, and the creaks and moans of the dying vessel punctuated the sound of rushing water.

The crew on board found themselves in another dire predicament as the *Minnow* began its slow, steady descent into the river's watery grave. Water rushed into the cabin and lower decks like a ravenous beast, eager to claim the skyship for the depths. Everyone knew they had minutes to act; their lives hung in the balance as the *Minnow*, torn red sails, depleted grey balloon, and shattered hull slowly succumbed to the river's cold embrace.

Beneath the river's tranquil guise, an enigmatic dinosaur's graphite spines, almost like sails, and long, narrow, spined tail with a paddlelike tip silently rose from the water's murky depths. It disrupted the serene surface, observed the newly arrived vessel and its occupants, and slipped back under the water's surface without being noticed.

Moments later, a sudden jolt underneath the water rocked the skyship wreckage, sending the passengers tumbling across the deck. From the turbulent waters, a spinosaurus revealed itself—its scales a canvas of dark and light-grey hues, its belly a pale yellow, while deep iris marked its visage and spine, trailing to the tail's tip. It bellowed a primordial roar, water cascading from its massive form as it shook its head, a display of primal vexation echoing through the mist.

"This way!" Mia yelled.

The passengers scrambled like rats on a sinking ship, desperately needing to get off the imperiled craft but also wanting to avoid the eyesight of the colossal spinosaurus that was ready to attack at the first sight of them. Impatient and hungry for a meal, the spinosaurus's massive jaws tore through the broken wooden vessel, sending shards of timber spiraling through the air, narrowly missing the frantic crew.

"Hold on!" Hogart yelled.

With a swipe of the dinosaur's mighty enlarged claws, the *Minnow* was overturned, now adrift on its side in the river. The spinosaurus savaged the craft with tooth and claw, pushing it around the water before disdainfully flinging a chunk of broken wood into the distance.

As the spinosaurus's three-clawed hand flipped the *Minnow* over, the crew clung desperately to guardrails of the upper deck and went around with it. The vessel that had once carried them was now a colossal weight above them, its shadowy form an ominous barrier between them and life-giving air. Under the water, they struggled to swim out of the path of the skyship that was sinking on top of them. With each passing second under the water's cold embrace, they battled against the pull of the sinking vessel, their lungs screaming for air. Above them, the wreckage of the *Minnow* continued to tumble and turn.

Above the water, the crocodilian behemoth continued its relentless assault on the *Minnow*, ferociously tearing into the vessel's hull. Each bite was catastrophic, sending the ship careening deeper into the gloomy depths, only to rise again to the surface in a desperate struggle for survival. The annoyed dinosaur prowled along the flank of the beleaguered craft, seeking any sign of life to emerge from within. Its growls reverberated through the air and water, a primal sound heralding danger. With sharp claws that churned the river into frothy white foam, it searched with unyielding intent, splashing waves in its wake. The beast's long snout plunged into the depths as it scoured for prey, and its roar echoed again when the search was futile.

Beneath the undulating waves, Suzu was trapped in a dire predicament. The sinking *Minnow* cast a dark shadow on her petite frame as vast as the ocean's depths. Desperation clawed at her lungs, and she battled against the relentless pull of the water dragging her farther under. She was losing air and strength, her head swaying into darkness.

Yet Mia's grasp was steadfast. With a strength born of camaraderie from the last couple of days together, despite any differences they may have had before, Mia clasped tightly onto Suzu's flailing hand. Together, the two women navigated through the aquatic labyrinth of falling wood, barrels, and crates. Safely away from the *Minnow*'s descent, the two women swam onward towards the promise of air and freedom in the pearly sparkle above the river's surface.

They emerged from underwater, gasping and panting for breath. Treading water, they frantically looked around at their surroundings. Garrison's swimming strokes cut through the lapping waves, his athletic, lean figure a beacon of hope that someone else had survived the crash as he moved towards them. Yet, in their hearts, a cold dread settled; Hogart and Mozo were nowhere to be seen. With the *Minnow*'s remnants being devoured by the monstrous entity, the trio gathered together, paddling fervently away from the mess that sought to claim them, too.

"Move faster!" Garrison cried.

"Where's Hogart?" Suzu shouted. "I'll kill him myself if he's dead."

"Mozo!" Mia screamed. "Where are you? Mozo!"

The towering and formidable spinosaurus locked its gaze on the trio yelling and treading water, instinctively sensing their vulnerability. With a sinister rumble that echoed through the heavy forest air, it began its deliberate approach towards them, circling the slowly descending skyship. The three swimmers, acutely aware of the coming threat, kicked into action, their strokes distressed and swift as they swam towards the distant promise of possible safety on the shoreline.

Mozo suddenly emerged from the depths of the turbulent water nearby, startling the swimmers. With a protective instinct as deep as the river he had surfaced from, Mozo faced the bigger spinosaurus. A scarlet blast of fire erupted from his maw, igniting the destroyed *Minnow* and forming a blazing barrier. The swimmers seized their chance, slipping away as Mozo's fiery dragon breath held the enormous beast at bay, blocking it from the escaping swimmers.

Hogart emerged from the depths, gasping loudly, his senses reeling under the crimson blaze of the fallen *Minnow*. Water filled his lungs, and his long tan coat floated up and wrapped itself around him like a blanket. Panic gripped him as he flailed for salvation amidst the chaos.

Desperately, Hogart clutched at the tilted skyship's wooden railing, the heat of the flames licking his skin. He shouted at the sting of the red-hot flames, instinctively detached from the boat, and splashed about in the water. Drifting a few feet away from the vessel, he got tangled in the mast lines floating on top of the water. Now entwined in the mast's treacherous lines, which danced on the water like eels coiling around his legs and torso, Hogart fought to free himself and avoid being dragged underwater with the sinking ship.

The spinosaurus zeroed in on what seemed like an effortless feast. Hogart, busy trying to separate the ropes and unaware of the looming threat, found himself in a precarious situation as the primal creature advanced on him. With a mighty heave, the dinosaur's razor claws scraped against the side of the boat, its massive head thudding against the vessel in a desperate bid to dislodge Hogart from his precarious perch. The *Minnow's* remains groaned under the spinosaurus's weight as it tipped the bow underwater, and its long tail thrashed, sending violent ripples through the water to shake free its anticipated prey.

Hogart's perilous predicament took an unpredictable turn. Just as the jaws of the spinosaurus threatened to clamp down on his hefty form, a sudden barrage of flaming arrows whizzed through the air, striking the beast squarely in its massive visage. The spinosaurus, caught off guard by this fiery assault, recoiled in bewilderment, granting Hogart a moment's respite. Another wave of numerous arrows, ablaze with unyielding ruby fire, rained down on the creature from hidden saviors, each impact causing the dinosaur to retreat farther from the desperate swimmers.

Amidst this unforeseen intervention, the persevering *Minnow* became an unintended target, its sinking wreckage now alight with spreading, wild flames. The entire structure of the cog skyship was punctured with arrows and ablaze, creating a natural fiery barrier on the water. The spinosaurus looked down on the rising flames nipping at its scales and roared in disgust. It shook its head violently, turned to leave the river, and then stomped off into the forest foliage.

With sheer determination and a little bit of luck, Hogart wriggled free from the twisted, smoldering mast ropes that once bound him to the flaming, sinking *Minnow*. Gasping for air and fueled by adrenaline, he propelled himself away from the brightly burning wreckage and swam through the water's cold embrace, making his way to the shoreline to join his friends.

Valsco

ogart's arms and legs were exhausted, the strength leaving him to the point where a small wave washed him up on the tan beach. He crawled forward on the sand like a lazy lizard until his shoulder hit a pair of small black boots. He wearily looked up, squinting his brown eyes to see the familiar form of a petite, jet-haired, olive-skinned woman looking disapprovingly down at him.

"Get up," Suzu said. "You're embarrassing me."

Hogart groaned softly and unhurriedly stood up next to Suzu, wiping the blend of river water and particles of fine sand away from his scruffy, round face. He could see his companion was not in a joking mood, her posture fixed for an attack. On the other side, a stern-looking and alarmed Garrison also appeared and stood vigilant beside him. At the forefront, Mia stood resolute, her silhouette outlined by the rising dandelion sun. The dragonet, Mozo, perched stoically on her shoulder, mirroring her readiness, while her sword gleamed menacingly in the morning sunlight.

Six soldiers of the Kayawa Empire, each mounted on a warhorse, surrounded the trespassers who had washed up on their coastline.

Each soldier was outfitted with silvery light shoulder and arm armor that led to black gauntlets. Their breastplates were a deep plum. Their thigh armor was black, just like their boots. Every man and woman carried an amber-tinged shield and a long silver sword. They formed a semicircle before the beleaguered group, the rumbling river behind them, so they were trapped, and there was no escape. The six riders were spread across the shore on their mounts an equal distance, but parted in the middle to allow a seventh rider to pass through.

An older white man, appearing physically fit for his late fifties, balding on top with close-cropped gray hair on the sides, rode in the center of the semicircle. He was also dressed in the same lightweight armor as the other riders. The only difference was that the chestplate was emerald, signifying a greater rank. His tiny flint eyes looked over the motley crew, specifically Mia and the small dragon poised on her shoulder to strike anyone at the slightest command. "Good morning," the man said calmly and evenly. "My name is Edburn Hardt, Kayawa Captain of the Guard. I would like to speak to you in private."

Mia slid her blade back into its sheath with a soft click. Her fingers found a spot between the two small curved horns protruding from the back of Mozo's head, lightly stroking it in gentle reassurance. With a silent nod, she sealed her unspoken accord.

Captain Hardt, meanwhile, descended from his steed, his boots thudding softly on the ground. He gave Mia a patient look that beckoned her without words. Side by side, they stepped away from the semicircle of Kayawa soldiers that parted like the sea, leaving the remaining trio rooted in confusion and curiosity.

Beyond the soldiers' human shield, the barricade snapped back into place with military precision, sealing off any stray whispers of the clandestine exchange that was about to unfold.

"What's this?" Hogart mumbled.

"I don't know," Suzu said softly.

"Maybe you were right about her from the beginning, my friend."

"Just when I thought we were getting along."

"Relax, both of you," Garrison said, his voice reassuring. "I believe we're in good company."

After enduring unnerving moments that stretched like hours, Mia finally inclined her head in a formal bow, signaling a silent concord. With measured steps, Captain Hardt retreated to the river's edge, where the rest of the waterlogged group awaited his counsel. The Kayawa horse riders seamlessly opened and closed ranks with the same military precision as he passed them. "You will come with us to Valsco, where you will be in the audience of King Kovlin."

"Very well," Garrison said. "Lead the way."

Captain Hardt mounted his steed, the subtle click of his tongue a familiar signal to the noble animal. Obediently, the horse pivoted, its hooves kicking up dust as it turned from the gentle lapping waves of the river. Behind them, the troops aligned themselves with precision, adopting a single-file formation that stretched back towards the water's edge. At the forefront, Mia was already striding confidently down a well-trodden dirt path, her steps sure and unwavering. Perched on her shoulder, Mozo seemed relaxed and surveyed their surroundings with keen eyes, his presence a silent guide for all who followed. The motley trio, seemingly forgotten about or of no concern, was at the convoy's tail end.

Within an hour of the journey, Suzu and Hogart noticed and silently acknowledged that Mia and Captain Hardt led the convoy together from at least fifty yards ahead. Walking side by side, they were constantly separated from everyone and appeared engaged in private conversation. The rest of the weary, lost group was escorted by the six Kayawa riders in front of them.

The caravan meandered tirelessly, a singular line etching its path across the expanse of nature's canvas. For what felt like an eternity, they traversed the vibrant tapestry of the verdant grasslands, where the hills rolled like gentle waves, and the plains stretched like endless seas. On the horizon, the sky kissed the ground in a tranquil aqua, while at their feet, a riot of wildflowers danced in the breeze, flares of bright marmalade, honey, and rose igniting amidst the lime-green grass. It was a world unmarred by time, a picturesque serenity that cradled their weary souls.

Hours later, as the radiant vermilion sun descended behind the distant horizon, casting a warm golden glow, the magisterial city of Valsco emerged amidst the lush meadows that swayed gently in the early evening breeze. The majority of structures were perched on a steep ledge above an expansive floodplain, which teemed with diverse flora and fauna. On the eastern shores, a collection of edifices clung to the robust banks of the Tain River bordering three cascading waterfalls that roar with vitality. To the west, the serene azure waters of an immense placid lake extended into the horizon, reflecting the sky's fiery palette and inviting peaceful contemplation. The architecture was sophisticated and harmonious, with elegant spires that reached towards the heavens and walls that echoed with history, integrating seamlessly with the natural surroundings and in unity with nature's grand tapestry.

Their senses were utterly overwhelmed by the lordly sight before them. Valsco, a sprawling cosmopolitan capital, loomed large, dwarfing most cities they had witnessed in their lifetimes. Esteemed by many travelers as a pinnacle of culture, Valsco boasted elegant architecture that sung in a unified, harmonious style. Its buildings, crowned with jade domes, exuded a handcrafted charm; proud tan ramparts stood guard; great swordlike spires reached for the heavens; and shining citadels highlighted the city's artisanship. High mooring towers with long observation platforms punctuated the skyline, offering panoramic views of the bustling streets below. The city's architectural unity was further exemplified by its sandstone-like block buildings, each roofed with chartreuse shingles that glistened under the sun's caress.

The company advanced steadily towards civilization, transitioning from the rugged dirt path to the city's structured cobblestone avenues. Without hesitation, they traversed the welcoming archway, guarded yet inviting, and emerged into the vibrant heart of a bustling metropolis. The warm wind resonated with the harmonious buzz of contented citizens, their laughter weaving through the streets like a melodious symphony, reflecting the city's flourishing spirit and communal joy.

The caravan pressed on with important business to attend, cutting through the labyrinthine heart of the ancient city. Towering tan stone walls rose on either side, casting long shadows over the cobbled streets that thrummed with life. Canopied litters carried by stoic bearers shuffled past, while merchants' calls melded into a cacophony of haggling over exotic wares. Monumental frost fountains sprayed a mist in flowing water droplets, and marbled statues stood sentinel, their gazes frozen in time. The atmosphere was heavy with the scent of exotic spices and the promise of knowledge wafting from small shops, grand museums, and hallowed universities.

Above, the sky was a tapestry of skyships acting as threads of commerce from distant lands, their hulls heavy with untold treasures. The riverport buzzed with activity as wealth from trade-minded neighbors was hoisted into towering mooring structures. Stables were bursting with horses and dinosaurs that needed food, caring, and rest.

On the ground, a symphony of movement played out; horse riders darted between slow-moving wagons while dinosaurs—brachiosauruses and triceratops—lumbered alongside them, their massive forms a stark contrast to the delicate dance of life around them. They pulled along objects of all shapes and sizes, contributing to the city's pulse—a rhythm set by the tireless beat of progress and time.

The escorted company came on a magnificent water fountain that danced with life before the marbled steps of the royal palace, its spray glistening like diamonds in the sun. The royal palace was a sprawling complex crafted from sandstone-hued blocks that rose into towers and rotundas, their cupolas sheathed in basil tiles. Dominating the complex was a triple-domed, drum-shaped colossus, overshadowed only by a slender tower that pierced the sky at the complex's zenith. Built against the sheer cliff face, the palace boasted numerous smaller watchtowers embedded in stone, where vigilant eyes scanned for threats from the valley's depths. It was the city's crown jewel, housing the monarch's family and welcoming foreign dignitaries with open arms.

Enveloping the regal abode, a sprawling garden unfurled its viridescent embrace. The entourage was ushered into a refined alfresco atrium, where the day's last light bled into the horizon, painting it with crimson, amber, and gold strokes. Regimented arbors stood sentinel, their foliage sculpted into living walls, while a mosaic of florals dappled the greenery with vibrant splashes of color—lilac, alabaster, amethyst, and cerulean. The chirping and chittering of birds flittering around was low, turning into a sweet, low birdsong.

A single bright cardinal carpet, rich in hue and soft to the touch, led to a grand, round, two-level dais in the center of the courtyard. This elevated platform was adorned with intricate patterns and symbols of power etched into its surface. On that dais sat a dignified gold throne, its frame glistening with the promise of authority and its burgundy cushions plush with velvet, inviting yet imposing. On the throne sat a single man garbed in regal robes that cascaded in folds of deep purples and shimmering golds. He was a handsome, bald, older gentleman. His white skin was etched with the faint lines of time, yet his thin, athletic build spoke of a disciplined life. Though he stood a couple of inches shorter than six feet, his presence filled the courtyard, his hazel eyes holding years of wisdom, and his strong and direct voice commanding attention with every word spoken. "I am King Kovlin of Kayawa," he said.

Mia strode with purpose, her gaze fixed on the grand throne ahead. As she approached, the murmurs of the court faded into hushed reverence. With a graceful fluidity born of deep respect, she lowered herself onto one knee; her head bowed in deference to the sovereign who commanded the room with an air of benevolent authority. "My lord, my name is Princess Karamia Vitta of Itonia. My father, King Jelia, sent me to ask for your help against the common threat of the advancing warmongering Zamana Empire."

"Princess?" Hogart said.

Suzu scoffed. "I knew there was something off about her."

"Princess Karamia," King Kovlin announced in a booming voice so all in the courtyard and beyond could hear. "From what I understand, I should be the one asking for your help."

Karamia stood stunned. "I don't understand, my lord."

"The state of the war has changed thanks greatly to you. It has been heard throughout all the lands of the daring young woman, along with a certain small dragon, freeing the innocent people held at Black Rock."

Suzu whispered harshly to Hogart, "She had help."

Hogart quietly shushed his counterpart, not wanting to raise anyone's ire.

"The result of the slave revolt at Black Rock is that the Zamana Empire's sea and air strength is now weakened," the king said. "The Zamana Empire has been placed in a position where they must completely withdraw from some occupied territories or cease their advances altogether. Well done."

"I am humbled by your words, my lord." Princess Karamia bowed.

Garrison felt a surge of urgency coming over him, compelling him to move boldly. Though possibly perceived as lacking courtesy, his actions were driven by a pressing need to act. "My lord, my name is Garrison—a Relic Hunter."

"Relic Raider, you mean," King Kovlin said. A slight, sharp undertone of disgust, annoyance, or deep mistrust was placed on the stigma of the title.

Garrison paused momentarily, flinching at the harsh directness of the derogatory label, and then found his voice. "There is a new threat that we must address. The hidden Kingdom of Tavter has been found."

"Indeed," the king said. "I had heard the rumor of that accursed city's resurrection days ago. I sent out a squadron of my best men to investigate. When my squadron arrived, scavengers and raiders were on the streets, looking to pillage anything they could find." King Kovlin looked directly at Garrison, almost accusingly. "You were too late, Relic Raider. There is evidence that bandits and thieves have already looted the treasure crypt. The Elemental Gemstone, the Land Gem, is missing from the terrible, wretched hand of the tyrannical despot King Dolaf."

Hogart and Suzu shifted uncomfortably on hearing those words. All they had ever sought through their endeavors was wealth and the kind of renown that comes with daring exploits. Yet their relentless pursuit of such treasures and vivid narratives of adventure had inadvertently steered the world towards a perilous and dismal fate. With heavy hearts and a silence born of regret, they acknowledged the possibility that their actions might have been a terrible mistake.

Then Hogart nudged Suzu slightly, giving her a reassuring nod and an acknowledging wink that their endless running and lustful quest for fortune and glory had finally ended. Suzu softly sighed, shrugged her slender shoulders, and nodded in agreement.

She advanced to the forefront with an adamant stride, positioning herself alongside Garrison and Princess Karamia. She reached into her V-necked tunic and delicately grasped the silver chain resting around her neck, bringing it out for all to see. A gentle press of the vibrant ruby and sapphire buttons on her ornate jewelry box in a specific sequence was followed by its unhinging, revealing the concealed emerald gemstone to the assembly gathered. "My lord Kovlin, the Land Gemstone is not missing. It's right here."

A furor went through the crowd like lightning, electrifying the atmosphere with anticipation and excitement. The atmosphere grew teeming with whispers, each word crackling with energy as it passed from one person to the next. It was as if the ground beneath their feet hummed with the collective pulse of their eager hearts.

"You're the ones that stole it!" the king growled.

"Stole?" Suzu said, acting surprised. "S-s-stole . . . ?"

"No, no, Your Highness," Hogart stammered. He came shooting to the side of his partner in plunder in verbal defense. "Safekeeping. My friend and I came on this little beauty; we knew it was a rarity, and would be important."

"So we kept it safe and traveled through many dangers, too numerous to count, may I add, to present it to you," Suzu added.

The king scoffed. "Oh?"

"For a . . . he-he . . . a small reward . . . Your Highness?" Hogart sputtered.

"If you . . . um . . . ah . . . feel so generous . . ." Suzu added.

The king stood tall from his throne and bellowed in a disgusted, loud voice. His eyes, fierce with authority, pierced the pair of misfits, who cowered under his gaze. "The fact that the two of you get to keep your heads should be reward enough!"

Suzu and Hogart bowed low. "Yes, my lord. Of course."

With deliberate care, Garrison lifted the gemstone from Suzu's open palm and examined it closely. Its surface was a tapestry of intricate cuts, each reflecting the sunlight in a dance of sparkling greens that rivaled the lushness of a spring meadow. He peered into its translucent heart, keen eyes tracing the delicate inclusions that whispered tales of the ancient world and time-locked secrets. The gem seemed to pulse with an inner life, its edges catching the light and throwing it back with enhanced vigor, as if it held a fragment of the very soul of nature. "It is true. This is one of the Elemental Gemstones, representing the land."

"We didn't know what we had with us, Your Highness," Hogart blurted defensively.

"What exactly is an Elemental Gemstone?" Suzu asked.

"The Dragon Wars were nearly a hundred years ago," Garrison said. "The Demon-God King, Shaitain, had a dark influence over King Dolaf of Tavter and tainted his mind with madness. In the name of the Demon-God King, the armies of Tavter waged war for years against the rest of the world. Losing the war, King Dolaf was directed by his master to look for supernatural means to conquer the world. When gathered together, the Elemental Gemstones have been rumored to open gateways to different worlds, dimensions, and planes of existence. King Dolaf was nearly successful in gathering all of them. However, an international band of exceptional individuals formed an inspiring team for the world: the Company of Heroes. They put aside their differences and stopped the armies of darkness."

"Why was this gemstone left in the hands of the tyrant king?" Hogart asked.

"At the end of the Dragon Wars, the four gemstones were separated, but the Land Gemstone was still in King Dolaf's possession. The Kingdom of Tavter isolated itself from the rest of the world. The mad king sat alone on his throne in a treasure vault, desperately clutching the Land Gemstone, vowing to fulfill his oath to his dark master, ignoring all the other surrounding valuable treasures he had stolen. As punishment and to eliminate the further risk of danger to the world, the Kingdom of Tavter was sentenced to vanish by the sorceress Laurisia's spell."

"And then these two misfits found it?" King Kovlin said.

"There have been rumors that Tavter can only be found with a magical artifact that honors a spearman named Lars Sill, one of the Company of Heroes, killed in the last battle," Garrison said. "A memorial statue of Lars Sill was built, with him holding his famous spear in his honor. Laurisia charmed the spear's tip and broke it off to signal the war's end. Due to his personal beliefs that life began anew with each dawning day, the artifact must be at the statue at sunrise for the Hidden Kingdom to be resurrected."

"And how did you two fools come about this important discovery?" King Kovlin asked.

The uncanny, mismatched duo looked at each other and shrugged. "Gambling."

King Kovlin scoffed loudly and waved his hand in disgust. "No matter. We are to travel to Tavter tomorrow morning. An emergency special council has been called amongst various countries to decide what to do with Tavter's proper and rightful ownership. You are all required to go with me. The Land Elemental Gemstone as well."

◆

The following day, under an indigo sky with greyish clouds, the weary group gathered to embark on the final leg of their arduous journey, returning to the Kingdom of Tavter. They congregated on the grand observation platform, which offered panoramic views of the sprawling kingdom below. They anxiously boarded the regal galleon skyship, an elegant vessel named *Royal Grace* adorned with the kingdom's colors and emblems, ready to soar through the skies.

The Kayawa sky flagship was a breathtaking craft. Its turquoise hull gleamed with polished silver trim and gold-leaf accents that reflected the sun's rays. The skyship's massive turquoise balloon boasted a white imprint design, and its gondola was crafted from the finest woods, fitted with large windows that offered views of the heavens and the landscape alike.

They ascended into the heavenly expanse, the *Royal Grace* an elegant silhouette against the sprawling sky canvas. Below, a mosaic of sapphire and turquoise lakes shimmered, bordered by forests ablaze with the beginning of autumn's fiery palette. With its billowing white sails and intricate rigging, the skyship floated over the undulating mountain range, its long shadow fleeting over the amber and crimson foliage. It continued its voyage across the jagged peaks that marked the realm's edge, venturing into the bordering country.

Hours later, the group beheld the spires, towers, and domes of the resurrected kingdom of Tavter looming ahead on the horizon. Encircling the resurrected kingdom were sprawling war camps. The outskirts were dotted with the encampments of various nations, each marked by their distinctive banners, fluttering symbols of their country. Amidst them, campfires flickered like stars fallen to earth, horses gathered close for warmth and sustenance, and guards stood in silent vigil. Overhead, a mere handful of skyships from different nations drifted, acting as silent sentinels in the sky.

Amidst the encampments, the notorious Zamana Empire's war tents, stamped with the dragon emblem, stood ominously, their presence a dark stain amongst the others. Within this foreboding atmosphere, Commander Tomap Sruz was observed in earnest discourse with a select few, their heads bowed in clandestine conversation. The Mistress of the Dark Arts was not visible, but a cold shiver ran down Mia's spine, knowing perhaps she was still alive and nearby.

Princess Karamia looked over the bustling camps, eyes scanning the vibrant throng for a hint of familiarity. The breeze was plentiful with the scents of campfire food, the melody of music, and the sounds of men and women alive with celebration. Yet, amidst the sea of faces and flurry of different languages, she searched for a symbol, any marker that whispered of her homeland. The flags that danced below in the gentle breeze were a mosaic of colors and patterns, but none bore the emblem she held dear in her heart. It was a poignant reminder that sometimes, even in a world so connected, one can feel like a solitary island adrift in an endless ocean.

The *Royal Grace* pulled in its propulsion sails and drifted purposefully towards the northern end of the old city. It descended towards a particular scaffolding platform, rapidly and crudely assembled, attached to an elegant, teal-domed, sand-colored square building. Mooring lines were tossed to the attendants waiting on the landing platform, securing the vessel. The ship docked, remaining adrift alongside the domed building, and lowered its ramp.

On the upper decks, Suzu and Hogart cautiously and optimistically approached a small gathering that was ready to depart for an immediate meeting—the Relic Hunter, the princess of Itonia, and the king of Kayawa—not knowing if they should approach at all. On sight, two greeted the pair with friendly smiles of camaraderie, while the last person looked on them disapprovingly with disdain.

"Princess Karamia is to come with me to the council meeting. The rest of you stay on board the *Royal Grace*," King Kovlin said.

"Forgive me, Your Highness, but I must come with you," Garrison said. "My knowledge of the gemstones may be useful to you in negotiations."

"Very well. But those two misfits stay here!"

"As you wish," Suzu and Hogart said together. They bowed low with courtesy. They were happy enough to be brought along and really had nothing to do with dignitaries of state anyway. They didn't mind being left behind momentarily on the skyship.

Princess Karamia walked down a set of stairs. She steadily and confidently strode towards the council chamber, her unannounced presence commanding the attention of all. King Kovlin, a figure of stoic authority, and Garrison accompanied her, their contours framed against the gleaming silver doors that guarded the entrance to the hallowed debating council chamber.

As they approached the threshold, a swift and discreet messenger approached King Kovlin. With a deference born of urgency, he leaned in to deliver his silent missive into the king's ear. The words spoken were unheard, but their significance was not lost; a subtle shift in the king's demeanor betrayed their weight. With a silent nod, an acknowledgment of the message's gravity, King Kovlin returned to Princess Karamia's side. There was a momentary exchange—a glance that spoke volumes in the silence between them. "I have the latest updates."

"Is my father present?"

"I have been informed that King Jelia has not arrived, Your Highness," King Kovlin said.

"What?" Mia said, alarmed. "Where is he?"

"He's on his way, but it will be hours before he arrives. Perhaps tonight at the earliest. I'm sorry, but we cannot wait any longer."

"But we have to wait until my father arrives."

"The others are impatient and, perhaps, fearful due to the turn in the state of the war with the Zamana Empire. They feel your country is well represented since you are here now, that you can make the decisions for your people."

Mia had always found solace in her father's wisdom, especially during the heated debates that shaped their kingdom's future. His absence at the upcoming discussion was a heavy burden, but Mia knew the crown's weight was now hers. As Princess Karamia, she would be forced to navigate the treacherous waters of politics, egos, and greed and make a decision that would steer the fate of her people in a positive direction. "I will," Mia said.

The silver doors swung wide, ushering the trio into a grand open chamber. Notably absent was any chair of prominence, a deliberate design proclaiming that here, within this noble court, all who gathered were peers, their voices carrying equal weight in the hallowed halls of discourse.

Dignitaries from all the lands in the region diplomatically greeted Princess Karamia as she walked in. Her presence surprisingly commanded the room, a silent symphony of respect and admiration flowing from every corner, especially after the recent events at Black Rock. Each bow and smile confirmed her unique grace and the peaceful harmony she brought to these diverse realms. Today, she was not just a princess; she embodied unity, a glimpse of hope in a divided world. As she took her place amongst the nobles, the summit of peace began.

"Are all the countries that are expected represented?" Chinsa, hailing from the esteemed country of Jasho, was a figure that also commanded attention. His stature was robust. His eyes, round and alert, were a deep black, like the midnight sky without its stars. His hair, equally dark, fell in a disciplined manner just above his shoulders. His smile was ever present, a bonfire of friendliness in a world that often lacked warmth. Adorned in a long robe of sienna, reminiscent of the earthy tones found in ancient Jasho tapestries, he stood proud. His charcoal shirt, which spoke of the impending dusk, completed his attire perfectly. The black pants and boots he wore were not just for show; they were the attire of a man ready for action at a moment's notice. Indeed, Chinsa bore the look of a noble warrior whose presence could change the course of history.

As if summoned by the question and an unseen force, the stately door at the chamber's far end flung open with a foreboding groan. A collective breath was held; the assembly of dignitaries stood frozen in silent anticipation. Into the hallowed space strode the youthful commander of the Zamana Empire, Tomap Sruz, his presence an ominous shadow that chilled the air. Sworn enemy to all, he commanded the chamber's attention with his mere arrival.

Tonio Ras, prince of the vibrant, dignified country of Thaimis, was the first to confront the new arrival. His slim build and medium height, highlighted by his jet hair and deep-mocha eyes, made him unmistakable. He wore a royal outfit in champagne and white tones, reflecting his innate elegance amidst the festive hustle. He stepped between Tomap and the assembly of delegates, providing a diplomatic shield. "Where is the witch that holds your leash, boy?"

"My country has suffered greatly at the hands of the Zamana Empire!" There stood a figure from the country of Fran—who seemed to have stepped out of a different era—a tall, skinny white man named Leon, his stature accentuated by the length of his long teal coat adorned with intricate brown embroidery that danced along the hem and cuffs like delicate vines. The coat flowed behind him as he moved, a whisper of elegance in the urban wilderness. His matching vest hugged his torso, its buttons gleaming like small, polished stones. Beneath it, a white puffy shirt billowed softly with each breath he took, its sleeves peeking out from under the coat's cuffs, frilled and free. Black boots, polished to a mirror shine, clicked against the marble floor, announcing his presence with each purposeful step. "What right do you have being here?"

Tomap stopped in the middle of the chamber. He gave all that surrounded him a hard, steady look as if he now commanded them as he would his soldiers. "I am here to claim what rightfully belongs to the Zamana Empire."

"Rubbish!" Leon cried out.

Chinsa took a brazen step towards Tomap. "If the claim to Tavter were that important to the self-proclaimed Mistress of the Dark Arts, she would have shown up herself."

"She is preoccupied in Black Rock rebuilding and overseeing the discipline of those that sought to overturn the Zamana Empire."

"You mean enslaving and torturing innocent people," Mia said.

"So, the hag overexerted herself, eh?" Chinsa said. His tone held a hint of suspicion, as if he wanted to explore a theory. "She needs time to recuperate after dabbling in the darker side of magic?"

Mia positioned herself next to Chinsa, displaying unity within the chamber against the Empire. "Keldace Vildan rose to power in a few years. She could not have done this without help. Whom does the Mistress of the Dark Arts serve?" Mia asked.

A cruel smile came across Tomap's lips. "Shaitain. The Demon-God King."

"Infidel!" Tonio Ras shouted. He drew his sword from its sheath.

In response, Tomap drew his sword as well. He pointed it at Tonio with a knowing smile, as if he had wanted the fight to happen all along. Tonio met his gaze, the atmosphere tense with the promise of impending battle. Around them, the dignitaries' clamor for peace became a distant echo, overshadowed by the gravity of the moment. Here, in the heart of the council chamber where peace accords were supposed to be signed, history would remember the clashing of wills as much as the clashing of swords.

A Passian woman commanded silence with a definitive bang of her staff that echoed through the chamber. She was none other than Elle Oh, whose elderly, petite stature belied her formidable presence. With a slim, athletic build, she moved with the grace of a seasoned performer, her chestnut eyes sparkling with intensity. Strands of grey interlaced with black in her hair served as a visual reminder of her experience and wisdom. Her attire was as striking as her demeanor. She was clad in a robed outfit that whispered of tradition and elegance. The lilac fabric draped over her form, adorned with a delicate floral arrangement that complemented her poise.

She was a vision of cultural heritage and contemporary strength, an embodiment of the rich tapestry that was Passi. "The Demon-God King was destroyed long ago. The threats of this crone, merely an apprentice to evil, are empty. She is nothing but a lost soul that will soon be taught respect. There is only the present business at hand."

"Who keeps the collected treasures of the Hidden Kingdom? More importantly, who rules the lost Kingdom of Tavter from this day forth?" From the heart of Gypro, amidst the timeless dunes and ancient pyramids, there stood a man draped in a tan cloak whose presence was as commanding as the towering monuments around him. Izzak, a name synonymous with the rich tapestry of the desert culture, carried the essence of his heritage with a dignified grace. He was six feet tall, with a stature that mirrored the grandiosity of the ocean sands itself. His hazel eyes held stories, reflecting a depth that was both enigmatic and inviting. With a slim build, he moved like a whispering breeze, his silhouette casting long shadows. "We should finish the task started long ago and burn it to the ground."

"Never! It's our city!" A midsize man called Vin stood firmly, his oily mustache a stark contrast against his fair skin. Balding on top, his stocky, stout frame carried an air of authority, hinting at a life of physical labor. Known for his short temper, he commanded respect and fear equally amongst the townsfolk. As the acting steward of Tavter, he bore the weight of his country's expectations on his broad shoulders. "It appeared in our territory by the magic of the sorceress Laurisia. The city, the historical significance of it, and all its riches are ours by right!"

"It is not yours or anyone else's! It was stolen from us!" From the rugged mountains of Cimmissia, where the air was as crisp as the untouched snow, a legend was born. Ah-knold, a man of imposing stature and undeniable presence, stood tall at six feet, two inches. His bodybuilder's physique, an exemplification to years of disciplined training, was accentuated by his striking blue eyes that mirrored the clear skies above. Adorned in scarlet with a gleaming golden collar, he wore attire that was a statement of power and a nod to tradition. The four straps connected to buttons across his chest were not just for show; they symbolized the four cardinal virtues he upheld in every aspect of his life. Completing his ensemble were black boots, which were sturdy and reliable, much like the man himself. "My country is ashamed of our past history with the Demon-God King. But not one of you can deny that we have persevered from those dark days, made amends, and have become a far better country."

"No one is denying the greatness that your country has contributed to the world. However, Tavter and all that comes with it cannot fall into the wrong hands." From the great country of Aliffica, even as a hologram magically emitting from a golden ring on the marble floor, the warlord Ames Te appeared, his presence commanding, his ebony skin a stark contrast to the piercing blue of his eyes. Standing six feet, two inches tall, his large, girthy frame mirrored Hogart's, exuding an aura of unyielding strength. His voice, low and deep, resonated with the power of his beautiful land. Long raven hair fell around his shoulders, framing his face and adding to his formidable appearance. Dressed in an all-black ensemble complemented by ashen armor that seemed to absorb the light around him, he carried himself with a warrior's grace. Two melee knives were strapped to his black belt, their hilts glinting subtly, hinting at the deadly skill of their bearer. "It was ruled by a tyrant that sought to end us all! Never again!"

The debates amongst the dignitaries raged on, each person drowning the other out of the conversation. In the gallant hall, voices clashed like swords, opinions as varied as the colors of a rainbow. The atmosphere was riotous with conviction, each statement a thread weaving into the fabric of discourse. There was no consensus in sight, yet the exchange was as vibrant as it was relentless, a passion that fueled their words.

Garrison walked silently out of the shadows, holding an emerald object alight in his hand to instantly gain the attention of all within the chamber. "Ladies and gentlemen, there is more to discuss than the possession of Tavter and its treasures."

The Land Elemental Gemstone, a symbol of the world's boundless bounty, was ceremoniously displayed before the assembly. This venerable relic, embodying the essence of terra firma, was unveiled to the collective awe of all present. Its multifaceted surface caught the light, casting prismatic shadows that danced like leaves in a gentle breeze. The stone's deep connection to the land was palpable, resonating with an ancient energy that whispered of verdant forests, sprawling mountains, and the untamed wilds that predated memory.

"The Land Gem!" Leon cried.

"One of the Elemental Gemstones," Tomap hissed.

Vin gasped. "It's come back to destroy us!"

The assembly hall buzzed with a low uneasy whisper amongst the gathered dignitaries. As tensions mounted, the whispers grew into pointed accusations, voices raised in heated dispute echoing off the hallowed walls with growing discord.

"May I make a suggestion that I believe will be agreeable to one and all?" Garrison said. His resolute voice broke through the swirling debates, gaining everyone's attention. "The Goldenwings Run. A fabled, dangerous long-distance horse race from decades ago will decide who gets to keep the Kingdom of Tavter and the Land Gem, one part of the four Elemental Gemstones. An obstacle course will be set throughout the streets of Tavter. One representative from each country. The finest equestrians from each country. Whoever is first to cross the finish, either rider or the country's horse without the rider, wins."

Within the grand chamber's walls, a resounding clamor arose as a multitude of voices crescendoed in unison, signaling a robust approval of the proposed idea.

"It is my duty, privilege, and honor to represent my people," Toni Ras said.

Ah-knold laughed loudly. "I will surely win for the glory of Cimmissia."

Mia inhaled sharply. "I am Princess Karamia Vitta of Itonia. I will race in the name of my country and will win against any tyrant in the name of freedom and peace."

Tomap flinched and then stiffened at the words. For him, a win was glory for the Zamana Empire, to capture the favor of Keldace Vildan, an assured promotion to captain, and a skyship of his own to conquer new lands. To lose was his death. There was not a third outcome. He looked at Mia, the young arrogant woman who led the revolt at Black Rock and, in his mind's eye, caused him to be in this unsettling position. A cruel smirk spread across his lips. "I accept any challenge to bring glory to the Zamana Empire."

"Then it is unanimously settled," Garrison said. "The Goldenwings Run will be at noon tomorrow."

⸺ ◆ ⸺

The silver half-moon appeared on a warm, peaceful night, and many white stars twinkled above the sienna desert landscape. Princess Karamia meandered solitarily through the resplendent terraces and gardens, her profile a solitary figure against the canvas of nature's artistry. A kaleidoscope of natural wildflowers danced in the warm breeze, their copper, freesia, and grape hues mingling with the serene light blue of sagebrush and the tranquil mint of shrubs.

Mia was an island unto herself in this moment of solitude, adrift in the sea of her private musings. As she wandered, doubt began to sprout within her mind's fertile ground. The fabled horse race loomed on the horizon, a challenge that stirred her spirit yet weighed on her heart. Could she claim victory against such daunting odds? Her decisions, made swiftly in her country's name, now echoed with the whispers of uncertainty.

As Mia strolled along the path, she heard a familiar monotone voice and saw a lone man standing in a tiny garden courtyard, softly murmuring to himself. Even from a distance, she could tell it was Garrison. He held a round gold amulet tenderly in his hands. With a grim and remorseful look on his face, Garrison looked at a holographic image emitting from the amulet of a tall blonde-haired woman in a white gown. She stood and smiled at him, even waving at him momentarily. The image was a short recording, repeating itself after ten seconds.

Sensing an unseen observer, Garrison hastily deactivated the device with a swift press of a button. The image of the woman disappeared. With a huff of irritation, he hastily shoved the amulet into his pocket, his actions tinged with the awkward rush of one concealing forbidden treasures.

Mia approached the Relic Hunter lightly, knowing she had disturbed a profoundly personal moment. "I'm sorry to disturb you. Is that the personal item so important to you that you had to risk your life at Black Rock?"

At first, it appeared that Garrison didn't know how to answer the simple question—or didn't want to answer—but he eventually found his voice. "Yes, Your Highness."

"A Remembrance Disk," Mia said. She recognized such a personal heirloom. A relative had shown her one a long time ago. It was rare, meant to keep an image of a lost loved one. Most chose to move on in life, but there were others who had such an item as a keepsake. "Who is she?"

Garrison seemed to stammer and search for the correct words. "My past."

"I am sorry about your loss."

"Thank you."

Mia sensed her intrusion and Garrison's need for solitude. With a soft, sympathetic smile, she retreated into the gardens. "I'll leave you to your thoughts."

Garrison's fingers trembled slightly as they ventured into the depths of his pant pocket. With Princess Karamia no longer present to cast a questioning gaze, he retrieved the small unassuming disk with a reverence reserved for the most sacred of relics. Activating it again, he watched the disk flicker to life, casting a luminous hologram of his beloved, forever captured in a moment of joyous greeting. In the loneliness of the garden courtyard, Garrison cradled the Remembrance Disk tenderly, a stark contrast to his other hand, which was balled into a tight fist of unresolved emotions. "We will be together again, Isla, my love."

Mia meandered leisurely through the garden, her path curving around a quaint cluster of low-lying hedges. Suzu and Hogart seemingly materialized along the garden's winding trail as she rounded the bend. Their presence was strikingly deliberate, indicating they had been lingering there briefly, evidently opting to stay in hopes of a discreet conversation with their mysterious, secretive fellow traveler.

"Princess, huh?" Hogart said gruffly.

Suzu smirked. "You couldn't tell us?"

"We might be a little rough around the edges . . ."

"I'm sorry, my friends," Mia said earnestly. "But it was my first adventure on my own. I didn't know you at the time."

Hogart scoffed. "We understand."

"We would do the same thing if we met us," Suzu said sheepishly.

"No harm done."

"Especially since we got our reward!" Suzu nearly jumped for joy.

"Five gold bars each!" Hogart shouted, matching his partner's excitement.

"Of course. You fulfilled your end of the bargain. Fortune and glory. That's your heart's desire. But why are you still here?" Mia asked.

"Well, um . . . we thought that . . ." Hogart stammered, ". . . since we started together . . ."

"We're staying for the race," Suzu said. "We want to see our friend win."

Mia appeared rather touched by the word "friend," not expecting it from the close-knit adventuring duo. The word hung in the air, heavy with meaning and unspoken promises of loyalty and camaraderie. It was a simple term, yet it carried the weight of countless shared experiences and unbreakable bonds forged in the fires of adversity. Being called a friend by these seasoned travelers was an honor many seemingly sought but few achieved. "Friend?"

"Yes, of course," Suzu and Hogart said together approvingly.

Finally, after all the traveling and adventures they have been through together, the three shared a laugh and a group hug. The journey had been long, filled with unexpected twists and turns, but the friendship truly made it memorable. As they stood there, wrapped in each other's arms, they knew that these memories would last a lifetime.

"You placed a gambling bet, didn't you?" Mia said.

Hogart and Suzu blushed brightly, knowing that they had been found out.

"We want to see you win," Hogart said lightly and truthfully.

A deliberate and loud cough resonated through the silence of the gardens, catching the attention of those nearby. Behind the joyous trio, a solitary figure stood with an air of patience. His presence was marked by big hooded eyes and long strands of mousy brown hair tinged with streaks of grey that echoed the fullness of his bushy beard. His tall, muscular build rose slightly over six feet, carrying an imposing, distinguished air that commanded attention. "Young lady," King Jelia said in a firm, outspoken voice, "you have a lot of explaining to do."

"Father!" Mia cried. She immediately sprinted over to his welcome arms and they embraced deeply.

Hogart and Suzu acknowledged the long-overdue, tender scene unfolding before them with an unspoken yet deeply felt mutual understanding. With a respectful nod, they retreated into the quiet embrace of the evening, their figures fading into the twilight. The sacred reunion space between parent and child was the king and Mia's alone, a private tableau etched against the backdrop of a world that continued to spin outside their moment of reconnection.

"My daughter," King Jelia said, "I am so pleased you are alright."

"There's no need to be concerned about me," Mia said. "I'm able to take care of myself."

King Jelia laughed lightheartedly, then a broad smile came to his face. "I'll always be concerned about my daughter's safety—no matter what you do or where you go."

"I know."

"But I fully realize you are intelligent, strong, and exceptionally resilient. That's how I raised you."

Mia laughed and hugged her father again.

"I also know that you can win the race tomorrow."

"T-then you heard about . . ."

"Yes. It was a wise decision to enter the horse race on behalf of our country."

"You're not going to appoint someone else to compete in the race?" Mia said, her voice sounding surprised.

"No. I support you and you alone. The truth is that you're the best rider I've ever seen in the saddle, barring no one."

"You're just saying that."

"No, so help me for telling the truth"—King Jelia chuckled lightly—"but it's true."

"Did it hurt to tell the truth to your daughter?"

"Ouch," the king said, pretending to be hurt. "Be kind to an old man."

Father and daughter laughed.

"I will tell you another truth. I believe in you, my daughter."

Mia blushed. Her heart was all aglow.

"I have to accept the fact that my little girl is becoming a young woman. My only final advice to you as a father is that you can achieve anything you want in this life. Always believe in yourself, and you can achieve greatness."

"Thank you, Father. I love you."

"To help you win," King Jelia said, "I brought along a friend."

Mia's horse since childhood, a majestic stallion with a coat that shimmered like obsidian under the sun's caress, clacked against the courtyard's cobblestones. The stallion's eyes, dark and deep as midnight pools, reflected wisdom beyond his years, and he carried himself with a pride befitting his royal charge. The stallion bowed in a silent show of loyalty to his mistress.

"Moonshadow!" She could not contain the excitement in her usually even tone about seeing her beloved horse. Mia embraced Moonshadow and lightly rubbed his neck. The stallion returned the affection with a jovial neigh.

The Goldenwings Run

Lying on a soft pile of butterscotch hay, Mia roused from her slumber and stretched lazily. The golden fingers of dawn crept through the gaps in the stable windows, casting a warm glow on the hay-strewn floor. The distant sounds of the stables stirring to life reached her ears, a symphony of anticipation for the day's festivities. Today was no ordinary day; it was the day of the Goldenwings Run.

As the sun climbed higher and the heat shimmered, the air swelled into a harmonious buzz. Mia rose, her movements gentle as she prepared for the day ahead. She brushed Moonshadow's glossy coat until it gleamed like midnight silk, the stallion nuzzling her in quiet appreciation. Then she carefully saddled Moonshadow, adorning him with an ornate tawny leather saddle that glistened in the light. Roused by the activity, Mozo stretched his leathery wings and glided over to Mia's shoulder. Together, they were a harmonious trio, ready to take on the world.

Mia and Moonshadow emerged from the shadowy confines of the stable into the fresh morning air. All the barns and pens were awakening, with the distant clatter of buckets and the soft murmur of individual voices blending with the chorus of the spectators. They passed the other horses, who nickered softly in their stalls, sensing the day's excitement ahead. Mia leaned forward, whispering words of encouragement to Moonshadow as they headed towards the racetrack.

"Your Highness. There you are!" Captain Hardt's familiar voice said. "They're about to start the parade. Follow me."

The air was alive with anticipation as the sun cast a buttery hue over the bustling streets. The once bleak town had transformed into a carnival of colors, with banners from different countries fluttering in the wind and the scent of street food mingling with the melodies of guitars and flutes. Mia rode atop Moonshadow, whose hooves clattered rhythmically against the cobblestone with the music. Mozo screeched merrily from her shoulder, adding his unique song to the symphony of sounds. Together, they strolled through the crowds, a tapestry of faces blurring past, each spectator alight with excitement, cheering and shouting words of encouragement for the race ahead.

The Kayawa captain and the Itonian princess turned a corner and entered a wide pedestrian street. A grand parade, a sight to behold, unfurled like a welcoming carpet down the street, its procession heralded by the jubilant fanfare. Clarinets and flutes weaved melodies that lingered in the wind, mingling with the thumping of drums, the blare of trumpets, and the laughter and chatter of the festive assembly. Dancers, adorned in a kaleidoscope of colors, moved with a grace that belied the complexity of their choreography. Each step and turn was a word in the visual language of celebration, telling tales of unity and joy. The midmorning sky transformed into a canvas of vibrant hues, and fireworks erupted, painting the heavens with fleeting beauty. Banners rippled like waves in the gentle breeze, their colors a tribute to the tapestry of nations represented in the stands.

Whimsical balloons bobbed and floated through the air, their shapes and designs as diverse as the people holding them. The countries' flags, a symphony of colors against the clear sky, seemed to sing a silent anthem of peace and camaraderie. Children ran alongside the procession and waved to the horse riders, their laughter a melody that completed the opus of festivity.

Mia departed her ally's side and moved to her position in the parade, her presence igniting cheers that rippled through the crowd. As she joined and settled into the parade route, set before the Kayawa captain, who was bringing up the rear, she was reintroduced to the familiar faces at the council meeting and to a couple of the new riders.

At the forefront of the horse riders lined up in the parade was Chinsa from Jasho. Dressed in jade racing attire, he exuded an air of adventure. His round silver helmet, equipped with protective earflaps, added to his gallant image. White leather gloves and black boots completed his ensemble, giving him a dashing look. He hung a riding whip at his hip on a black belt. His friendly smile was unfaltering as he greeted the revelers.

Next was Tonio Ras of Thaimis. His attire spoke of practical elegance—a black riding jacket paired with a shirt, the ensemble completed by black leather chaps draped over pants, all anchored by sturdy black boots. Atop his white steed, he was a vision of grace. With a flourish, he waved to the enraptured crowd.

Leon, from peaceful Fran, wore a long teal coat and vest with intricate bronze embroidery. His white puffy shirt billowed slightly as a gentle breeze passed, offsetting his polished black boots. With a graceful wave to the onlookers, he acknowledged their cheers and admiration.

The festivities died quickly, and a low chorus of jeers and sneers erupted at the next rider. The atmosphere thickened with tension as Zamana Commander Tomap Sruz came into view. His crimson-and-black armor, a scarred tapestry of battles fought and won, was proudly displayed on his robust and youthful form. Yet there was a glint in his black eyes, a silent promise that he was more than the sum of his scars. Today, he would ride not for the glory of the Zamana Empire but to prove that valor knows no allegiance and even the scorned can rise to victory.

The jovial spirit of the assembled audience, primarily locals, was rejuvenated by the sight of the newest rider. Brynn Krist, representing the Kingdom of Tavter, rode into view. At nearly six feet, her athletic contour was crowned by a cascade of long jet hair. She epitomized allure, ensnaring gazes as she effortlessly commanded her dark cocoa steed. Clad in a mauve riding jacket, meticulously buttoned from neck to waist, she cut a striking figure against the backdrop of fervent spectators. Her white pants and black boots completed the ensemble, exuding elegance and agility. She acknowledged the unfurled sea of ivory and violet banners from the homeland, waving in her honor, with a warm smile and a gracious wave.

Next in line was another new face. Jak Chann of Passi, a man of medium stature with black hair. He boasted a slim, athletic build that complemented his equestrian skills. His attire was dazzling, with a bright yellow-and-champagne riding outfit that captured every gaze. With a swift motion, he and his steed executed a spinning trick in the saddle that was so fluid it seemed they were one. The crowd held their breath, witnessing a moment of pure harmony between rider and horse, and clapped in overwhelming approval.

Hailing from the sandy lands of Gypro, Izzak awaited the start, deep-brown eyes reflecting a calmness that belied his stoic nature. His lean build was poised with a focused grace, seemingly unfazed by the spectator chaos. Clad in a pristine pearly shirt and pants, he was draped in a long maroon robe with an elegant gold-and-blue lining, a silent statement of his homeland's stature. His grey steed, adorned in the same harmonious colors of his robes, seemed ready to run at the slightest command.

The audience ceased clapping and descended into a loud murmur of indecisiveness. Envision a titan amongst men and women, his physique sculpted like that of an ancient statue. Towering and splendid, Ah-knold gazed at the crowd, his artic eyes as deep and fathomless as the ocean. Atop his gargantuan obsidian steed raised in Cimmissia, which carried itself with the dignity of a war-torn general, he rode with an unyielding stoicism. His sneer was not merely malevolent but etched with the wisdom of countless victories. Cloaked in a glorious crimson riding robe that cascaded over his broad shoulders, he bore six stripes of gold across his chest to mark his triumphs.

A new rider represented the marvelous land of Aliffica, a woman bearing a commanding presence. Graj Nes stood out in any crowd with her androgynous allure and striking features. Imposing with a statuesque frame, her presence was accentuated by her ebony skin that contrasted sharply against the snug russet riding pants and jet-black boots she confidently strode in. Her attire, a bronze leather V-top, tastefully studded, dared to bare her midriff and showcase her muscular arms. Silver gauntlets clasped her forearms, much like Mia's, catching the glint of sunlight and the eye of curious onlookers.

Mia approved of the wild woman's style and laughed lightly. She waved to the crowd and was aware of Mozo's fluttering departure from her shoulder. The dragonet, a streak of lavender against the azure sky, ascended to the royal stand where King Jelia awaited, his presence commanding even from a distance. Garrison's stern face broke into a rare smile as Mozo landed on his shoulder, a soft chirp acknowledging the gathered dignitaries. Suzu whispered a greeting to the dragon, her eyes alight with the historical event unfolding. Hogart nodded in silent approval, his nervous gaze fixed on the course.

Mia turned in her saddle, her gaze lingering on the stalwart figure of Captain Edburn Hardt, her ally bringing up the rear of the parade. He saluted Kayawa King Kovlin, who was also in the stands area. More than a mere gesture, the salute was a silent acknowledgment of the unspoken bond between the monarch and his protector. The crowd's murmur grew into vivacious applause for a moment, acknowledging the solemnity of the gesture.

As the vibrant procession diverged, the air thrummed with the rhythm of retreating drums and the soft shuffle of dancers' feet. The flag-bearers, their colors a blur against the city's backdrop, broke off and disappeared down the labyrinth of side streets. Each country's representatives retreated from the main thoroughfare, their duties fulfilled, leaving behind a trail of national pride and cultural splendor.

Meanwhile, the horse riders, a diverse international group united by the thrill of competition, advanced towards a single rope stretched across the dirt track. Their steeds, powerful and eager, sensed the excitement in the air, their hooves kicking up dust clouds as they trotted to the rope. The riders, clad in their traditional cultural racing silks, adjusted their reins and tightened their gloves, with each thought focused on the race ahead. The dirt track, a simple, unadorned path, was about to become the stage for an age-old contest of speed and skill.

The eleven champion riders, each proudly representing their country, lined up behind the simple thin rope stretched across the horses' chests. All the horses were becoming restless, each acting ready to burst. Some were prancing about in anticipation, some were stomping the dirt in frustration, some were frothing at the mouth in expectation, and all were more than prepared to run. Last-minute, steely glances were cast by the riders, fists tightening around the reins, and faces set in grim determination. The riders settled in their saddles, trying to calm their nerves and mounts. The starter dropped the thin rope to the dirt ground—and they were off!

The collected crowd, already buzzing with anticipation and excitement, roared in approval as the individual horses sprang forth as one. Eleven riders started down the unknown obstacle course ahead, galloping away at full speed, each trying to gain an early advantage.

The racetrack was alive with the thunderous clamor of hooves and the fervent shouts of riders coaxing their steeds into a frantic dash to get a good starting position in the race. But to their frustration and dismay, all the riders found themselves ensnared in a tight-knit cluster very quickly. Unable to move freely, the riders flicked their riding crops back and forth to encourage their horses to run faster. Eleven equine athletes, manes whipping like banners in the wind, jostled for dominance and the lead on the delineated path, their bodies brushing against each other in the heat of competition. As they barreled towards the first long stretch, the crowd's roar crescendoed, mirroring the tumultuous energy of the race.

Highly annoyed by being stuck in a swarm, all riders took extreme measures early in the race to get ahead. Instead of flicking the riding whip against their horse's hide, each rider could whip their opponent—and brazenly started to do so. A couple of quick hits were exchanged between riders to create running space, developing a more dangerous atmosphere for all eleven riders and horses involved.

Ah-knold, a colossus of muscle and might, thundered forward, closing the gap to his first adversary: the agile and wiry Jak of Passi. Their steeds pounded the earth in unison, racing at breakneck speeds. With a calculated ferocity, Ah-knold drew his right arm back, poised to strike with the force of a tempest. Yet Jak anticipated the looming threat with a dancer's grace and a seasoned warrior's alertness. He leaned backwards in his saddle in one fluid motion, eluding Ah-knold's thunderous blow by a hair's breadth.

Jak instantly erected himself in an unexpected countermove and swiveled adeptly in his saddle. With a swift and fluid motion, he swung his right leg in a wide, sweeping arc through the brisk air, delivering a resounding kick to his adversary's robust chest. The strike's impact, potent and precise from Jak's compact stature, would ordinarily send a rider tumbling from their mount. However, it barely registered against the hulking figure's impenetrable exterior.

Graj, the ebony warrior from Aliffica, rode valiantly beside Princess Karamia, ensuring they maintained a steady pace. Graj used the riding whip as a weapon and struck out at Princess Karamia. She landed a blow across the princess's upper arm, making her scream and react in pain, briefly losing her grip on the reins. Graj rode alongside the princess and flicked the riding crop at her, trying to land a couple more hits on her opponent. Ready for the attack, the princess leaned away, and the lash struck her armor gauntlet, protecting her from harm. As they swiftly approached a grand broken structure in the middle of the course, their paths diverged, each taking a different route around it.

In an unexpected twist, the exuberant, cheering crowd in the stands along the course morphed into an unanticipated and unwanted element of the competition. A duo of overzealous spectators leapt onto the course in a peculiar exhibition of daring and fervor. These two individuals embarked on a frenzied jaunt down the track, jubilantly flailing their arms in the air, bringing a bold act of excitement to the race. While foolish, their reckless abandon or sheer audacity added an unpredictable element to the race as the riders navigated around the runners.

The thunder of hooves crashed down on the pair of idiots. Amidst the exciting flurry, one nimble runner seized good fortune and a fleeting chance, scaling to the safety of a balcony and being hoisted by the collective effort and goodwill of eager onlookers. Alas, fate and fortune were not as kind to the other. In a harrowing moment, the second runner suffered a blatant, glancing shot from the boot of Tavter's envoy, Brynn Krist, whose steed brushed past the slow-moving man in haste, casting the runner aloft in a dramatic arc and sent him spiraling into an unwitting ballet, cradled by the gasping crowd and the sea of hands.

Tomap marked his first unwilling target, Leon of Fran, and closed his galloping horse on him. He pulled out a small hidden knife from his belt, galloped on the side of Leon's horse to match his speed, and lashed out at the slender man with the thin, sharp blade.

Alarmed at the sight of the small knife, Leon instinctively panicked and jerked away erratically to avoid being cut. The sudden shifting in the saddle threw the rider off-balance, and the constant momentum and his body's light weight continued his downfall. The Franman screamed as he helplessly dangled on the side of his racing steed. Satisfied with Leon's dire predicament, Tomap broke off in search of his next target.

In an unforeseen twist of fate, Leon found himself in a precarious position. His left foot, trapped by the stirrup, left him hanging off the horse's flank. Each length the steed galloped eased the foot's hold slightly, inching Leon closer to the unforgiving, deadly embrace of the passing ground below. Leon struggled, arms flailing in desperation. He reached up to grasp the saddle horn with all his might, seeking salvation in the form of the saddle's steady leather.

Once a vast canvas of shifting sands, the crudely outlined racetrack abruptly morphed into an unyielding mosaic of rigid cobblestones. Leon's breaths were ragged, his hands tearing through the air for the saddle horn as his eyes fixated on the foreboding heap of stones strewn across his path. With a desperate surge of adrenaline, he scrambled a second time to regain his rightful place in the saddle, fully aware that any delay could result in a hazardous collision with the jagged rocks awaiting his fall.

With a soft grunt, Leon reached skyward, his fingers clasping the saddle's horn in a desperate bid for survival. For a fleeting moment, he hoisted himself, but his grip faltered, fingers sliding off the horn, and he teetered perilously closer to the unforgiving ground below. Summoning what seemed to be his final reserve of strength, Leon made one more valiant effort. He secured a firm hold on the saddle's horn, pulled himself up, and righted himself just as his steed skirted past the jagged rock pile.

The inaugural leap of the perilous circuit was a masterclass in deception: a seemingly innocuous, slender brook, its waters deceptively calm and surface beguilingly narrow. Yet all eleven intrepid riders handled this first challenge with aplomb, their steeds barely skimming the water's edge. With the initial hurdle behind them, they surged onward, their pace unrelenting as they traversed the ancient cobblestone path, now a mosaic of equal stone and sand.

Izzak glided effortlessly by Princess Karamia. He had a broad grin on his bearded tan face and gave a casual yet chivalrous salute to the competition. As he raced forward and positioned himself before the visibly irked princess, Izzak deftly slipped between the next two riders in front of him, Tonio Ras and Jak. Unbeknownst to Izzak, the riders from Thaimis and Passi had formed a fleeting alliance between them solely for this race.

The unknown partnership unfolded in a unified act. Tonio and Jak positioned themselves on either side of the lone rider, forcing Izzak to keep between them. They edged closer and inward, creating a dynamic formation that prevented Izzak from maneuvering and allowed synchronized movements and matching speeds for the other two riders. In an impressive display of skill, Tonio used his riding whip to strike Izzak in the face with one swift stroke. It stunned and distracted him enough for Jak to ride in closer, perform an acrobatic feat by swinging gracefully around in his saddle, and knock Izzak off the horse with a single solid kick to the chest.

Izzak, reeling from the successive blows dealt by the duo in unison, was violently dislodged from his steed. His battered form tumbled onto the racetrack directly in the path of Princess Karamia. Unfazed by the sudden hindrance, she deftly maneuvered Moonshadow to sidestep the fallen rival, careful to prevent any harm. As Izzak's dazed gaze lifted from the dirt, catching the princess's fleeting figure, she flashed a triumphant smile and tossed back a comradely salute.

Izzak, with every ounce of his will, heaved himself up from the gritty embrace of the racetrack, his legs trembling like palm fronds in a storm. Bitter curses spilled from his lips, a tempest of fury directed at the deceitful tactics of his less-than-honorable adversaries. With determination etched on his face, he lurched towards his loyal steed, only to collapse under the cruel betrayal of his as-yet-unnoticed fractured limb. Yet, even as agony wracked his body, Izzak's spirit, as untamed as the desert winds, refused to yield. He would mount his horse and chase victory, or so was his resolve until reality dawned— his mare had chosen the path of tranquility over the chaos of the race. Thus, amidst the cacophony of the Goldenwings Run, Izzak's journey ended abruptly, not with glory for the desert land of Gypro but with the silent resignation of defeat.

Ten riders left the first casualty of the horse race far behind and approached the second significant jump of the course, their steeds pounding the ground. Before them lay a collection of fallen grey stones, remnants of a once towering building now reduced to a distorted wall that cut across the track. This accidental barrier, born from destruction long ago, now served as a current test of skill and courage. As they neared, each rider steadied their mount, preparing for the leap. With hearts racing and muscles tensed, they soared over the rubble, each defying gravity in their own style, leaving behind nothing but a cloud of brown dust.

After the daring leap over the rugged ashen stone barrier, the riders reined in their spirited horses, decelerating from their frenetic gallop. They had arrived at the threshold of a treacherous bend, which ushered them into a quaint series of lean lanes nestled within a cozy residential area known as "the Narrows."

A meticulously crafted course wound through the labyrinthine network of slender cobblestone alleys nestled amidst the dense cluster of urban dwellings. The thoroughfares, a mere fifteen feet across, permitted only a duo of riders to navigate the convoluted path in a serpentine fashion side by side at one time. The Narrows, with its ever-evolving topography, presented a formidable, treacherous challenge to the competitors. Within the initial stretch of three hundred yards, the racers were compelled to barrel down a tight passageway and execute an abrupt right-hand turn leading into a gentle arc spanning a brief expanse, followed by an immediate sharp veer to the left.

To escalate the challenge of this section of the circuit, intricate water fountains emerged on the course, demanding nimble navigation around or through them. Also scattered haphazardly along the serpentine route were diminutive carts, overturned barrels, and heaps of debris piles, each a dangerous hurdle requiring dexterous vaults to surmount. Meanwhile, to make matters worse, the breeze buzzed with the deafening, raucous cheers of impassioned onlookers crowding every balcony and rooftop along the route, their collective excitement adding a palpable intensity to the race.

Unintimidated by any man almost twice his size and feeling the need to prove his worth to the Zamana Empire by eliminating the biggest competition, Tomap closed in on the most significant threat in the race: Ah-knold. His mount sprinting on the left side next to the giant black mare and matching speeds, Tomap removed his hidden knife from his belt again and slashed away at the big man, catching him on the upper right arm with the tip of the blade.

Reeling by the sudden, surprising, brazen attack, Ah-knold initially jerked away and lost his reins for a moment, shifting awkwardly in his saddle and completely forgetting about the constricting confines they were speeding through. His opposite shoulder grated a short distance along a rough wooden wall, further physically harming the brute from Cimmissia. Slowed by the deadly encounter and now behind the Tavter rider, Brynn Krist, the sizeable man rebounded quickly and regained composure.

Ahead of the pack, Graj and Captain Hardt were the epitome of a competitive spirit, their steeds galloping neck and neck as they vied for the lead. But in their spirited struggle, they became entwined in blind rivalry, each one's determination becoming the other's obstacle. As they approached the next sharp street corner, their battle peaked, resulting in a two-person pileup that was both lethally chaotic and unwittingly comical. They scrambled around and around the corner, limbs and riding crops entangled, each flick of frustration only serving to hinder their progress further. Meanwhile, the rest of the riders seized the opportunity, whizzing past the duo caught in their private world of competition.

"I'm losing the race because of you, old man!" Graj growled.

As the brown dust settled on the track, Graj and Captain Hardt realized their fierce fight had cost them dearly. Locked in a battle of wills, they had lost sight of the actual competition. They untangled themselves from the clash with a mutual nod and surged forward. The race was not over, and they had ground to make up. Once leaders, their momentary duel had relegated them to chasers, but determination burned within them to reclaim their positions.

Leon of Fran approached the minor obstacle of a few crates in his path, the street beneath his horse a blur of tan and mocha. With a graceful leap, he soared over it, his steed momentarily weightless. In midair, he encountered Jak of Passi, their paths crossing in the game of chance. Jak struck out with a fist, landing a punch to the slender man's face. Landing deftly, Leon recovered and sped up to his adversary before the next collection of crates on the road. Jumping over the second crate obstacle, Leon returned the favor by side-kicking the petite man in the torso. Jak dangled slightly in his saddle until he executed a flawless trick, spinning back into the saddle with the simplicity of a seasoned performer. The Goldenwings Run became his stage, and he, the undoubted star.

Of all the racers, Chinsa's joy was unmistakable, his grin wide as he raced amidst his rivals' wild shenanigans. But his delight faded when Brynn pulled up alongside, her steely gaze dripping with threat, and a nasty look of menace on her beautiful face. In an unexpected move, she turned in her saddle, facing him, and delivered a brutal, swift kick to his face. Chinsa tumbled from his saddle, the force of the blow sending him sprawling on the track.

The portly man from Jasho shakily got up to see his trusted horse happily trot down the course without him. He then heard horse hooves beating louder within his ears and looked behind him to see Ah-knold bearing down on him with his mighty mare. Alarmed, Chinsa scampered down the stone street. He searched desperately for any opening, any crevice to shield himself from the impending doom of being run over and trampled to death.

With no refuge in sight, Chinsa's gaze shot upwards to a pedestrian balcony where hope flickered—dangling hands were outstretched, ready to hoist him to safety. The balcony was abuzz with life; people shouted words of encouragement, their hands waving Chinsa to them. Gasping for air, his legs wobbling like jelly, Chinsa lunged forward and clutched at salvation. Fingers intertwined with those of strangers, he was heaved up from the brink of disaster. He climbed over the railing to safety just as Ah-knold thundered below on his horse. Though he was the second contestant who had been ousted from the Goldenwings Run, Chinsa's spirit soared, cradled by the swift and selfless acts of those entertained by the race.

The labyrinthine alleys of the Narrows, ever-changing and bewildering, seem to relish their role as a relentless architect of confusion and peril, all for their cryptic amusement. Yet this twisted game found a pause when the nine valiant riders, survivors of the maze's capricious whims, emerged around a city block. A shallow expanse of water lay before them, stretching three hundred yards along the designated path—a remnant of grandeur from an oversize, fractured frost fountain. With no path around, the steeds had to brave the fountain's pool, wading through the water just inches deep.

As the thunder of hooves echoed off the confining stone walls, the racers neared the glistening white fountain, its waters shallow but their spirits not. A few spectators, caught in the rapture of the wild race and celebration, once again vaulted over barriers and cascaded down from their balconies. They daringly dashed within the restricting track boundaries, arms waving excitedly in the air, their laughter mingling with the cheering approval of the clapping audience. Wisdom prevailed for most, who clambered back to the safety of their balconies with outstretched hands and a collective effort. However, a single daring runner stubbornly insisted on sprinting down the track and weaved through the race's narrow gauntlet, flirting with destiny's unpredictable embrace.

Amidst the thunderous applause and the pounding hooves on the racetrack, an unforeseen event unfolded. The lone pedestrian, lost in the excitement of the Goldenwings Run, dashed down the track just as Brynn rounded a street corner and galloped at full speed. In a heart-stopping moment, Brynn's steed collided with the civilian.

The impact sent a shock wave through the stands, and spectators leapt to their feet to view the outcome. Brynn and her mount were catapulted into the pool. The fountain water exploded skyward, droplets catching the sunlight like diamonds flung from the hands of fate. A loud splash echoed, enhancing their perilous fall.

But even as the ripples fanned across the surface, Brynn was in motion, wrestling with reins and gravity to right herself and her horse. With a mighty effort, both horse and rider clambered from the pool, soaked but unbroken. The crowd's roar of approval was deafening, a tidal wave of sound that washed over them, spurring them onward.

As they rejoined the fray, Brynn noticed that a couple of her competitors had seized this chance to advance, their figures growing smaller in the distance. With grit, Brynn urged her horse forward, reclaiming their rhythm. They'd fallen to fifth place, but hope was not lost; the race was far from over.

Thankfully for all the horse riders, the confining Narrows finally ended and opened to a broader race course—a field of burnt grass. A right turn lay at the end of this natural grassland. Competitors accelerated along a stretch of reprieve, bracing for the notorious leap over a man-made obstacle called "the Ditch." It was a daunting barrier with a stone wall that spanned four feet in height from the ground, fifteen in breadth, and three in depth after the wall.

In a heated moment, Tomap galloped fiercely alongside the innocent Leon of Fran for a daring second encounter. Their steeds snorted in defiance as the two different but seasoned horse riders, with their stirrups clinking and clothes billowing, started to clash with their riding crops in a thunderous fury that echoed across the city. After they swiftly exchanged a few glancing strikes, a small collection of debris in the middle of the route separated them momentarily.

Immediately after passing the debris, Tomap and Leon shouted at their steeds, charging inward towards each other with a ferocity that shook the grassy ground beneath them. Their steeds snorted and neighed, muscles rippling with power as they closed the distance. Riding crops drawn and eyes locked, they resumed the vicious duel in a whirlwind of motion, each rider parrying and thrusting in a fight to be the victor.

As they approached the fringe of the Ditch, Tomap shouted in a rage and struck Leon across the center of the chest with the riding whip. Stunned by the savage blow, Leon fell off his horse and into the deep ditch. On impact, the frail, slender man's neck snapped sickeningly.

The surrounding crowd's exuberant cheers abruptly halted, their festive, triumphant melodies ceasing mid-note. A discomforting hush descended on the assembly aligned in the streets, stands, and balconies, the situation's true gravity dawning on each spectator as they witnessed the race's perilous turn. The twisted, motionless figure on the track cast a pall over the crowd, a tangible sense of danger now permeating the atmosphere. Three competitors had already been eliminated from contention, yet this marked the first loss of life—a sobering moment that quelled any urge to celebrate. No solitary cry of encouragement or solitary applause pierced the respectful silence; instead, a collective muted exhale of relief resonated as each remaining rider conquered the legendary, infamous hurdle.

After the Ditch jump, the competition intensified at the Goldenwings Run. Tomap, with unmatched skill, gained and maintained his lead. The others trailed, each harboring a fierce tenaciousness to triumph. Their names etched into the annals of the race: Jak Chann, known for his swift maneuvers; Ah-knold, whose steadiness was legendary; Princess Karamia and her steed's fiery spirit; Tonio Ras's strategic mind; Brynn Krist, with her unyielding will; Captain Hardt, whose resilience shined; and lastly, Graj Nes, whose boldness knew no bounds. Despite past tragedies that befell some racers, their legacy fueled the current riders' resolve to claim victory, regardless of the sacrifices required.

Ah-knold, with his usual aggressive gusto, bumped into Brynn Krist. As the horse whinnied in distress, the sudden jolt sent Brynn teetering over dangerously in her saddle, her arms flailing in a frantic bid to grab the saddle horn for balance. The scene unfolded in slow motion as Brynn's grip on the saddle horn and reins loosened, and she found herself hanging off the side of her steed, suspended in a moment of pure adrenaline and angst.

Mia, in a display of equestrian prowess, urged Moonshadow into a swift gallop, closing the gap between her and a fellow rider in distress. With deft agility, Mia extended one arm to steady Brynn, while her other hand maintained a firm grip on the reins. As Moonshadow raced forward, Mia's arm became a pillar of support, allowing Brynn to regain her hold on the saddle horn. Together, they surged ahead, Mia's unwavering, steady arm ensuring Brynn's safe return to her rightful place atop her steed.

In an odd spectacle of perverse thankfulness, Brynn contorted herself atop her steed, opting for a side-saddle position directly opposite Mia. With a devilish grin curling her lips, Brynn kicked the unsuspecting princess sharply in the face, mirroring the vile act once inflicted on Chinsa. The unexpected assault caused Mia to jerk the reins, decelerating Moonshadow's stride and allowing her sly rival to gain the lead. Brynn, content with the turmoil she'd sown, whirled back around, seating herself correctly, and galloped away with a hearty laugh.

Mia wobbled uneasily in the saddle for half a minute, shifting along with the movement of the quick strides until she regained her composure and balance. Settling firmly in the saddle, she swiped a small trickle of scarlet blood away from her lip. She tightened her grip on the reins and urged Moonshadow on with a determined, fierce cry.

The remaining eight riders now entered an empty merchant quarter, their steeds deftly traversing a gentle curve that veered slightly to the right. Beyond this turn, they encountered an incline, subtle yet challenging, beckoning them upwards for about a hundred yards.

As the riders reached the top of the steep incline, the sight of the long, slender wooden bridge caused a stir of excitement. It stood as evident hasty craftsmanship, its structure an unfinished construction of wood and open air. The racers' hearts pounded in anticipation; this was no ordinary course stretch. They would have to maneuver through this precarious path to reach the next stage of the course.

The bridge was a gauntlet of disorganization. Wooden crossbeams loomed like silent sentinels before gaping holes that promised peril. Weakened planks groaned underfoot, threatening to give way at the slightest misstep. Piles of unclaimed lumber lay scattered, a forest's worth of obstacles in their path.

The horses galloped between the equipment and the open spaces with each thunderous stride. Their hooves struck a rhythm against the wood, a drumbeat that echoed over the river water beneath them. The riders were focused, guiding their steeds with finesse, their eyes fixed on the solid ground that awaited on the other side of the bridge.

As the procession of riders advanced in an almost linear formation, Ah-knold's giant steed inadvertently jostled Brynn, sending her veering perilously into an off-limits construction zone. The robust equine, spurred by unbridled momentum, shattered the frail wooden barrier, oblivious to the reason behind its placement. The moment's urgency swallowed Brynn's cries for her horse to halt. Steed and rider plummeted through the weakened planks in a heart-stopping instant, cascading into the churning river depths below.

Brynn and her horse survived the plunge and emerged victorious against the river's rushing current. As they reached the sanctuary of the riverbank, the horse, with a mighty shake, cast off the clinging water droplets like a cloak of liquid pearls. With her garments clinging to her shapely form, Brynn crawled from the river's embrace, sparing a few moments to ensure her equine companion bore no scars from their ordeal. Then, with a blazing fire in her brown eyes and a storm brewing in her heart, she released a torrent of unrefined, fervent invectives in her native tongue, each bitter word a sharp, pointed dagger aimed at the deceit of her competitors.

The seven steadfast contenders, still vying for victory, emerged from the bridge's shadowy lip. As they did, the path before them broadened amidst the academic and business edifices of Tavter, flattening into a vast expanse of unadulterated ground akin to the classic equestrian circuits of lore. Simultaneously, the thrum of anticipation from the onlookers resumed—a cacophony of excitement that had lain in wait. Enthusiastic spectators erupted into more cheers at the merest glimpse of the equine athletes thundering by.

The broad, expansive track, layered with fine, sunbaked dust, meandered gently to the left. The dwindling number of riders steered their mounts into a legendary stretch of the city known as the "Crescent Moon Curve." This iconic section earned its name from the course's subtle yet persistent leftward bend that stretched far into the distance, mimicking the slender arc of a crescent moon.

The atmosphere was intense as the wildly cheering crowd's attention was riveted on the track's latest twists. With a deft maneuver, Tonio slipped past Tomap, seizing the lead pole position amidst roaring approval. Not to be outdone, Princess Karamia surged ahead of Ah-knold, Moonshadow slicing through the competition like a dart. The spectacle intensified as some riders, caught in the heat of competition, engaged in impromptu fights. Riding crops clashed against riding crops in a frenzied ballet, only to untangle as quickly as they connected, each rider peeling away to focus once more on the curving track ahead.

In one exchange, Graj attacked Captain Hardt with a new weapon: the extended baton. She swung the three-foot baton at the captain's head and barely missed with her first attempt. After the second failed attempt with the baton, the captain retaliated by striking the young woman with a side kick to the torso. It was not a surprising move, but was strong enough that Graj lost her balance and found herself hanging upside down along the side of her horse.

Using the saddle's stirrups for support, Graj twirled herself forward like a wheel on the horse's side, launched away from the trampling hooves, and landed solidly on her feet. The ebony warrior ran along the course for a few paces as her horse instinctively slowed down for her to catch up. She vaulted perfectly back onto the saddle of the faithful horse trotting alongside her, speeding off again in pursuit of a historic win.

Jak, driven by a surge of boldness, opted for a direct offensive against the smug commander, Tomap. With a calculated maneuver, Jak steered his steed to ride abreast of his adversary. He pivoted in his saddle, executing an intricate sequence of acrobatic prowess. Suspended upside down, clinging to the horse's flank with only one foot anchored in the stirrup, Jak launched a devastating downward kick. The force of the blow was so tremendous that it sent Tomap tumbling from his mount.

Tomap, with a daring grip, seized the saddle horn in the nick of time, contorting his frame in a backwards arch as his boots grazed and trailed the dusty track. Upright yet reversed, he clung to the horse's flank, his feet dragging, carving a path through the track. Onward, he persisted in this treacherous ballet, with sand scattering and spitting beneath his heels. Then, with an agile leap, Tomap ascended to the saddle again, securing his seat, and surged forward.

As Mia observed Jak and Tomap's dynamic exchange, a spark of inspiration ignited within her. The princess, battling against the whipping gusts, attempted to cloak herself invisibly, but the relentless wind thwarted her efforts. With a swift half turn in her saddle, she faced the rear. Clutching the fabric of the cloak, she draped it over herself, her fingers grazing the brooch. She instantly vanished from sight, her presence obscured from every eye of those watching the thrilling race.

The prince of Thaimis remained steadfast amidst the track's carnival-like fervor, his focus unyielding. Yet, in a twist of fate, the horse named Moonshadow bounded forward, flanking Tonio and his horse, revealing an empty saddle. Tonio's laughter boomed across the track, mirthful at the delightful spectacle. The arrogant, haughty Princess Karamia of Itonia had been unseated and was out of the Goldenwings Run.

Suddenly, an unseen force struck Tonio's handsome, firm chin with a robust and solid punch. Mia followed this with a couple more solid punches to the face. Still having the advantage of being invisible, she performed a deft side-saddle maneuver and kicked Tonio in the torso. Tonio toppled over in his saddle by the force of the kick, clinging desperately onto the saddle horn to stop his descent, and was dragged alongside his horse's flank. Mia spun around in the saddle to face forward, the whipping wind taking off the effects of the invisibility cloak, and she rode away.

With his body aligned upright but backwards along the horse's flank, Tonio Ras clutched the saddle horn with desperate fervor, his feet skimming the dirt track's surface for an extensive stretch of the course. In an agile maneuver, he successfully vaulted atop the saddle once more. Incensed by the audacious ambush, Tonio's steely gaze swept his surroundings, seeking retribution. His eyes locked with an ally in proximity, Jak, and the silent accord re-formed in the quest for vengeance against the noble princess. "Jak!" Tonio barked. "Squeeze play on her!"

Hearing the harsh command despite the thundering hoofbeats, Mia twisted in her saddle to look behind her. She witnessed the petite man from Passi, Jak, quickly ride abreast of her on the left flank and Tonio galloping along the right. The same unspoken alliance between the two riders, responsible for Izzak's downfall as the race's initial casualty, appeared poised to ensnare her with a similar deadly ploy.

Tonio and Jak, with a sly gleam in their eyes and mischievous smirks, coaxed their steeds closer and inward to Princess Karamia, the distance between all three steeds dwindling. Their hands gripped their riding whips tightly, the threat of an imminent strike on the princess hanging in the air like an ominous storm cloud. But Mia, with experience and wisdom sparking her instincts, sensed the peril. In a fleeting heartbeat, she disrupted Moonshadow's rhythmic gallop, guiding him with a subtle touch to skirt around and past the encroaching danger, evading the would-be assailants with grace.

Tonio and Jak narrowly missed their intended mark, causing their steeds to collide in a tumultuous clash. They found themselves entangled in a brief but intense scuffle, their frustration boiling over as they jostled against one another. The forced deceleration of their horses only fueled their growing ire. What started as a competitive spark quickly ignited into a blazing row, with harsh words escalating into a flurry of hard fists, shattering any camaraderie and alliance.

Amidst their mounting fury, the riders lost sight of the race's true challenge—the track itself, which was fraught with perils. Their focus was consumed by animosity; they overlooked an upcoming hazard: an extensive, sprawling mass of debris strewn across the course's center. This arduous barrier, splitting the path into two distinct lanes, demanded swift navigation and clearheaded strategy.

As they approached this critical juncture, the new adversaries were compelled to part ways, each veering off into separate trajectories. The obstacle served as an unexpected ceasefire, momentarily suspending their quarrel and forcing them to confront the race's inherent dangers.

Once past the stretch of piled debris cluttering the track, Tomap emerged alongside Tonio as if magically conjured by the air, his steed's hooves thundering in unison with Tonio's. Like a lion, youthful and brimming with fierce resolve, Tomap leapt from his mount to the back of Tonio's mare with the skill of a circus acrobat. Atop the singular beast, a tumultuous struggle ensued, each man vying for dominance. With an arm wrapped around the throat in a viselike grip, Tomap sent Tonio tumbling into the unforgiving embrace of the passing dirt racetrack below. Claiming victory atop his adversary's steed to the watching crowd's vocal disapproval, Tomap signaled his horse to come closer with a sharp whistle, transitioning back to his saddle with seamless agility and without breaking stride.

Mia twisted in her saddle, glancing over her shoulder to gauge the positions of her competition in the spirited contest. A good twenty paces back, veering to her left, was Jak, his features etched with a troubling glint of malice, intent on abruptly halting the princess's gallant charge. Yet, in a swift and surprising turn of events, Mia noticed another contender, Ah-knold, who had stealthily drawn up alongside the more petite man.

Amidst the clamorous arena's sudden spike in interest, Jak's senses heightened as he perceived the looming threat. With a quick and graceful motion, he attempted an audacious maneuver; his right leg arced over the saddle and through the air, aiming for the burly chest of his adversary. But Ah-knold, expecting the acrobatic maneuver with a keen eye and quicker reflexes, intercepted the airborne limb. He purposefully steered his steed aside, seizing control of the situation—and Jak's leg. With a forceful tug, he uprooted Jak from his saddle as if he were plucking a feather from a bird and, with a powerful heave, sent him plummeting to the passing dirt track below. The horse, still tethered to Jak by the reins, lost its footing and collapsed in a heap atop its fallen rider, dust billowing around them.

Both rider and horse tumbled into an untimely mess before Captain Hardt's steed. With agility born of necessity, the captain of the Kayawa guard urged his mount skyward, leaping over the tangled duo. Behind him, Graj Nes of Aliffica, wild as the winds and plains of her homeland, surprisingly reined in her charge. Her advance was thwarted by the disarray before her, placing her far behind the rest of the riders.

The five riders remaining in the Goldenwings Run reached the end of the Crescent Moon Curve, where they confronted the inevitable, almost expected, change in the course: a maddening shift from velocity to viscosity, their steeds' hooves clattering in protest against the reluctant descent. The downward slope, a grudging adversary, taunted with its steepness, leading to a quaint obstacle—a two-foot merlot-brick garden wall standing sentinel at the hill's base. With a leap of faith over this immovable barrier, they found reprieve on the other side. The world flattened into a vast expanse of sage, the grass scorched yet resilient underfoot, beckoning the riders onward.

With a fearsome yell and a sharp kick, Ah-knold and his massive horse surged forward. Ah-knold pierced through his opponents like an undeniable, sharp blade cutting between Princess Karamia and Tomap, who separated but did not fall. Ah-knold was now being brutish, knocking into both of them with a glancing shot and making them lose the combined lead to him. Seeing an opportunity he could not ignore, Captain Hardt took advantage of the situation and followed closely behind the proverbial human plow, now taking second place in the race.

The riders were forced to guide their horses towards a towering sand-colored structure, its outlines etched against the blue sky. The building's grandeur was marked by an oversize, open, oval portal, inviting them into its depths. As they galloped through this grand archway, the riders were thrust into the middle of an expansive beer tavern, wildly alive with the spirit of camaraderie.

There was a small stage nestled to the right of the entrance, where a five-piece band erupted in a jazzy symphony with each arriving rider, their melodious notes drifting through the air. Here, the atmosphere was rich with the scent of roasted meats and spiced ales. The long tables that were once orderly had been arranged now to skirt the room's edges, serving as impromptu pedestals for the crowd. They stood atop both table and chair, craning for a glimpse of equine grace thundering by. The walls were lined with an assembly of hundreds of patrons and revelers whose cheers rose and fell like the ocean's tides, their faces alight with joyous anticipation and drink. Above, the second floor teemed with an exuberant audience perched on beams and rafters, hoisting their drinks in a raucous salute to the rhythm below. The tavern was enveloped in harmonious melodies, a tapestry of sound that wrapped around the audience in an embrace as warm as the fires that glowed in the hearth, and exuberant laughter, the very essence of high-pitched merriment reverberating off the stone walls.

As the riders galloped through the middle of the crowded tavern, wondering with suspicion why the gathered crowd was so heartily joyous, they could scarcely believe the sight that waited before them. An open hole, gaping like a monstrous maw, had been torn through the heart of the structure, cleaving it in twain over the churning river below. It was as if the building itself, when it had been resurrected, was split asunder by some great, unseen force. Now, the riders faced a daunting challenge: to leap across the watery abyss between the two sundered halves of what was once a grand architectural marvel.

Ah-knold, still the frontrunner in this thrilling race, was the first to brave the leap across the yawning chasm. The onlookers, a sea of anticipation, watched with bated breath as the moment of truth neared. Then, as Ah-knold and his mighty steed launched into the air, a collective gasp morphed into an exhilarating "whoa," stretching out as long and spirited as the jump itself. The pair, bound by gravity and their combined mass, flirted with danger, barely clearing the gap. The mare, muscles quivering, stumbled on the brink of disaster, trying to avert a dangerous fall.

The crowd's anticipation built. Their collective breath was held in suspense as they watched the unfolding drama. The horse, sensing the precarious edge of the pit, gathered its strength in a final valiant effort. With a powerful lurch, it freed itself from the edge, its erratic movements sending Ah-knold tumbling from his perch. The burly man's descent into the river below was met with an uproarious cheer from the onlookers, who commended the noble steed for its instinctual self-preservation. A few spirited spectators even offered a toast to the river, a few drinks poured over the side of the open hole in a good riddance jest to the rider, along with a few obscene gestures, celebrating the horse's triumph over adversity.

The building erupted in a chorus of cheers and jeers as the first rider's defeat catalyzed a boisterous celebration. Each new challenger was greeted with a raucous salute from the motley crew, their spirits buoyed by the intoxicating mix of danger and revelry. Captain Hardt, the beloved hero of the Kayawa Empire, soared across the gap with a grace that belied the peril, igniting the crowd into a howling frenzy. Mere moments later, Tomap took his turn, his notorious reputation preceding him. He was the instant target of a barrage of mockery, vulgar sneers, and more colorful, obscene gestures.

Oddly and amusingly, as she passed by, Mia could see the individual rosy-cheeked faces as each reveler hoisted their drink and cried out for joy almost in slow motion. She easily cleared the open space as Moonshadow safely overcame the obstacle. This simple goodwill gesture, a positive acknowledgment by the community of good people, gave Mia renewed inspiration and hope. She had to *believe* in herself. She *could* win this race.

Speeding through the rest of the crowd and out of the interior of the tavern building, Mia could tell that Graj also made it safely behind her with the last approving, roaring round of drunken cheers and wild applause. In front of Mia, about fifty yards ahead, was Tomap Sruz. The exact distance ahead of the soldier of evil was Captain Hardt.

As the race progressed, the terrain underwent another dramatic transformation; the firm ground gave way to a vast expanse of sand that meandered to the right, extending for a considerable distance.

The competitors then approached a straight section, where a deliberate water dousing had transformed the track into a challenging, muddy mess. At the end of the stretch, a mere five hundred yards away, lay a deceptively shallow water trap strategically placed just before an imposing three-foot stone barrier.

The racetrack buzzed with exhilaration as the crowd's cheers crescendoed, mirroring the thundering hooves. In a spontaneous burst of insanity, four bronze metal pendulums swung from nearby low-hanging rooftops, their outlines etched against the sky before touching down across the course's periphery. The track became a haze of motion as the four pendulums swung back and forth before the racing steeds, their swooshing sound soaring through the wind.

As Captain Hardt braided through this section of the course, guiding his horse harmlessly past two pendulums, he turned in his saddle to look behind him. The only other rider in sight, fifty yards behind and closing in on the lead fast, was Tomap. The ruthless commander, racing hard on his horse, angrily side-kicked one of the pendulums Captain Hardt had purposely avoided into a stone wall.

Turning his attention back ahead, Captain Hardt saw two pendulums pass harmlessly in front of him. Two waterjet streams joyously erupted from both sides of the track in front of the upcoming fence. This forced the racing horses to jump over both an increased pool of water and the immovable stone fence barrier.

Captain Hardt, with unsuspected agility, vaulted over the paired obstacle. His form was so flawless it was as though the barrier were a mere figment. Yet, in the wake of his expert maneuver, Tomap surged forward to complete the jump and ride abreast of the noble captain with a burst of spirited vigor that startled even the seasoned onlookers. With a wild cry torn from the depths of his fervor, the impetuous youth hurled a backhanded strike with a riding whip held in the fist at the throat of the older military man. The force behind the blow was such that it unseated the captain with brutality, sending him tumbling into the unforgiving ground, his descent appearing as if it killed him on impact.

The Kayawa captain executed a series of barrel rolls along the rugged track in a futile attempt to cushion his fall, each more audacious than the last. As he skidded to an abrupt stop, the silence of the aftermath was punctuated only by his soft groans. Despite the severity of his injuries, he was alive. He rose to his feet with great effort, each movement deliberate and unsteady. As he took a tentative step forward, an intense pain surged through his right leg. It was clear that the bone had significantly suffered, though whether it was fractured or wholly broken was yet to be determined.

Captain Hardt, his ears tuned to the relentless rhythm of approaching hoofbeats, propelled himself forward. Each stride sent a jolt of agony through his seasoned frame, his right leg bearing the brunt of his battle-worn history. Yet, with gritty perseverance, he pressed on, the discomfort increasing with each labored step. A low balcony loomed ahead where an assembly of outstretched arms and encouraging shouts beckoned him to hasten his escape from certain death. As the distance closed, a sea of helping hands reached down, clasping firmly onto Captain Hardt, hoisting him to safety as he left the tumultuous Goldenwings Run behind.

Merely five seconds later, Mia glided beneath him, swiftly trailed a half-minute later by the enigmatic wild woman, Graj. Present, too, was Ah-knold's formidable, giant mare, barreling ahead as though its master still commanded her from the saddle, vying for victory. Spooked by the colossal black mare's aura, the unmounted Kayawa steed abandoned the contest. It rushed to the side of the track, leapt over a diminutive stone barrier aligned with astonished onlookers, and rushed recklessly forward amidst the dense sea of shrieking spectators.

Mia leaned forward, whispering words of encouragement, urging Moonshadow to quicken his pace and aim to overtake the current frontrunner, Zamana Commander Tomap Sruz. They approached a new obstacle: the shattered remnants of a once sublime statue. With grace befitting his name, Moonshadow leapt, clearing the debris effortlessly.

The obstacle preceded a treacherous turn, yet Moonshadow landed and surged forward, his stride unbroken. This remarkable maneuver allowed Mia to draw level with Tomap. Now neck and neck, the duo charged into the next stretch: a straightaway of sienna grass seemingly charred by fire, their figures casting long shadows as they raced towards victory.

Mia was focused on the course ahead, ignoring the opposition, when she felt the first biting sting on her arm. Tomap yelled as he flicked his riding crop at the princess. The long lash of the whip crashed across and around her long arms and upper torso multiple times, stinging and flaying the flesh.

Mia's left arm shot up in defense, her silver bracelet shimmering in the sunlight as it met the onslaught of blows, a welcome, needed barrier against the relentless aggression. But the whip was cunning as if it were alive, coiling around her forearm with a viper's grip. Tomap, sensing his advantage, yanked back hard on the weapon. The horses, locked in their equal forward charge, became unwitting accomplices in Mia's plight. Mia was wrenched from her saddle with a forceful tug from Tomap, only her right foot entwined within the stirrup's embrace keeping her from death.

A tug-of-war ensued, growing more intense with each passing second. A fierce fight proceeded back and forth, neither side yielding, as the ominous shadow of a sizeable, stacked debris pile loomed ever closer on the track. Realizing that the commander of the Zamana Empire was purposefully dragging her straight towards impending doom, Mia's heart raced; she pulled at the whip wrapped around her silver forearm bracelet with renewed vigor, her desperation mounting as she struggled to break free from its unyielding grip.

Knowing that the princess was conveniently caught, Tomap held the whip handle firm in his hands and pulled with all his strength. His ruthless efforts almost took Mia completely off her saddle, making her scream as if her arm were being ripped out of its socket. Unknown to Tomap, Mia's right hip injury resurfaced, festering with every mighty tug. Her right foot was inescapably caught in the stirrup, the only thing that kept her from being pulled off and falling to the merciless passing ground.

Swiftly closing in on the debris pile, Tomap maneuvered his horse so that he would pass on the left side. Mia passed on the right, with her left arm stretched out in the middle between them. Moments away from having her arm ripped off from riding full speed into an immovable structure, she bellowed with fury and pulled at the whip wrapped around her wrist in one last desperate attempt. The right hip injury was now like a piercing arrow stuck into her torso, shooting pain throughout the body. She finally broke free, wrangling and snapping the lash of the entangled whip away just before colliding with a stack of crates that safely passed her.

Separated but still in the lead for the Goldenwings Run, Mia and Tomap still faced two back-to-back fence jumps on the course. Still even in the race, interweaving with each other, they entered a straightaway.

Tomap momentarily let go of the reins and removed another hidden three-inch knife from his belt. Continuing to ride alongside an unaware Mia, with one swift movement, he drove the knife into her lower right thigh.

Mia's cry pierced the air. Clinging to Moonshadow's reins, she fought the urge to succumb to the agony that threatened to overwhelm her senses. Each heartbeat was a reminder of the wound, as blood rhythmically pulsed from the gash, staining her clothes in a vivid crimson. Her fingers trembled as they brushed against the cold steel of the knife embedded in her flesh; even the slightest touch sent waves of unbearable pain radiating through her body.

With gritted teeth, she raised her eyes, only to see another challenge looming on the horizon of this treacherous race. The last obstacle bore down on her with unforgiving speed, demanding every ounce of resolve she had left. "Run, Moonshadow! Don't stop!"

The Rolling High Bar, an infamous and daunting fence obstacle, reigned as a highlight of the Goldenwings Run, meticulously designed to captivate and delightfully amuse the crowd. This demanding challenge derived its moniker from the unpredictable trio of robust alabaster wooden beams that teetered between towering heights and low depths at random intervals. Equestrians were forced to navigate this peril with extraordinary precision and dexterity, leaping over a chosen beam while it could, without notice, alter its elevation—a true test of their mettle and their mounts' prowess.

Moonshadow, with unwavering confidence, strode towards the imposing High Roller. His pace was steady. With a powerful leap, he ascended, aiming to soar over the bar with ease. Yet, as he took to the air, the wooden bars beneath him began their treacherous rotation. The sable stallion's hind legs grazed the beam at its apex, sending a jarring shudder through his frame.

This unforeseen contact propelled Mia from her saddle, her body nearly somersaulting over Moonshadow's robust neck. She clung to her steed post-jump, her fingers gripping deep into his mane. The stakes were perilously high; a slip would spell disaster.

Seizing the grand opportunity to finally rid himself of the annoying, boastful princess from Itonia, Tomap directed his horse to gallop alongside Moonshadow. Taking his riding whip in hand once more, he swung, viciously, wildly, in an attempt to kill Princess Karamia. The princess was stuck dangling from the foot, caught in the saddle's stirrups, and holding on to her running horse's neck. Some of the swings missed, but some hit hard as Moonshadow ran full pace down the track.

With no other options, Mia grabbed the hilt of the knife in her thigh. Her screams were loud enough to overcome the noise of the watching crowd as she wrenched the knife from her leg. Holding the blade firm, she stabbed Tomap in the unprotected portion of his crimson-armored torso.

Screaming in tremendous torture and jerking violently away, Tomap fell off his saddle. As he plummeted, his foot got caught in the stirrup, causing the racing horse to drag him along the rugged, harsh, dirty ground for a lengthy distance. Flopping and bouncing off the ground, he finally got his foot untangled from the stirrup and dropped abruptly onto the gritty course.

Summoning the last of his strength, a bloodied, beaten, and battered Tomap defiantly picked himself off the ground and shakily stood up, hearing a dreadful, piercing war cry fill his ears. The brash, arrogant man wearily looked up in time to see the fierce ebony woman of Aliffica, Graj Nes, wild-eyed with vengeful bloodlust for her country, bearing down on him alongside Ah-knold's riderless, mighty mare.

With nowhere to run and brave enough to accept the inevitable outcome, Tomap stoically stood his ground on the track and held firm before the coming stampede. The commander of the Zamana Empire was immediately knocked down and trampled by the passing hooves of the other horses, his body lying deathly motionless within the murky shroud of dust afterward.

In the lead, yet oblivious to the grim final fate that befell her rival, Mia was locked in a desperate struggle for her own life, her foot anchored in the stirrup. Her fingers grasped at the saddle horn with determination. With renewed urgency, she lurched upwards in a single concentrated effort and held on to the saddle horn. Steadying herself, she rose slowly but resolutely in the saddle as the trail curved dangerously to the right, morphing into a treacherous dirt track.

Now firmly established atop her steed, Mia shouted joyfully. She spurred Moonshadow forward with infectious enthusiasm, coaxing every last ounce of energy from her mount. As the black stallion galloped at a breakneck pace, the watching spectators' cheers swelled in a crescendo. Nearing the climactic end of this heart-pounding, endurance-laden, deadly race, she smiled as the finish line approached ahead.

Moonshadow gallantly crossed the finish line. A wave of cheers erupted, heralding the first champion of the legendary Goldenwings Run in decades. Princess Karamia, atop her noble steed, basked in the glory of victory, her name echoing in a chorus of admiration from the diverse assembly of spectators. Flags representing myriad nations danced fervently in the stands, mirroring the moment's excitement—a kaleidoscope of confetti cascaded from the heavens, painting the sky with vibrant hues. Meanwhile, a cascade of fireworks ascended, igniting the atmosphere with spectacular bursts of various bright colors reflecting this historic event's joyous spirit.

A vibrant chorus of trumpets sliced through the exuberant cheers, their golden notes soaring high above the clamorous crowd—drums thundered in unison, leading to a crescendo met by the cymbals' shimmering, splashy crash. An opulent wave of celebratory fanfare flooded the city's streets and stands, signaling the commencement of a grand awards ceremony in the wake of the spirited horse race.

Under the sun's golden glow, Moonshadow pranced with unrestrained joy, his hooves tapping a rhythm on the track to match the festive melodies that filled the air. The crowd's cheers grew louder, a warm welcome that echoed through the open square. With a gentle nudge, Mia brought her horse to a standstill before the ornate steps leading to the grand reception stage. Despite the sharp twinge in her leg, she dismounted with elegance and care.

Mia tore off a piece of clothing from the bottom of her shirt, long enough to wrap and address the wound. She felt a piercing sting with every step on the stairway. She straightened her back, embodying resilience, her eyes fixed forward and alight with courage. She approached the summit gracefully, pain and triumph intertwined in her poised stride, embracing the discomfort as a mere shadow in her triumphant moment.

Soothing the stinging affliction of the glorious victory, Mia spied the top of the stairs—where her family and friends eagerly awaited. Her father's face genuinely appeared as if he could not be prouder of his daughter, beaming with pride. He held the prized Land Elemental Gemstone aloft, ready to bestow it on Mia.

Standing to King Jelia's right on the platform were her adventurous new friends: the comical, bumbling duo Suzu and Hogart. Both had broad smiles on their faces. Perhaps because of their additional winnings, but more than likely, they were happy for their once mysterious traveling companion. Surprisingly, Mozo was perched on the big man's broad shoulder, playfully nuzzling through the long charcoal hair into his ear.

Garrison Ogan, the Relic Hunter, remained stoic on the platform to the monarch's left. The veteran archaeologist's stillness was striking, his square-jawed face a mask devoid of emotion. It was as though Garrison harbored a personal, silent gratitude for the fortunate turn of events at the Goldenwings Run—a competition he proposed— yet nothing more betrayed his deepest private thoughts. On Mia's ascent to the stair's peak, Garrison offered a subtle, polite nod in her direction, a silent gesture of courteous recognition and approval.

With a hearty laugh and approving, wide smile, King Jelia handed the mystic, magical emerald Land Elemental Gemstone to his young daughter. Princess Karamia shouted with joyous glee, holding the small highly prized jewel high over her head in sweet victory. The assembled multinational crowd roaringly approved of the winning gesture, signaling hope and peace for the once hidden Kingdom of Tavter and all good people worldwide in the coming days.